Royal and Ruthless

ROBYN DONALD
ANNIE WEST
CHRISTINA HOLLIS

Published in Great Britain 2015
by Mills & Boon, an imprint of Harlequin (UK) Limited,
Eton House, 18-24 Paradise Road, Richmond, Surrey, TW9 1SR

ROYAL AND RUTHLESS © 2015 Harlequin Books S.A.

Innocent Mistress, Royal Wife, *Prince of Scandal* and *Weight of the Crown* were first published in Great Britain by Harlequin (UK) Limited.

Innocent Mistress, Royal Wife © 2008 Robyn Donald
Prince of Scandal © 2011 Annie West
Weight of the Crown © 2011 Christina Hollis

ISBN: 978-0-263-25204-0
eBook ISBN: 978-1-474-00383-4

05-0315

INNOCENT MISTRESS, ROYAL WIFE

BY
ROBYN DONALD

Robyn Donald can't remember not being able to read, and will be eternally grateful to the local farmers who carefully avoided her on a dusty country road as she read her way to and from school, transported to places and times far away from her small village in Northland, New Zealand. Growing up fed her habit; as well as training as a teacher, marrying and raising two children, she discovered the delights of romances and read them voraciously, especially enjoying the ones written by New Zealand writers. So much so that one day she decided to write one herself. Writing soon grew to be as much of a delight as reading—although infinitely more challenging—and when eventually her first book was accepted by Mills & Boon she felt she'd arrived home. She still lives in a small town in Northland, with her family close by, using the landscape as a setting for much of her work. Her life is enriched by the friends she's made among writers and readers, and complicated by a determined corgi called Buster, who is convinced that blackbirds are evil entities. Her greatest hobby is still reading, with travelling a very close second.

CHAPTER ONE

RAFIQ DE COUTEVEILLE looked directly at Therese Fanchette, the motherly, middle-aged woman whose razor-sharp mind oversaw the security of his island country in the Indian Ocean. In a level voice he asked, 'Exactly what sort of relationship does this Alexa Considine have with Felipe Gastano? Are they lovers?'

Therese said neutrally, 'They are sharing a room at the hotel.'

So they were lovers. Rafiq glanced down at the photograph on his desk. Fine featured, medium height and slim, the woman was laughing up at the man he'd had in his sights for the past two years. She didn't look like Felipe Gastano's sort, but then, he thought with ice-cold anger, neither had Hani. His sister, now dead. 'What have you discovered about her?'

'Not much, but I've just been talking to a source in New Zealand. I taped the conversation, of course, and I'll make a written report after I've had the information verified.' She straightened her spectacles and checked her notes. 'Alexa Considine is twenty-six years old, and in New Zealand she is known as Lexie Sinclair. Until a year ago she was a veterinarian in a rural practice in the north of the country. When her half-sister—Jacoba Sinclair, the model—and Prince Marco of Illyria became engaged, it emerged that Ms Considine is actually the daughter of the dead dictator of Illyria.'

'Paulo Considine?' At her nod, Rafiq's brows lifted. 'How did the daughter of one of the most hated and feared men of the twentieth century grow up in New Zealand?'

'Her mother fled there when the children were very young. She must have had good reason to be terrified of her husband. According to the news media, neither girl had any idea of their real identity until they were adults.'

'Anyone who knew Considine had reason to be afraid. Go on,' Rafiq said, his eyes once more on the photo-graph.

'She has spent the past year working with the peasants in Illyria, healing their animals and teaching classes at the veterinary college she's helped set up under Prince Alex of Illyria's patronage.' Therese looked up. 'It ap-pears he used her obvious innocence of her father's sins to break the ancient system of blood feuds in his country.'

Yes, Alex of Illyria was clever enough to stage-manage the situation to his advantage, Rafiq thought, his mind racing.

So Felipe Gastano had brought Alexa Considine to Moraze. What the *hell* was her family thinking to allow it? Her cousins were sophisticated men of the world; they must know that Gastano lived on the edge of society, using his wits, his handsome face and the faded glamour of an empty title to dazzle people. The tabloids called Count Felipe Gastano a great lover. Rafiq knew of a woman who'd killed herself after he'd stripped her of her self-respect by seducing her and then introducing her to drugs.

But perhaps Alexa Considine had something of her father in her. In spite of her work for the peasants, she could be an embarrassment to the Illyrian royal family.

Possibly she didn't need protection because she knew very well how to look after herself...

He had to know more before he worked out how best to exploit the situation. 'She and Gastano have been lovers for how long?'

'About two months.'

Rafiq's dark gaze travelled to the handsome face of his enemy. Although he doubted that Gastano felt anything much beyond a cynical, predatory lust for any woman, he had a reputation for pride. He had always demanded beauty in his amours.

But Alexa Considine—Lexie Sinclair—was not beautiful. Attractive, yes, even striking, but without the overt sexuality the man had always favoured. So why had he chosen her to warm his bed?

Brows drawing together, Rafiq studied the photograph of the woman on Gastano's arm. It had been taken at a party in London, and she was laughing up at Gastano's good-looking face.

The illegitimate son of an aristocrat, the man had assumed the title 'Count' after the real count, his half-brother, had died from a drug overdose. Gastano might well consider that the Sinclair woman's connections to the rich and powerful Considine family—tainted though they were—would give him the social standing he'd spent his life seeking.

That certainly made sense. And now Gastano's arrogance and his conviction that he was above suspicion had delivered him into Rafiq's hands.

Transferring his gaze to the crest on the wall of his office, Rafiq reined in a cold anticipation as he surveyed the emblem of his family—a rampant horse wearing a crown that held a glitter of crimson, signifying the precious fire-diamonds found only on Moraze.

Rafiq would not be his father's son—or Hani's brother—if he failed to use the situation to his advantage.

Revenge was an ugly ambition, but Hani's death should not be in vain.

As for Alexa Considine—she might have been innocent before she met Gastano, though it seemed unlikely. Her half-sister had worked in the notoriously amoral world of high fashion, so maybe Alexa Considine had a modern attitude to sex, taking partners as she wanted them.

But if not, he'd be doing her a favour. Felipe Gastano was no considerate lover, and once his world started crumbling around him he'd fight viciously to save himself. She'd be far safer out of the way.

Besides, he thought with cold satisfaction, it would give him great pleasure to take her from Gastano, to show the creep the limits of his power and influence before the trap closed around him.

Mind made up, he said evenly, 'This is what I want you to do.'

Mme Fanchette leaned forward, frowning slightly as he outlined his instructions. When he'd finished she said quietly, 'Very well, then. And the count?'

Rafiq's voice hardened. 'Watch him closely—put your best people onto it, because he's as wary as a cat.'

He got up and walked across to the window, looking down at the city spread below. 'Fortunately he is also a man with a huge sense of self-esteem, and a sophisticate's disdain for people who live in small, isolated countries far from the fleshpots of the world he preys on.'

From beneath lowered lashes, Rafiq watched the woman in the flame-coloured dress. Cleverly cut to reveal long legs, narrow waist and high, small breasts, the silk dress angled for male attention. But Alexa Considine's face didn't quite fit its skilful, not entirely discreet sensuality.

The photographs hadn't lied; she wasn't a top-class beauty, Rafiq decided dispassionately—although, like every other woman attending the official opening of Moraze's newest, most luxurious, highly exclusive hotel, she was superbly groomed. Her cosmetics had been applied expertly and her golden-brown hair cut by a master to make the most of her features. However, apart from that eye-catcher of a dress, she stood out, and not just because she was alone.

Gastano, Rafiq noted, was across the other side of the room flirting with a film star of somewhat notorious reputation.

Interesting…

Unlike every other woman in the place, Alexa Considine wore no jewellery. And she looked unawakened, as though no one had ever kissed that tempting, lushly opulent mouth—sensuous enough to make any red-blooded man fantasise about the touch of it on his skin.

Rafiq's gut tightened. Swiftly controlling the hot

surge of desire through his blood, he scanned her fine-boned face with an impassive expression. It seemed highly unlikely that her features told anything like the truth. Mme Fanchette's source in New Zealand had come up with a blank about any possible affairs, but that didn't mean Alexa was an innocent. At university no one would have taken much notice of her love life.

And she was certainly Felipe Gastano's mistress, so that grave, unworldly air had to be spurious, a mere trick of genetics from somewhere in her bloodline.

Yet her cool self-possession challenged Rafiq in some primal, instinctive way. What would it be like to banish the composure from those regular features, set those large, slightly tilted eyes aflame with desire, feel those lips shape themselves to his...?

It took an effort of will to look away and pretend to scan the crowd, carefully chosen for their ability to create a buzz—a gathering wave of gossip and comment that would reach the ears of those who wanted privacy and opulence when they holidayed.

Rafiq had himself vetted the guest list, and apart from the woman in the sunset-coloured dress everybody in this Indian Ocean fantasy of a salon wore their sophistication like a badge of belonging.

Standing alone in the elegant, crowded room, she was attracting interested glances. Rafiq had to rein in a disturbing urge to forge his way through the chattering mob and cut her out, like a stallion with its favourite mare.

As he watched she turned and walked out through the wide doors into the warm, tropical night, the light from the chandeliers gleaming over satiny, golden-amber hair.

Across the room Gastano looked up, said something

to the film star, and set off after his mistress. Rafiq fought back a raw anger that drove him to follow Gastano, and moved with the lithe gait of a man in complete control of his body.

He should leave it to the security men, of course, but he wanted to see them together, Gastano and Alexa Considine. That way he'd know for certain the truth about their relationship.

It was, he thought cynically as he stepped out onto the wide stone terrace, a perfect night for dalliance— the stars were as big as lamps, the sea gleamed like black silk shot with silver, and erotic perfumes from the flower farms of Moraze drifted lazily through the palms.

Stopping in the shadow of a vine heavy with flamboyant scarlet blossom, Rafiq watched the count walk up to Alexa Considine, and fought a primitive impulse to follow the man and best him in a territorial contest of overt masculine power.

The impulse startled him. Even in his amours he never allowed himself to be anything other than self-possessed, and this proprietary attitude towards a woman he didn't even know—and planned to use—was an unwelcome development.

Of course, it couldn't be personal—well, it was, he thought with a slow burn of anger, but it was between him and Gastano. Attractive though she was, the woman was merely a bystander.

Frowning, he noted her reaction to the count's opening remark, scanning her face for emotions as she turned from her contemplation of the lagoon.

Although Rafiq had a hunter's patience, he must have made some slight movement, because the woman looked over the count's shoulder. Her eyes widened momentarily, only to be hastily covered by long lashes.

Not in fear or surprise, he thought, but in warning. A very cool customer, this one. No, he didn't have to concern himself about her feelings; she was fully in command of them.

Narrowly he inspected the regular features highlighted by the silver witchery of starlight. Her sensuous mouth was compressed, her detached expression not altering as Gastano bent his head down to her.

The count's voice was pitched too low for Rafiq to hear what he said, but the tone was unmistakeable—intimate and smoothly caressing.

The woman's brows lifted. 'No, I haven't changed my mind.'

Again the count spoke, and this time Rafiq caught a few words. He stiffened.

Speaking in English, the count had said, 'Come, don't be so angry, my dearest girl,' accompanied by a lingering, significant gaze.

She tossed back a crisp comment and walked past him, her spine straight as she headed for Rafiq.

'Hello,' she said in English, her voice clear and steady. 'I'm Lexie Sinclair. Isn't it a gorgeous evening?' Not giving him time to answer, she turned to include the count and asked in a pleasant tone, 'Do you two know each other?'

Full marks for social skills, Rafiq thought sardonically. Aloud he said, 'Of course.' Without offering a hand, he favoured the other man with a slight unsmiling inclination of his head. 'Gastano.'

'Ah, sir, how delightful to meet you again.' The count's voice was a mixture of impudence and false man-to-man heartiness. 'I must congratulate you on yet another superb investment—I can tell you now that this hotel will be a huge success. I've already had two film stars singing its praises, and at least one minor European royal is planning to bring his latest mistress here for a week's tryst.'

He switched his attention to the woman, letting his eyes linger on her face, and went on in a voice where the impertinence had transmuted into charming ruefulness. 'Alexa, I must introduce you to Rafiq de Courteveille. He is the ruler of this lovely island, and all who live here, you know. But I must warn you to beware of him—he is well known to be a breaker of hearts. Sir, this is Alexa Considine, who prefers to be known as Lexie Sinclair. Perhaps she will tell you why.'

With an ironic smile, he bowed to them both then walked back into the hotel.

Aware of the anger that tightened her neat features, Rafiq took Alexa's arm. Ignoring her startled resistance, he walked her towards the edge of the wide, stone-flagged terrace.

A volatile mixture of irritation laced with apprehension had prompted Lexie's decision to make use of this stranger. If she'd known that he was the hereditary ruler of Moraze she'd never have dared; she'd probably shattered protocol. It had been kind of him to ignore her lack of manners.

So why did she feel that her impulsive approach to him had set something dangerous in motion? Resisting a faint, foolish urge to turn and run, she stole a rapid sideways glance at his face and dragged in a silent breath. A silver wash of starlight emphasised boldly angular features, strong and thrusting and uncompromising.

Dead gorgeous, she thought with involuntary appreciation, her heart picking up speed. In superbly tailored evening clothes he carried himself like an autocrat, his six-foot-several-inches of lean manhood almost intimidating.

Against such steel-hard authority, Felipe's glamorous sophistication suddenly seemed flashy and superficial.

Sedately, she said, 'It's an honour to meet you, sir.'

'My name is Rafiq.' He smiled at her, his dark eyes intent.

Lexie's pulse rate accelerated further, and an odd twist of sensation tightened her stomach. Trying to curb her runaway response, she struggled to remember what she'd read about the man who ruled this small, independent island state.

Not a lot. He didn't make the headlines, or figure largely in the tabloids. Felipe had referred to him contemptuously as 'the tinpot fake prince of a speck of land thousands of miles from civilisation.'

But Felipe's jeering dismissal of the man beside her had been foolish as well as wrong. Rafiq de Couteveille walked in an aura of effortless power based on formidable male assurance.

Her mind jerked away from the memory of the moment that morning when, tired after the long flight from Europe, she'd discovered that Felipe had organised for her to spend the week in a room with him.

It had been a shock. She'd already decided she wasn't in love with Felipe, and by going back to New Zealand she'd be ending their relationship.

The week in Moraze on her own was to have been a holiday, seven days to reorient herself to her real life as a country vet in Northland. Being met by Felipe at the airport had been unexpected. But when he'd swept her off to the hotel he was staying in, and they'd been shown into a suite with flowers everywhere and a bottle of champagne in a silver bucket prominently displayed, she'd realised with dismay and a certain unease that he'd set the scene for seduction.

Still, she'd been civilised about it, and so had Felipe, when she'd told him that no, she wasn't going to join him in any sensual fantasy.

He hadn't argued. Felipe never did. He'd taken her rejection with a smiling shrug, observing that it didn't matter, that he'd sleep on one of the very comfortable sofas. That was when she'd found out that he'd cancelled her booking at her own, much more modest hotel some miles away. It had been impossible to get a room to herself—it was the holiday season and all the hotels were fully booked, an apologetic clerk told her.

It hadn't been the first time Felipe had suggested they make love, but before it had always been with a light touch so she'd never felt pressured.

This time there had been something about his humorously regretful acceptance that didn't ring true; he'd sounded satisfied, almost smug. Oh, she wasn't afraid, but right now she felt a long way from home, and rather vulnerable and wary, whereas before she'd always been at ease with him.

Well, almost always.

He'd talked her into accompanying him to the party, only to abandon her after the first half-hour. It seemed very like punishment.

Yes, she thought—deliberate and rather vindictive. That sense of unease grew. Because she was out of place in this assembly of famous faces she'd seen in newspapers and gossip columns. Others were complete strangers, but they too wore fabulous clothes and even more fabulous jewels, and they all seemed to know each other.

'You are all right?' the man beside her asked in a deep, cool voice that ruffled across her skin like dark velvet.

'Yes, of course.' Goodness, was that her voice? Pitched slightly too high, the words had emerged almost breathlessly.

'Should I apologise for disturbing you and your friend?' Rafiq de Couteveille asked.

'No, not at all,' she said, again too quickly. She fixed her gaze on the lagoon, placid and shimmering beneath the tropical night.

She stole a glance at Rafiq de Couteveille, and a hot shiver worked its way down her spine, igniting her nerves so that she was acutely, almost painfully aware of him. Like her he was looking out across the lagoon, and in the darkness his arrogantly autocratic profile was an uncompromising slash across the star-gemmed sky.

Both he and Felipe were exceedingly good-looking, but the difference between them couldn't have been greater.

Felipe had dazzled her; after the hard work of proving herself to the Illyrians, he'd accepted her without comment, made her laugh, introduced her to interesting people and generally entertained her with a light touch.

And, until she'd been presented with the *fait accompli* of that huge double bed, she'd taken him at face value.

Perhaps she should have seen the signs sooner—like the moment, after they'd been seeing each other for a month or so, when he'd noticed she was tired and told her he could get something that would take away her tiredness…if she wanted him to.

After one glance at her stunned expression he'd laughed softly and with affection, before apologising charmingly, saying that he'd only been testing her.

Then she'd believed him. Now she wondered whether he'd been lying. In spite of seeing so much of him, she really didn't know Felipe at all. Her hands tightened on the balustrade.

'There is something wrong. Can I help?'

Could Rafiq de Couteveille read minds? 'I'm fine,' she said briskly. After all, she didn't know this man either.

'Do you know Gastano well?'

'I've known him for a couple of months,' she said with restraint.

'It appears you are close to becoming engaged to him.'

'What?' He was watching her keenly, those dark eyes uncomfortably piercing. 'I don't know where you got that idea from,' she said more forcefully than she'd intended, startled by her instinctive rejection of the possibility.

His straight brows rose, but his voice was smooth when he said, 'You don't find the idea of taming a man like that intriguing?'

Turning her gaze to the pool and the gracefully curved trunks of the palms beyond, she said abruptly, 'I don't find the idea of taming *any* man intriguing.'

And she stopped, because this was an odd conversation to have with a man she didn't know.

'It's supposed to be a universal female desire,' he observed.

A note in his words told her he was amused—and strangely, she found that a relief. 'Not mine,' she told him brightly. 'What made you think that we were about to become engaged?'

'I heard it somewhere,' he said. 'Perhaps whoever was discussing it misunderstood—or possibly I did. So what *is* your desire?'

The flicker of excitement deep inside her leapt into a flame. He was flirting with her.

She should go back inside. Actually, she should leave this party. But that suite upstairs, with its one huge bed, loomed like a threat. Shrugging off that worry, she smiled up at her companion. Although his lips curved in response, she couldn't see any humour there. He was watching her, his chiselled face enigmatic in the starlight, his expression speculative.

Did he know what was happening to her? Could he feel it too—that keen awareness, the anticipation, hidden yet potent, the whispered instructions she didn't dare obey?

Hastily, before she could react to a treacherous impulse to lift herself onto her toes and kiss his excitingly sensuous mouth, she said demurely, 'Only a foolish woman tells a man her innermost desire.'

'My innermost desire at this moment,' he said, his deep voice investing the conventional words with an edge that sent Lexie's pulse racing into overdrive, 'is to discover if your mouth tastes as good as it looks.'

Lexie froze, her widening eyes taking in his honed features.

His smile twisted into something close to cynicism. 'But not if it goes against your principles.'

'No—well—no,' she stammered, barely able to articulate.

'Then shall we try it?' He took her startled silence for assent, and bent his head to claim her lips in a kiss that was surprisingly gentle.

At first.

But when her bones melted his arms came around her and he pulled her against his lean, powerful body— and all hell broke loose.

That cool, exploring kiss hardened into fierce demand and Lexie burned up in his arms, meeting and matching his frankly sexual hunger. Stunned by an urgent, voluptuous craving, she almost surrendered to the adrenalin raging like a bushfire through her.

She felt the subtle flexion of his body, and knew that he too wanted this—this headstrong need, mindless and sensuous. Desperately, she fought to retain a tiny spark of sanity as a bulwark against the white-hot sensations his experienced kiss summoned inside her.

Yet when he lifted his head and drawled, 'Shall we go further down into the garden?' it took every ounce of her will power to refuse.

In a ragged voice she muttered, 'No.'

He let her go and stepped back. Embarrassed, shocked and angry with herself, she whirled and set off for the bright rectangles of light that indicated the doors onto the terrace.

'One moment.'

Startled into stillness by the decisive command, she stopped and half turned.

He was right behind her. A long-fingered hand lifted to tuck a lock of hair behind her ear, and somehow he managed to turn the simple gesture into a caress that sent more forbidden excitement drumming through her.

'You don't look quite so storm tossed now,' he said, that sardonic smile tilting his lips again as he surveyed her face. 'But a trip to the powder room is advisable, I think.'

'I—yes,' she said, forcing her voice into its usual practical tone. 'Are you coming inside too?'

'Not for a few minutes,' he said gravely. 'My body, alas, is not so easily mastered as yours.'

'Oh.' Hot faced, she took off to the sound of his quiet laughter behind her.

Rafiq watched her go, frowning as his *aide-de-camp* passed her in the doorway, the man's presence breaking in on thoughts that weren't as ordered as he'd have liked.

Dragging his mind away from Lexie's sleek back and the gentle sway of her hips, he said abruptly, 'Yes?'

'Your instructions have been followed.'

'Thank you,' Rafiq said crisply, and turned to go inside. Then he stopped. 'You noticed the woman who passed you on the way in?'

'Yes, sir.' When Rafiq's brows lifted, the younger man expanded, 'She is also under s—' He stopped as Rafiq's brows met over his arrogant nose. Hastily he went on, 'She is staying at the hotel with Count Felipe Gastano.'

He stepped back as another man approached them, saying to Rafiq, 'You're leaving already, sir?'

Rafiq returned the newcomer's smile. He respected any man who'd hauled himself up from poverty and refugee status, and this man—the CEO of the construction firm that had built the new resort—was noted for his honesty and philanthropy. 'I'm afraid I must,' he said. 'I have an early call tomorrow.'

They exchanged pleasantries, but as Rafiq turned to go the older man said, 'And you will consider the matter we discussed previously?'

'I will,' Rafiq told him with remote courtesy. 'But I am unable to make the decision; there must be consultations with the council first.'

The older man said shrewdly, 'I wonder if you will ever regret giving up the power your forebears took for granted?'

Rafiq's broad shoulders lifted in a negligent shrug. 'In the eyes of the world Moraze might be only a smallish island in the Indian Ocean. But its few-million citizens are as entitled to the privileges and responsibilities of democracy as any other free people, and if they don't want them now they will soon enough. I am a practical man. If I hadn't introduced self-government, power would eventually have been taken away—either from me or from one of my descendants.'

'I wish all rulers were as enlightened,' the other man said. He paused before adding, 'I know my daughter has already thanked you for your magnificent birthday gift, but I must thank you also. I know how rare fire-diamonds are, and that one is superb.'

'It is nothing.' Rafiq dismissed his gift with a smile. 'Freda and I are old friends—and the diamond suits her.'

They shook hands and Rafiq frowned, his mind not on the woman who'd been his lover until six months previously but on Alexa Sinclair Considine, with the gold-burnished hair and the steady gaze, and a mouth that summoned erotic fantasies.

And her relationship with a man he loathed and despised.

She was no longer in the room, Rafiq realised after one comprehensive glance around the large salon. And neither was Felipe Gastano.

CHAPTER TWO

UP IN the palatial bedroom, Lexie could still hear the faint sound of music. Moraze was as glorious as its discreet publicity promised—a large island, dominated by a long-extinct chain of volcanoes ground down by aeons of wind and weather to become a jagged range of mountains bordering a vast plateau area.

Just before landing the previous day Lexie had leaned forward to peer at the green-gold grasslands. She'd hoped for a glimpse of the famed wild horses of Moraze, only to sink back disappointed when lush coastal lands came into view, vividly patched with green sugar cane and the bright colours of flower farms.

Now, standing at the glass doors onto the balcony, she remembered that the island's heraldic animal was a rearing horse wearing a crown. Her mind skipped from the horse to the man it signified, and she lifted her hands to suddenly burning cheeks.

That kiss had been scandalously disturbing, so different from any other she'd ever experienced that it had overwhelmed her.

Why? Yes, Rafiq de Couteveille was enormously attractive, with that compelling air of dangerous assurance, but she was accustomed to attractive men. Her sister Jacoba was married to one, and Marco's older brother was just as stunning in a slightly sterner way. Yet neither of them had summoned so much as an extra heartbeat from her.

It wasn't just his leanly aquiline features, boldly sculpted into a tough impression of force and power, that had made such an impression. Although Felipe Gastano was actually better-looking, he didn't have an ounce of Rafiq's dangerous charisma. She couldn't imagine Felipe on a warhorse, leading his warriors into battle, but it was very easy to picture Rafiq de Couteveille doing exactly that.

Or she could see him as a corsair, she thought, heart quickening when her too-active imagination visualised him with a cutlass between his teeth as he swung over the side of a vessel...

According to the hotel publicity, in the eighteenth century the Indian Ocean had been the haunt of buccaneers. Moraze had been threatened by them, and had also used them in the struggle to keep its independence. Eventually the corsairs had been brought to heel, and Moraze's rulers were at last able to give up the dangerous double game they'd been forced to play.

But no doubt the corsairs had left their genes in the bloodlines of the people of Moraze. Certainly Rafiq looked like a warrior—stern, hard and ruthless if the occasion demanded it.

However, fantasising about him wasn't any help in dealing with her most pressing problem. Frowning, she stepped back inside. What the hell was she to do?

She wished she could trust Felipe to sleep on the sofa, but she didn't. If she chose the bed, she suspected he might see it as an invitation for him to join her, and she did *not* want an undignified struggle when he finally decided to come up for the night.

Making up her mind, she pulled the light coverlet from the foot of the bed, grabbed a pillow, changed into cotton trousers and a shirt and curled up on the sofa.

She woke to music—from outside, she realised as she disentangled herself from the coverlet. Vaguely apprehensive, she glanced towards the closed bedroom door and grimaced. Once she'd finally fallen asleep, Rafiq de Couteveille had taken over her dreams to such an extent that she was possessed by an odd, aching restlessness.

The light she'd left on glowed softly, barely bright enough to show her a note someone had slipped under the door. Heart thudding, she untangled herself and ran across to retrieve it.

My dear girl, she read, *I am sorry to have inconvenienced you. As it upset you so much to think of sharing a room with me, I have thrown myself on the sympathy of good friends who have a suite here. Because I do not trust myself with you.*

Felipe had signed it with an elaborate *F*.

Lexie let out a long breath. She could have slept in the bed without fear, it seemed. It was thoughtful of Felipe.

Or perhaps, she thought, remembering the way he'd more or less ignored her at the party last night, this too was a little punishment?

Surely he wouldn't be so petty?

It didn't matter; the clerk had promised her a room of her own tomorrow—today, she amended after a glance at the clock. Felipe's consideration should have appeased her, but his assumption that he could manipulate her into bed had crossed a boundary, and she knew it was time to tell him that their friendship would never develop any further.

Surprised at the relief that flooded her, she realised she'd been resisting a creeping sense of wrongness ever since he'd offered to buy drugs for her.

So her decision had nothing to do with the fact that he seemed far less vital—almost faded—next to the vital, hard-edged charisma of the man who'd kissed her on the terrace.

Felipe's kisses had been warm and pleasant, but conveyed nothing like the raw charge of Rafiq's...

'Oh, *stop* it!' she commanded her inconvenient memory.

Irritated, she poured herself some water to drink, and carried it across to the glass door leading onto the balcony.

The music that had somehow tangled her dreams in its sensuous beat had fallen silent now, the only sounds the sibilant whisper of a breeze in the casuarinas, the sleepy hush of small waves on the beach, and the muted thunder of breakers against the reef. As far as she could see the lagoon spread before her like a shadowy masquerade cloak spangled with silver.

She drank deeply, willing herself to relax, to enjoy the breeze that flirted with her hair, its hint of salt and flower perfumes mingling with a faint, evocative scent of spices, of ancient mysteries and secrets hidden from the smiling beauty of daylight.

It was almost dawn, although as yet no light glowed in the eastern sky. Feeling like the only person in the world, she took a deep breath and moved farther out onto the balcony.

The hair on the nape of her neck lifted, and unthinkingly she stepped back into the darkness of the overhang, senses straining as her eyes darted back and forth to search out what had triggered that primitive instinct.

Don't be an idiot, she told herself uneasily, there's no one out there—and even if there were it would be some sort of night watchman.

Moving slowly and quietly, she eased into her room and pulled the glass door shut, locking it and making sure there was no gap in the curtains.

But even then it was difficult to dispel that eerie sense of being watched. She marched across to the bathroom and set the glass down, washed her face, and then wondered how she was going to get back to sleep.

Half an hour later she gave up the attempt and decided to email her sister Jacoba.

Only to discover that for some reason the internet link wouldn't work. Thoroughly disgruntled, she closed down her laptop and drank another glass of water.

It seemed that Felipe had decided to continue his charade of rejection. After breakfast in her room the butler hand-delivered a note that told her Gastano had business to attend to in Moraze's capital, and would see her that evening.

Suddenly light-hearted, Lexie arranged the transfer of her luggage to a new room, then organised a trip up to the mountains, eager to see the results of the world-famous bird-protection programme.

It was a surprise to find herself alone in the small tourist van with a woman who informed her she was both driver and guide.

'Just you today, *m'selle,*' she confirmed cheerfully. 'I know all about this place, so, if you got any questions, you ask.'

And know about Moraze she did, dispensing snippets of information all the more intriguing for having a strong personal bias. Lexie plied her with questions, and once they reached the high grasslands she looked eagerly for signs of the horses.

'You like horses?' the driver asked.

'Very much. I'm a vet,' Lexie told her.

'OK, I tell you about the horses.'

Lexie soaked up her information, much of which concerned the legendary relationship between the horses and the ruler.

'As long as the horses flourish,' the guide finished on the approach to a sweeping corner, 'Our Emir will also, and so will Moraze.'

She spoke as though it were written law. Lexie asked curiously, 'Why do you call him the Emir?'

'It's kind of a joke, because the first de Couteville was a duke in France. He got into trouble there, and after a couple of years of roaming in exile he found Moraze. He brought an Arabian princess with him.' She gave a thousand-watt smile. 'Their descendants have kept Moraze safe for hundreds of years, so you better believe we look after those horses! We don't want anyone else taking over our island, thank you very much.'

Lexie gasped with alarm as the guide suddenly jerked the wheel. The van skidded, the world turned upside down, and amidst a harsh cacophony of sounds Lexie was flung forward against the seatbelt. It locked across her, the force driving the breath from her lungs, so that she dragged air into them with a painful grunt.

The laboured sound of the engine and a strong smell of petrol forced her to ignore her maltreated ribs. A cool little wind played with her hair, blowing it around her face. She forced her eyes open and saw grass, long and golden, rustling in the breeze.

The car had buried its nose in the low bank on one side of the road, and when she tried her door it refused to open. She turned her head, wincing at a sharp pain in her neck, to see the driver slumped behind the wheel. The woman's harsh breathing filled the vehicle.

'I have to turn off the engine,' Lexie said aloud. If she didn't it might catch fire.

Easing herself around, she freed the seatbelt and groped for the key. She could just reach it. With shaking fingers, she twisted rapidly, hugely relieved when the engine sputtered into silence.

Now she had to see if the driver was all right. If it was a heart attack she could at least give CPR. But first she had to get out, which meant crawling over the poor woman, possibly making any injuries worse…

She reached for the driver's wrist, hugely relieved when the pulse beat strongly beneath her shaking fingers. And then she heard the distant throb of a powerful engine, a sound she identified as a helicopter.

The pilot must have seen the wrecked car because the chopper altered course. The clack-clack-clack of the engine filled the air, and seconds later the craft landed in a haze of dust and wind. Immediately a man leapt down, ducking to avoid the rotors as he ran towards her. Lexie put her hand up to her eyes and closed them, then looked again, blinking hard.

Even at this distance she knew him. Rafiq de

Couteveille—the man who had kissed her only last night...

Stunned, her stomach hollow, Lexie watched him yank open the driver's door and crouch beside her. After one quick glance at the unconscious woman, he transferred his gaze to Lexie's face.

'You are all right?' he demanded, pitching his voice so she could hear him above the noise of the helicopter.

Lexie nodded, ignoring the sharp stab of maltreated muscles in her neck. 'I think she might have had a heart attack.'

He bent his attention to the crumpled woman beside her. Was he a doctor? No, he didn't look like a doctor.

The driver stirred and muttered something in the local Creole French, then opened her eyes.

'Don't worry,' Rafiq de Couteveille said. 'We'll have you both out soon.'

No sooner said than done; within a few minutes the driver was free and being carried across to the chopper by two men, and Rafiq was saying, 'Let me help you.'

'I can manage, thank you.'

But he eased her past the wheel, his strong arms gentle and controlled. In spite of the shivers racking her when he set her carefully on her feet, her breath was shallow and her colour high.

And all she could think of was that she must look a real guy. 'Thank you,' she said as crisply as she could.

Something flickered in the dark eyes—green, she realised in the clear light of the Moraze day. Not just ordinary green, either—the pure, dense green of the very best pounamu, New Zealand's prized native jade.

'So we meet again,' he said with an ironic twist to his beautifully chiselled mouth.

He was too close. Taking an automatic step back-wards, she turned slightly away, her brows meeting for a second as another twinge of pain tightened the mus-cles in her neck.

Sharply he asked, 'Where are you hurt?'

'I'm not—the seatbelt was just a bit *too* efficient.' Her smile faded as she asked anxiously, 'Is the driver all right?'

'I think so.'

Lexie swallowed to ease a suddenly dry throat. 'I'm so glad you happened to be passing.'

He responded courteously, 'And so, Alexa Considine, am I.'

'Lexie. My name is Lexie,' she told him. 'From New Zealand,' she added idiotically.

She shivered, then stiffened as he picked her up and strode towards the chopper.

'I can walk,' she muttered.

'I doubt it. You're in shock. Keep your head down.'

Her face turned into his shoulder; she inhaled his dark, male scent. He ducked, and it was with faces almost pressed together that they headed for the chopper door. Lexie shut her eyes.

She felt safe, she thought raggedly—safer than she had ever felt in her life.

Which was odd, because every instinct she pos-sessed was shouting a warning. Somehow she'd man-aged to forget that he had his own particular scent—faint, yet hugely evocative. And although her ribs were still complaining, memories flooded back in sensory overload as the remembered impact of that kiss burned through every cell in her body.

The noise of the helicopter's engines thundered

through her, turning her shivers into shudders; by the time the chopper lifted off, she was white to the lips.

At least she'd managed not to throw up, she thought distantly after they landed in the grounds of a large building in the capital city.

The following hours passed in a blur of movement and noise, at last relieved by blessed peace when she was delivered to a solitary bed in a small, cool room overlooking the sea. She looked up from the pillows as Rafiq de Couteveille came in with a slender woman at his side—the doctor who'd supervised her tests.

'How are you now?' he asked.

'Better, thank you.' Except that her throat had turned to sand. Huskily she asked, 'How is the driver?'

'Like you, she doesn't seem hurt apart from mild shock,' Rafiq told her.

'Does she know what happened?'

He scanned her face with hard green eyes. 'An animal apparently ran out in front of the coach.'

'I hope it wasn't hurt,' she said quietly.

The woman beside him smiled. 'Probably not as much as you are. Our animals run fast. Although you have bruises, you do not have anything cracked or broken. However, you're still suffering a mild case of shock, so it seems a good idea to keep you in here for tonight.'

Rafiq de Couteveille asked, 'Is there anyone I should contact?'

If her sister Jacoba heard about this she'd be on a jet to Moraze immediately. Crisply, Lexie said, 'No. I'll be fine, and I presume there's no reason why I shouldn't see out the rest of my holiday?'

He looked at the doctor, who said, 'None at all, with

a few precautions. I'll tell you about those tomorrow before you leave hospital.'

'I do need to notify someone about where I am,' she objected, feeling rather as though someone had run over her with a steamroller.

'I will contact the count,' Rafiq de Couteveille said calmly. 'The doctor feels that you need to be left alone tonight, so don't expect visitors.' When Lexie frowned he told her, 'The hotel is sending along toiletries and clothes. I will leave you now. Do everything you are told to do, and don't worry about anything.'

Silenced by the authority in his tone and bearing, Lexie watched him stride out of the room beside the doctor, tall and utterly sure of himself, the superbly tailored light suit revealing a body that made her foolish heart increase speed dramatically. How could one man pack so much punch?

And how had he appeared up on those grassy plains—literally from out of the blue?

Like a genie from a bottle, she thought, and gave an involuntary smile, because the image was so incongruous. Rafiq de Couteveille bore all the hallmarks of an alpha male—it would be a very clever magician who managed to confine him.

And it would take a special sort of woman to match that impressive male charisma—someone elegant, sophisticated, worldly.

Someone completely unlike Lexie Sinclair, a vet from New Zealand who'd never even had a lover!

Which inevitably brought more memories of that kiss—explosive, exciting and still capable of causing a delicious agitation that temporarily made her forget her tender ribs and stiff neck.

It almost seemed like fate, she thought dreamily, that they should meet again…

Oh, how ridiculous! Coincidences happened all the time—everyone had stories of the most amazing ones that meant nothing at all.

Forget about him, she told herself sternly.

When she eased out of bed the following morning an inspection of her body revealed some mild bruising over her ribs. She was also stiff, although movement would ease that. However the shakiness that had startled her after the accident was gone.

And although the doctor was cautious she said there was no reason why she shouldn't leave, cautioning her to take things easy until the bruises had faded and she felt completely well.

So she dressed in the outfit that had arrived from the hotel the previous evening with her toiletries, and sat down rather limply on the chair. Presumably Felipe would come and get her, and she just didn't feel like dealing with him at the moment.

A knock at the door made her brace herself. 'Come in,' she called, getting to her feet and squaring her shoulders.

But it wasn't Felipe. When Rafiq de Couteville walked in, his lithe form immaculate in superbly tailored casual clothes, her heart performed an odd gyration in her chest, quivering as it finally came to rest.

'Ready to leave?' he asked, dark eyes cool and measuring.

Later she'd wonder why on earth she hadn't asked him what he was doing there.

'Yes, of course.' Oddly breathless, she picked up the small bag with her clothes from yesterday.

'You will be more comfortable once you get home,' he said calmly. At her hesitation, his brows met for a second across his nose. 'Come—they'll be wanting this room soon.'

'I can't ask you to drive me back to the hotel,' she said inanely. 'Felipe—?'

'But you aren't asking me,' he pointed out with a smile that pierced her fragile shell of independence.

When she still didn't move he held out an imperative hand.

With a meekness entirely foreign to her, Lexie handed over her bag.

CHAPTER THREE

COOL, firm fingers gripped Lexie's elbow. Rafiq said, 'Shall I ring for a wheelchair?'

'Of course not,' she spluttered, and started walking.

But once out beneath Moraze's brilliant sun she was glad to sink into the air-conditioned comfort of the waiting vehicle.

He took the wheel, which surprised her; she'd have presumed the ruler of a place with several million inhabitants would have a limousine with a chauffeur. Instead he drove a late-model car, sleek, and with all the accoutrements of luxury.

Hanging on to the remnants of her composure, she said steadily, 'This is very kind of you.'

'It is the least I can do,' he said, adding with a smile that barely tucked in the corners of his sculpted mouth, 'We value our tourists. It is a pity your trip to the jungle was cut short. When you are fully recovered I will take you there.'

Lexie stared straight ahead, refusing to allow herself to feel any excitement at the prospect. They were passing beneath an avenue of tall palms, and the shadows of their long, slender trunks flashing across her eyes set up such an unpleasant rhythm that she turned her head away.

Unfortunately this gave her an extremely good view of Rafiq de Couteveille's profile in all its autocratic purity. Whatever interesting meld of races and cultures had given him that face, it was disturbingly beautiful in a very masculine way—a compelling amalgam of angles and curves and hard-honed lines that spoke of formidable power.

And perhaps just a hint of cruelty? She would not, she thought with an inner shiver, closing her eyes, want to make an enemy of him.

His voice broke into her thoughts. 'Here, take these.'

Eyes flying open, she realised he was holding out his sunglasses. 'I can't—you'll need them,' she said, unwilling to wear something so intimately connected to him.

He shrugged. 'You are not accustomed to this sun. I am.'

And very much accustomed to getting your own way, she thought dryly.

But then rulers were notorious for that. Reluctantly she accepted the spectacles and perched them on the end of her nose.

They made an immense difference. She said quietly, 'Thank you. I'm not usually so wimpish.'

'You are too harsh on yourself. There is a difference between being fragile and being a wimp, and an accident always leaves one shaken. Why don't you put your head back and rest quietly?'

It was couched as a question, but clearly he expected her to obey. And because it was simpler she did, waiting for the hum of the engine to calm her.

Only to find the impact of the man next to her negated any soothing effect. Rafiq de Couteville got to her in a way no other man ever had, his presence alerting unsuspected sensory receptors in her mind and body, so that everything seemed suddenly more vivid, more exhilarating, more *more*, she thought with a surge of apprehension.

She didn't need this. Because she'd spent so much of her time studying, she'd missed out on the social aspect of university life. But she'd watched with considerable bewilderment when heartbroken friends suffered agonies over young men she'd considered shallow and inconsiderate.

Eventually she'd decided there had to be something missing in her. Possibly growing up without a father had somehow stunted her response to men.

In a way, that was why she'd let herself be beguiled by Felipe. It had been such a relief to discover that she *could* enjoy flirting with a man!

But this—this was entirely different—a driving, uncontrollable reaction that was dangerous and altogether too tantalising.

If this was how lust started, she thought wryly, she could at last understand why it was so difficult to resist. She catalogued her symptoms: racing heartbeat, a kind of softening of the muscles, a fluttering in her stomach that hovered between apprehension and excitement, a keen attentiveness and heightened physical responses.

And an involuntary reaction to the memory of his mouth on hers that still embarrassed and shocked her.

Yes, it sounded like the first stages of attraction, all right. And of course it was doomed, because Rafiq de

Couteveille was a kind of king, even though he didn't have any title.

No, not a king—a sheikh, she decided, watching him through her lashes. His profile was strongly marked and arrogant, and when he walked she could almost hear the swish of robes about that lean, powerfully muscled body. In spite of the superb tailoring of his clothes and his luxurious car, there was something untamed about him, as though he lived by a more elemental code.

Beneath the sophisticated exterior he was a warrior, and she sensed a warrior's uncompromising determination. Clearly he was of French descent, but Rafiq was an Arabic name, and she'd bet that Moraze's ruler had familial links to both cultures.

'Are you feeling all right?'

Lexie's eyes flew open. 'Yes, fine, thank you,' she said a little disjointedly.

Rafiq snatched a sideways glance at his passenger, then fixed his gaze on the road ahead. Her exquisite skin was still pale, and her ribs would probably be painful beneath the seatbelt. 'It's not very far now.'

Smoky eyes hidden by his sunglasses, she leaned forward, a frown showing in her tone. 'I don't remember this part of the road.'

Rafiq shrugged. 'Possibly because you have not seen it before. When the doctor and I discussed your condition, we agreed it would be better for you to spend the next few days in a place with more peace than the hotel could provide. So you will be staying with me.'

And he waited with interest and a certain amount of anticipation for her response.

Her head swung around. She snapped off the sunglasses to glare at him, eyes gleaming the blue of a Spanish sword blade, her lush mouth compressed in outrage. 'Why wasn't I included in this discussion?' she demanded tautly.

'It wasn't necessary,' Rafiq replied, intrigued in spite of himself.

She could be a consummate actress. And she could be truly in love with Gastano. In which case, she'd thank him one day for this abduction.

After scrutinising him as though she couldn't believe what she'd heard, her delectable mouth opened, then closed again, to bite back what were clearly intemperate words.

Fully aware of her seething resentment, Rafiq kept his eyes on the road ahead and waited.

In the end she said through gritted teeth, 'There is no need to treat me like a halfwit just because I've been in a minor—a *very* minor—accident.'

'I'm sure your family would agree with me that you need a few days' respite after a nasty experience,' he said blandly. 'Should I contact them to check?'

'No!'

'Why not?'

After a second's hesitation, she said reluctantly, 'My sister is six months' pregnant. She'd insist on flying out here, and the trip would exhaust her. I'm sure you and the doctor are only thinking of my wellbeing, but I'm perfectly capable of looking after myself. You don't have to feel any sort of responsibility for me.'

'Possibly not, but the hotel management said they were not equipped to deal with someone convalescing, and it was agreed that this was the best solution.' He allowed that to sink in, ignoring her mutinous expression to finish, 'You will spend several days at my home—which is big enough to give you all the privacy you desire—and once the doctor has given you the all-clear you can go back to the hotel.'

After considering this she said briefly, 'In that case, I should let Count Gastano know where I'll be.'

Rafiq controlled the curl of his lip, despising himself for wanting to believe she was just a naive New Zealand girl entangled by the count's deceptive charm. His brows drew together. This wildfire, highly inconvenient attraction couldn't—*wouldn't*—be allowed to distract him from his reason for keeping her tucked safely away where she couldn't contact the self-titled count.

'Gastano has already been told about your accident.' Rafiq let that sink in, then said, 'I believe he has business here that will keep him occupied for some days. Then you can join him again.'

Steadily she said, 'It doesn't sound as though I have any choice in the matter.'

'I'm sorry if my decision conflicts with your independence.'

'Well, it does.' Her voice was crisp and cool. 'However, I've never thought banging my head against a wall was a sensible way of working through a situation. Thank you for the hospitality. I'm sure you won't mind if I avail myself of it for as short a time as possible.'

Lexie hoped the final snide comment might pierce his armour-plated inflexibility, but when he gave her a smile that almost banished her justifiable resentment she realised he was still fully in control.

And that smile was an epiphany—filled with charm and sexual magnetism, it was the sort of smile that led to broken hearts and despair.

Grimly, Lexie concentrated on the scenery until her body stopped singing.

Fortunately the scenery was worth looking at, with everything that was exotic about the tropics—brilliant sky, deep aquamarine lagoon, vivid flowers and the intense green of the countryside, coconut palms bending gracefully over white sand, and mountains purple with heat haze...

Determined not to be impressed, she decided it was just like a picture in a travel magazine.

Besides, if it came to a competition, New Zealand had some of the best beaches in the world. And pretty good mountains too, jutting into as blue a sky, and displaying every bit as much boldness and drama as these peaks did.

The man beside her said, 'I have never been to New Zealand, but I believe it's very beautiful.'

Was he a mind reader? 'It is,' she said woodenly, and let the conversation lie there, dead on the floor.

His smile was wry. 'So what particular part of the country do you come from?'

'I grew up in Northland.'

'It's a long way from there to Moraze.'

Dampening down her impulse to use the manners her mother had drilled into her, she confined her answer to a few noncommittal words. 'Indeed it is.'

If he had the nerve to mention that kiss, she'd— she'd tell him straight it was a one-off, an indiscretion she had no intention of repeating.

He didn't. Instead he asked, 'Do you specialise in a certain sort of animal in your veterinary practice?'

'Domestic animals,' she said, adding reluctantly, 'But it's a country practice, so I also deal with a lot of farm animals.'

'Horses?'

'Sometimes,' she admitted.

How did he know she was a vet?

She tried to remember where her profession was given in her passport, then recalled writing it in the arrival form she'd filled in as they came towards Moraze.

So he'd checked her travel documents—or more likely had ordered someone else to check them.

All right; security was a concern to those who were rich and famous enough to attract obsessive or downright dangerous people. Nevertheless, the thought of anyone poking around in her life gave Lexie an uneasy feeling.

Keeping her gaze defiantly on the view outside, she was about to observe tartly that as he knew all about her there was no need for further conversation, when she realised she couldn't be rude to a man who'd gone out of his way to be kind to her after the accident. Also, he was going to be her host for a few days.

She searched for something innocuous to say and finally came up with a subject. 'I went diving the day I arrived. The reef fishes are absolutely gorgeous—like living jewels.'

'You are interested in jewels?' he commented dispassionately.

Perhaps that was the way everyone referred to the fish here and he found it trite. Well, she didn't care.

Of course, Moraze was famous for the rare and exquisite—and extremely valuable—fire-diamonds found in gravel beds washed down from the mountains. Perhaps he thought she was hinting; no, how could he?

'Most people are. Off Northland's east coast we have a very interesting mix of sea life. A warm current sweeps south from the tropics, and we get a mixture of tropical and temperate fauna.'

OK, so she sounded like something out of a text-book, and was probably boring him to bits. It served him right. If he'd taken her to the hotel, instead of con-spiring with the doctor behind her back, he'd have been rid of her by now.

'It sounds most intriguing,' he said smoothly, re-turning the waves of a small group of children walking down the road.

A few metres further on he turned into a drive and the big car passed between gates that had slid back silently at the press of an unknown button. Lexie looked around for a sentry box, but clearly security nowadays was much more technical and far less conspicuous. Ahead, the drive began to climb steeply through a tangle of greenery.

'We're almost there,' Rafiq told her.

He lived in a castle. Perched on the edge of a cliff overlooking the lagoon, it frowned down over a scene as beautiful as it was deserted.

Lexie drew a sharp breath. 'I don't know much about the architecture of castles, but that looks like something out of the Middle East.'

'It's a mixture of Oriental and European styles.'

The car eased to a halt outside a huge set of what appeared to be bronze doors, sculpted and ornate, with a grid of iron spikes poised above to grind down in case of an attack. Rafiq switched off the engine.

In the silence the sound of the waves on the reef echoed in Lexie's ears. A manservant came swiftly out through a side door and went to the boot of the car, and one of the big bronze doors swung slowly open.

Rafiq looked at her, heavy-lidded eyes narrowing as

he scanned her face. 'Moraze was known to Arab sailors, but because it wasn't on their trade routes and had nothing they wanted they rarely came this way. The first settlers were led by a distant ancestor of mine, a French nobleman who had the temerity to conduct an affair with his monarch's much-prized mistress. Nowhere in Europe was safe, so he travelled farther afield, and eventually found refuge here with a somewhat motley crew of adventurers and sailors and their women.'

Fascinated, Lexie said, 'I wouldn't have thought the King of France's mandate stretched this far.'

He smiled, and the skin at the back of her neck tightened, lifting the tiny hairs there. For a second she thought she saw his ancestor, proud and gallant and tough as he shepherded that motley crew to Moraze.

Rafiq told her, 'By then it wasn't the French king he was concerned about. On his travels my forebear stole an Arabian sheikh's most precious jewel—his daughter—and as she was more than happy to be stolen they needed a refuge they could defend.'

'When did all this happen?'

'Several hundred years ago.'

Fascinated, she asked, 'What happened to the French king's mistress?'

He looked surprised. 'I believe she was married off to some elderly duke. Why?'

'I just wondered,' she said. 'I hope she liked that elderly duke.'

'I don't think anyone ever enquired,' he told her dryly.

As though bored by the discussion, he got out and came around to open her door. With the same automatic courtesy he took her arm as they went up the steps and through the door into a vast, tiled hall. She'd expected grim stone inside, but the far end of the hall was high glass doors that opened out onto a terrace bordered by shrubs and trees.

'Oh, how lovely!' Lexie stopped without thinking.

Rafiq said smoothly, 'I'm glad you like it. Let me show you up to your room.'

The staircase was wide and shallow, but by the time she reached the top her ribs were letting Lexie know they'd had a difficult time recently, and the tide of anticipation had receded, leaving her flat and exhausted. Exasperated by her weakness, she had to force her legs to take the final few steps.

He left her with a maid at the door. 'Your clothes have been brought here from the hotel. Cari will show you where everything is,' he said, and that hard green gaze rested for several charged seconds on her face. 'You look a little pale; I suggest a rest, perhaps even a nap, then some refreshments when you are ready for them.'

Her room turned out to be more like a suite—something from an *Arabian Nights* tale of love lost and won, she thought, gazing at the huge bed covered in sleek silk, its sensuously curved headboard picked out in gilding. Translucent curtains softened the light from the sea, and the silk Chinese rug was in restful shades of blue, green and cream that echoed the colours of the ocean without competing with them.

And everywhere—in the window recesses, on the exquisitely carved desk, in a massive urn on the floor—were flowers, mainly white and cream, their scent sweet and seductive on the warm air.

Lexie felt totally out of place in her white jeans and simple tee-shirt. This room looked as though it had been built for a languorous concubine in flowing, transparent robes, a woman with only one aim in life— to please her lord.

That thought tightened something deep inside her. Hot cheeked, she thought with defiance that the room— and the maid—would just have to get used to her downmarket wardrobe. Apart from her flame-coloured silk and a couple of simple dinner dresses, she'd brought only holiday clothes to Moraze.

The maid spoke English reasonably well, and after showing Lexie the dressing room, took her into a splendid marble fantasy of a bathroom dominated by a huge, freestanding bath.

'Heavens! It's almost a swimming pool!' Lexie exclaimed.

Cari laughed, and gestured at a pierced marble screen, almost hidden by pots of lush greenery. 'Behind there is the shower—very modern,' she said eagerly. 'Perhaps you would like one now before your rest?'

'I would very much, thank you.'

Sighing happily, Lexie stepped into the shower and washed herself, carefully skimming the sore spots. Since her sister had married into the Illyrian aristocracy Lexie had become accustomed to luxury. But Rafiq's castle, she thought as the water swept away her aches, was something else again, its exotic beauty out of this world.

Just like Moraze.

Rafiq's story about his ancestors had added to the island's unusual charm. With herds of elegant wild horses and rare, exquisite fire-diamonds, transcendent beauty and isolation, Moraze was a fairy-tale place, a spellbound island that might disappear overnight into an enchanted mist...

Scoffing at her unusual flight of fancy, Lexie turned off the water and wrapped herself in one of the embroidered towels the maid had placed for her.

A rest would put paid to these feverish fantasies, she thought stoutly, wincing as she rubbed herself down. She inspected her bruises, then shrugged. Because of the seatbelt she'd got off lightly, and she was a fast healer, so the marks would soon be gone.

Yet it wasn't just her ribs that had had a workout; her heart felt ominously fragile, as though it was under attack.

When she arrived back in the bedroom the maid had drawn back the covers on the bed; smiling, she pointed out a waiting jug of water and a glass. Lexie waited until she'd left the room before climbing gratefully into that enormous, decadent bed.

She slept deeply, without dreams, for almost an hour. Rubbing her eyes, she swung her feet onto the floor and realised she felt hugely better.

'Almost normal,' she said with satisfaction, examining her clothes. Carefully hung in the dressing room, they looked rather pathetic. As well as the orange silk dress, Jacoba had insisted on buying her several resort-style outfits, but what on earth did a reluctant guest in a castle wear?

And should she substitute a complete make-up for her usual lip-gloss?

No; she didn't want to look as though she was trying to attract…well, anyone.

Defiantly ignoring a quickening of her pulse, she chose one of Jacoba's purchases. The relaxed cotton trousers sat lightly on her hips to emphasise her long legs, and the silk shirt's subdued pattern repeated the soft camel colour of the trousers. The cosmetics she left at a tinted moisturiser and some lip-gloss.

Before she rang the bell for the maid she walked across to a window and looked out. Sheer stone walls fell away from the windows that opened onto an infinity of sea and sky, framed by the panelled white shutters.

The maid escorted her downstairs again and out onto the long terrace, where Rafiq de Couteveille sat in the shade of a spreading tree that carpeted the flagstones with brilliant purple petals. The sultry scent of gardenias hung heavy and erotic in the lazy air. Lexie's betraying heartbeat kicked up another gear when her host lifted his impressive height from a chair and inspected her with one of his intent, penetrating surveys. Prickles of awareness shot down her spine.

'Yes, that's better,' he said, and indicated the chair beside him. 'Are your ribs painful?'

'Only when I twist,' she told him, her voice as prosaic as she could make it. She avoided that piercing scrutiny by lowering herself into the chair. 'How is the driver?'

The sooner she got better, the faster she'd get away from this man. He attracted her in ways that scared her.

Like Jacoba, her half-sister, Rafiq possessed more than superficial good looks. Jacoba's character illuminated her stunning face, and Rafiq's formidable authority endowed his aquiline features with strength as well as charisma. It was a potent combination that made Lexie feel very vulnerable.

Rafiq told her, 'She is at home with her family, recovering fast. She sent her apologies, and her thanks for the flowers you ordered for her.'

'I'd have liked to see her, but they wouldn't let me.'

He frowned. 'The doctor told me you had to rest as much as possible.'

'I will.' Carefully steering her thoughts away from the personal, she straightened her shoulders and laboured on with brittle composure. 'This must be a very old building. Is it where your ancestors originally settled?'

'No, they built the much grimmer fortress that now overlooks the capital city. This began as a watchtower, one of a chain along the coasts that were always kept manned.'

'That Arabian princess's father must have had a long arm,' she said flippantly.

He shrugged. 'Moraze has always needed good defences.'

'I didn't realise there had been pirates on the Indian Ocean,' she admitted. 'I really don't know much about its history.'

'Why should you? If you are interested I have books I can lend you, but like most histories it is long and bloody and dominated by force. Through good luck and considerable cunning, my ancestors kept the island safe until eventually the corsairs—and other threats— were either assimilated or crushed.' He looked up as a maid appeared with a tray. 'I noticed that you drank tea at the hospital, so I ordered that, but say so if you'd prefer coffee or a cold drink.'

He noticed too much.

And oddly, that last meeting with Felipe popped into Lexie's brain. How much had Rafiq seen or heard?

She should have realised that the count's practised charm hid your average, garden-variety wolf, she thought ironically. Then she wouldn't be feeling quite so foolish.

Oh well. She'd learned something her friends at university could have told her years ago: some men weren't to be trusted.

'Tea will be lovely, thank you,' she said sedately.

What followed was all on the surface, the conversation of two people who knew little of each other, yet Lexie sensed undercurrents. Partly it was a feeling of something held back, of being swept into events over which she had no control.

But most of her tension, she decided with rueful frankness, was rooted in the explosive memory of that kiss.

CHAPTER FOUR

WARINESS tightened Lexie's skin. Unable to resist the temptation, she stole a look at Rafiq, colouring when she met greenstone eyes slightly narrowed against the sun and clinical in their detachment. A superstitious shiver ran through her—fierce, uncaged, almost desperate, forcing her to glance away hastily before those perceptive eyes homed in on her inner turmoil.

What would it take to break through his iron control?

More than she was prepared to risk, she thought bleakly. His air of authority wasn't just a family heirloom handed down from hundreds of years of unquestioned rule. Sure, some of it might be due to the potent effect of strongly handsome features backed by wealth and power, but underpinning it was an indefinable aura of masculine competence.

This man could make a woman ache with desire and scream her satisfaction in his arms.

Lexie's cup jangled musically in the saucer as she set both down, and her tone was a little too abrupt when she asked the first thing that came into her head. 'How long have you ruled Moraze?'

'For ten years,' he said readily enough, adding, 'Since I was twenty. My father died young.'

'I'm sorry,' she said quietly, turning her head to admire the crimson blossoms of a hibiscus close by.

Rafiq's gaze sharpened. Those clear-cut features might appear to reveal every emotion, but her silences were enigmatic.

So her father was a sore point.

Well, he admitted silently, if his sire had been notorious for his perfidy and cruelty, he too would avoid mentioning him.

He waited before saying, 'Life can be cruel. Tell me, what decided you to become a vet?' And he watched her through half-closed lashes, noting the tiny, almost unnoticeable signs of her relaxation.

She answered his question without hesitation. 'I love animals, and I wanted to be able to do something for them.'

'Very altruistic of you,' he drawled, irritated by her pat answer.

She flashed him a direct look, following it with a cool, 'Of course, it pays well too.'

'The training is long and very expensive, I believe.'

'I managed,' she returned, her level tone a contrast to the challenge in her eyes. 'I was lucky—I had a regular holiday job, and my sister helped a lot.'

Jacoba had worked as a model from the time she turned sixteen, determined to earn enough to care for their ill mother. Her extremely successful career had also helped with Lexie's tuition and boarding fees.

In spite of Jacoba's insistence that it wasn't necessary, Lexie was slowly reimbursing her. The past year's leave of absence had meant a hiatus in her repayments, but she'd be able to start again when she got back home.

No doubt Rafiq de Couteveille had swanned around enjoying himself with some easy option at college. Not for him the worry of sordid, boring things like where the next meal was coming from, or whether a good daughter would be staying at home to care for her mother rather than putting her own ambitions first.

She enquired sweetly, 'Where did you go to university?'

'Oxford and Harvard,' he said. 'With some time at the Sorbonne.' He added with a twist of his lips that revealed he'd guessed what she was thinking, 'My father valued education highly.'

'On Moraze as well as in his family?' she asked even more sweetly, then wished she'd remained silent.

Her urge to dig at his impervious facade was becoming reckless. And recklessness was something she didn't do.

In a level, unemphatic tone that managed to refute her snide insinuation, he said, 'Of course. Moraze has an excellent school system, and my father set up a scholarship scheme that offers promising students access to the best overseas universities.'

'Do you lose many to the lure of bigger, more sophisticated places?'

'We might, if they weren't bonded to come back here to work for five years; usually after that they're incorporated back into the fabric of our society. If not, they are then free to leave to pursue those goals.'

Lexie nodded, eyes widening as he got to his feet. Tall as she was, he towered over her so that she felt crowded. No, *dominated*, she thought, settling back into her chair and trying to look confident and at ease.

'I must go now,' he told her. 'If you need anything at all, tell Cari.'

An odd emptiness took her by surprise. 'I'm very grateful for everybody's kindness,' she said, and tried to sound her usual practical self as she went on, 'I assume I'll get a bill from the hospital—'

'No.'

'But I have travel insurance—'

'It isn't relevant,' he interrupted again, brows drawing together.

Head held so high it made her neck ache, Lexie got to her feet. Was he implying that he'd pay for it? Rich and powerful he might be, but she was an independent woman. 'Surely Moraze's health system bills travel insurance companies? In an island that depends on tourists—'

'We do not *depend* on tourists,' he said. 'We have an extremely good and progressive offshore banking system, and we have invested heavily in high-tech industries. Along with sugar, coffee and our gems, these are the pillars of our prosperity. Tourists are welcome, of course, but my government and I have taken note of the problems that come from too heavy a reliance on tourism.'

She would *not* let that aristocratic authority intimidate her. Steadily, each word bitten out, she said, 'Perhaps you would let me finish?'

A black eyebrow climbed, and his reply was delivered with a cool, autocratic politeness that reminded her he was almost a king. 'Of course. My apologies.'

'I pay my own way,' she said with brittle emphasis. 'And I pay my insurance company to cover me while I'm travelling.'

He measured her with one of those penetrating green

surveys, then shrugged dismissively. 'I will make sure someone deals with it. I suggest that for the rest of today you take things quietly. There is a pool here, if you wish to swim, although it would be sensible not to go into the water until tomorrow.'

Lexie fought back a pang of humiliating disappointment, because that didn't sound as though he was coming back to the castle. She said with what she hoped was some dignity, 'Thank you very much for everything you've done.'

'It is my pleasure,' he said formally with a half bow, before turning on his heel to stride away.

Very much the man in control, she thought, subsiding back into the chair.

Very much the ruler of his own kingdom.

But why had he been so kind? If it *was* kindness that had persuaded him to bring her here to convalesce.

What else could it be? She gazed around at vivid flowers soaking up the sun, her gaze following a bird bright as a mobile bloom that darted from one heavily laden bush to another.

Uneasily she wondered if the kiss had had anything to do with his consideration. No; he'd given no indication that he even remembered that wild embrace.

Perhaps he was so accustomed to kissing women he'd forgotten. It had almost certainly been a whim, put behind him once he'd realised she didn't know much about kissing.

This holiday had seemed such a good idea; the chance to decide once and for all whether she and Felipe had a future together.

Now she wished she'd flown straight back home to New Zealand. Felipe's attempt to pressure her into his bed had convinced her she definitely didn't want any sort of future with him, and meeting Rafiq had stirred something dark and disturbing in her, making her yearn for some unknowable, unattainable goal.

Therese Fanchette said, 'You asked for a check to be kept on Count Felipe Gastano.'

Not a muscle moved in her ruler's face, but she felt the chill from across the big desk.

Eyes chips of green ice, Rafiq rapped out, 'So?'

'Information has come in about the Interpol operation.'

Rafiq's voice gave away nothing of the cold anger biting into him. 'Is he aware of what's happening?'

'Not so far, as far as we can tell. His emails have been intercepted, of course. There has been nothing to suggest that anyone in his organisation has yet discovered our plans.'

Rafiq dampened down his spurt of triumph. 'We need a couple of days. Has he tried to contact M'selle Considine?'

'So far he has made several telephone calls to the castle. Your people have said she is still resting.'

'It is strange that he knew I was involved in her rescue, yet he has made no attempt to contact me.'

Therese Fanchette was one of the few people who knew the reason for Rafiq's caution. She frowned, and said slowly, 'Which leads one to suppose that he wants to keep out of your way. One of Gastano's closest associates is convinced that he plans to marry M'selle Considine.'

Rafiq's head came up and he stared at her. 'Is this good information?' he demanded. 'Not just gossip?'

'I don't deal in gossip; this is as good as it gets. The source mentioned that the date had been set. Has M'selle Considine said anything about that? Or about Gastano?'

'Nothing,' he said briefly. 'Continue keeping him under observation. I want to know exactly what he is doing, where he goes, who he sees, and I want to make sure that he is unable to contact M'selle Considine for at least another couple of days.'

Therese inclined her head. 'Her phone calls and email are being monitored, as you requested. If he tries to contact her we will know immediately.' After a slight pause she said, 'With respect, sir, I still think it would be better to let them communicate with each other and see what we can learn.'

'I don't.'

She gave him what he called her grandmother's look, and his mouth quirked, his expression lightening. 'I know how you feel,' he admitted. 'I rarely have hunches, but something tells me to keep her under wraps for the present. If it achieves nothing else, the knowledge that his prospective bride is my guest and incommunicado should keep his mind off his overseas affairs.'

With a reluctant smile, Therese said, 'So far your hunches have been one-hundred-per-cent accurate, so I'd be stupid not to accept this one.'

'I realise it's likely to make things more difficult for you.' After another speaking look from her, his smile widened. 'But I'm sure you'll cope.'

When he was alone again he sat back at his desk and stared at the gold pen in front of him.

One part of him was icily furious that Gastano had dared set foot on Moraze, the other was bleakly satisfied—because now the count was in unfamiliar territory where the rules were different.

Greed bolstered by overconfidence often led to mistakes, Rafiq thought with ruthless pragmatism. And coming to Moraze was the first mistake Gastano had made in a long time.

Rafiq got to his feet and walked over to the window, glancing up for a moment at the rampant stallion on the wall of his office, the badge of his house and the symbol of his family's rule. Everything he did was for Moraze's welfare.

So, was Lexie what she seemed to be, the complaisant lover of a high-flying criminal, in line to be his wife?

Or was she an innocent dupe, rather charming in her lack of sophistication?

If she wasn't a partner in Gastano's schemes, discovering the true nature of her lover could hurt her. But Rafiq knew he couldn't afford to be squeamish; he needed an edge over Gastano, and if the man planned to marry her this could be it.

Had Lexie been an innocent when she'd met the count?

A surge of lethal fury took Rafiq completely by surprise. Implacably, he fought it back, forcing himself to think analytically. It seemed unlikely. She'd spent years studying to be a vet, and, although universities were by no means hotbeds of vice, she was a very attractive woman with a swift, reckless sexual response that hinted at considerable experience.

Some of it gained in Gastano's bed, he reminded himself ruthlessly.

The memory of the kiss they'd exchanged still had the power to arouse Rafiq. What had been a rather sardonic whim on his part had changed the instant his lips met hers. She'd been vividly, tantalisingly passionate, and he'd lost himself in her open sensuality.

That kiss had been surprisingly hard to break away from—and even harder to forget.

His household offices were in the old citadel, built on a spur of volcanic rock that overtopped the city by some hundred or so metres, so he had an excellent view of the business district. His gaze skimmed the glittering water of the port, and the bright trees that lined the business area, then beyond to the houses clinging to the surrounding hills.

Logically, dispassionately, he considered the situation, examining it from all angles until he finally came to a conclusion. It was a difficult one, but he had been trained to make difficult decisions, even ones that threatened to exact a personal cost.

As the sweet-scented tropical day drew to a close, Lexie felt so much better she thought quite seriously about heading back to the hotel. Common sense decided that tomorrow would probably be a better day. The maid had insisted she rest again before dinner, closing the shutters even while Lexie was trying to persuade her that she wasn't tired.

'The Emir says it is necessary,' Cari said firmly.

Rafiq the Emir. It suited him, Lexie thought with an odd little shiver.

To her astonishment she did sleep again, lulled by the distant thunder of the waves on the reef, waking to a feeling of lazy wellbeing, a kind of hopeful anticipation, as though something wonderful was in store, something she'd waited for without even realising it...

'Just watch yourself,' she said aloud.

But that rash eagerness persisted even after she'd got up, even though she knew Rafiq wasn't coming back. Irritated by the wistful tone of her thoughts, she made an impatient gesture.

So she was attracted to him. Why should that startle her? Plenty of other women at the party had watched him from the corners of their eyes, avidly appreciating his superb male assets. Like this castle, her suite, her bathroom, he was straight out of a fairy tale—a ruler, strong, and more than a little intimidating.

He'd asked her if she liked the thought of taming a man.

Flushing, she went to brush her hair. The answer was still no, but it would be...exciting to discover whether *his* imperious control was unbreakable.

Meeting—being kissed by—Rafiq de Couteveille had summoned a hidden, shameful yearning.

To be beautiful.

There, she'd said it, but only in her mind. To rub in how completely ridiculous she was being, she forced the words through her lips: 'I'd like to be beautiful. I'd like him to look at me the way Marco looks at Jacoba. Even once would do.'

A swift, derisory glance at the mirror revealed why that would never happen. 'There's nothing *wrong* with you—you're just *ordinary*,' she said, pronouncing the word like a curse.

She stared more closely at her reflection, clinically cataloguing her assets.

Good skin, though it turned sallow if she didn't choose the right colours to wear.

Fine features, but without anything of Jacoba's witchery.

OK eyes, darkish blue, set off by black brows and long lashes.

Hair that was wavy and thick, boring brown with gold highlights in the sun.

And although she had quite a reasonable figure, she lacked any lush curves; slim and athletic was probably as good as it got.

Lexie curled her lip. All in all—*forgettable*.

And the kiss they'd shared had clearly meant so little to Rafiq he'd relegated it to some dark cupboard in his memory, never to be opened again.

Which was what *she* should do, she decided, ashamed by her neediness. It embarrassed her that the independence she'd taken so much for granted had crumbled at one touch from a man's practised mouth.

She was Lexie Sinclair, and she was a vet—a *good* vet—and she'd be a better one before she finished. Always she'd gratefully left the limelight to Jacoba and followed her own less-spectacular dreams. Being thrust into the Illyrian spotlight had shocked her, and awakened a difficult conscience within herself, one that forced her to do what she could to alleviate her father's bitter, brutal legacy. She was proud of what she'd achieved in her year in Illyria. But now it was over she craved privacy, and the chance to get on with the life she'd planned.

So how the heck had she ended up in a royal palace on an exotic island in the Indian Ocean, with the most handsome prince in the world as her reluctant host?

'Sheer chance. And you'll soon be out of here,' she told herself. 'Then you can forget about this interlude.'

But even as she turned away and dressed she knew she'd never forget Rafiq de Couteveille.

The tropical twilight was draping the hills in a hazy robe when she made her way down the stairs. At the bottom of the flight, a table stood with a huge vase of flowers, some completely alien to Lexie. Entranced by their colours and shapes, she stopped to admire them, but her attention was caught by a photograph beside the urn.

A girl—in her mid-teens perhaps, and clearly a close relative of Rafiq. Her bright, beautiful face was a softened version of his features.

From behind, Cari said, 'The Emir's sister.'

'I didn't know he had a sister,' Lexie said rapidly, warned by a note in the older woman's voice that something was amiss.

The maid looked sadly at the photograph. 'Her name was Hani. She is dead since two years,' she said. 'I will show you to the courtyard.'

'I know the way to it.'

'I think not. You sat with the Emir in the garden. This is different.'

Lexie followed her into an arcaded square, where a fountain played musically in a grassy lawn sectioned into quarters by gravel paths. Flowering shrubs were set out in patterns, the formal style tempered by luxuriant growth and the penetrating, languorous perfumes of the tropics. Along the wall that looked out over the sea was another arcade, deeply shadowed.

After telling the maid that she needed nothing, Lexie was left alone to watch the darkness come, surprised that it brought no coolness. Within minutes the sea was cloaked and the stars sprang out, forming their ancient patterns in the velvet sky.

An ache chilled her heart. How had that vital, laughing girl died? Straightening up, she turned to go back inside. Her skin tightened when she saw Rafiq walk out, and wildfire anticipation flared to life in her guarded heart.

This was what she'd been waiting for.

A faint tremor tempered her first undisciplined emotion when Rafiq came towards her—tall, powerfully built and compelling as a panther. He looked austere, as harshly forbidding as that long-ago desert sheikh who'd lost his favourite daughter to a French exile.

No words formed in her brain; silent, except for the thudding of her heartbeat in her ears, she watched him approach and wished she'd worn something more sophisticated than trousers and a shirt.

Because she felt stupid just standing there and staring, she tried for a smile, holding it pinned to her lips for a few seconds too long to be natural.

He stopped a few feet away and treated her to another trademark survey, swift and unwavering, his gaze ranging across her face.

One foolish hand started to move in an instinctive attempt to shield herself. Hastily she controlled the betraying gesture, straightening her arm.

'Have you a headache?' he demanded sharply, crossing the intervening space in three long strides.

'No.'

But he'd already taken her chin in his hand and was examining her face carefully, running his fingers through the hair at her temple where her own hand had strayed. Something sparked in the dark green eyes, and Lexie felt herself melting, her bones turning heavy and lax, a tide of honeyed sensation stirring inside her.

In a quick, panicked voice, she said, 'I'm perfectly all right. My head didn't get hurt.' Her neck still spasmed when she turned it incautiously, but apart from that she felt remarkably fit.

He let her go and stepped back, his mouth held in an uncompromising line. 'So I see. Cari tells me you have slept again. You look better.'

'I do, thank you.' Self-consciously she cleared her throat because something had caught in it, turning her normally clear tones husky.

'Good. Come and sit down. Would you like something to drink?' When she hesitated, he smiled and added, 'Without alcohol, if you prefer that.'

'It sounds perfect.' She tried to hide a treacherous surge of dizziness at that killer smile.

Something had changed, she thought as he took her elbow in an automatic gesture. She didn't exactly know what, but some instinct sensed a softening—well, no, an awareness—in him that hadn't been there before in spite of his consideration for her.

Rafiq sat her down, silently appreciating her smooth, lithe grace as she sank into the comfortable chair he held.

'This courtyard was built by one of my ancestors for his bride,' he told her when Lexie looked around with a soft sigh of pleasure. She was very tactile, responding immediately to beauty. Would she be as open and ardent when she made love?

Ruthlessly he disciplined his unruly mind. 'She was from the south of Spain, and he wanted to give her something that would remind her of home, so he built her a serenity garden, something like the one in the Alhambra. She loved it, as did later wives.'

'So this place has been a home for a long time?'

He nodded. 'After the corsairs were defeated, yes, it

became the residence of the oldest son. Until a hundred years or so ago, the actual ruler still lived in the citadel above the capital.'

He handed her a glass of juice, cool and refreshing. 'I hope you enjoy this. It's mostly lime juice, but there is some papaya there, and a local herb that's supposed to heal bruises.'

'It's delicious,' she said after a tentative sip. 'That citadel looks pretty grim. I doubt if the wives of the heirs ever wanted to leave this lovely place for it.'

Stepping back, Rafiq tore his gaze from her lips and fought back a surge of desire. He'd watched hundreds of women drink a variety of liquids, and none of them had ever affected him like this woman.

Masking his intense physical reaction with cool detachment, he answered, 'It was largely rebuilt in the nineteenth century, and is now used as offices for my household.'

He looked down, noting her interested expression, and wondered angrily what it was about her that bypassed the strictures of his brain and homed straight onto his groin. Taken feature by feature, she wasn't even beautiful. Superb skin enlivened by smoky-blue eyes and a mouth that more than lived up to its sensual promise did make her alluring. But he'd made love to some of the world's most beautiful women without feeling anything like this primitive desire to possess that gripped him whenever he saw Lexie Sinclair.

CHAPTER FIVE

RAFIQ enquired, 'You are interested in history?'

Lexie gave a rueful little smile, wondering what was going on behind the angular mask of his features. 'Because we're such a young country, most New Zealanders are impressed by anything that's more than a couple of hundred years old.'

'Moraze has a history stretching back a couple of thousand years, possibly even longer,' he told her. 'Certainly, the Arabs knew of its existence well before the end of the first millennium—its name is from the Arabic, meaning East Island, because it lies east of Zanzibar.'

East of Zanzibar—oh, the phrase had magic, she thought dreamily. *Anything* could happen east of Zanzibar. You could meet an excitingly dangerous man and discover things about yourself that shocked you.

You could even find your ultimate soul mate…

Hastily she dragged herself back to reality. 'I'm surprised they didn't exploit the fire-diamonds. Surely any trader worth his salt would have realised how incredibly valuable they were?'

Thick, black lashes covered Rafiq's hard eyes for a second before he shrugged. 'Before they are cut they look like mere pebbles, so they weren't discovered until a hundred years or so after the first de Couteveille arrived. If you're interested, there are ruins of unknown origin in the hills of the escarpment further to the north.'

'Really?'

'When you're fully recovered I will take you there,' he said casually.

A feverish thrill tightened Lexie's skin. He was watching her, and as their eyes met he smiled, a slow movement of his mouth that sent even more chills of excitement through her. He sounded as though he was looking forward to the promised excursion as much as she was.

Help! Thoughts chased through her head in tumultuous distraction. She took a swift breath and said sedately, 'How very intriguing. Does anyone have any theory on who built them?'

'Theories abound,' he informed her dryly. 'Some say they are the original Atlantis, some that they were made by the Trojans when they fled Troy, some that the people who built them came from China.'

'Are they being excavated?'

'Yes.'

He told her about the ruins and the museum, and university teams that had combined to excavate them. He astonished her with tales of the furious war of words that had broken out between two extremely opinionated archaeologists, a battle fought through the media, until finally Rafiq had threatened to ban both of them from ever coming to Moraze again.

'It seems incongruous for people whose profession is to find the truth to be so hidebound and one-eyed,' Lexie said thoughtfully.

'Egos often get in the way of the truth. Egos and greed.'

The words fell into the scented air, flat and cold and uncompromising, so much at variance with the soft hushing of the water in the fountain and the overarching infinity of the sable sky above that Lexie shivered. 'Greed? Surely archaeologists don't profit financially from their discoveries?'

'Profit need not be financial. An interesting set of ruins well-excavated will build a reputation. Greed for the possible rewards of a big discovery can override common sense, and sometimes even lead to destructive actions.'

It sounded like a warning—one directed at her.

Did he know about her father? Greed and ego had led him to do monstrous things.

Shaken by the nausea that always affected her when she thought of the man who had sired her, Lexie sipped more of the delicious juice and said colourlessly, 'I suppose you're right.'

Dismissing the subject, Rafiq got to his feet. 'Are you ready for dinner?'

'Yes, thank you.' But she stood too fast; the abrupt movement sent a jab of pain through her neck, making her clamp her lips together.

She didn't think he'd noticed, but it took him only a second to reach her, his hands gripping her shoulders from behind as he asked, 'What is it? What's the matter? This is the second time you've almost fainted.'

'I didn't.' Her voice sounded thin and far away, so she swallowed and tried again. 'I must have twisted my neck in the accident. It's fine, but every now and then the muscles remind me of it. It's nothing.'

His grasp eased, but he didn't let her go, still so close that she could discern his subtle, potent male scent.

'Perhaps this will help,' he said quietly, his thumbs moving in slow circles on the nape of her neck.

Sensuous little chills raced down her spine. Lexie closed her eyes, but that made her pulse rate soar even higher; an odd weakness in her bones threatened her with an undignified collapse. Resisting the temptation to lean back, she forced her eyes open and stared belligerently ahead, blinking to clear the dreamy haze from her sight.

Break it up right now, caution warned. She said curtly, 'I'm perfectly all right, thank you.'

'Are you?' A raw note in the words caught her attention as he turned her to face him.

She looked up into an angular visage, all hard lines and intensity. What she saw there drove every thought into oblivion.

Green eyes blazing, he bent his head. 'You don't look *all right*. Shall I carry you to your room?'

'No!' Sheer panic raised her voice.

Panic—and a wild response that blazed up from nowhere, licking through her like the best brandy, burning away inhibitions and restraint in a conflagration of need.

'Your eyes give your words the lie.' He dropped his narrowed gaze to her mouth. 'And that delicious mouth makes promises I want to collect on.'

Struggling for control, she shook her head.

'Say it,' he said in a harsh voice. 'Tell me you don't want me as much as I want you.'

Lexie's breath stopped in her throat. Her muscles locked as she met his gleaming gaze with a challenge she couldn't hide.

'Say no—or take the consequences.' This time he spoke more gently.

Wordlessly she lifted a hand to his cheek.

Half smiling, he teased her with kisses on the corners of her willing mouth. An inarticulate little sound from her made him smile, but in answer to her wordless plea he deepened the kiss, and his arms clamped her against the lean strength of his body.

The tension between them was now revealed for what it was—a fierce sexual charge that hungered for this, for more...

Rafiq lifted his head to tilt hers back, so that he could kiss the length of her throat, stopping only a fraction above the neckline of the prim silk shirt she'd bought half a world away in Illyria.

Lexie's heart literally jumped; she was sure she felt it move in her breast, then settle back into place before he said against her skin, 'You have the mouth of a siren.'

His faint accent intensified so that he sounded exotic—almost barbaric. 'And you kiss like one. Where did you learn that?'

'I don't—I don't think you *learn* to kiss,' she parried breathlessly, aware only that she couldn't let him see how much that final caress had shattered her once-safe world.

One black brow arched. 'Perhaps not,' he drawled.

And he kissed her again, mercilessly stoking the craving that ate into her, a wild, primal longing for union, a desire that burned hotter and even hotter until she was aching, her body poised and eager, her mind clouded as though with drugs.

Alarm bells rang. When he lifted his head and let his gaze slide downwards, she realised that her inner turbulence was physically revealed; her breasts had peaked, demanding a satisfaction only Rafiq could give her.

Shocked, she pulled back. For a second she thought he was going to keep her in his arms by force, but then he gave a twisted, rather sardonic smile and let her go.

'No,' he stated rather than asked.

'Dinner must be ready.' Although her voice was hoarse and uneven, she met his gaze steadily, without flinching.

His laughter held no amusement. 'Indeed, and one should never keep the servants waiting. This way.'

He extended his arm. After a moment's hesitation Lexie laid her fingertips on it, feeling the slow flex of his muscle beneath them with a voluptuous thrill—half forbidden desire, half fear.

This was *dangerous*, she warned herself silently as they walked across the great hall.

'You are afraid of me?' His tone was aloof, at odds with the penetrating look he sent her.

'No,' she said rapidly. 'Of course not.'

The person she was terrified of was herself. She appeared to have no resistance to Rafiq's particular brand of potent masculinity, and her abandon startled and dismayed her.

Stiffly, her voice as brittle as her tight-strung body, she said, 'I don't normally make a habit of kissing near strangers like—like that.' The last few words rushed out. Aware that she'd probably revealed more than she wanted him to know, she straightened her shoulders and stared straight ahead.

'I guessed as much.'

His worldliness shattered what remained of her composure. Was he insinuating that she was transparently inexperienced?

Well, she was, she thought stoutly, and what did it matter whether her untutored response to his kisses had told him so?

He finished with forbidding emphasis, 'And you need not worry—I do not force women.'

'I... Well, I'm sure you don't,' she said warily, then stopped when she saw where he was leading her. 'Oh—oh! Oh, how *lovely.*'

They'd gone up one floor and through a small salon that opened out into air lit by lamps, their warm glow illuminating a wide, stone terrace, and a row of arches on the seaward side that were latticed with stone delicately carved into flowers and leaves. Shrubs and trees cooled the terrace and shielded it from prying eyes. At one end a lily-starred pool surrounded a roofed pavilion, connected to the terrace by a stone bridge. Behind floating, gauzy drapes, Lexie discerned the outlines of furniture.

'Another whim of yet another besotted ancestor,' Rafiq explained with a touch of irony. 'He rescued his wife from a corsair ship; she loved to swim, and he loved to join her, so he built this pool and made sure it couldn't be overlooked.'

The kisses they'd exchanged suddenly loomed very large in Lexie's mind. Was he indicating...?

A sideways glance at his face banished that vagrant thought. He wasn't even looking at her, and it was impossible to read anything from his expression.

Rafiq looked down and caught her watching him. His lashes drooped, and she asked too hastily, 'Why was she on a corsair ship? Was she a pirate too?'

He stopped by the bridge. 'She was the daughter of the British governor of a West Indian island, snatched

for ransom, but the captain found her appealing enough
to keep her. When the Caribbean got too hot for him,
he fled to the Indian Ocean. She waited until they approached Moraze, intent as they were on plunder, then
managed to wound her abductor severely enough to
escape and swim ashore.'

Startled, Lexie looked up from her contemplation of
the water lilies. They weren't growing in the pool, as
she'd first thought, but had been cut and floated on the
water, a medley of white and palest yellow. Their scent
teased her nostrils. 'She must have been a very resourceful woman.'

Her companion showed his teeth in a smile that held
more than a hint of ruthlessness. 'I come from a long
line of people who did what they had to do to survive,'
he said evenly. 'Some weren't particularly scrupulous,
or even likeable; some embraced revenge without compunction if it served their plans. She hated her captor.'

A little shiver snaked down Lexie's backbone, and
memories of her father's actions clouded her eyes. 'Very
few people can claim to have only saints in their lineage.'

He smiled cynically. 'Agreed.'

'So what happened to the governor's daughter after
she swam to Moraze?'

'My ancestor found her hiding on shore. She told him
of the corsair's plans, and with his men he captured the
ship, killing the man who'd abducted her. Apparently she
and my ancestor quarrelled furiously for several months,
then astonished everyone by marrying.' This time Rafiq's
smile showed real amusement. 'They had a long and
happy life together, but they were not a peaceful couple.'

'I'm glad she found happiness after such an ordeal,'

Lexie said. 'As for peace, well, some people find peace boring.'

'Are you one of them?' he asked, indicating that they should cross the bridge.

Lexie frowned. It sounded like a throwaway question, yet somehow she sensed a thread of intention, of significance, in his words that made her feel uneasy and dangerously vulnerable. Was he exploring her personality, or just keeping the conversation alive?

Almost certainly the latter, common sense told her, and yet...

Because the silence threatened to last too long, she set out briskly across the bridge. 'As a vet I don't like too much excitement—it tends to involve going out in the middle of the night in filthy weather to deal with sick, very expensive animals and their frantic owners! But I certainly enjoy variety.'

There, that was innocuous enough, surely? She didn't want to get into anything heavy here. Although they'd kissed—and he'd seemed to enjoy those kisses—she wasn't going to let herself fall into the trap of believing they'd meant anything more to him than the superficial response of a virile man to a woman of the right age to mate.

A woman whose instant arousal, she thought with a burning shame, must make it obvious she found him irresistible.

But then, he'd be used to that response—it probably happened in every female who set eyes on him.

And to quench the flickering embers of desire she'd better stop this train of thought right now. So she asked, 'What about you?'

'I enjoy moments of peace,' Rafiq said, his tone giving nothing away. 'But I think a life of unalloyed tranquillity and harmony could become tedious after a while. I relish a challenge.'

'Oh, so do I,' she responded, and changed the subject abruptly. 'The water lilies here must be different from the ones at home. Ours fold up at dusk.'

'So do ours.' He smiled. 'I believe the petals of these ones are held in place by candle wax. It is a local tradition.'

A few steps brought them to the pavilion, where Rafiq held the drapes back with a lean hand. 'Do you play chess?'

'Badly,' she replied, walking into the airy space and looking around. 'I don't think I'd be even the mildest challenge to anyone who can think more than two moves ahead.'

But several hours later, after they'd eaten, she was sitting on the edge of her chair and glowering at an elaborate chessboard, her mind working frantically.

Rafiq said evenly, 'You lied.'

Her head came up, and she met his half-closed green eyes with a flash of fire. 'I don't lie.'

'You said you were no challenge.' His voice was amused.

'You're winning,' she pointed out. 'In fact, I can't see how I'm going to get out of this situation.'

He lifted his brows. 'If you want to know—'

'No! Give me another few minutes to see if I can do it.'

His quick grin—so unlike his usual air of sophisticated forcefulness that it startled her—was quickly controlled. 'Go ahead,' he invited.

Frowning, Lexie puzzled over the board, saw what

seemed to be the perfect move, and almost made it—until further intense thought revealed it would involve a check to her king a few moves further on.

Rafiq had a poker player's face; not a single emotion escaped his control. She was acutely, violently aware of him at his ease in the cane chair, long limbs relaxed, the light from a dozen soft lamps highlighting the arrogant sweep of cheekbones, the tough jawline and the hooded green of his eyes.

Lexie's breath caught in her throat. Behind him she could see several elegant loungers, and a day bed—a sinful thing, more than big enough to hold two people during the hours of a lazy tropical siesta. A puff of breeze smoothed over her skin, sensitising it...

Every coherent thought died a swift and unappreciated death, drowned by a sensuous recklessness. *I want you*, she thought, the need so violent she wondered for a panicky second if she'd actually said it.

Colour burned her cheeks. She had to get out of there, away from this man—away from this love nest with its scented flowers and gentle lamplight. Abruptly she said, 'Do you mind if I call it a day? I'll concede if you'll tell me how to get out of this.'

One black brow climbed, but he showed her.

As they blocked out the moves, he said in a casual voice, 'In two days' time I will be attending a special function—the opening ceremony for another hotel, but this time the celebrations are for those who worked on the building, and those who will work in it. A people's party, much less formal than the affair you attended the other night. If you feel up to it, would you like to come with me?'

Completely taken aback, she flushed again, search-

ing for words. 'I feel fine, but I don't want to intrude…
I'll be quite happy here, you know.'

His all-too-potent smile sent erotic little shivers
through her. 'There will be music and dancing and excellent food, and very few speeches.'

Torn, Lexie hesitated. Being with Rafiq was starting
to mean far too much. A sensible woman would find
some good excuse to refuse.

Deciding that being sensible was vastly overrated,
she strove for some of his confidence. 'I'd love to come.
It sounds like great fun.'

'I hope so.'

Rafiq wondered what was going on behind that
serene face. She didn't realise that she was actually a
prisoner in the castle; he hoped she never would.

Not for the first time he wondered how an intelligent,
accomplished woman like her had been duped by
Gastano. Was she bored with the man? She hadn't tried
to contact the count, and certainly she'd shown no signs
of missing him.

Which could mean that to her the relationship was
as superficial as Gastano's charm.

It seemed likely. Rafiq's mind ranged back to the first
time they'd met; she'd been offhand with the count, and
in spite of Gastano's presence she'd been acutely aware
of Rafiq.

As physically aware as he'd been of her.

Lust at first sight, he thought, controlling a cold, humourless smile. His jaw hardened as Lexie began to
pack away the chessmen in their carved box.

Did she know Gastano intended marriage? It didn't
seem likely. Or was this her way of showing Gastano
that she'd wanted no more than an affair with him?

If so, she had no understanding of her lover. Her family connections would be worth more than gold to the count. As her husband, he'd have entrée into a milieu he'd long coveted—the charmed world of royal power and influence.

The count would be furious if he thought the woman he'd targeted as a ticket to respectability and even greater power was slipping through his fingers.

And furious men made mistakes.

Gastano had already tried to establish contact with Lexie. Rafiq recalled Gastano's email note, written in a tone he probably intended to be disarming, but with enough innuendo to summon a shockingly forthright and very territorial response from Rafiq. And although he couldn't find a logical reason for it, he still felt strongly that hiding her away from Gastano was the only way to keep her safe.

Because of Hani? He dismissed that thought. His sister had been naïve; Lexie was not. Even if she had been when she met Gastano, two months as his mistress would have put paid to any innocence.

The question Rafiq couldn't ask nagged at him. Had she responded to Gastano with the same wildfire passion she'd revealed in his own arms?

The thought made his fists clench. Watching the way the golden lamplight shifted and shimmered across her bent head as she carefully sorted the chessmen, Rafiq wondered again if his objectivity was being hijacked by his response to her. Those smoky blue eyes, half-hidden by her long, black lashes, might mask her thoughts, but nothing could disguise that softly sensuous mouth.

His gaze hardened as Lexie slid the queens into

place, capable fingers moving swiftly, her lashes casting shadowy fans on her exquisite skin.

Lexie looked up to find her host's dark eyes on her, intent and speculative, as though trying to see into her soul. Her nerves sparked and colour heated her cheeks.

'You look tired,' he said quietly. 'How is your neck?'

Her colour deepened. 'It's fine, thank you. It just catches me now and then.'

She took her time about closing the case that held the chess set, fiddling with the catch until she regained some composure. But although her skin was cool once more, the fire inside her still burned with a fierce, hungry flame.

Getting to her feet, she said a little shortly, 'It's been a lovely evening. Thank you.'

He rose with her, looking down from his considerably superior height with a smile that didn't reach his eyes. They walked in silence across the bridge and back through the castle.

Lexie wished she could be as controlled. His nearness was delicious torture. She both longed for the door of her room and resented its imminence, torn between this dangerously addictive arousal and the knowledge that the chemistry between them meant nothing more than uncomplicated, old-fashioned animal magnetism.

Looked at from a biological point of view, she thought, trying hard to be dispassionate and scientific, the volatile attraction pounding through her bloodstream and alerting every cell in her body was a natural urge stimulated by hormones that somehow knew she and Rafiq would make splendid children together.

Something deep inside her melted.

Ruthlessly she told herself it didn't mean she was in

love with him. He certainly wasn't in love with her. It was simply a matter of genes, the need to perpetuate the species—all the things she'd learned in her long and expensive university training.

And although her response to him was a fiery torment, it didn't really mean much. Worldwide, there were probably millions of men she could feel this way about.

She'd just never met one before.

Anyway, when she married she wanted what Jacoba had—a man who adored her and accepted her as his equal in every way.

Not someone who saw her simply as a sexual partner.

Rafiq's voice broke in on her ragged thoughts as they reached the door of her room. 'That is an interesting expression.'

She stiffened, her brain searching for something innocuous to say. Lamely—and too quickly—she said, 'I was thinking about a biological... Ah, about biology.'

His lips curved in a wry, humourless smile, and his eyes were darkly shaded. 'So was I.' The last word was spoken against her eager, expectant mouth.

His previous kisses had been explorations, she thought dimly; this one wasn't. He knew what she wanted, and when she gave a muffled groan and surrendered, he gathered her even closer so that she could feel his physical reaction—the electric intensity of his desire, the erotic difference between her female softness and his male power.

A rush of adrenalin sharpened her senses as her body sprang into exhilarating life. Shivering with delight, she forgot everything but the sheer physical magic of his embrace and her mindless, primal response. His body heat, the strength of his hands on her, the faint, intrinsic scent of him, the tactile excitement of his skin beneath her seeking fingers—all combined to add sensual fuel to that inner fire burning away inhibitions and caution.

CHAPTER SIX

Rafiq loosened his arms and rested his cheek on the top of Lexie's head, gently rocking her in his arms while she came back to earth.

'It is too soon,' he said, his voice oddly harsh. 'And although you are like wildfire in my arms, there are smudges under those beautiful eyes, and I think you are trying to stifle a yawn in my shoulder. Good night, Lexie. Sleep well. Tomorrow I will take you on the trip that was cut short by the accident.'

She might see something of the famed wild horses of Moraze. Lexie should have been delighted. To her shock and dismay, all she could summon was mild enthusiasm. Stifling a small sound of protest, she composed her expression into serenity and eased back, feeling foolishly bereft when he let her go with insulting ease.

'I'll look forward to that.' Oh Lord; her voice was breathy and soft, as though she were mimicking Marilyn Monroe!

Without meeting his eyes, she directed a swift, shaken smile at him and turned into her room, nerves jumping when she closed the door. She leaned back against the carved wood, striving to force strength into her lax bones.

This whole situation was too dangerous. She shouldn't have allowed those passionate moments in his arms, moments charged with a carnal magic that still ached through her.

Allowed them? She'd welcomed them, surrendered to them, wallowed in the erotic excitement of them, until in the end she'd had no defences left. The intensity of her emotions, the sensations Rafiq made her feel, scared her. When he touched her she lost herself, became someone different, an alien person with no shame and no control.

Lexie wrenched herself upright and walked across to a window, staring out across the lagoon to the white line of the reef.

Slowly she dragged air into her lungs. These bewildering days on Moraze were teaching her that she wasn't capable of an easy relationship with lots of lust followed by a cheerful goodbye once it was sated.

'Not my style,' she said a little bitterly to the silent room. Certainly not with Rafiq…

But at least she'd learned one thing about him: he didn't want just casual sex either. Because he could have had her right there and then, and he'd known it, yet he'd pulled back.

She set her jaw. Because her resistance was so easily breached, there must be no more of this perilous intimacy. After tomorrow she'd leave the castle. And she'd make it clear she wasn't in the market for, well, anything. He wouldn't press her; Rafiq de Couteveille was a sophisticated man, and there were plenty of sophisticated, experienced women who'd be more than happy to satisfy his urges.

And that sharp stab of emotion was *not* jealousy, or—worse still—anguish at the thought!

'There!' Rafiq pointed over her shoulder, his voice urgent. 'Can you see them?'

'Yes.' Thrilled, Lexie lifted the binoculars he'd lent her and examined the small herd.

Not at all spooked by the vehicle, the horses lifted their heads and serenely surveyed them. A couple of skittish youngsters danced sideways, their coats gleaming in the tropical sun, only to subside and snatch another mouthful of grass. The stallion, master of his harem, clearly realised that no harm would come to them from this particular vehicle. Although he kept a watchful eye on them, his stance showed his trust. Even the wise old mare that led the herd had already dropped her head to graze again.

Lexie stole another glance at the arrogant line of Rafiq's profile as he watched the herd. The angular lines of his face intent yet relaxed, he looked as though the sight of the herd satisfied a hunger in his soul. Her heartbeat picked up speed. How would she feel if he ever gazed at her like that?

Angry with herself at such futile longing, she lifted the binoculars to her eyes again. 'How long have they been on Moraze?'

'The bride of the first de Couteveille brought some of her father's horses with her. They were set free up here, and here they've flourished ever since.'

Like the de Couteveilles, she thought. She said on a

sigh, 'I'll always remember this day. Thank you so much.'

'It has been my pleasure,' he said calmly, and set the four-wheel drive in motion. As they started on the winding descent to the fertile lowlands, he asked, 'Which did you enjoy most—the jungle animals in the mountains, or the horses?'

She laughed. 'That's an unfair question, but I was fascinated by the jungle animals, and can't help wondering how on earth their ancestors got here.'

'Biologists are working on their provenance,' he told her. Without any change in tone he went on, 'So you liked the horses better?'

Surprised at his perception, she admitted, 'Yes. They're so wild and free, and so lovely. I suppose I envy them.'

'Perhaps we all do.' He sent her a glance that set her toes tingling. 'But you have independence. Or are you planning to give it up?'

Startled, she said quickly, 'No.'

His glance sharpened before he returned it to the road ahead. 'What appeals to you so much about the thought of freedom?'

'Surely it's everyone's desire?' She looked ahead to the vehicle that accompanied them, driven by a bodyguard with another by his side. Living like that would stifle her. How did Rafiq stand it?

'Most people seem content to settle into comfortable servitude,' he observed.

'Perhaps. And perhaps they're happier than those who long for freedom.' She looked up. 'Are you content with your chains?'

'Tell me what you think to be my chains.'

'Well, you're forced to live as the ruler of Moraze. Don't you ever have the urge to break free?'

His gaze flicked across her face, then returned to the road ahead. 'Sometimes,' he said, shrugging. 'And you? What chains hold you?'

Lexie bit her lip. Like him, servitude to her fore-bears, but she wasn't going to tell him about her father. 'Oh, nothing really,' she said lamely, wishing she hadn't embarked on this.

She stared around, then said, 'Oh! I recognise this place—it's where we crashed!' Frowning, she leaned forward to examine the road and the grassy bank as they passed the spot. 'I wonder why I didn't see the animal that ran out in front of us.'

'It's possible you did see it, but because of the shock you don't remember,' Rafiq said coolly. 'The driver has recovered completely, by the way.'

'I still feel guilty because I didn't go to see her,' Lexie said without thinking.

He shrugged. 'You have high standards of behaviour. She did not expect it.'

Something in his tone made her say crisply, 'Simple courtesy isn't exactly a high standard.' And without finesse she steered the conversation in another direction. 'Tell me, what should I wear to the hotel party? I don't know the sort of thing that would be appropriate.'

He sent her another enigmatic glance, almost as though she'd surprised him. 'The dress you wore the night we met would be perfect.'

The flame-shot silk Jacoba had bought for her? Lexie loved that dress, and not just because the colour brought out a richness in her hair, and gave her skin a glow it didn't normally have. In it she felt like someone else—a different, bolder, more confident person.

Torn between a desire to look her best and a cowardly caution, she hesitated, fixing her gaze on the scenery as Rafiq steered the vehicle around a set of hairpin bends.

When they'd been safely and skilfully negotiated, she asked, 'Are you sure?'

'I am,' he said, and smiled, a slow, amused curl of his beautiful mouth that sent excitement flickering through her. 'Colour is important here,' he went on. 'It seems to be a tropical thing. In cooler climates, people wear more subdued hues.'

'Possibly because we have paler colouring, and vivid shades tend to wash us out.'

'But not you,' he told her with the confidence of a man who saw nothing unusual in discussing clothes with a woman.

The crisp note of challenge in his tone brought up her chin. 'Then I'll wear the dress.'

Only to stop there, because she didn't know what to say next.

Although he didn't seem to be flirting with her, there was definitely an appreciative glint in the greenstone gaze when it skimmed her face before returning to the road.

'Whatever you wear you will look good,' he said almost dismissively as he guided the vehicle around another hairpin bend.

Lexie didn't know whether it was a compliment or a sop to her rare lack of confidence.

'Thank you,' she said spiritedly, wishing she'd dated more often, even indulged in a couple of affairs. Surely experience would have given her some idea of how to deal with him?

Probably not, she thought with a touch of cynicism, watching the trees flash by—a coastal forest sparser than the jungle. Rafiq de Couteveille, ruler of Moraze, was no ordinary man.

'The jungle reminded me of New Zealand,' she said absently. 'Those massive trees with their huge trunks reaching for the sky, each notch and fork filled with epiphytes—just like home!'

'Rain forest looks similar the world over. I've seen photographs of New Zealand trees; I was most impressed with the size and the majesty —the authority—of those huge trees that grow in the north. Kauri, are they not?'

'Yes. Northern New Zealand's iconic tree, along with the coastal pohutukawa, and true lords of the bush.'

She looked away again, longing to be safely back home, away from all this perilous beauty, the constant sensation of being watched and somehow under siege.

Sheer imagination, of course. And although she was out of her depth with Rafiq she wasn't green enough to take his embraces seriously, no matter how powerfully she was affected by them.

Yes, he'd been kind—well, taking her into his home after the accident was more than simple kindness—but that didn't mean anything. He'd probably have been just as considerate—without the kisses!—if she'd been fifty and grey-haired.

The road straightened once they reached the fertile plains, rich with sugar cane plantations and farms where flowers grew in ribbons and rainbows of saturated colour—seductive, scented orchids, the polished brilliance of anthuriums, and the erect, surreal stems of ginger in all their bold, vibrant hues.

Lexie let out her breath on a soft sigh. 'This is so beautiful.'

'Indeed,' he said calmly, and sent her another sideways glance. 'Are you tired? There is a place you might like to see a little farther on.'

'I feel fine.' An understatement if ever there was one; her mind and senses were at full stretch, intensely stimulated by his potent, compelling presence.

He touched a button and spoke in the local language to the car in front. A few moments later he slowed the car, took a sharp intersection and headed up into the mountains again through jungle that got more and more dense as they climbed.

'We are going to a lake that occupies an extinct volcanic crater,' he told her. 'The islanders believe it is the home of a particularly beautiful but extremely dangerous fairy, who has been known to amuse herself by seducing young men and then sending them away. They become afflicted with love for her, and drown as they try to swim back to her arms.'

Lexie repressed an odd little shiver to ask lightly, 'And does this happen often?'

He sent her an amused glance. 'Not within living memory, but that may be because most young men are careful not to go there until they are married. She isn't interested in married men, apparently.'

'You're not afraid?' she asked with a teasing smile, then wished she hadn't.

His response was sardonic. 'Not a bit,' he said coolly. 'I have yet to meet a woman I'd drown for.'

Her heart clamped tight. He was warning her off—why?

Last night when he'd stopped their lovemaking she'd been impressed because she'd thought it meant he didn't want just sex from her. Had she misread his consideration?

Perhaps his blunt statement of a moment ago was intended to convey that he didn't plan a serious relationship.

Was there a sophisticated way to tell him flatly that she wasn't foolish enough—even in her dreams—to have hoped for that…?

No, she thought, mentally cringeing. But he knew that she wanted him. Last night her wild response to his kisses had shocked her into planning a retreat, but that had been cowardly. Rafiq was the first man she'd ever wanted– sexy as hell, considerate, intelligent, compelling and trustworthy.

Who better to be her first lover?

And Lexie made a decision—a reckless, possibly even dangerous decision—one she knew might well cause her heartbreak.

But she also knew that, no matter the grief, she'd never regret making it. Just once in her life she'd throw away caution and follow her desires.

It would be worth it, she thought, controlling the breath that came too rapidly. She turned her head, pretending to be contemplating the scenery, and knew that next time they kissed she'd— Well, she thought nervously, she'd let him realise that she didn't need to be cosseted. She was a free and independent woman, and she wanted him.

The crater lake was almost round, surrounded by

thick jungle, and on one side a semi-circle of cliffs. In spite of the sunlight a faint mist hovered over it, and the only sound was bird song, faint and eerily distant.

'I can see why the legend grew up,' Lexie said, glancing around. 'It's a very potent place. Is the water still hot?'

'No, but that mist is nearly always there.' He looked down at her, ignoring the security car that had preceded them, and the bodyguard standing with his back turned as he swept the jungle with binoculars. 'I imagine crater lakes are not unusual in New Zealand.'

'There's a dormant volcanic field not far from where I live, and one of the extinct volcanoes has a crater lake, with eels as thick as your arm in it.' She gave a lopsided smile. 'It's an evocative place too, but that might be because by the time people have climbed its very steep sides they're exhausted!'

He laughed and took her elbow, steering her back to the car. 'We must go now. I have a meeting I can't miss tonight.'

They had nearly reached the castle when he said casually, 'I won't be in for dinner tonight, but tomorrow night I know of a charming little restaurant where we can eat, if you'd like to go. The chef is a genius.'

Hiding her disappointment, she told him, 'That would be lovely, thank you.'

Safely up in her room, she sighed, hugged herself, and went into the opulent bathroom to run a shower. She should, she thought, make it a cold one; for a few seconds she'd wondered whether there was any chance that Rafiq was courting her—to use an old-fashioned term.

Fortunately common sense soon banished that

hope. But he couldn't fake the hunger he felt. That was genuine.

Excitement burned in the pit of her stomach, completely different from the way she'd felt when she'd realised Felipe was interested in her. She'd been flattered, and she'd enjoyed his company, had found him attractive, but it now seemed very pallid and ordinary compared to the way Rafiq affected her.

As she dried herself down she wondered what Felipe was doing. Since the accident she'd thought very little about him—when she was with Rafiq she didn't have room in her mind for anyone else.

And she was still angry with Felipe for thinking he could railroad her into sleeping with him.

Still, perhaps she should try to contact him, to tell him finally that it was over. But then he'd made no attempt to get in touch with her, and since he'd only planned to stay a couple of days, he might even have left Moraze. She'd probably never see him again, a thought that brought an unexpected sense of relief and freedom.

And as she ate her solitary dinner she recalled the warning Rafiq had delivered while they were at the perilous pool.

'I have yet to meet a woman I'd drown for...'

Odd how much that hurt.

Get used to it, she thought staunchly, because she wasn't going to play the coward's role again and change her mind.

Lexie spent the next morning in luxurious laziness with a couple of books Rafiq had sent up to her room via the maid, with a brief note apologising for his absence. One was a novel written by a famous author from

Moraze, the other a beautifully produced guide to the island with fabulous photographs and a very entertaining history. She then tired herself by swimming lengths in the pool, and napped in the heat of the day, determined to be alert that night and prove that she was fully recovered from the very minor results of the accident.

For dinner she wore a sleek resort dress in a subdued gold that brought out the lights in her hair. She didn't look too bad at all, she decided, adjusting the neckline. The skirt fell to her ankles, and the sash belt clung to her narrow waist.

Tiny hot shivers tightened every nerve in her body. Later she and Rafiq would be alone together. Perhaps they'd kiss, and she'd know once more that aching, bittersweet delight in his arms.

And this time, instead of following his lead, she'd let him know—subtly, she hoped—that she was ready for the next step.

Whatever that might be…

Rafiq drove them to the restaurant in an unmarked car. By mutual consent they kept the conversation light, speaking mostly of the island and its beauty. A few miles inland they came to a large building throbbing with lights, and almost jumping with music. Lexie was glad when they passed it by.

He said, 'Since the sugar industry was rationalised years ago, some of the old mills have been transformed into places like this where the locals can get together to sing and dance and play music. They're now being discovered by tourists, but I thought that you might prefer somewhere smaller and more intimate. You agree?'

It was a good sign that he'd read her so accurately,

though right this minute she'd probably have agreed if he'd told her the moon was falling into the sea. Sedately she said, 'It sounds perfect.'

The rest of the short journey was made in silence, although a vibrant awareness hummed between them as Rafiq turned the car down a narrow road that led back towards the coast again. Palms swayed languidly above, and the salty tang of the sea mingled with the flower perfumes that saturated these coastal lowlands. Lexie kept her eyes on the white line of the reef around a headland that jutted like a giant castle, gaunt against the star-dazzled sky.

She could wait; in fact, this slow build-up would make their kisses even sweeter, more fiery. Half eager, half apprehensive, she wondered if tonight…?

Rafiq's car was clearly well known; they were met by a man who indicated a secluded parking spot away from the small courtyard.

How many other women had Rafiq brought here? Lexie squelched the jealous little query. Live for the moment, she advised herself fiercely as she went with him into the vine-hung restaurant.

Afterwards, looking back, Lexie would always remember it as an evening of enchantment. They ate superb seafood and drank champagne, and he honoured her with his plans for the future of his country, although he first warned her, 'I'm likely to bore you.'

Lexie's brows rose. Nothing about him would bore her—and she suspected he knew it. Furthermore, she'd had enough of protecting herself. She didn't care any more. 'As a citizen of another small island nation—with about a million fewer people than Moraze—I'm interested in how you see its future.'

'I hope it will eventually be an independent and self-sustaining country under its own prime minister,' he said promptly. 'But there is some time to go before we reach that point. Democracy isn't well-established here; my father and grandfather were benevolent autocrats of the old school, so it's been left to me to introduce changes, and old habits die hard. It will probably take another generation before the reforms are so firmly bedded in that the citizens of Moraze will both choose and be their own rulers.'

'And you don't regret giving up power?'

He shrugged. 'No.' He scanned her face and said, 'The band's striking up. Would you like to dance?'

On Moraze, it seemed, ballroom dancing was the established mode. Fortunately Lexie had accompanied a friend to classes while they were at high school. If she'd known then that someday she'd be dancing a waltz with the ruler of an exotic island in the Indian Ocean, she'd have paid much more attention to the steps, she thought as she got up with him.

Heart thumping, she went into Rafiq's arms, felt them close around her, and gave herself up to the sensation. He moved with the lithe, powerful grace of an athlete, keeping perfect time. In his strong arms, his body only an inch or so away from hers, Lexie found the sexual magnetism that crackled between them both compelling and dangerously disturbing.

Part of her wanted to get these preliminaries over and go back to the castle to lose herself in this voluptuous recklessness. Another part treasured this subtle communication of eyes and senses, this aching, unsatisfied physical longing that promised an eventual rapturous release in each other's arms.

At first they talked, but eventually both fell silent; Rafiq's arm tightened across her back, and her breath came faster and faster between her lips as their bodies brushed and swayed and were taken hostage by the music.

Lexie forgot there were others there, that although the lights were dim and subdued they could be seen. Eyes locked onto Rafiq's darkly demanding ones, she danced in a thrall of desire.

He said, 'Let's get out of here.'

In a voice she didn't recognize, she said, 'Yes.'

CHAPTER SEVEN

BUT once in the car Lexie sat still, hands clasped tightly in her lap, until Rafiq ordered, 'Do up your seatbelt.'

'Oh,' she said, feeling stupid, and fumbled for it.

He said something harsh, leaned over her and found it, slamming the clip into the holder.

Lexie's breath locked in her throat while she waited for him to straighten up. Instead he bent his head and kissed her, and fireworks roared into the sky, wiping everything from her mind but this delicious, intolerable need. Her hands came out to grasp his shirt as her mouth softened beneath the hungry demand of his lips.

Until faintly the sound of an engine percolated into her consciousness. Lights flashed across her closed lids. She realised they were real lights, not the fire in her blood, and reluctantly opened her eyes.

Rafiq lifted his head. After an incredulous second he said in a raw, goaded voice, 'This is—not my usual style.' When she didn't answer he gave a ghost of a laugh and finished, 'Not yours, either?'

'No,' she admitted.

He set the car in motion, saying grimly, 'I think you must be sending me mad.'

'I know the feeling.'

He flashed her another fierce glance, then smiled, reached for her hand, and tucked it beneath his on the wheel, only releasing it when they reached a small town on the way home. Lexie let it rest in her lap, oddly chilled by the subtle rejection. Of course, it might merely be that he needed to concentrate more—but what if he was ashamed of wanting her?

Was that why he'd taken her to the tiny, out-of-the-way restaurant? After all, she was the daughter of one of the century's most despised dictators...

Oh, for heaven's sake, she thought, angrily resentful of the hurdles her mind kept setting up for her heart, he almost certainly doesn't know who your father is! And you're *not* responsible for Paulo Considine's actions.

Why should Rafiq be ashamed of her? She scrubbed up quite well, and the gown she was wearing made the most of her slim, athletic figure and her colouring. Jacoba would make her look very second-rate, but then Jacoba had that effect on every woman!

Rafiq had simply chosen somewhere discreet, and she was grateful to him for being so understanding.

And soon she'd be in his arms and her reservations would be banished.

The thought should have filled her with dismay, but although it was strange to realise that she'd lost her control so completely to a man she barely knew, she felt nothing but happiness, deep and sure and powerful.

Anyway, she was beginning to find out more about him. He was kind and thoughtful, as well as being incredibly sexy. He was also extremely intelligent, and he wanted the best for his country and his people.

She sat up straight and looked through the side window at the starlit night. Pride was a hard thing to deal with, she thought with a wry smile, but at the moment it was all she had—pride and this unwanted, out-of-character desire that had blossomed so swiftly.

And would, she knew, come to nothing; the best thing she could hope for was for it to burn out in the fierceness of passion. She didn't expect Rafiq to reciprocate. He'd be embarrassed if he knew just how eager she was to discover what making love with him was like.

Better by far for him to believe she was enjoying a torrid affair with him, a holiday fling...

'What are you thinking?' he asked, stopping the car outside the huge doors of the castle.

'Just—drifting.' Her cheeks heated at the lie.

He switched off the engine and smiled ironically at her, moonlight outlining the autocratic angles and lines of his features. Her heart swelled, and she let herself be carried away by the wave of hunger that had been threatening to break over her all evening.

This, she thought with a desperate recklessness, was worth any pain that might lie in the future. *Anything.*

Inside the castle, Rafiq suggested a nightcap. 'We have our own distillery here. I know you enjoy wine, but at least once you should try Moraze's rum. It is mellow, and filled with the essence of flowers.'

After the first small sip, she agreed, 'You're right; it's delicious.' Tension bit into her, and she walked over to a window, clutching the glass as she gazed out onto the lagoon, that shimmered silver beneath the black sky. 'I'll always remember Moraze like this,' she said on a half sigh. 'It's everyone's secret ideal of a tropical island, filled with flowers and sunshine and laughter.'

And moonlight, and passion...

Rafiq's voice came from close behind her. 'It's not all charmingly romantic. We have the occasional hurricane, and there have been tidal waves. And although the islanders' smiles are warm, they also cry.'

She turned her head slightly, nostrils flaring at the subtle, evocative scent—pure alpha male—that teased them. 'That's life, isn't it?' she said lightly. 'Always the bitter with the sweet. But for tonight I think I'll let my inner romantic indulge herself.'

He bent his head and kissed the back of her neck, sending tiny, sexy shivers through her. 'It will be my pleasure to allow her full rein,' he said, and let his teeth graze her skin.

The shivers transmuted into arrows of golden anticipation, darting from nerve end to nerve end to summon responses from every cell in her body. Whatever happened, she had this, she thought, turning to meet his intent eyes. And for tonight, this was enough.

'Kiss me,' he commanded between his teeth. 'For hours I've been watching your mouth, imagining it under mine. Kiss me.'

Smiling, she took his face between her hands. Her fingertips tingled as they shaped out the forceful lines of his jaw, traced his beautiful, relentless mouth, travelled along the high, aristocratic sweep of his cheekbones. Excitement beat high in her, filling her bloodstream with stars, summoning a witchery of desire that ached through her in a slow, languorous tide, melting her bones.

Rafiq bent his head, and flames sparked between them as his lips came down on hers.

With an odd sigh of relief Lexie sank against him,

surrendering herself to the magic of this moment, this place—this man.

It satisfied some more than physical hunger when she felt his body harden against hers, his arms tighten, and the muted thunder of his heart drown out hers. To know that she could do this to him was an aphrodisiac in itself.

'You're sunlight and moonlight in my arms,' he said against her mouth, punctuating each word with a kiss. 'Golden and warm. Yet behind those blue, sunlit eyes there are secrets, depths as deep and mysterious as a star-shadowed night.'

'No secrets,' she said, but she'd lied and he knew it. She saw the change in his eyes.

And because she couldn't bear to spoil this, she qualified with a wry smile, 'No important secrets, anyway. Just the usual things no one wants to admit to.'

He held that mercilessly penetrating look for a moment more, then his dark lashes came down and he smiled, an almost humourless quirk of his lips.

'We all have secrets,' he said, and kissed her again before putting her away from him, and saying in a cool tone that set a distance between them, 'I think you need rest. You say you are completely recovered from the accident, but there are still traces of shadows beneath those lovely eyes.'

Although disappointment and frustration ached through her body, she smiled and nodded and went with him.

At her door he picked up her hand and kissed the palm, then closed her fingers over it. 'Sleep well,' he said quietly, and left her.

Hours later, she thought grimly that any darkness

beneath her eyes was due to the time she spent awake each night, sleep driven away by highly coloured, erotic fantasies.

But when sleep finally came it somehow transmuted the keen frustration of the previous night into serene acceptance. The next day Rafiq took her for a picnic to a secluded bay on one of the royal estates. They ate in the soft, whispering shade of the casuarinas, and swam in milk-warm water, and even though they barely touched, Lexie had never been so happy. It was delicious to be given time, to feel no pressure from him at all, even though she knew he wanted her.

He made no secret of it. His glances, his smiles, the narrowed regard that set her heart pounding, all told her so. Their lovemaking, she thought dreamily as she got ready for the hotel party that night, would come when they were both ready. Until then she was content to float along in this passion-hazed dream.

Of course she wore the flame-coloured dress with its matching high-heeled sandals, and applied cosmetics with the skill and expertise she'd learned from her sister. When she was ready she stepped back from the enormous mirror and gave her reflection a swift, secret smile.

Be careful—be very careful—her mind warned, but she knew her heart wasn't going to listen. Her emotions seemed to be riding a roller coaster, the gentle acceptance of the day banished by a cocktail of adrenalin and anticipation pulsing like drugs through her veins.

At the bottom of the staircase she spared a compassionate glance for the photograph of his sister Hani. Why didn't he mention her?

Perhaps the grief of her untimely death was still too raw.

When she entered the salon, Rafiq was talking into a mobile phone, speaking with forceful authority in the local Creole French.

He looked up as she came in, and to Lexie's astonishment, and a forbidden, heady delight, she got her look—a green glitter of stunned, intense desire.

Only for a moment—he gathered himself together almost immediately—but her foolish, wayward heart rejoiced while he terminated the conversation and snapped the phone shut.

For the rest of her life she'd hug to her heart the memory of that split second of passionate hunger.

'That colour does amazing things to you.' His voice was controlled and level. 'Do you understand French?'

'No. I do speak Maori.' And Illyrian, but she wasn't going to admit to that—it could lead to questions she didn't want to answer.

They took the coast road to the new hotel. Lexie looked around her with interest when they drove in, making a small sound of pleasure at the flowers and festoons of coloured lights that decorated the place.

From beside her Rafiq said, 'There are always two openings for any new hotel on Moraze. The first is for the people who actually do the building, and then there is a more formal one, like the one you attended the other night, where publicity is a factor. That was rather stuffy; this will not be.'

The year she'd spent in Illyria had accustomed Lexie to royal occasions, but the moment she walked in with

Rafiq she realised how right he was—this was indeed something special.

Smiles and cheers and applause greeted their arrival. Without the burden of being the only child of the dictator who'd terrorised the onlookers, it wasn't difficult to smile back, to relax in the warmth of their greetings.

Until she saw a face she recognised.

She must have flinched, because Rafiq demanded sharply, 'What is it? You are not well?'

'I'm perfectly all right.' After all, why on earth should she be afraid of Felipe Gastano?

He came towards them with a smile on his too-handsome face, and the air of someone completely sure of his welcome. 'Dearest Alexa,' he said smoothly as he bent to kiss her cheek.

Rafiq pulled her a little closer to his side and the unwanted kiss went awry.

Something glittered a second in Felipe's pale eyes, but the smile stayed fixed as he nodded to Rafiq. 'I am sorry,' he said in an apologetic tone that grated across Lexie's nerves. 'I was so pleased to see an old friend that I forgot protocol. Sir, it is a pleasure to be here on this auspicious occasion.'

Rafiq said, 'We're pleased to see you here.'

An apparently sincere greeting, yet somehow the calm words lifted the hairs on the back of Lexie's neck. She sensed a very strong emotion beneath his glacial self-control, and wondered if she was the cause of it.

Felipe didn't seem to notice. Still smiling, he transferred his gaze to Lexie, held her eyes a moment, then turned back to Rafiq. 'I thought I'd like to see whether my friend Alexa was enjoying all that Moraze has to offer its guests.'

Lexie stiffened, wondering exactly what he meant by those enigmatic words.

The noise level soared suddenly, fuelled by a group of musicians who'd gathered around a bonfire blazing on the sand.

'I hope you enjoy the evening,' Rafiq said coolly. 'After a few short, official speeches there will be dancing on the beach.' His narrow smile gleamed. 'Our local dances are a feature of the entertainment here.'

'I'm sure I shall find them very interesting,' Felipe said, fixing Lexie with a significant look.

She met it with hard-won composure, both relieved and glad when he stepped back to let another couple be introduced.

As Rafiq had promised, the official part of the evening was short, punctuated by champagne toasts and much good cheer, and then the party really got going. Down on the beach, the band struck up again in impressive rhythm, guitars and keyboards vying with older instruments—a triangle, gourds with seeds inside, and an insistent drum.

'The hotel dancing troupe will do a demonstration first, but later everyone will join in,' Rafiq told her as the crowd moved onto the sand, the better to watch the spectacle. 'You will find it a little different from western dancing; in the *sanga*, people do not touch.'

Watching the dancers—women in brightly coloured cropped tops and full skirts that reached their ankles, and men in white pirate shirts knotted at the waist above tight breeches—Lexie decided they didn't need to.

Because the *sanga* was erotic enough to melt icebergs.

The women began it, holding out their full skirts

while they approached the men with sensuous, shuf-
fling steps. They swayed to the music, bare feet moving
in an intricate rhythm, smiles bold and challenging as
they danced from one partner to another, choosing and
discarding until eventually they settled on one particular man.

When that had happened, the drum beats began to
build to a crescendo and the dance took an even more
provocative turn. Both women and men taunted and
teased their partners, hip movements suggesting a
much more intimate encounter, smiles becoming
slow and languid as the dancers gazed into each
other's eyes.

The insidious spell of the dance—the rhythm set up
by the drums and the primitive imperative of the fire,
the heat and the gorgeous, primal colours of the
women's full, flounced skirts—set fire to something
basic and untamed within Lexie. Her cheeks burned and
her eyelids were heavy and slumbrous.

And then, with the drumbeats reaching a frenzied
climax, only to abruptly halt, the world seemed sus-
pended in dramatic silence. After several seconds
people began to applaud, releasing the dancers from the
erotic spell of their own contriving. Many relaxed,
laughing, calling out jests to the crowd; others walked
off together—still not touching, Lexie noticed.

Carefully avoiding Rafiq's scrutiny, she looked
across the leaping flames of the bonfire and met Felipe
Gastano's cynical smile.

She nodded, wishing she'd never been so silly as to
go out with him, wishing—oh, wishing a lot of foolish
things, she thought bracingly, trying to still the constant
thrumming of her heart.

No wonder people talked of going troppo! This had to be the dangerous enchantment of the tropics.

As though sensing her restlessness, Rafiq said, 'Would you like to see around the hotel? The gardens and pool area are magnificent.'

'I'd love to,' she said, grateful for the chance to get away from too many interested eyes.

They walked there through a grove of casuarinas, the long, drooping needles whispering together in the scented breeze. Lexie recovered some of her composure as she admired the glorious gardens and a pool out of some designer's Arabian dream, only to lose it when they walked back to the beach and Rafiq said, 'A moment.'

She stopped with him, looking up enquiringly. He was smiling, but the intent expression of his eyes warned her what was coming, and her blood sang inside her.

Quietly he said, 'I neglected to tell you how very lovely you are.'

The kiss was merely an appetiser, one snatched before they rejoined the crowd, but she longed for more. The screen of trees was thick enough to hide them from anyone on the beach, but she hadn't thought Rafiq was the sort of man to indulge in almost-public displays.

Emerging from the feathery shade of the grove, she felt slightly embarrassed, as though everyone knew about that kiss.

From beside her Rafiq said, 'I'm afraid I must leave you for a few minutes.' A swift lift of his brows summoned a younger, good-looking man to stand beside her. 'You will enjoy discussing the dancing with Bertrand,' he said after introducing them.

Which she did. Bertrand was respectful and knew a lot about the dances of Moraze, revealing that different areas had different versions, some more restrained...

'And some—ah—less so,' he finished with a cheerful smile. 'But you won't be seeing any of *them* tonight. Everyone is on their best behaviour because our ruler is with us.'

She encouraged him to talk about Rafiq. Not that he needed much encouragement, she thought with a wry, inner smile after five minutes. Clearly he thought his ruler only one step below the gods!

'You are laughing at me,' he said, and grinned before becoming quickly serious. 'But I am truly beholden to him. Without his intervention, I would have been cutting either sugar cane or flowers in the fields. He sits on the board that chooses the ones deserving of further education, and although I was a bad boy at school, he persuaded them to give me a chance. Everyone else thought I was beyond help; he did not. I would die for him.'

His words were simply stated, without false bravado.

'It's a lucky ruler who can inspire such loyalty,' Lexie said, meaning it. She too had experienced Rafiq's consideration and his honesty.

Bertrand drew himself up. 'It is a lucky subject who can follow such a leader,' he said. He glanced over her head and frowned. 'Oh, I will have to leave you only for a moment. I must find someone to keep you company.'

'No,' she said crisply. 'Off you go; I'll be perfectly all right.'

He dithered, then said, 'I won't be long.' After an apologetic smile, he bowed and left her.

Smiling to herself, Lexie watched him being swallowed up by the crowd as he angled towards a middle-aged woman who stood alone.

'He is one of Prince Rafiq's security men,' a voice said from behind her. 'And that woman is his superior.'

Lexie suddenly felt alone and unprotected, her skin tightening in response to an imaginary threat.

'Hello, Felipe,' she said lightly. 'I always thought security men were eight-feet tall with necks wider than their heads.'

'The muscle men, perhaps—the grunts. The others come in all sizes and shapes, and I think this one will receive a chastisement from Prince Rafiq for leaving you.'

'I'm in no danger,' she said evenly, turning her head to look up at him.

His smile was as charming as ever, his eyes as appreciative, his tone low and flirtatious, yet he left her completely cold.

'Of course you're not,' he agreed. 'But you know how it is with these rich, powerful aristocrats—they see perils in every occasion.' He gestured at the milling crowd, a little noisier than it had been before, its laughter ringing free. 'Even in such a friendly group as this—all devoted subjects.'

He transferred his gaze to her face, surveying her with an intensity that was new and unsettling. 'Did you know that the word in the bazaars is that Prince Rafiq is very interested in his house guest?'

'Rumour is—as always—hugely exaggerated,' she said evenly, and made up her mind. This wasn't the perfect occasion, but he needed to know. 'Felipe, I need to tell you—'

'Not now,' he interrupted curtly.

He wanted something; she could feel it—a fierce lust, though not for her personally, she realised with a sudden flash of insight.

It had never been her—he'd always seen her as means to some unspoken end.

Before she could finish he went on, 'And not here. It can wait until later, when de Courteville releases you.'

'I'm not a prisoner,' she said automatically, eager to get this odd, worrying exchange over and done with. 'And I think this is as good a time and a place as any to say goodbye.'

Felipe Gastano smiled, but although the skin around his eyes crinkled they showed no emotion. 'So that is it?' He shrugged. 'Well, it was fun while it lasted, was it not?'

Relieved yet still wary, she said, 'I certainly enjoyed it.'

'I thank you. Perhaps I did not—quite—get what I thought we both wanted, but I also enjoyed our time together. However, before I go, there is something *I* must tell *you*. After your little accident, I tried to get in touch with you, but it seems you are not able to be contacted by telephone or email.'

'What do you mean?' In spite of the flames of the fire, she felt cold, and the chattering around her seemed to die away.

'Just that it seems someone is monitoring your communications with the outside world.'

'I'm sure you're wrong,' she retorted.

His smile was condescending. 'Why don't you ask de Couteville? He comes now, and if I read him right he is not happy to see us talking together.'

Indeed, Rafiq sent her a keen glance as he approached, but although his tone when he greeted Felipe again was cool, it certainly wasn't brusque. Felipe chatted a little about the hotel development before Rafiq and Lexie moved on.

From then on they were never alone. They stayed another hour, saw another dance, this one even more sensual than the first, and then it was time to go.

On the way back to the castle Lexie was aware of a certain air of constraint in Rafiq. He was courteous, amusing, interesting—and unreachable.

Felipe's observations gnawed at her mind. She wanted to confront her host with them, yet another part of her brain told her to be sensible. Why on earth would Rafiq monitor her phone calls?

Eventually, as they drove in through the gates, she said, 'Felipe said he's been trying to contact me, but the staff were uncooperative.'

'I'm afraid they probably were,' Rafiq said coolly. 'I have people who are trained to handle the media, and they dealt with all the calls about you. I gave your sister's name to them, which is why she was put straight through, but I gained the impression that you wouldn't want Gastano to have free access to you. If I was wrong, I will of course add him to the list.'

Hastily Lexie said, 'No, it doesn't matter, thank you. He won't be calling again.' As for the emails— even if Felipe did have her correct address, they'd been known to disappear into cyberspace for days, sometimes weeks, at a time. Curiosity and a certain relief drove her to ask, 'Were there many approaches from the media?'

'Quite a few. Some of the big news agencies have

stringers on the island, and of course news travels fast.' His tone hardened. 'I didn't think you'd like to be discussed in the gossip columns.'

Distastefully, she replied, 'You were right.'

Her brief encounter with gossip writers and paparazzi had sickened her of the whole industry. In Illyria she'd been shielded from the worst of their excesses, but she'd seen the havoc they could create, and she wanted no part of it. Besides, she had a feeling that if Jacoba found out she was staying with Moraze's ruler she'd send Prince Marco down to check him out.

The last thing she wanted was for Rafiq to discover who her father had been.

Honesty warred with shame. Perhaps she should tell him—right now. Yet the words froze in her throat. The sins of the fathers were indeed visited on their sons— and their daughters, she thought wearily, remembering how suspicious the Illyrians had been of her. Mud stuck; occasionally she even found herself wondering if she'd inherited any of her father's brutality.

No, much better to leave things as they were. Then Rafiq might remember her as an ordinary woman, not as the child of a monster.

Once inside the castle, Rafiq asked, 'How did you enjoy the evening?'

'Very much,' she told him, her tone more brittle than bright. 'It was interesting to meet the people who'd actually worked on the project. And their singing was fantastic.'

'What did you think of the dancing?'

His voice was amused, and his eyes half-hidden by his lashes. They were walking towards the terrace with the pavilion and the pool, and she could feel that forbidden, intoxicating anticipation chipping away at her control.

'It was very sexy,' she said firmly. 'And amazingly athletic! At times I thought they might dislocate their hips.'

He threw his black head backwards and laughed, the sound full and unforced. 'Did it give you the desire to try it?'

'I know my limitations,' she said. Curiosity drove her to ask, 'Can you do it?'

'Every Moraze-reared person can dance their version of our national dance,' he said gravely. 'Our nurses teach us it in our cradles—or so they say.'

They walked across to the pavilion, its translucent draperies floating languidly in the sea-scented breeze. A moon smiled down, silvering everything in a soft, unearthly light—the pool, the white-and-pink water lilies, the shimmering expanse of gauze that surrounded them and shut out the world.

Lexie swallowed something that obstructed her throat and said chattily, 'I think you'd probably need to learn it in the cradle to be able to do it without falling over or making a total idiot of yourself. And constant practice must be necessary to give your hips and legs that flexibility.'

'Don't be so wary—I am not like the dancers at the hotels who sometimes lure tourists onto the sand to show them how very lacking in flexibility their hips are. And to dance properly you need drums and music.' He looked down at her, his eyes gleaming and intent. 'But I would like to teach you,' he said deeply.

'Teach me what?'

CHAPTER EIGHT

LEXIE swallowed again, her throat closing. He was talking about dancing, not making love. He didn't even know she was a virgin, and she had no intention of telling him.

In a voice she barely recognized, she said, 'Unfortunately, I don't think I'll be here long enough to learn—to dance, that is.'

'You're very graceful, so I'm sure you have a natural aptitude,' he said, his smile cool and subtly mocking.

'I don't know about that.' This banter with its tantalising undercurrents was new to her. Nervously she glanced away, eyes widening as she saw that the table had been set with trays of small delicacies and what was clearly a bottle of champagne.

'I thought we should toast your stay on Moraze,' Rafiq told her. 'I noticed that you didn't drink anything stronger than fruit punch at the party, but I'm hoping to tempt you with some champagne.'

Lexie knew she should refuse. In this magical glimmer of moonlit enchantment, any sensible woman would make sure her brain was in full control.

But then a sensible woman would have seen danger

in the prospect of an evening with Rafiq, and would have pretended a fragility she didn't feel. And once at the party, no sensible woman would have allowed herself to be carried away by the erotic rhythms and hypnotic drumbeats of the dancing, the whirl of colour and the open sensuousness.

And even a halfway-sensible woman would have avoided any sort of post-party drinks, and said a briskly cheerful goodnight at the door of her room before shutting said door firmly on him.

All right, so she wasn't sensible. She certainly wasn't going to walk back to the arid, lonely refuge of her bedroom.

To the crackle and heat of bridges burning behind her, she said, 'I'm easily tempted,' adding hastily when she realised what she'd implied, 'To champagne.'

Colour burned across her cheekbones and she fought back embarrassment, holding her head high and her smile steady.

One black brow lifted to shattering effect. Without saying anything, Rafiq turned to ease the top off the bottle. Instead of a pop it emitted a soft sigh—of satisfaction?

Don't even think about satisfaction! Small sips, Lexie promised herself as he poured the sparkling wine into long, elegant flutes. She'd take tiny little sips, at long, long intervals…

And when she got back to real life she'd remember this evening—this whole stay on Moraze—without regret. Instead she'd feel gratitude that the man who summoned those reckless, dangerous impulses from her was a man of honour and integrity.

'So,' Rafiq said calmly, handing her a glass, 'We drink to your continued good health.'

After one tiny, wholesome sip, she said, 'Oh, that's superb wine.'

'It is French, of course. Moraze produces some excellent table wines, but for champagne we rely on France.' He set his glass down. 'I'm glad you like it.'

Lexie made the first comment that came into her head. 'New Zealand makes good wines too.'

'Indeed it does. I have drunk a very supple, subtle Pinot Noir from the south of the South Island, and some extremely good reds from an island off the coast of Auckland.'

'Waiheke. It has its own special microclimate.'

Her innocuous words were followed by silence, far too heavy with unspoken thoughts, unbidden desire.

Desperately Lexie broke it. 'I'm no connoisseur, but I do like the wines made in Marlborough from Sauvignon Blanc grapes. In the north of the North Island, where I live, wine growers are also trying out unusual varieties of grapes to see which cope best with the humidity and the warmth.'

Oh, *brilliant*, she thought in despair. Talk about banal!

'Shall we stop fencing?' Rafiq suggested, his amused tone laced with another emotion, one that sent shivers of excited recognition through her.

'I wasn't aware we were,' she lied, hoping she sounded crisp and fully in control.

He held out his hand for her glass, and when after a moment's hesitation she handed it over, he set it beside his own on the low table. The moonlight glimmered on his white shirt, lovingly enhancing the breadth of his shoulders, the narrow waist and hips, the arrogant angles and planes of his features. Whenever she'd ridden a roller coaster she'd felt like this: both exhilarated and terrified.

'Of course we were,' he said, straightening up to smile at her. 'We are like swordsmen, you and I, continually duelling for advantage. But it is time to bring an end to it.'

Once again her stomach did that flip thing. A hot rush of sensation drove away memories and common sense. When he looked at her like that she was aware of nothing but the drumming of her heart in her ears, and the relentless heat of desire building like a storm through her. Honey-sweet, potent as the strongest rum, powerful and frightening, it shook her to the core.

Eyes dilating endlessly, she watched his smile harden, and her breath locked in her throat at the slow slide of his hands up her arms.

'Your skin is finer by far than the silk you're wearing. For this whole interminable evening I have been wanting to touch it,' he said in a low, harsh voice, and bent his head to kiss the place his fingers had caressed.

Sharp as joy, acute as pain, pleasure shot through her at the touch of his mouth. When he slid his hands across her back and pulled her against him, she sighed his name and met his seeking, demanding kiss with open passion.

It ended too soon. He lifted his head and looked at her, green eyes glittering, and in a tone that was almost angry said, 'That is the first time you've allowed yourself to say that.'

Somehow the simple act of pronouncing the two syllables that made up his name was almost more intimate than the kisses they'd exchanged. 'You've never told me I could,' she said huskily.

A smile curved his sculpted mouth. 'I didn't know

New Zealanders held to such strict rules of etiquette. In fact, I believed the publicity—that you are a laid back, ultra-casual lot.'

But her mother had not been a New Zealander, she'd been Illyrian, and she'd brought up her daughters to be more formal than their friends.

Rafiq went on, 'We've kissed—that gives you the right to call me whatever you want.' And he kissed her again, this time lightly. 'And me the right to call you sweet Lexie—no?'

Sweet? Was he indicating that he knew she was a virgin, and that it was all right? Forcing a smile, she said, 'I don't think I'm sweet. Practical, perhaps...'

But a practical woman wouldn't be like this, locked in his arms, her body rejoicing at the hardness of his, her heart pounding so heavily he must feel it.

'Do you feel practical right now?' His voice was low and tender.

She closed her eyes against him, afraid that he'd see just what she was feeling—total surrender, a desperate, wanton abandonment of all the rules she'd lived by until she'd met him.

'No,' she admitted, gaining confidence from the thudding of his heart against her. Whatever he thought, he couldn't hide the fact that he wanted her.

'So—how do you feel?' And when she didn't answer, he laughed softly. 'A little wild?'

He punctuated each word with teasing kisses, but she sensed the inner demands driving him, and something unregenerate and fierce flared up to meet and match his hunger.

'Reckless?' he murmured, his mouth poised so close to hers that their breaths mingled.

'Yes,' she said simply, knowing what she'd just agreed to, knowing that after this there would be no going back—knowing, and not caring, because there was nothing in the world she wanted as much as learning about Rafiq in the most intimate way of all.

Later? Oh, she'd deal with *later* when it came.

She gave a squeak of astonishment as the world swooped, and he lifted her high in his arms and carried her across to that sinful double day bed.

Beside it he lowered her to her feet, sliding her down his lean, powerful length so that his need for her became blatantly, erotically obvious. Shivering, afire with sensation, she couldn't drag her eyes away from his narrowed gaze, which darkened with an elemental need that banished all her shyness with its heat.

'This pretty dress is a seduction in itself,' he said deeply. 'I've been wanting to slide these tiny, taunting buttons free, push them back so that the silk frames you...'

As he spoke his hands followed his words. Prey to an intensity of feeling she'd never experienced, she ignored the colour burning her skin and shrugged free of the bodice. And then stopped, acutely conscious that the only thing between her breasts and his deft, insistent hands was her bra.

Should she undo it?

Almost before the thought had formulated she felt his hands at the catch—knowledgeable and far too skilful at this, she thought on a spurt of sharp jealousy that kept her head high when he eased her bra away.

He stood looking at her, the dark, fierce hunger in his eyes satisfying something primitive and untamed in her.

On a raw note, he said, 'You are—perfect,' and took her eager mouth, bending her back over his arm so that his lips slid easily from hers to the demanding, importunate tips of her breasts.

The hot caress of his mouth splintered every inhibition. Moaning, lost in a carnal haze, Lexie's hands clenched helplessly in the fine fabric of his shirt as his mouth worked erotic magic on her.

'No,' she muttered when he lifted his head.

'What?'

He bit it out with such harshness she forced her eyes open, and saw the sudden rigidity in his features. 'Don't stop,' she said on a gasp.

But he held her eyes in a measuring stare. 'You are sure?'

'Of course I'm sure.' Frustrated, she stumbled over her next words. 'If you stop, I just might kill you.'

Strong arms closed around her again, and he set her on the bed. Shivering with anticipation so keen it came close to pain, she watched him shuck off his shirt. Lamplight gilded his skin, picking out the smooth swell and flex of muscles as he dropped the garment to the ground. But when his hands moved to the belt of his trousers she looked away, suddenly and shyly aware of her total lack of experience.

Should she tell him? Would he think she was some sort of frigid freak? Worse still, would he be overcome by an outdated chivalry and refuse to make love to her?

Clamping her mouth to hold back the confession that threatened to tumble out, she kicked off her shoes, not caring whether they landed on the stone terrace beside the bed or in the pool a few feet away.

Lithely, Rafiq came down beside her, muscles shifting and coiling, a study in gleaming bronze power. Lexie swallowed to ease a dry throat as the sheer size of him struck home. Without the civilising influence of his superbly tailored clothes, the difference between her female slenderness and his forceful masculinity overwhelmed her.

But that initial qualm was immediately eased by his gentleness as he began to slide the dress down her body.

Only to stop when he saw the faint shadows on her ribcage. She said quickly, 'They've just about gone now.'

'I don't want to hurt you.' He bent his sleek black head and kissed them, his lips sending darts of sensation to her very soul.

'You couldn't hurt me.' When he hesitated, she held her breath in an agony of supplication.

He said, 'I will be very careful, and you must tell me if there is any pain.'

'I will.'

Her eyes flew open in dismay as another thought presented itself. What if he thought she was using contraceptive medication?

As though he'd read her mind, he asked, 'Are you protected, my sweet one?'

'No,' she mumbled, rigid with embarrassment.

'It is no problem.' He got off the bed.

Lexie knew she should be relieved, and was shocked to discover that the thought of carrying Rafiq's child sent a subversive pang of longing through her.

Keeping her eyes away from what he was doing, she looked downwards. Her gaze stopped on the thong her sister had insisted she wear under the silk dress.

Should she take it off?

Colour mantled her skin, and desire ebbed under the weight of her embarrassment. How on earth did people ever make love with all these things to think about?

'What is worrying you?'

It was scary just how easily he could read her. 'Nothing.'

But once she was in his arms again, and his mouth on hers wreaked the familiar havoc to her busy mind, the need came back, swift and sure and compelling. Her virgin fears and worries vanished in an intense, voluptuous craving for something only Rafiq could give her.

'You taste like desire,' he said. 'Warm and silken and mind-blowing.'

His hand touched her breast, and she was unable to prevent a convulsive jerk of response.

'What is it?' he demanded.

'I just... I can't... I want you so much,' she finished in a rush, scarlet with an odd sort of defiance, but determined to be honest.

His laughter was deep and intimate. Her hips thrust upwards in an involuntary plea and demand for something she craved so much she could feel the wanting in her bones.

Against her skin, he murmured, 'So fierce you are, so responsive, so passionate, my dove. But shy—I won't break if you touch me.'

Almost dazed by the ferocity of her need, she smoothed a hand over his chest, her fingertips tingling at the resilience of his skin, the subtle shift and move of the muscles and tendons, their power and promise.

'Yes,' he whispered, his warm breath tantalising the sensitive tip of her breast. 'Touch me, Lexie, as you want to—and as you want to be touched.'

Cautiously she ran a coaxing, tentative hand across his shoulder, her fingertips thrilling at the heat of his fine-grained skin, the coiled strength that called to something deep inside her. Her breath came quickly; she bent her head so that her hair fell across him in a golden-amber flood, and then she kissed the path her fingers had made, rejoicing at the sudden thunder of his heart.

Emboldened, she opened her mouth and licked him, savouring his taste—a hint of salt, faint musk, all vital male.

Passion was a painful flame, an exciting demand, a surge of sensation through her so intense it was all she had room for. She said in an aching voice, 'You are beautiful.'

'Ah, no.' Rafiq sounded oddly shaken. 'That is for me to say to you. But *beautiful* does not convey enough—you are lithe and graceful, a woman of flame and satin and desire. The moment my eyes found you, I knew that this was inevitable.'

And he kissed her again, banishing her final fears and worries so completely that she willingly followed wherever he led, her body arching in uncontrollable urgency as he showed her what pleasure points lay in her breasts, her waist, the tiny hollow of her navel, the sleek curves of her hips...

And the removal of the thong became an erotic experience that almost banished all of her shyness.

But when his black head moved lower, she stiffened. He dropped a final kiss on the plane of her stomach and looked up, his eyes unexpectedly keen.

Colour flooded her skin. Rafiq smiled slowly, almost cruelly, and stroked one lean, long-fingered hand from the hollow of her throat. A thread of fire followed that deliberate claiming, radiating between the high peaks of her breasts, across her stomach, finally erupting when he cupped the wildly sensitive mound at the junction of her legs.

It was a gesture of pure possession—a statement of ownership—and oddly it gave Lexie a confidence she'd never have achieved otherwise.

Eyes holding his, she mimicked the sweep of his hand, letting her fingers linger on the antique pattern of hair across his chest, discovering the small, masculine nipples. The dark flush across his high, patrician cheekbones made her even bolder; she slid her palm across his flat, taut abdomen, relishing the hardening of muscles beneath her touch.

Narrow hips beckoned. Carefully, lovingly, she outlined them, bending to kiss the lean contours of his body.

And then her confidence faltered, faded. He was acutely aroused, and she literally didn't know what to do next.

He laughed quietly, darkly glittering eyes registering her embarrassment without censure. Silently he moved his hand and, as she bucked beneath his probing fingers, he found the passage that waited for him so eagerly, and explored it with a gentleness she found unbearably stimulating.

A soft, almost guttural sound broke past her lips. Gripping his shoulders, she felt the slickness of sweat beneath her hands, but this time she was too lost in the shatteringly sweet sensations he was conjuring to understand what was happening to him.

She needed—her whole body yearned for—*some-*

thing. Connection, completion, she thought inadequately, a unity she could only imagine, yet it was what she'd been waiting on for these long years past.

'Rafiq,' she breathed, her fingers clenching on him as he moved over her.

'Yes, my sweet one. Wait just a little time.' His voice was laboured, hoarse, as he turned away.

Lost in the turmoil of her senses, she closed her eyes, but when he poised himself over her again she opened them, and slid her hands down his back to his hips, then smiled and pulled him down.

He dragged in a harsh breath. His half-closed eyes locked with hers, so that she thought she was falling into the centre of a green firestorm, as he slowly, carefully, eased himself into her.

For a split second pain threatened, and she tensed, but then he broke through that tiny invisible barrier. Shivering, she felt sensation flood through her in a wave of heat, of joy, of seeking that something wonderful that still lay ahead of her, and again she arched into him in speechless supplication.

Rafiq's jaw clenched and, as though her movement had snapped the last shred of his self-control, he pressed home with a single, powerful thrust. Almost sobbing with pleasure, she soared at each welcome intrusion, up and up, and over a barrier into an ecstasy that shook the foundations of her world.

Almost immediately he followed her into that rarefied region, and when his climax was over he asked in a raw voice, 'Why the tears, my lovely girl?'

'I didn't know,' Lexie said unevenly, surprised to find that she was crying.

He rolled over onto his side, raising himself on one

arm to look down into her face. Shaken to her centre, she closed her eyes, because she couldn't see anything in his expression to match the tumult of emotions rioting through her—a kind of relief, fierce exultation, wariness, and a sweet exhaustion.

Obviously he felt nothing like that; once more he was fully in control, the arrogant framework of his face even more pronounced, the green eyes hard and accusing.

'Was that the first time you've had an orgasm?' he asked.

Flushing, she turned her face away, and resisted when an inexorable finger turned it back. He didn't hurt her, but she knew he was scanning her face for every nuance, every fleeting emotion.

'Look at me,' he commanded.

'No.'

Her heart thudded in the silence, until he said, still in that cool, controlled tone, 'Or was that the first time you've made love?'

He couldn't know. There was no way he could know. There had been only one swiftly vanishing second of pain...

But why did it matter so much to her that he shouldn't know?

'Is it important?' she parried, wishing her voice wasn't so thin.

No muscle moved in his face, but her heart quailed. However, his tone was grave when he replied, 'I think it is, if it was the first time for you. I could have been gentler—?'

'I didn't want *gentle*,' she flashed, determined to put an end to this hugely embarrassing conversation.

Weren't men supposed to roll over and go to sleep after sex?

But then, Rafiq de Courteville wasn't like other men. In that moment she realised that she was in even greater danger than she'd imagined.

The danger of falling in love, if she hadn't already done so.

In words brittle with desperation, she said, 'I'm sorry if it wasn't—'

'Hush.' He stopped the tumbling words with his mouth, in a kiss that brought every emotion and thought to a crashing halt, vanquished by the turbulence of sensation and remembered rapture.

Rafiq lifted his dark head so that his words were spoken against her lips in the lightest of kisses. 'It was—' He paused, as though choosing what to say next, then went on, 'Much more than I expected. I hope that for you it was good too.'

CHAPTER NINE

Lexie breathed, 'It was wonderful. Couldn't you tell?'

Rafiq's smile was wry. 'Some women fake orgasms very well, but yes, I could tell. I'm glad.'

And without saying anything more he got up and stooped for his clothes, giving her a last view of his powerful back and leg muscles shifting in smooth harmony, the light of the lamps casting golden highlights and coppery shadows over his lean, magnificent body.

He looked both alien and heartbreakingly familiar, a man of sophistication backed by raw power, his combination of bloodlines and cultures so different that the only thing they had in common was this passionate desire.

Lexie's heart clamped into a hard knot in her chest. What now?

Without hurrying, he got into his trousers and slung the shirt over one broad shoulder. She couldn't read his expression; he'd retreated behind the bronze mask of his face to a place where he seemed entirely unaware of her.

Chilled, she sat up and reached for her dress. Perhaps the movement broke his introspection; he came across and picked it up from the floor to put it beside her.

'Not a good way to treat such a pretty thing,' he said conversationally, his eyes hooded and enigmatic, and walked away to the table where the champagne flutes gleamed in the lamplight.

Hastily scrambling into her clothes, Lexie wondered dismally what on earth she was supposed to do now.

What followed was a tense ten minutes spent in sophisticated conversation with Rafiq—conversation Lexie could match only with taut, disconnected answers.

So she felt relief and disappointment in equal measure when he walked her back to the door of her bedroom.

There he paused, and said with a humourless twist of his lips, 'This is not how I envisaged the end of the evening, but I think we both need a night of sleep before we talk.'

Eyes raking her face, he finished, 'Before that, I should repeat that I enjoyed very much our evening together—all of it. I hope you did too.'

She flushed, wanting only to be taken in his arms again, to be reassured in the most basic of ways that he was telling her the truth.

But that wasn't going to happen. 'I've already told you I did,' she said, her tone aloof and edged with more than a hint of defiance.

He laughed softly, and for a transparent second she thought he was going to put paid to the tumbling whirlwind of her thoughts and emotions with another sensuous kiss and the addictive security of his arms.

Then his face closed against her, and he stepped backwards with an inclination of his head. 'Goodnight. Sleep well,' he said formally.

'Goodnight.' She closed the door on him before the hot tears could reach her eyes.

As always he'd been considerate, but even though he'd liked making love to her he might still be regretting that it had happened. After all, there was a huge difference between an experienced woman of the world, who knew how to conduct an affair with style and grace, and a virgin with no skills or experience when it came to matters of sex.

He might even now be trying to find a way to tell her that it was over—a kind, *considerate* way, of course—she thought on a spurt of fresh anguish.

She woke the next morning with one decision fixed in her mind: she'd go back to the hotel.

'No,' Rafiq said unemotionally when she told him at breakfast on the terrace that overlooked the lowlands.

Lexie's brows shot up. Pleased with the cool crispness of her tone, she stated, 'I'm not asking your permission. I'm perfectly well, so the hotel no longer has any reason to object.'

He leaned back. A stray ray of sun struck across his face, and she glimpsed a corsair, dark and dangerous—a leader of men even more desperate then he was.

'It is not possible,' he said evenly. 'Your accommodation has been given to another guest.'

Stunned, she closed her mouth with a snap. 'Who made that decision?'

'I told them to,' he said with a controlled assurance that grated across her nerves. 'The hotel opening was a huge success—bookings have come in from all over the world. It would have been foolish not to take advantage of that. Why do you want to leave the castle?'

'Because there's no longer a reason for me to be here.' She stared at him, her eyes sending a challenge she didn't care to voice. 'My stay was only ever temporary. I'm fine, my ribs are fine—' Colour burned her skin but she ploughed on, 'As you know.'

When Rafiq got to his feet in one swift movement, she had to stop herself from flinching. He loomed, and although Lexie knew she had nothing to fear from him she had to resist her immediate impulse to leap up so that she faced him on slightly more equal terms.

He was deliberately being intimidating, she realised, her hand closing around the handle of a knife. *Why?*

Calmly, yet with an edge of authority to his voice as though reasoning with a rebellious teenager, he said, 'There is no need for you to go. I understand your feelings, and I agree—this has happened so fast that we don't know each other very well. But fleeing is not the way to deal with it.' His eyes dropped to her death grip on the handle of the butter knife. 'I refuse to believe that you are afraid of me.'

'I'm not!' She dropped the knife back onto her plate. The sharp little chink broke into the soft air like a small explosion.

No, she wasn't afraid of him; she just wanted him so much that her last shreds of prudence dictated flight, before she made a total fool of herself by falling madly and hopelessly in love with him.

'Perhaps you should be,' he said, and the silence between them became suddenly charged with a menace that sent shock waves through her.

Disbelievingly, she stared at him as he leaned down and caught her wrist, urging her upwards. His mouth came down on hers; she resisted for a second, then sank into his warmth and strength, even as part of her mind fought this insidious entrapment.

The sensations—potent, arousing—were the same, yet she knew something was different. Behind his passion she sensed an icily restrained anger and a determination that made her extremely wary.

When he released her she commanded furiously, 'Don't ever do that again.'

He examined her with hooded eyes, flinty and cold. As she watched the anger faded, and he said something in a raw, harsh voice in the local language.

Lexie didn't have to understand it to know that he was swearing.

Between his teeth he said in English, 'I will not touch you again until you ask me to.'

'I— All right,' she snapped, hoping her uncertainty wasn't humiliatingly obvious.

He scanned her face, his own devoid of expression. 'I am not normally so crass,' he said curtly. 'You affect me in a way I haven't had to deal with before. I'm sorry.'

Lexie bit her lip, trying to repress a forlorn hope. Surely he couldn't mean that he was as lost to emotion as she was? She didn't dare hope that.

His eyes hardened. 'Tell me, do you want to leave because we made love?'

After a few tense seconds she decided that the truth was the only way to go. 'Yes.'

Not because of their loving—never *that*—but because afterwards the odd sense of alienation, of rejection, had pained and confused her.

Rafiq watched her expression, still shuttered against him, and wished again he'd managed to rein in his hungry desire. Making love had infinitely complicated the situation; he felt smirched by his own behaviour, although it had never occurred to him that she could be a virgin.

He couldn't let her leave the castle because Gastano still wanted her, and he was dangerous.

After witnessing that carefully stage-managed kiss at the party last night, the self-titled count must know he'd lost his passport to the world of the very rich and privileged. During the past twelve hours he'd have learned that his world was shattering around him, the empire he'd built with such ruthlessness in chaos, and Interpol hot on his heels.

And although he might not yet know that the man who'd taken Lexie from him was responsible for all that, he would very soon. He'd react with all the viciousness of a cornered rat.

Warning her would achieve nothing; she clearly had no knowledge of Gastano's criminal life, and why should she believe Rafiq?

Unless he told her about Hani...?

Not now, he thought. Everything in him refused to reveal his sister's humiliation and suicide. But although he hadn't been able to protect her, he could make sure Lexie was safe.

Choosing his words carefully, he said, 'I promised a few moments ago not to touch you until you asked me to. I made that promise in anger, but it holds. You will be perfectly safe here.'

Lexie sensed rather than saw the inflexible line of his mouth, and wondered what was going on behind the handsome, arrogant features.

Fighting back a bleak disappointment, she said, 'I know that. It's— You were right, everything's happened so quickly...'

So quickly it didn't seem possible that the emotions that gripped her could be true. Until she remembered that her sister had taken one look at Prince Marco of Illyria and instantly fallen into lust.

And although that initial fierce attraction had grown into love, just because it had happened for Jacoba didn't mean it was going to be her fate too.

Rafiq smiled, and the green eyes—so uncompromising a minute ago—warmed. 'It will be difficult keeping my hands off you, but by the exercise of great—*immense*—restraint I think I can manage it.'

And he lifted her hand to his mouth and kissed it, then turned it over to press another kiss into the palm.

A painful delight throbbed through her. Somehow their lovemaking the previous night had made her even more sensitive, as though she'd been trained to react infinitely more strongly to his powerful presence.

If she were cautious or even sensible, she'd leave the castle and find a room in another hotel. She'd run fast and far—as far as New Zealand—from this reckless delight.

But she wasn't going to. Whatever happened she would always be glad that she'd met Rafiq, that her initiation to sex had been so wonderful, that here on this magical island east of Zanzibar she'd found something rare and precious, something she wasn't going to let fear forbid her.

'Perhaps,' she said solemnly, those swift kisses still tingling through her bloodstream. 'But how do you know I'll have the same self-control?'

'I rather hope you don't.' The deep voice was amused and tender. 'But not today; I have a council meeting that will take all day. So relax.'

* * *

He didn't come home until after she'd gone to bed, but he'd rung twice, and at the sound of his voice she'd melted. Rafiq. Always and for ever Rafiq, she thought later, lying in bed alone and watching the stars drift slowly across the velvet sky as she remembered the previous night. Eventually she slid into sleep, and into turbulent dreams.

Several hours later Rafiq asked abruptly, 'Where is M'selle Sinclair?'

'She went up to her room shortly after she had dinner, sir.'

'Thank you.' He strode up the staircase, slowing a little when the passage forked to go to Lexie's room.

Damn, he wanted her! After that moment's hesitation, he went on past. In his own room he swore beneath his breath when he saw the red light blinking on the communication device that connected him to the head of security.

'Yes?' he barked into it.

'Sorry, sir, but there's just been an attempted robbery in the strongroom at the citadel. It looks like an inside job on the fire-diamond vaults.'

Rafiq's head came up. Harshly he ordered, 'Go on.'

He listened keenly as she concisely laid out the evening's events. 'A man armed with the correct passwords infiltrated the citadel and got as far as the vaults before the alarms finally picked up his presence.'

Mind racing, Rafiq demanded, 'Where is he?'

Chagrined, she admitted, 'He gave us the slip in the old town.'

So he was a local. No outsider would be able to navigate the narrow alleys of the original town.

Mme Fanchette confirmed this. 'We've got a good

shot of him on tape. He's a petty thief—been in trouble since he was a kid, and he's now deep in hock over gambling debts.' She paused. 'The man he owes has been seen talking to Gastano.'

Rafiq digested that. 'Have the passwords been changed?'

'As we speak.'

'But if we don't know who the traitor in the household is, we'll have to assume that he—or she—will also be told of the changes.' His frown deepening, Rafiq thought rapidly before commanding, 'I want the watch on Gastano reinforced; he's wily and he's ruthless. And step up the security at the castle as well as the citadel.'

'You think M'selle Sinclair is in danger?'

'Possibly.'

Driven by a need to know that Lexie was safe, Rafiq strode down the hall towards her room. Once he was sure of that, he'd set a guard at her door. Although he'd chosen her room to make sure she couldn't escape, the sheer walls on the seaward side would also make it impossible for anyone to reach her that way.

But if Felipe Gastano had suborned someone in the household to get those passwords, he could have access to someone in the castle as well.

Rafiq opened the door quietly. The room was in darkness, although the shutters were still open. He could see the stars through the tall windows, and hear the muted thunder of the sea on the reef.

And something else—a soft weeping that lifted the hairs on the back of his neck.

Get out of here, he told himself, angry because he knew he wasn't going to abandon her to such distress.

His voice woke Lexie from a nightmare of loss and

disillusion, of frantic fear and terror. She reached blindly for him, feeling the side of the bed sink as he sat down on it, and then the safe haven of his arms closed around her.

Stroking her hair, he murmured, 'Hush, hush, it's all right, Lexie. It's just a nightmare, just a bad dream, and you're awake now.'

'You were gone,' she sobbed. 'I couldn't find you—they wouldn't let me go—but I knew you were dead…'

'I am very much alive.' His confident voice eased the horror that still gripped her. He picked up her hand and held it against his heart. 'Feel that? It's my pulse, and it's not going to stop for many years yet.'

Brokenly, mouth against his throat, she said, 'Oh, thank God. Thank God…'

And she reached up and kissed him, relief making her bold.

When he pulled away, she whispered, 'No. Oh, please.' And his mouth hardened on hers and she knew it was going to be all right.

They made love with a rapacity that should have shocked her, and then slowly, gently, with a sweet tenderness that made her heart sing and weep at the same time.

When he eased away from her, she clung openly.

Rafiq laughed, a sexy sound that sent more shivers of delight through her. 'So valiant now,' he teased, and ran a light, infinitely provocative finger from the hollow at the base of her throat to the dimple of her navel.

Lashes drooping over her eyes, she savoured the rills of anticipation from that light, unsatisfying touch. She looked up into a face that hardened subtly, the autocratic framework exposed by tanned skin.

I love you so much, she thought achingly.

She kissed along his jaw, lips tingling at the slight friction of his beard while heat began to build again in the pit of her stomach.

'Yes,' he said deeply. 'You like that. So do I.'

His seeking hand cupped the soft mound of her femininity, then two fingers slid into the moist recess and she arched against the intimate caress, her breath coming rapidly between her lips, the heat transmuted into a wildly erotic complex of sensations.

But this wasn't what she wanted—a quick release.

No, she wanted him to remember her, to never be able to walk into this room again without her face coming to him, and her voice echoing in his ears.

Emboldened, she pushed at his shoulders. 'Lie down,' she said, and bent her head and kissed him, using that slight leverage to ease him back.

She felt his mouth curve beneath hers, and then he obeyed, settling onto the sheets, heavy-lidded eyes smouldering.

Long and lean and golden, he sprawled across the bed beneath her, the smooth definition of relaxed muscles beneath his sleek skin belying the power she knew he commanded, the blazing male potency that called to everything female in her.

Absorbed in sensation, she explored him with increasing boldness, delighting in the contrast of textures and the swift contraction of muscles beneath her fingertips, the way his eyes promised the most carnal of retribution, the thinning of his beautiful mouth as he fought her effect on him.

A film of moisture across his forehead sent her pulses racing. She lowered her head and touched tiny butterfly kisses there, then licked across the path her lips had taken.

Hoarsely, he said, 'You're killing me.' And when she hesitated his mouth twisted and he went on, 'But stopping would kill me faster.'

'I just want to please you.' She dropped another kiss on each shoulder, bunched now, and iron-hard beneath her seeking mouth.

He gestured down his body. 'You must see you're succeeding.'

Indeed she could. Desire burned her cheeks, and she reached out a hand, cupping him, caressing the silken shaft that had given her such erotic pleasure.

He said unevenly, 'Much more of that, and you'll unman me.' His arms were outstretched, the muscles corded and tight, his hands curled into fists.

'I don't think anyone could unman you,' she said in a tone to match his, and opened her lips to his fierce demand, before a wild impulse pulled her away to climb over him and stretch herself the length of his taut body.

He didn't move, not even when she slid herself down, shivering with pleasure as she took him into her. She caught the green glitter beneath his lashes, welcoming the colour along his high, autocratic cheekbones.

Concentrating hard, she began to clench and unclench inner muscles in a subtle massage. His lashes lifted; he pinioned her gaze with such single-minded intensity, she felt he was reading her soul.

Eyes locked, bodies still, the only sound was the mingled harshness of their breathing. Lexie continued the voluptuous torment, ratcheting up the sensual tension, until the only thing she could feel was the molten pleasure rising like the tide through every cell.

And then it broke over her, a wave of such passionate delight that she gave a muffled cry, and her body stiffened in a rictus of ecstatic release.

Rafiq's hands whipped up to support her; he made a guttural sound that mingled with hers, and his powerful length arced beneath hers, hands on her hips forcing her down as he joined her in fulfilment.

When it was over he held her against him and they lay spent in silent communication. Dazed, Lexie understood that something significant had happened, but she didn't know exactly what. It seemed to her that they had forged a link that might never be broken.

For her, anyway.

Much later, when she was almost asleep, she felt him move. Grief tore at her; without thinking, she whispered, 'Stay with me.'

But he said gently, 'My sweet one, I don't want the staff to know I have been with you. Let me go now.'

Humiliation woke her properly. Keeping her eyes closed, she mumbled, 'Oh, of course.'

Rafiq heard the note of chagrin in her voice and gritted his teeth as he dressed. All he wanted was go back to her, lose himself in her warmth and her passion, but he needed to check the castle security.

Something he should have done *before* he came to her room.

When Lexie woke the next morning it was to a lonely breakfast out on the terrace. Forcing fresh fruit salad and toast past her lips took effort and concentration.

She'd asked where Rafiq was, and had been told that he was working at the citadel. Well, of course; rulers had to rule, and no doubt that was what Rafiq did every day.

But once more she faced the bitterness of rejection. Was she being too sensitive? Probably. Last night had been the high point of her life so far, yet clearly to him it had meant so little he hadn't even bothered to join her for breakfast.

'Stop it,' she muttered, startling a small bird that had settled on the edge of the balustrade. Her mouth quirked as it opened its bright orange wings and fluttered to a safer perch on a potted gardenia not too far away. 'Sorry, birdie, it's not your fault.'

This was all so new to her, but obviously it wasn't to Rafiq. And she'd been the lucky recipient of his over-developed sense of responsibility, so she shouldn't be surprised or disappointed at his absence.

She was finishing a cup of delicious local coffee when she heard the chatter of a helicopter coming fast from the capital.

A pang of embarrassment clutched her. What had seemed so natural and thrilling last night suddenly appeared in a different light. Would Rafiq think she'd been forward and needy when she'd writhed in desperate rapture in his arms? Or when she'd explored his body with greedy adoration? Or, most pathetic of all, when she'd pleaded with him to stay with her?

Was he secretly despising her? Or wondering how to get rid of her?

And did he realise—as she had when she'd woken that morning—that their mutual passion had been so great they'd forgotten to take any precautions against pregnancy? She'd counted the days of her cycle, relaxing when she found it was highly unlikely she'd been fertile, even though the thought of carrying Rafiq's child under her heart melted her bones.

ROBYN DONALD   145

Heat stung her skin. She got up and walked nervously to the shade of an arbour, watching the black dot that was the chopper grow rapidly as it headed purposefully towards the castle.

Should she go down, or wait for Rafiq here?

She decided to wait.

The maid Cari appeared, obviously looking for her. And just as obviously flustered, holding her handbag. 'Miss, it is the Emir—he has sent the helicopter to pick you up. From the upper terrace!'

Joy flooded through her. 'Oh—I'd better go, then!'

Wondering why on earth Rafiq had chosen that particular landing ground, she accepted the bag and hurried with the maid up onto the upper terrace, where the water lilies held their satiny cups up to the sun.

Noise filled the air and she had to half close her eyes against the wind blasting from the rotors as the chopper landed. Someone inside pushed back the door, painted with the stallion of the royal house of Moraze in all its menace and grace, the crown on its head glittering with fire.

The same man beckoned. Without hesitation, Lexie ran across.

Strong hands hauled her inside and stuffed her into a seat. The chopper took off instantly, and the door closed before she had time to fix her seatbelt. Frowning, she did up the belt and turned towards the man next to her.

An odd apprehension kicked her beneath the ribs when Felipe Gastano lifted a thumb to her and mouthed words she couldn't hear.

CHAPTER TEN

GASTANO'S smile broadened as Lexie shook her head and put her hands to her ears. When he tossed her a pair of earphones she clapped them on, only to realise they weren't connected to the communications system.

Ice touched her skin. Something, she thought feverishly, was wrong. Rafiq didn't like the count; he wouldn't have sent him for her.

Her eyes flicked to the man piloting the chopper. He wore an official flying suit, the emblem of the rearing horse clear on it. Only this horse had wings. Chastened, Lexie let out a small huff of air.

She was being over-dramatic. After all, what on earth could there be to be afraid of? This was a Moraze Air Force helicopter, and the pilot was clearly a serviceman. Besides, Felipe was no threat to her.

So why did she now feel an instinctive unease in his presence?

Folding her hands tensely in her lap, she looked down at the countryside, the green of sugar cane fields giving way to the jungle of the escarpment. Perhaps Felipe had been offered a chance to see the famed horse herds?

Indeed, once they'd reached the plateau, she leaned forward and to her delight saw a herd below. They didn't seem alarmed; after a quick gaze upwards they resumed grazing, as though the helicopter was a regular sight in their sky. For some reason, that made her feel better.

But when the chopper headed for a collection of buildings, she frowned as it banked and dropped towards the ground.

It looked like ruins. Some sort of industrial complex, not very big—a sugar mill on a back country road, perhaps. Indeed, when she looked down she could see that there had once been a house there, but it had been burned to the ground.

Startled, she searched for signs of people, but nothing moved in the shrubby vegetation around the stone buildings. The cold patch beneath her ribs increased in size.

What was going on?

The chopper landed with a slight bump and a whirl of dust. The engines changed pitch, and Gastano indicated that she get out.

Lexie made up her mind. She shook her head.

Felipe's smile widened. He groped in a bag at his feet to produce a small, snub-nosed black pistol that he aimed straight at her.

The colour drained from her skin. Instead of words the only sound she could make was a feeble croak of disbelief, and then something hit her, and in a violent pang of pain she lost consciousness.

Lexie huddled on the stone floor, reluctantly accepting that this was no nightmare; tied at the wrists and the ankles, she was propped up against a wall in what looked like an abandoned sugar mill somewhere in Moraze. Forcing herself to ignore the thumping of her head and the nausea, she tried to work out what had happened.

Why had Felipe snatched her from the castle?

A swift glance revealed that she seemed to be alone, but instinct stopped her first impulsive attempt to free her hands. Instead she strained to hear—something, *anything!*

But the only sounds were placid, country noises— a distant bird call, low and consoling, and a soft sigh of wind seeping through the empty windows, sweet with the fragrance of flowers and fresh grass.

A second later she stiffened. A faint whisper—alien, barely there—grated across nerves already stretched taut. Lexie froze, trying to draw strength from the solidity of the stone building, the fact that fire and desolation and the inexorable depredations of the tropics, hadn't been able to turn it into a complete ruin.

That faint, untraceable sound came again and once more she strained to pinpoint it. Was it a thickening of the atmosphere, a primitive warning that bypassed more advanced senses to home in on the inner core that dealt with raw, basic self-preservation?

Or was she fooling herself?

Slowly, carefully, hardly daring to breathe, she inched her head around. Nothing moved in the gloom, but she knew she wasn't alone in the shadowy building. There were plenty of places to hide—behind the wreckage of machinery seemed the most likely.

Footsteps from outside swivelled her head around. Rafiq, she thought in anguish, wondering how she knew it was him. If her senses spoke truly, he was walking into a trap. Surely he wasn't alone? Panic knotted her stomach as she tried to work out what to do.

Scream a warning? But was that what Felipe wanted? He hadn't gagged her.

The footsteps stopped, and her mind ricocheted from one supposition to another. Possibly Felipe thought he'd hit her hard enough to keep her unconscious for longer.

And knowing Rafiq, he'd come in whatever she did, she thought, stifling her panic. But surely— oh, God, *surely*—he wouldn't come here alone and without weapons?

Head pounding, she struggled to hear more.

And caught it—the barest whisper of motion from outside the doorless building.

Lexie bit down on her lip. Rafiq had to know she was here; he wouldn't have come otherwise. She mustn't call out.

But oh, it was so hard…

A jerky flow of movement caught the corner of her eye. Not breathing, she whipped her head around and saw the dark figure of Gastano take a step from behind the machinery so that he could see the doorway more clearly.

Her heart juddered to a stop when she realised he was still holding the pistol. So he meant to kill Rafiq.

Everything else forgotten, she opened her mouth, only to have her yell forestalled by Gastano's voice, bold and arrogantly satisfied.

'So you came, de Courteveille. I knew you would— stupidly chivalrous to the end.'

For a second Rafiq's silhouette in the open door

shuddered against the light, then blended into the dimness inside.

Lexie closed her eyes, nausea gripping her. That moment of clarity had revealed he carried no weapon.

And then he spoke, his voice cool and dispassionate. 'Now that M'selle Sinclair has fulfilled her function as bait, I suggest you let her go. She's not necessary to you any longer.'

With a wide smile, Gastano strolled over to stand above Lexie like a conqueror. 'I have no intention of letting either of you go until you agree to my terms. Come closer—you are too far away.'

He's getting off on this, Lexie realised with sick fear.

And he was totally confident that he held all the cards.

Holding her breath, she watched Rafiq move silently towards them. It was too dark for her to see his face, but she could tell from his gait that he was ready for anything that might happen. She opened her mouth to tell him that Gastano was armed, but was forestalled by her captor.

Sharply he said, 'That's close enough.'

Rafiq took another step, and Gastano swung the pistol around until it was directed straight at Lexie. He swung it back to fix onto Rafiq, and said between his teeth, 'You will do everything I say, when I say it, or suffer the consequences. Take one step backwards.'

Rafiq didn't move, and Gastano prodded her with his foot. 'If you do not, then Alexa will die,' he said calmly. 'Oh, not now, and not quickly—she will die at my disposal. The same way your sister did.'

Hani? Into Lexie's mind flashed the photograph of the girl, vivid, bright, her face full of impudence and joy. Rafiq's sister. And Gastano? Bile caught in her throat.

Gastano's eyes never left his antagonist's face, and she could feel the confidence oozing from him. 'It was quite clever of you to realise that I had plans for Alexa. But you underestimated me.'

Gastano's laugh was a taunt as he switched his gaze back to Lexie for a second.

'You should perhaps have been a little more careful of her feelings before you made love to her, *sir*.' He pronounced the last word with a gloating emphasis that made it an insult. 'Women are inclined to be upset when they are made use of so flagrantly. But I'm sure she suspected that there had to be an ulterior motive to your lovemaking. Alexa knows she is no beauty—unlike your charming but so naïve sister.'

And while an appalled and horrified Lexie was digesting this, he finished on a sneer, 'Besides, you are no better than I am. You decided that the best form of revenge would be to seduce the woman I intend to marry. You were wrong—I still intend to marry her, and neither you nor she will prevent it.'

The fear gripping Lexie slowly receded before an icy realisation. She thought she heard her heart break, shatter into a thousand brittle pieces in her breast, each one stabbing her with a pain that would never go away.

At the centre of this war between the two men was Gastano's treatment of Rafiq's sister.

Lexie herself was merely a bystander, a pawn used by both men in a battle that had nothing to do with her. Rafiq's lovemaking must have been a coolly calculated move to at least shake what he thought might be her loyalty to Gastano.

But he'd come to rescue her.

Rafiq stood like stone, his hands clenched at his sides, his eyes never leaving the man. 'You bastard,' he said gutturally, his voice low and shaking with fury, hands so tightly clenched Lexie could see the whiteness of his knuckles in the gloom. 'You'll rot in hell for what you did to Hani.'

Gastano shrugged dispassionately. 'She had choices,' he said with callous indifference. 'No one forced her into my bed. No one forced her to take drugs or to prostitute herself so that she could pay for them.'

Ruthlessly Lexie pushed the choking sense of betrayal to the back of her mind. Rafiq had to have some sort of plan. And here on Moraze he had the advantage of local knowledge.

The count understood that too, so he was pushing Rafiq, trying to get him off balance. But a glance at Rafiq's face, drawn and darkly anguished, shook her.

It appeared Gastano was succeeding.

Yet although Gastano might pretend to despise Rafiq he was watching him closely, his finger poised on the trigger of the revolver.

As long as he kept that unwavering focus, Rafiq was in danger.

Her pulses quickened. 'I wouldn't marry you if you were the last man in the world. You're just a gutless bignoter,' she said contemptuously.

Gastano swung around. At any other time she might have laughed at the shock in his face, but as soon as the pistol wavered from its lock on Rafiq, she lashed out with her bound feet, catching the count more by luck than good judgment on the side of the kneecap.

He lurched sideways, his finger tightening on the

trigger. Ducking reflexively, she felt the wind of the bullet against her cheek. Her eyes clamped tight shut and her heart pumped so loudly she couldn't hear anything else.

A choked sound forced her eyes open in time to see Rafiq fell Gastano with one blow. The count went down into a limp heap; Rafiq dropped on one knee to check him out, then got up and headed towards her in a lethal, silent rush. She gasped as he grabbed her and hurled her brutally behind what seemed some sort of press.

'Are you all right?' he demanded, running his hands over her with a gentleness so at variance with the brutality of the blow he'd delivered, she could only stare dumbly at him.

A flurry of shots echoed through the building.

'Silence,' Rafiq growled into her ear, shielding her with his body as she struggled to get up.

A voice called out in the local language. Rafiq answered, holding her still as a man raced around the side of the vat.

His answer to Rafiq's swift question was one succinct word.

Rafiq eased up, supporting her while he rapped out an order. The newcomer pulled a knife from somewhere on his person and handed it over, and Rafiq slashed the cords that held her wrists and ankles together.

Chafing her wrists gently, he said, 'You are safe now.'

'I'm all right,' she muttered, still stunned by the abrupt change of situation. She dragged in a sharp breath as the blood began to return to her hands and feet.

'He fooled me into thinking he was truly unconscious.' Ignoring her shivers, he began on her ankles, his fingers soothing yet firm. 'I should have been more careful. He had a knife, and was heading for us when one of my men shot him. It was too quick a death for one so foul, but the best outcome, nevertheless. Otherwise he'd have had to be put on trial.'

Intuitively Lexie guessed why he hadn't wanted that—the details of his sister's degradation would have become common knowledge. He needed to protect her reputation.

She opened her mouth to speak, and he demanded, 'Did he hurt you in any way?'

'Except for hitting me on the head, no,' she said huskily.

He swore harshly, then demanded, 'Were you unconscious?'

'Yes.'

'Do you have a headache now?' He leaned forward and raised her eyelid, staring intently and impersonally into her pupils. 'No, they don't seem dilated, but you could have concussion. Stay still.'

Frowning, she said, 'I did have a headache, but I feel better now.'

'Adrenalin,' he said, getting to his feet.

Desperate to know, she asked, 'Tell me, who—how did whoever shot him get here?'

'There are three army snipers here. The plan was that I should keep him occupied while they crept into place, but you put paid to that. They had only just got here when you lashed out at him—we were lucky one got a clear enough sighting to be able to knock him down.'

'I see,' she said numbly, wincing as feeling cascaded painfully back into her feet and hands. 'How did you get here so quickly?'

His expression hardened. 'He sent a message from the helicopter. I came up in another one.'

A man came through and said something. Rafiq shook his head and gave a swift order, then got to his feet.

'We will soon have you out of here,' he promised, and moved noiselessly away.

Feeling sick, she eased back against the wall, dragging the damp, slightly musty air into her lungs. It smelt sweet and thick and heavy with the scent of past sugar harvests, the faint, spirituous flavour making her gag.

She realised she was shivering; icy tremors seemed to soak right down into her bones. Shock, she thought distantly, and set herself to mastering it. By the time Rafiq came back she'd managed to regain enough composure to control everything but her chattering teeth.

'Don't try to talk,' he commanded as he picked her up and carried her out towards the waiting helicopter.

Back at the hospital she had a shower, a medical checkup that revealed she didn't have concussion, and an injection to counter any infection in the abrasions around her wrists and ankles.

Also, she strongly suspected the next morning, waking up in the hospital bed, some sedative to give her the night of dreamless sleep she'd just enjoyed.

Late that morning she was sent back to the castle in a limousine, with a very solemn Cari and a bodyguard.

She didn't see Rafiq for another two days. He sent her a note saying that because of the fallout from Gastano's death he'd be busy, and that he wanted her to do nothing but recover.

Misery ate into her, but she told herself stoically that

she needed time to get her strength back—strength to leave Moraze and Rafiq without making an idiot of herself.

On the morning she woke with a clear head, she said to Cari, when the maid brought her breakfast tray, 'I'm getting up today.'

'Yes, the doctor is coming this morning to make sure you are recovered.' Carefully Cari positioned the tray over Lexie's knees.

Lexie opened her mouth, then closed it. She knew it was no use fighting Rafiq's dictates. And anyway, it was sensible to get an all-clear. 'And after that I'm getting up properly.'

Instead of leaving, the maid stood, her hands held tightly behind her back. In a subdued voice she said, 'If I had thought just a little I would have known the helicopter was not sent by the Emir. He would never have told it to land on the terrace.' She bit her lip, anxiously scanning Lexie's face. 'I thought it was so romantic. I am truly sorry.'

'It's all right,' Lexie said hastily. 'You weren't to know. Don't worry, Cari. Apart from this bump on the head, I wasn't hurt, and all's well now.'

But once alone, she pushed the tray away. Although she felt the effects of Gastano's wickedness like a smeary feather brushed over her spirit, it was Rafiq's betrayal that shattered her.

She took a deep breath because she just had to accept that, grit her teeth and get on with life. If she faced facts and kept her head high, she'd cope.

But although she'd always known that he didn't love her, it hurt in some shrinking, vulnerable part to know that his actions had been a cynical exercise in revenge.

Poor fool that she was, she'd treasure the memories for the rest of her life, but Rafiq? Well, after she'd left Moraze, he'd probably never think of her again.

Or only as the unwitting agent of change who'd helped him avenge his sister's death.

Stoically she forced down breakfast and endured the medical check-up, which resulted in a complete clearance. It took all of her strength to smile and thank the doctor. When she got back to New Zealand she could indulge in whatever form of breakdown she preferred, she thought drearily, but until then she had to stay in control.

Late in the afternoon, Rafiq came to see her. After she'd satisfied his queries about her health, she said firmly, 'I'm ready to go home now. Can you recommend a good travel agent?'

He paused, then said, 'There are some things I need to explain to you.'

Rapidly, before he had time to go further, she said, 'Look, it doesn't matter. I understand why you did what you did. Your sister—'

Not a muscle moved in the arrogant face, and his voice was cool and flat as he cut her off. 'My sister died because of Gastano. I suspect he targeted her for the same reason he chose you—because she had access to a world he desired above everything else. Also, he enjoyed defiling innocence.'

Humiliated, she stared at him. He was almost certainly right.

Stone-faced, Rafiq said, 'Did you know he was a drug dealer?'

'*No!*' Her skin crawled.

He searched her face keenly. 'Did he ever offer you drugs?'

'Once,' she said quietly, so appalled she felt physically ill. The conversation in the ruins had played through her mind over and over, and she'd accepted that Felipe must have had something to do with the drug trade, but the thought still horrified her. 'I didn't think he was a user, but I supposed that he knew how to get them. Even in New Zealand drugs are easy enough to get if you really want them. It never occurred to me he was a dealer.'

Rafiq's brows drew together. 'Sit down,' he commanded, and when she stayed defiantly upright he caught her up and carried her to a chair.

In the strong grip of his arms the familiar magic washed over Lexie, drowning out everything but aching need and memories of passion. Until Rafiq deposited her onto the chair, with care but no tenderness, as though he couldn't wait to get rid of her.

Hope died a wretched death. She could have crossed her arms over her breasts and rocked with wailing despair, but pride kept her upright, steadied her gaze, forced her lips to move. 'Do you believe me?'

'Of course,' he said with a faint air of surprise. 'Like all men of his stamp, Gastano could read people—it must have been obvious to him that you were not a good candidate for addiction.'

'Was *he* an addict?'

'No. As you heard in the old sugar mill—' He paused a moment before finishing in a level, emotionless tone, 'He turned my sister into one.'

'I'm so sorry.' Totally inadequate though her words were, it was all Lexie could think of to say.

Still in that clinical, dispassionate tone, he went on, 'When she realised that the man she thought she loved had deliberately betrayed her and seduced her, she could not live with the pain and humiliation and she committed suicide.'

Lexie said again, 'I'm so very sorry.'

'She was eighteen at the time, in her first year at university.'

CHAPTER ELEVEN

THE nausea that had slowly dissipated over the past couple of days returned to Lexie in a rush.

Rafiq continued in a flat, lethal tone, 'Gastano didn't know that before she died she sent me a letter telling me about their secret affair, her dependence on the drugs he'd fed her, and her shame and humiliation and horror at her foolishness. He believed I knew nothing about him, which gave me the edge when it came to hunting him down.'

His air, his voice, even his measured words, gave no hint of his attachment to his sister—but she could see a little below that controlled surface now, and she understood his bleak determination to bring Gastano to book.

Not only did she understand it, she thought bleakly, she applauded it.

If only it hadn't cost her her heart.

Rafiq's voice was cool and clinical. 'Gastano is— was—the kingpin of a cartel that shipped heroin and cocaine to Europe and North America. He was assessing Moraze as his next staging post.'

Rafiq had spent the past days and most of the nights

working with his government and the security service. He looked at Lexie's intelligent face and thought wearily that, just for once, he wished she'd accept the easy answer.

But that wasn't Lexie. And he owed her the truth before they moved on from this.

'He was an arrogant man, vain and secretly insecure,' he said austerely. 'Possibly because he was illegitimate; the title he used was not his but his half-brother's, who died in suspicious circumstances.'

Horrified, she demanded, 'You mean—did he *murder* his brother?'

'I don't know. I think not—but the real count died of a drug overdose.'

'Nothing—not growing up illegitimate, not *anything*—excuses dealing in drugs.'

She stopped, acutely conscious that her own father had killed without compunction, and spent years plundering a country at the whim of inner demons that nothing else could satisfy.

Rafiq filled in her sudden silence. 'Who knows the secret workings of a man's mind?' he said sombrely. 'I'm not sorry he is dead, not sorry I've spent the past two years working to bring him down. His damned drugs have killed more people and ruined more lives than anyone can count.'

He paused, and she looked up to meet his narrowed eyes. 'But I am very sorry you were caught up in it. That was never my intention.'

'I understand now why you acted the way you did.' she said abruptly, 'I didn't know he planned to marry me. I had no intention of marrying him.'

Soon she'd leave Moraze, and once she got home

she'd be able to put this behind her, she thought. How could she blame Rafiq for doing what he could to protect his subjects and his sister's memory? He wouldn't be the man she loved if he'd done anything else.

His seduction of her might have been coldly calculated, but set against the misery and degradation that Felipe had already caused, and the prospect of him using Moraze as a staging post for his filthy merchandise, she couldn't blame Rafiq for using whatever weapons he had.

She looked at him and asked slowly, 'Did you know he planned to marry me?'

'I learned of it after you came here,' Rafiq said curtly.

'If you knew that, you must have known I wasn't in any danger from him. Why on earth did you come unarmed to the sugar mill?' Lexie asked, furious with him all over again for taking such a risk.

'It wasn't as dangerous as it seemed. I was almost certain he wouldn't kill me.'

'How could you be so sure?' she demanded, her voice angry. 'You had no right to put yourself at risk like that!'

He sent her a sardonic glance. 'To my knowledge he had never actually murdered anyone himself. There was always someone to do it for him, you see. It is much easier to say "get rid of this person" than actually do the act yourself. Besides, after seeing me kiss you the night before, he judged that he could use you as leverage to force me to do what he wanted here on Moraze. I couldn't allow that to happen.'

He frowned, and she felt her heart bump into overdrive, singing with a painful joy because she loved him. He didn't love her; it was his overdeveloped sense of responsibility that had brought him to her rescue.

In a hard voice he resumed. 'The snipers had a fix on him—you didn't need to recklessly throw yourself in the path of danger by kicking at him.'

'*You* were the reckless one,' she retorted, stung. 'You had no weapons, and just acting on the hunch that he wouldn't kill either of us was sheer madness.'

His broad shoulders lifted. 'It was a desperate situation,' he said calmly. 'Besides, Moraze has been my responsibility for more years than I care to count; I owe it much.'

And there, she thought wearily, was her answer in a nutshell: everything he'd done, including seducing her, had been for the honour of his sister and the protection of his country. *Everything*—their passionate lovemaking, the hours of honey and fire in his arms, the slow discovery of each other—had been an unspoken lie.

For him. Not for her. She was leaving her heart in his keeping—unnoticed, unwanted, but lost to her for ever.

Rafiq's face hardened even further. In a cold, controlled voice, he said, 'I will not insult you with excuses for my actions. At first I suspected that you were his lover—'

'With no proof,' she flashed.

His eyes didn't soften. 'It seemed more likely than not. And I deliberately manipulated circumstances to separate you from him—partly because, although I knew him to be dangerous, I didn't know how he'd react when he realised that his empire was shattering around him.'

'And partly to keep his mind off the fact that it was happening,' she said, engulfed by intense tiredness.

His mouth compressed, but he agreed calmly, 'That too.'

'It was a clever move, and it worked. He must have been furious when he realised you were just as capable as he was of separating sex from the things that really matter.'

She'd intended her words to cut, but Rafiq shrugged them off without any visible reaction. 'I must also apologise to you.'

Pride wasn't much armour, but it was all she had left, and it drove her to forestall the inevitable. 'I'm glad you achieved what you wanted. And although it's a terrible thing to say, I can't be sorry that Felipe is dead.'

Because she suspected that Rafiq would never have been safe if the other man had lived; the count's ego and malice would have seen him work to bring down the man who'd bested him.

She hesitated. 'It gives me the creeps to know I once thought he was fun to be with.'

'He traded on his charm and his *savoir faire*.' He dismissed Gastano with a single movement of his hand and looked at her. 'Forget about him. My government and I have worked hard to contain the fallout from all this, and succeeded in great part. Now that it is over, there is one thing left for me to do.'

Eyes widening, she watched him come towards her, his eyes hooded and unreadable in his hard face. Her heart began to beat faster, and the hope she'd thought so dead burst into flames inside her. Uncertainly she said, 'What—what is that?'

He stood for a moment, looking down at her with a hooded gaze. Was he going to suggest they continue their affair?

What would she answer? Part of Lexie wanted nothing more than to lose herself again in the fiery passion summoned by his lightest touch. But any affair with him would eventually end, leaving her bereft.

He said gravely, 'I have never done this before, so perhaps I am clumsy, but I would like very much for you to marry me, Lexie.'

Sheer untrammelled joy fountained through her, and then—as quickly as it had come—faded. The photograph of his sister, virginal and betrayed, flashed in front of her eyes.

He'd been shocked and startled to discover that Lexie had never had a lover. And Gastano's jibe that seducing Lexie made him no better than the count would have stung.

Scanning his composed face, she searched for some sign of love, something akin to the violence of her own emotions. Her heart quailed when she read nothing. He even looked slightly amused, as though he knew what she felt, and expected nothing more than her vehement agreement.

What she couldn't see was any sign of tenderness, of love.

It was then that Lexie realised that there are worse things than a love betrayed. A treacherous little hope whispered that in time Rafiq could learn to love her— only to be quickly rejected. Lexie's hungry heart wanted more than a comfortable, sensible affection.

Oh, it would be a reasonably suitable marriage, she thought bitterly; after all, even though her father had been a murderous monster, she was related to one of the oldest ruling families in Europe.

She had no money and few social graces, but hell, her sister had learned how to cope with life as a princess; she could too.

Only she wasn't going to.

A *sensible* marriage? Never! She longed for the fiery incandescence of uncontrollable love, the sort that lasted a lifetime, a love that would match hers.

In a subdued voice she told him, 'It's a great honour, but I'm afraid I can't accept.'

Rafiq's expression didn't change. If anything, more was needed to convince her that he felt nothing more for her than a convenient passion, it was this.

He said on a note of irony, 'Perhaps I need to convince you.'

And he pulled her into his arms, locking her there with relentless desire. Fighting back a white-hot hunger, Lexie drew on all her strength. She had to stop this before it went any further—and she knew how to do it. Rafiq's icy pride was a weapon for him, but also a weak point.

Quietly, her voice level and bleak, she said, 'You can make me want you. But when it's over, I'll still refuse your proposal.'

Then, because her emotions threatened to burst through the dam of her own pride, she folded her lips, trying fiercely to project her utter conviction.

To her astonishment he smiled and bent his head. She expected a kiss that echoed the violence of her emotions, but when it came, it was a soft whisper of sensation across her lips that broke through her defences, so raggedly and hastily erected.

Against her mouth he said softly, 'Are you going to refuse me, my dear one? Surely you can't be so cruel…?'

'Please,' she whispered, aching with anguish. 'Don't do this to me.'

'But see what you do to me.' His voice was tender, yet she heard the satisfaction in it as he pulled her a little closer so that she could feel the wild response of his body, lean and hard and supplicant against hers.

This, she thought, was truly the end. She looked at him, her eyes glittering, and said between her teeth, 'All right, then—one last time, and on my terms. I'll be leaving Moraze tomorrow.'

He froze, his eyes narrowing as he looked down at her. 'You mean this?'

'Yes. It's over, Rafiq.' She lifted her head high.

He knew he could manipulate her with sex—and she couldn't bear the thought of a loveless marriage, based only on that. When he became accustomed to her, as he would, would there be other women?

Perhaps not; he was an honourable man, but she would not be seduced into an existence that would eventually result in a kind of death of the spirit.

'It might not be,' he said curtly. 'There is the fact that last time we made love we did not use any protection. That was my responsibility, and I failed you.'

With steely determination, she said, 'It's highly unlikely that I'm pregnant, but the possibility is no reason for marriage.'

'What better reason for marriage can there be?' he demanded, his face like stone.

Lexie had to respect him for not lying to her, but oh, if he'd said—just once—that he loved her she might surrender.

He'd carefully avoided that.

Hoarsely she said, 'If I am pregnant, I promise I'll let you know.'

'If you are pregnant you will marry me,' he returned with icy authority. 'My child will not grow up illegiti-mate like Gastano.'

'Our child—if there is one—will not grow up like him at all! What do I have to do to convince you that I know what's best for me? And it's not marriage with you. I will *not* be harassed or coaxed or seduced or intimidated into it.'

Just in time she stopped herself from adding, *Your sister might have died because she was betrayed, but I'm not quite so weak.*

It would be spiteful and it would be wrong, because her will power was already fading.

He said, 'I could stop you from leaving Moraze.'

'You wouldn't dare!' She stared at him, and something cold slithered the length of her spine. He looked ruthless, as tough as any of his ancestors of old, capable of anything. 'Yes, you would,' she said slowly, heavily.

She bared her teeth at him. 'If the sex—because that's all you'd get—is so important to you, then I can't see why we shouldn't enjoy each other one last time before I go.'

Silkily he answered, 'No reason at all. But once you leave I'll hold you to that promise. If you are pregnant, I want to know immediately.'

Colour flooded her skin, then vanished. Dismissing the immediate outcry from some distant, barely heard part of her that must be common sense, she said crisply, 'Of course.'

And she lowered her lashes to mask the anguish in her eyes, and kissed his throat.

His familiar taste summoned an instant response, hot and compelling and heady, a surge of desire that swept through her and obliterated any weak appeal to prudence and caution, and all the boring concerns that might stop her making love to Rafiq before she walked out of his life.

'I'm glad we understand each other so well.'

Something cynical and dangerous in his tone lifted the hairs on the back of her neck, but before she had time to react he lifted her and carried her across to the huge bed.

Mouth on hers, arms tight around her, he lowered her so that her feet came to rest on the carpet.

'So,' he said coolly, holding her a little away from him, his eyes intense and compelling, 'Indulge me. Strip for me.'

His smile stirred more bitter pride in her. 'Only if you do it for me as well,' she retorted, head high, eyes challenging him in the most elemental of battles.

'Perhaps we should do it for each other,' he suggested. He kissed the spot where her neck met her shoulder, and then bit delicately, his teeth sending frissons of excitement through her.

So they did, interspersing the removal of each garment with kisses that grew more and more urgent, with caresses that banished her inhibitions—until in the end they came together in a conflagration of reckless hunger so intense Lexie burned up in it, her body an instrument of such extreme pleasure she forgot everything but the violence of her own sensations as he made himself master of her every reaction.

Her ecstatic release scared her; she lay panting in his arms, shocked at the strength of her feelings, her body still hungry for something he couldn't give her.

When she could speak again she unclenched her hands from the sheets and whispered hoarsely, 'You didn't—you haven't...'

Her voice trailed away as she met his eyes. Ruthless, utterly determined, they made her flinch. 'Not yet,' he said, his voice harsh and raw. 'Not yet, my dove, my beautiful woman…'

And he began all over again. That searing, primal look warned her. She braced herself to be plundered, but this time—ah, this time—it was slow and erotically voluptuous. Like the conqueror he was, he made himself master of her body, his hands coaxing, his mouth taking its fill of the satin perfection of her breasts, of every inch of her skin except for the place that longed for him.

Frustrated, she reached for him, but he pushed her hands above her head and held them in a loose grip while he bent his head to continue the exquisite, gentle torture, knowing with experience and a sure male instinct which were her most sensitive pleasure points, exactly how long to work each one, and when to leave and find the next…

Helpless, she began to whimper with anguished pleasure, muttering, 'Please—oh, please, Rafiq—now…now…'

And then he took her in a stark, slow thrust; almost she convulsed around him, but he eased out, leaving her bereft, aching with loss, until he took her again, this time even deeper, even slower…

She struggled, but he said steadily, 'It is hard, I know, but wait. Just wait.'

So she did, and he continued his slow, erotically charged strokes until at last she could hold back no longer. Her body arched uncontrollably—she cried out his name as ecstasy swept over her and through her.

After he'd left her she wept for his cruel tenderness, his total, complete consideration and absorption in his exploration of her body, the way he'd skilfully coaxed her into ecstasy before sending her soaring beyond it into a place she'd never been before.

And would never find again, she knew. For the rest of her life she'd long for that place, the security of his arms, the knowledge of his hunger for her—and know that it wasn't enough.

She wanted his love: total, unconditional, without strings. The way she loved him.

And as she couldn't have it, she'd just have to learn to live without it.

They met the next morning for an oddly formal farewell.

Lexie thanked him for his hospitality. In turn, he thanked her for her help, and finished, 'I ask you not to speak of what has happened here.'

'Of course I won't,' she said rapidly. When she got home she was going to try her hardest to forget everything about the island. She met his keen, intimidating scrutiny with a direct look. 'And you don't have to thank me—I did nothing but complicate things!'

'You kept your head in a situation that must have terrified you.'

With an irony that hid the sound of her heart cracking again, she said, 'I should have known—actually, I did know—that you had a plan. I was just afraid that he might kill you before you were able to carry it out.'

For a second she caught a glimpse of that desert ancestor, autocratic and powerful and ruthless. 'Thank you.' Without pausing, he went on, 'I want to hear from you as soon as you know whether or not you are pregnant.'

'Very well.'

He said with an undernote of menace, 'Don't put me to the trouble of coming after you, Lexie.'

She stiffened. 'Don't worry about that,' she said pleasantly. 'I won't.'

Their eyes locked. 'I'm glad,' he said with silky distinctness. 'If at any time or place you need help—whatever sort—contact me.'

'Thank you,' she said, knowing it meant nothing. Oh, if she asked, he'd move heaven and earth to do what he could for her, she was quite sure.

But she'd never ask.

He smiled, its irony echoing hers. 'Thank you, Lexie. Goodbye.'

And it was over. She was taken to the airport in a discreet car and settled into a first-class seat. As the huge jet lifted over the grasslands, she watched a herd of horses galloping, galloping, galloping, and thought bleakly that at least she'd seen them.

The shrill summons of her mobile phone woke her from a deep sleep. Wearily, she groped for it and muttered, 'Hello?'

'Lexie, get out here fast. Sultan's Favourite's in trouble.'

Exhaustion fled in a rush of adrenalin. 'What?'

'The foal's not coming easy.'

'Be there in ten.'

Fingers clenched on the steering wheel, she drove through the night to the stables owned by a good friend of hers. 'How is she?' she demanded on arrival, scanning the mare—who, she was grateful to see, looked as comfortable as any female could in her condition.

It was a condition Lexie didn't share. She'd been back in New Zealand for a month—long enough to establish that she wasn't pregnant. As soon as she'd known, she'd sent a formal registered letter to Rafiq to tell him that he was free of any prospect of fatherhood. His reply had been equally formal. He wished her everything good in her life. And he was sincerely hers, Rafiq de Couteveille.

The irony wasn't lost on her, but she'd suppressed the pain, forcing it down until it was merely a deep-seated ache. Sometimes it came to the surface in dreams of loss and anguish, but mostly she could function as though she'd never been anywhere east of Zanzibar.

'I think she's OK now,' her friend said with a wry smile. 'I panicked.'

But the marc needed help, and it was almost dawn when Lexie drove back home. Fortunately it was the weekend and she wasn't on call, so she could go back to bed once she got home.

Sleep didn't come easily anymore. She wondered how much longer she was going to be tormented by this fierce hunger for a man who'd used her. How was it that film stars and the glamorous people who filled the gossip magazines seemed able to flit from lover to lover without wasting time on grief?

No such luck for her. She rolled over onto her back and stared at the ceiling. She'd hoped that the aching emptiness inside her would soon dissipate, but so far time had only intensified it. Fill her days with work as much as she could, she still missed Rafiq.

One day she'd see a notice of his engagement to some suitable woman, and then she'd be forced to get on with her life.

A week previously she'd decided she'd had enough. Mourning a love that had never had a chance was a futile waste of time; from now on, she'd ignore it and

live life to the full instead of moping like some
Victorian heroine intent on devoting the rest of her life
to the memory of a lost love.

So when a newly separated partner in her practice
asked her to accompany him to a formal dinner, she'd
accepted. He was a dear, and still very much in love
with his wife, so she didn't fear any sort of advance.

But if she wanted to stay awake during the dinner with
him the following night, she'd have to get some sleep!

Eventually she dropped off, enough so that con-
cealer hid the shadows under her eyes, and the evening
passed pleasantly enough.

'Thanks for coming with me,' her date said on the
way home. 'I'm not looking forward to Christmas.
What are you doing?'

'I'm on duty,' she said cheerfully.

He nodded as they turned into her gateway. 'I enjoyed that evening more than I expected to. Thanks to
you, mainly,' he said. 'Lexie, if it's an imposition say
so, but do you mind if I make use of you shamelessly
for this festive season? There are several other functions
I can't get out of…'

She'd had more enthusiastic offers, but she understood. She too had functions she couldn't avoid. 'OK,'
she said lightly, and opened her door.

But he got out and came around the car to her. 'I'll
see you to the door,' he said with a wry attempt at a
smile. 'I haven't entirely forgotten how to behave.'

He waited until she'd unlocked it, and then said, 'I
enjoyed tonight so much I'm quite looking forward to
our next date.'

Lexie waved as he turned the car and set off down
the drive again. It was a beautiful night, and she stood

for a few seconds to admire the stars, thinking of the same stars in a depthless tropical sky.

Stop it, she told herself fiercely, and stepped back.

Then froze as a piece of shadow detached itself from beneath the jacaranda tree and came towards her.

'Just as well he didn't try to kiss you,' Rafiq said in a lethal voice.

The initial flash of terror was superseded by a triumphant joy so fierce that she pressed one hand over her heart. As he strode silently towards her in the starlight, she couldn't speak.

And when she did her voice was thin and uncontrolled. 'It's none of your business who I kiss.'

He stopped just in front of her. 'You really believe that?' he asked in a low, fierce growl.

And at her defiant nod he said thickly, 'Then you need to learn otherwise,' and hauled her into his arms, his mouth coming down on hers with a famished hunger that smashed through every shaky defence.

Passion soared through her, unleashed and formidable, sweeping away common sense and all the rational arguments she'd used to bolster herself through the long, dark days since she'd left Moraze.

But when at last he lifted his mouth from hers, and framed her face with his lean strong hands, eyes fiercely intent as he scanned her, she asked beneath a harsh indrawn breath, 'What are you doing here?'

'I am starving to death without you,' he said just as quietly, but with an intensity that brought warmth, and a wild hope with it.

CHAPTER TWELVE

'RAFIQ,' she said on a broken little sob. 'I don't want an affair.'

He said jaggedly, 'I cannot bear your tears. Rage at me, little cat, show me the spirit you've kept intact all through this. But I beg you, don't weep.'

Lexie couldn't control her shock. His unexpected arrival had finally tipped her over the precipice she'd been negotiating for the past weeks. She gulped as more tears clogged her throat, and then she felt the longed-for strength of his arms around her, his warmth enclosing her as he rocked her back and forth, murmuring soft, comforting words in the language she didn't understand.

Until finally her tears slowed and she could think again.

Then he said deeply, 'So it has been as bad for you as it has for me?'

'I don't know how bad it's been for you,' she retorted with a flash of spirit.

He tipped her chin and examined her face, a gleam of satisfaction gilding the dark green eyes. 'Very bad,' he said succinctly. 'Until you left, I didn't realise how much I was going to miss you. I hoped you were missing me just as much, but if you were, you didn't show it.'

'How do you know?' she demanded, startled by his words.

He looked arrogantly sure of himself, a conqueror fully in command. 'Surely you didn't think I would let you go so easily?' he asked, his brows lifting. 'Of course I made sure you were all right.'

'You had me watched?' Lexie tried very hard to be outraged; it shouldn't have been difficult, but her natural anger was softened by a treacherous glow of pleasure.

'Checked,' he corrected, his jaw jutting. 'If you had been happy, if you'd showed no signs of missing me, then I would have accepted your decision.'

She tried to pull back; he held her for another second, then let her go. 'Really?' she said disbelievingly.

Shrugging those broad shoulders, he conceded with an enigmatic smile, 'Not without seeing you again. Everything happened so fast between us, and then you discovered that I had used you, and naturally you were furious and hurt. And there was the possibility of a child to complicate the situation. You needed time to think, to regroup, to discover for yourself what your emotions were. But always I planned to come and ask you to marry me again.'

Lexie heard his words as though in a dream. She stared at him and said furiously, 'Just what do you feel for me? Apart from passion?' Colour heated her cheekbones, then faded abruptly, so that they stood out starkly beneath her hot blue eyes. 'That's not the best base for something as serious as marriage, but you've never shown any indication of feeling anything more.'

He looked at her as though she was mad, his eyes blazing above a face suddenly stark. 'I love you,' he said between his teeth. 'Of course I love you—how could you not have known? I asked you to marry me, Lexie!'

'You asked me to marry you because you found out I was a virgin,' she retorted tensely, her heart thudding so hard she had to focus on speaking clearly. 'And because you thought I might be pregnant!'

Her whole future depended on this. He had to be sure—as sure as she was. And she had to be sure, too, that his sister's wretched fate hadn't driven him into that astonishing proposal.

Because it had to be faced, she said more steadily, 'You couldn't bear to be associated with Gastano in anything, especially not the seduction of a virgin. And then we made love without protection.'

Appalled, she watched his hands clench at his sides. He surveyed her with menacing eyes, their glitter so intimidating she had to stop herself from taking a step backwards. After a few seconds, he dragged in a deep breath and his fists relaxed.

'I did not *seduce* you,' he rasped. 'We made love. There is a difference. For me there was always love.'

'I can't believe that,' she said desperately, wanting so much to accept what he was saying she could feel the need like a huge hunger inside her. 'You despised me because you thought I'd been Felipe's lover.'

'I tried very hard *to* despise you,' he corrected with a grim smile. 'From the moment I saw you in that flirtatious orange dress, I wanted you, but even then I felt more for you than the transient lust of a man for a sexy woman.'

'How do you know?'

He gave her another arrogant look, one mingled with frustration, then, in a gesture as brutal as it was unexpected, hammered a fist into one cupped hand. 'I felt—doubt, confusion, anger. All those—and something else. For the first time in my life, I did not know what it was I was feeling, and the loss of control made me angry.

'So, yes, I suspected that you were far more experienced than you were, but the woman I kidnapped did not live up to my expectations. You were warm and thoughtful; after the car crash, you insisted on finding out how the driver of the car was, and you sent her a card and flowers. She is one of my best agents, by the way. You showed no signs of interest in anything but Moraze and the horses, the people—almost everything around you but me!'

Lexie couldn't stop her incredulous laugh. 'You must have known—you're an experienced man, and every time you touched me or kissed me, I lost it.'

His anger faded. He smiled, but with irony. 'Ah, but you regained that infuriating composure very quickly. I would like to be able to tell you when love happened, how it happened, but it came so swiftly, stealing my heart before I knew it was in danger. Even after we made love the first time, I thought I was safe. Until in the sugar mill, when it seemed that Gastano held all the cards in his hands, and I knew that if I couldn't rescue you I would die a lonely man.'

That simple statement and the tone it was delivered in—as stark and uncompromising as the stripped anguish in his eyes—almost satisfied Lexie's desperate need to be convinced.

Yet still she couldn't quite dare to believe him.

Instead she turned and unlocked the door, saying over her shoulder, 'You'd better come inside. It's summer here, but it must be cold for you after Moraze.'

What would he think of her cottage? He followed her in, closing the door behind him. She stood silently, devouring him with her eyes, as he inspected the small living room with its doors opening out onto a brick terrace.

'It looks like you,' he said at last, then turned and smiled at her. 'Warm and practical, yet with charm and spirit. When did you know you loved me?'

'I knew for sure when I thought Gastano was going to kill you. That's why I kicked out at him; I realised that life without you wouldn't be worth living.'

Rafiq held out his hand. She took it, and his fingers closed around hers, warm, confident, strong and protective. But he didn't take her into his arms.

Instead he said in a low, implacable voice, 'I loathed Gastano for what he did to my sister—he stripped her of her innocence, degraded her until she believed that she was worth nothing. But I didn't feel that I had done that to you after we made love. I felt—transported, as though this was new and happening for the first time, as though I suddenly knew why I had been born.'

She said quietly, 'So did I.'

Although his fingers tightened around hers, he still didn't kiss her. 'I knew I couldn't touch Gastano legally. I probably could have arranged his assassination, but that would have made me as bad as he was.'

'No,' she said jerkily.

He shrugged. 'I felt so. Also, it would have left his organisation ripe for being taken over by someone as evil as he was. But I wanted him to pay for what he did—and I wanted to make sure no more innocents would suffer degradation at his hands. To do that, I had to get him to Moraze. I didn't realise you were coming too, or that he intended to marry you.'

Lexie nodded, and scanned his beloved face. 'So you lured him there.'

'But then I decided to keep you out of circulation, hoping that would infuriate him enough to make him show his hand.' He gave a grim smile. 'Well, that was what I told myself. The real reason was because I couldn't bear the thought of him talking to you, kissing you, making love to you. So I organised that accident.'

She lifted her brows, trying to hide the warmth of joy his words caused. 'You're a devious man.'

Rafiq's voice hardened. 'But even though I knew he would turn feral when he realised things were going down, I didn't expect him to steal the helicopter and force the pilot at gunpoint to fly to the castle.'

'I see,' she said, nodding, then frowned. 'What happened to the pilot?'

'He was shot.'

Lexie flinched, and he finished with lethal determination, 'That was why I told my men to shoot to kill.'

'Yes,' she said sombrely. 'When you said that his death was too quick and clean, I agreed, but I understand even better why you felt that way.'

'I'm glad,' he said quietly. 'Now, as I have told you everything, will you please marry me and make me happy?'

Horrified, Lexie felt tears glaze her eyes. 'I wish I could, but I have something to tell you. It's about my father—you don't know who he was.'

'Of course I do,' he said coolly, his frown easing.

She met his eyes, green and steady and direct, then

gave a pale imitation of a smile. 'Yes, of course you do. But have you thought things through? If we marry everyone on Moraze will discover that my father was a monster. You didn't want Hani's reputation sullied.'

'Let them say what they want to say. It will not affect us,' he said with the magnificent self-assurance that came from centuries of autocratic rule. In a voice that quietened all her fears, he said, 'I don't care about anyone who will judge you for what your father did— I care only about you. If you will marry me, Lexie, I will love and cherish you all our life together until I die. Neither of us can change our past, but together we can forge a future that will put the memories where they belong—behind us.'

Heart swelling with joy, she smiled at him. 'Then let's do that.'

It took all of Rafiq's iron discipline to control himself. 'I want you to learn to love Moraze as I do,' he said. 'All you have known of it has been a kind of imprisonment—but at home now the flame trees are flowering, and the air is languid and heavy with promise, and there are glories you have never seen waiting for you.'

'I'll love anywhere you are,' she said, the words a vow.

His expression softened. 'And you will be happy,' he said in a deep, harsh voice she'd never heard before. 'I swear it.'

She lifted a misty gaze to him. 'So will you,' she said, not holding back the tears as at last he took her into his arms.

'All right,' Princess Jacoba Considine said, frowning. 'Twirl.'

Obediently Lexie twirled, the silk of her creamy-gold dress swirling around her in a gentle sussuration.

Jacoba inspected her with the unsparing scrutiny of a woman famed the world over for her fashion sense. 'You look utterly, astoundingly gorgeous. Rafiq is going to faint when he sees you.'

To giggles from the two maids who had helped her into her wedding dress, Lexie said with a grin, 'He's not into fainting. I'll settle for him being gobsmacked.'

The maids giggled again, and Jacoba glanced at the clock. 'OK, time to get this show on the road,' she said cheerfully. 'We have exactly three hours before my son announces his desire for his next sustenance.' She examined the Considine tiara. 'I believe that thing weighs half a tonne, but it's worth it.'

'Anything is worth it for Rafiq,' Lexie said quietly, and went out of the room to where Prince Marco, her brother-in-law and distant cousin, waited to escort her to her marriage ceremony.

Much later, in a pavilion overlooking a lagoon scattered with stars, she looked at her husband.

'Come here,' he commanded, holding out his hand as his eyes narrowed in the intent, penetrating gaze that always set her pulse drumming. 'Have I told you how wonderful you looked today as you walked up towards me in the cathedral?'

She smiled shakily, heated anticipation building inside her. Since her arrival in Moraze they hadn't made love, and the time spent away from each other had sharpened her hunger into something close to desperation.

'Not until now,' she said, walking to him over a floor strewn with the petals of tropical flowers. Their scent hung like a blessing in the warm, smooth air.

She cupped his face in her hands, saw the answering glint of passion in his eyes, and knew with rock-solid certainty that this was the start of a long and happy life together.

'I love you,' she said, resting her forehead on his chest, inhaling his beloved scent, taking simple comfort from his formidable strength and presence.

'As I do you. With everything I am, everything I have, for eternity.'

He spoke the words like a vow; to her they were more precious than the magnificent fire-diamond jewellery he'd given her, more precious than anything else in her life.

Then Rafiq kissed her, and all thought of jewels vanished in the magical potency of that kiss, and the glorious promise of their future together in Moraze.

'East of Zanzibar,' she murmured when she could talk again. 'When you told me Moraze got its name because it means east, I thought anything could happen east of Zanzibar—even something so wildly romantic as finding a soul mate. I didn't really expect it to happen, though.'

He leant his cheek on the top of her head. 'But it did. To both of us,' he said in a voice dark with satisfaction, and together they walked hand in hand towards a future as bright and glittering as the fabled fire-diamonds of Lexie's new country, the country that held her heart.

PRINCE OF SCANDAL

BY
ANNIE WEST

Annie West spent her childhood with her nose between the covers of a book—a habit she retains. After years preparing government reports and official correspondence she decided to write something she *really* enjoys. And there's nothing she loves more than a great romance. Despite her office-bound past she has managed a few interesting moments—including a marriage offer with the promise of a herd of camels to sweeten the contract. She is happily married to her ever-patient husband (who has never owned a dromedary). They live with their two children amongst the tall eucalypts at beautiful Lake Macquarie, on Australia's east coast. You can e-mail Annie at www.annie-west. com, or write to her at PO Box 1041, Warners Bay, NSW 2282, Australia.

For Karen, Reeze and Daisy,
who celebrate with me
and who understand all the rest.
Thank you!

CHAPTER ONE

RAUL stared unseeingly out of the chopper as it followed the coast south from Sydney. He shouldn't be here when the situation at home was so delicately poised. But he had no choice.

What an unholy mess!

His hands bunched into fists and he shifted his long legs restlessly.

The fate of his nation and the well-being of his subjects were at risk. His coronation, his right to inherit the kingdom he'd been born to and devoted his life to, hung in the balance. Even now he could scarcely believe it.

Desperately the lawyers had sought one legal avenue after another but the laws of inheritance couldn't be overturned, not till he became king. And to become king...

The alternative was to walk away and leave his country prey to the rivalries that had grown dangerous under the last king, Raul's father. Civil war had almost ripped the country apart two generations ago. Raul had to keep his people safe from that, no matter what the personal cost.

His people, his need to work for them, had been what kept him going through the bleak wasteland of disillusionment when his world had turned sour years before. When paparazzi had muckraked and insinuated and his dreams had shattered around him, the people of Maritz had stood by him.

He would stand by them now when they most needed him.

Besides, the crown was *his*. Not only by birthright. By dint of every long day, every hour he'd devoted to mastering the myriad royal responsibilities.

He would not renounce his heritage. His destiny.

Tension stiffened every sinew and anger simmered in his blood. Despite a lifetime's dedication to the nation, despite his experience, training and formidable capacity, it had all come down to the decision of a stranger.

It scored his pride that his future, his country's future, depended on this visit.

Raul opened the investigator's report, skimming familiar details.

Luisa Katarin Alexandra Hardwicke. Twenty-four. Single. Self-employed.

He assured himself this would be straightforward. She'd be thrilled and eager. Yet he wished the file contained a photo of this woman who would play such a pivotal role in his life.

He closed the report with a snap.

It didn't matter what she looked like. He wasn't weak like his father. Raul had learned the hard way that beauty could lie. Emotions played a man for a fool. Raul ruled his life, like his kingdom, with his head.

Luisa Hardwicke was the key to safeguarding his kingdom. She could be ugly as sin and it would make no difference.

Damn! The cow shifted, almost knocking Luisa over. Wearily she struggled to regain her footing in the bog at the edge of the creek.

It had been a long, troubling morning with early milking, generator problems and an unexpected call from the bank manager. He'd mentioned a property inspection that sounded ominously like a first step to foreclosure.

She shuddered. They'd fought so long to keep the small farming co-operative going through drought, illness and flood. Surely the bank couldn't shut them down now. Not when they had a chance to turn things around.

Overhead came the rhythmic thunder of a helicopter. The cow shifted uneasily.

'Sightseers?' Sam shouted. 'Or have you been hiding some well-heeled friends?'

'I wish!' The only ones she knew with that much money were the banks. Luisa's stomach coiled in a familiar twist of anxiety. Time was fast running out for the co-op.

Inevitably her mind turned to that other world she'd known so briefly. Where money was no object. Where wealth was taken for granted.

If she'd chosen she could be there now, a rich woman with not a financial worry in the world. If she'd put wealth before love and integrity, and sold her soul in that devil's bargain.

Just the thought of it made her ill.

She'd rather be here in the mud, facing bankruptcy with the people she loved than be as wealthy as Croesus, if it meant giving up her soul.

'Ready, Sam?' Luisa forced herself to focus. She put her shoulder to the cow. 'Now! Slow and steady.'

Finally, between them, they got the animal unstuck and moving in the right direction.

'Great,' Luisa panted. 'Just a little more and—' Her words were obliterated as a whirring helicopter appeared over the rise.

The cow shied, knocking Luisa. She swayed, arms flailing. Then her momentum propelled her forwards into the boggy mess. Wet mud plastered her from face to feet.

'Luisa!' Are you OK?' Her uncle, bless him, sounded more concerned than amused.

She lifted her head and saw the cow, udder swaying, heave onto firm ground and plod away without a backward glance. Gingerly Luisa found purchase in the sodden ground and crawled to her knees, then her feet.

'Perfect.' She wiped slime from her cheeks. 'Mud's supposed to be good for the complexion, isn't it?' She met Sam's rheumy gaze and smiled.

She flicked a dollop of mud away. 'Maybe we should bottle this stuff and try selling it as a skin tonic.'

'Don't laugh, girl. It might come to that.'

Ten minutes later, her overalls, even her face stiff with drying mud, Luisa left Sam and trudged up to her house. Her mind was on this morning's phone call. Their finances looked frighteningly bleak.

She rolled stiff shoulders. At least a shower was only minutes away. A wash, a quick cup of tea and...

She slowed as she topped the hill and saw a helicopter on the grass behind the house. Gleaming metal and glass glinted in the sun. It was high-tech and expensive—a complete contrast to the weathered boards of the house and the ancient leaning shed that barely sheltered the tractor and her rusty old sedan.

Fear settled, a cold hard weight in her stomach. Could this be the inspection the banker had mentioned? So soon?

It took a few moments before logic asserted itself. The bank wouldn't waste money on a helicopter.

A figure appeared from behind the chopper and Luisa stumbled to a halt.

The sun silhouetted a man who was long, lean and elegant. The epitome of urbane masculinity.

She could make out dark hair, a suit that probably cost more than her car and tractor put together, plus a formidable pair of shoulders.

Then he turned and walked a few paces, speaking to someone behind the helicopter. His rangy body moved with an easy grace that bespoke lithe power. A power that belied his suave tailored magnificence.

Luisa's pulse flickered out of rhythm. *Definitely not a banker.* Not with that athletic body.

He was in profile now. High forehead, long aristocratic nose, chiselled mouth and firm chin. Luisa read determination in that solid jaw, and in his decisive gestures. Determination and something completely, defiantly masculine.

Heat snaked through her. Awareness.

Luisa sucked in a startled breath. She'd never before experienced such an instant spark of attraction. Had wondered if she ever would. She couldn't suppress a niggle of disturbing reaction.

Despite his elegant clothes this man looked...dangerous.

Luisa huffed out a choked laugh. Dangerous? He'd probably faint if he got mud on his mirror-polished shoes.

Behind the house, worn jeans, frayed shirts and thick socks flapped on the clothes line. Her mouth twitched. Mr stepped-from-a-glossy-magazine couldn't be more out of place. She forced herself to approach.

Who on earth was he?

He must have sensed movement for he turned.

'Can I help you?' Her voice was husky. She assured herself that had nothing to do with the impact of his dark, enigmatic stare.

'Hello.' His lips tilted in a smile.

She faltered. He was gorgeous. If you were impressed by impossibly handsome in a tough, masculine sort of way. Or gleaming, hooded eyes that intrigued, giving nothing away. Or the tiniest hint of a sexy cleft in his chin.

She swallowed carefully and plastered on a smile.

'Are you lost?' Luisa stopped a few paces away. She had to tilt her chin up to look him in the eye.

'No, not lost.' His crisp deep voice curled with just a hint of an accent. 'I've come to see Ms Hardwicke. I have the right place?'

Luisa frowned, perplexed.

It was a rhetorical question. From his assured tone to his easy stance, as if he owned the farm and she was the interloper, this man radiated confidence. With a nonchalant wave of his hand he stopped the approach of a burly figure rounding the corner of the house. Already his gaze turned back to the homestead, as if expecting someone else.

'You've got the right place.'

She looked from the figure at the rear of the house whose

wary stance screamed *bodyguard*, to the chopper where the pilot did an equipment check. Another man in a suit stood talking on a phone. Yet all three were focused on her. Alert.

Who were these people? Why were they here?

A shaft of disquiet pierced her. For the first time ever her home seemed dangerously isolated.

'You have business here?' Her tone sharpened.

Instinct, and the stranger's air of command, as if used to minions scurrying to obey, told her this man was in a league far beyond the local bank manager.

An uneasy sensation, like ice water trickling down her spine, made her stiffen.

'Yes, I need to see Ms Hardwicke.' His eyes flicked to her again then away. 'Do you know where I can find her?'

Something in that single look at her face, not once dropping to her filthy clothes, made her burningly self-conscious. Not just of the mud, but the fact that even clean and in her best outfit she'd feel totally outclassed.

Luisa straightened. 'You've found her.'

This time he really looked. The intensity of that stare warmed her till she flushed all over. His eyes widened beneath thick dark lashes and she saw they were green. The deep, hard green of emeralds. Luisa read shock in his expression. And, she could have sworn, dismay.

Seconds later he'd masked his emotions and his expression was unreadable. Only a slight bunching of sleek black eyebrows hinted he wasn't happy.

'Ms *Luisa* Hardwicke?'

He pronounced her name the way her mother had, with a soft s and a lilt that turned the mundane into something pretty.

Premonition clamped a chill hand at the back of her neck. The accent *had* to be a coincidence. That other world was beyond her reach now.

Luisa wiped the worst of the dirt off her hand and stepped forward, arm outstretched. It was time to take charge of this situation. 'And you are?'

He hesitated for a moment, then her fingers were engulfed in his. He bowed, almost as if to kiss her hand. The gesture was charming and outlandish. It sent a squiggle of reaction through her, making her breath falter. Especially as his warm, powerful hand still held hers.

Heat scalded her face and she was actually grateful for the smearing of dirt that concealed it.

He straightened and she had to arch her neck to meet his glittering scrutiny. From this angle he seemed all imposing, austere lines that spoke of unyielding strength.

Luisa blinked and drew a shaky breath, trying to ignore the butterflies swirling in her stomach and think sensibly.

'I am Raul of Maritz.' He said it simply but with such assurance she could almost imagine a blare of trumpet fanfare in the background. 'Prince Raul.'

Raul watched her stiffen and felt the ripple of shock jolt through her. She yanked her hand free and took a step back, arms crossing protectively over her chest.

His mind clicked up a gear as interest sparked. *Not* the welcome he usually received. Fawning excitement was more common.

'Why are you here?' This time the throaty edge to her words wasn't gruff. It made her sound vulnerable and feminine.

Feminine! He hadn't realised she was a woman!

From her husky voice to her muddy boots, square overalls and battered hat that shadowed her grimy face, she had as much feminine appeal as a cabbage. She still hadn't removed the hat. And that walk! Stiff as an automaton.

He froze, imagining her in Maritzian society where protocol and exquisite manners were prized. This was worse than he'd feared. And there was no way out.

Not if he was to claim his throne and safeguard his country.

He clenched his teeth, silently berating the archaic legalities that bound him in this catch-22.

When he was king there'd be some changes.

'I asked what you're doing on my land.' No mistaking the animosity in her tone. More and more intriguing.

'My apologies.' Automatically he smiled, smoothing over his lapse. It was no excuse that the shock of seeing her distracted him. 'We have important matters to discuss.'

He waited for her answering smile. For a relaxation of her rigid stance. There was none.

'We have nothing to discuss.' Beneath the mud her neat chin angled up.

She was giving *him* the brush-off? It was absurd!

'Nevertheless, it's true.'

He waited for her to invite him in. She stood unmoving, staring up balefully. Impatience stirred.

And more, a wave of distaste at the fate that decreed he had to take this woman under his wing. Turn this unpromising material into—

'I'd like you to leave.'

Raul stiffened in indignation. At the same time curiosity intensified. He wished he could see her without that mask of mud.

'I've travelled from my homeland in Europe to speak with you.'

'That's impossible, I tell you. I have no—'

'Far from being impossible, I made the trip for that sole purpose.' Raul drew himself up and took a pace closer, letting his superior height send a silent message. When he spoke again it was in a tone that brooked no opposition. 'I'm not leaving until we've concluded our business.'

Luisa's stomach twisted in knots and her nerves stretched to breaking point as she hurried through the house back to the veranda where she'd left her visitor.

The crown prince of Maritz, her mother's homeland, here at her house! *This couldn't be good.*

She'd tried to send him away, turn her back rather than face anyone from that place. The memories were too poisonous.

But he'd been frighteningly immovable. A single look at that steely jaw told her she wouldn't succeed.

Besides, she needed to know why he was here.

Now, armoured as best she could manage by scouring hot water and clean clothes, she tried to stifle rising panic.

What did he want?

He filled up her veranda with his larger than life presence, making her feel small and insignificant. His spare features reminded her of pictures of the old king in his youth—impossibly handsome with his high cut cheekbones and proud bearing. From his top notch tailoring to his air of command, this man was *someone*.

Yet royalty didn't just pop in to visit.

Disquiet shivered through her. A shadow of the stormy past.

He turned to her. Instantly she felt at a disadvantage. With those chiselled aristocratic features and that uncompromising air of maleness he was...stunning. Despite her wariness, heat ricocheted through her abdomen.

His eyes narrowed. Luisa's heartbeat pattered out of kilter and her mouth dried. With a jolt of shock she realised it was the man himself, as much as his identity that disturbed her.

Luisa laced her fingers rather than straighten her loose shirt, her only clean one after weeks of rain. She wished she could meet him on equal terms, dressed to the nines. But her budget didn't run to new clothes. Or a new hairdryer.

She smoothed damp locks from her face and pushed back her shoulders, ignoring the way her stomach somersaulted. She refused to be intimidated in her own home.

'I was admiring your view,' he said. 'It's lovely countryside.'

Luisa cast her eyes over the familiar rolling hills. She appreciated the natural beauty, but it had been a long time since she'd found time to enjoy it.

'If you'd seen it two months ago after years of drought you wouldn't have been so impressed.' She drew a deep breath, fighting down the sick certainty that this man was trouble. Her skin crawled with nervous tension but she refused to let him see. 'Won't you come in?'

She moved to open the door but with a long stride he beat her to it, gesturing for her to precede him.

Luisa wasn't used to having doors opened for her. That was why she flushed.

She inhaled a subtle, exotic scent that went straight to her head. Luisa bit her lip as tingles shot to her toes. None of the men she knew looked, sounded or smelled as good as Raul of Maritz.

'Please, take a seat.' She gestured jerkily to the scrubbed kitchen table. Luisa hadn't had a chance to move the buckets and tarpaulins from the lounge room, where they'd staved off the leaks from the last downpour.

Besides, she'd long ago learnt that aristocratic birth was no measure of worth. He could sit where her friends and business partners met.

'Of course.' He pulled out a chair and sank into it with as much aplomb as if it were a plushly padded throne. His presence filled the room.

She lifted the kettle, her movements jerky as she stifled hostility. She needed to hear him out. 'Would you like coffee or tea?'

'No, thank you.' His face was unreadable.

Luisa's pulse sped as she met his unblinking regard. Reluctantly she slid into a chair opposite him, forcing herself into stillness.

'So, Your Highness. What can I do for you?'

For a moment longer he regarded her, then he leaned forward a fraction. 'It's not what you can do for me.' His voice was deep, mellow and hypnotic, holding a promise to which she instinctively responded despite her wariness. 'This is about what I can do for you.'

Beware of strangers promising gifts. The little voice inside sent a tremor of disquiet skidding through her.

Years before she'd received promises of wonderful gifts. The future had seemed a magical, glittering land. Yet it had all been a hollow sham. She'd learned distrust the hard way—not once but twice.

'Really?' Her face felt stiff and she found it hard to swallow.

He nodded. 'First I need to confirm you're the only child of Thomas Bevan Hardwicke and Margarite Luisa Carlotta Hardwicke.'

Luisa froze, alarm stirring. He sounded like a lawyer about to break bad news. The voice of warning in her head grew more strident. Surely her ties with Maritz had been completely severed years ago.

'That's right, though I can't see—'

'It pays to be sure. Tell me—' he leaned back in his seat but his eyes never wavered from hers '—how much do you know about my country? About its government and states?'

Luisa fought to remain calm as painful memories surged. This meeting had a nightmare quality. She wanted to scream at him to get to the point before her stretched nerves gave way. But that glittering gaze was implacable. He'd do this his way. She'd known men like him before. She gritted her teeth.

'Enough.' *More than she wanted.* 'It's an alpine kingdom. A democracy with a parliament and a king.'

He nodded. 'My father the king died recently. I will be crowned in a few months.'

'I'm sorry for your loss,' Luisa murmured, struggling to make sense of this. *Why was he here, interrogating her?* The question beat at her brain.

'Thank you.' He paused. 'And Ardissia?'

Luisa's fingers clenched as she fought impatience. She shot him a challenging look. He was like a charming bulldozer, with that polite smile barely cloaking his determination to get his own way.

'It's a province of Maritz, with its own hereditary prince who owes loyalty to the King of Maritz.' Her mouth twisted. 'My mother came from there, *as I'm sure you know.*'

She shivered, cold sweeping up from her toes and wrapping around her heart as bitter memories claimed her.

'Now, my turn for a question.' She planted her palms on the table and leaned forward, fixing him with a stare. 'Why are you here?'

Luisa waited, her heart thudding hectically, watching him survey her beneath lowered brows. He shifted in his seat. Suddenly she wondered if he were uncomfortable too.

'I came to find you.' His expression made her heartbeat speed to a pounding gallop.

'Why?'

'The Prince of Ardissia is dead. I'm here to tell you you're his heiress, Princess Luisa of Ardissia.'

CHAPTER TWO

RAUL watched her pale beneath her tan. Her eyes rounded and she swayed in her seat. Was she going to faint?

Great. A highly strung female!

He thrust aside the fact that anyone would be overcome. That his anger at this diabolical situation made him unreasonable.

She wasn't the only one whose life had been turned on its head! For years Raul had steered his own course, making every decision. Being fettered like this was outrageous.

But the alternative—to turn his back on his people and the life to which he'd devoted himself—was unthinkable.

'Are you all right?'

'Of course.' Her tone was sharp but her eyes were dazed.

They were surprisingly fine eyes, seen without that shadowing hat. Blue-grey a moment ago, now they sparkled brilliant azure. Like a clear summer sky in the Maritzian Alps. The sort of eyes a man could lose himself in.

She blinked and shifted her gaze and Raul was astonished to feel a pang of disappointment.

He watched her gnaw her lip. When she looked up and flushed to find him watching, he noticed the ripe contours of her mouth. With the grime washed away, her features were pleasant, regular and fairly attractive.

If you liked the artless, scrubbed bare style.

Raul preferred his women sophisticated and well groomed.

What sort of woman didn't take the time to style her hair?

Pale and damply combed off her face, it even looked lopsided. Anyone less fitted for this—

'I can't be his heir!' She sounded almost accusing.

His brows rose. As if he'd waste precious time here on a whim!

'Believe me, it's true.'

She blinked and he had the sense there was more going on behind her azure eyes than simple surprise.

'How is it possible?' She sounded as if she spoke to herself.

'Here.' Raul opened the briefcase Lukas had brought. 'Here's your grandfather's will and your family tree.'

He'd planned for his secretary, Lukas, to take her through this. But he'd changed his mind the moment he saw Luisa Hardwicke and how unprepared she was for this role. Better do this himself. The fewer who dealt with her at this early stage the better.

Raul suppressed a grimace. What had begun as a delicate mission now had unlimited potential for disaster. Imagine the headlines if the press saw her as she was! He wouldn't allow the Maritzian crown to be the focus of rabid media gossip again. Especially at this difficult time.

He strode round the table and spread the papers before her.

She shifted in her seat as if his presence contaminated her. Raul stiffened. Women were usually eager to get close.

'Here's your mother.' He modulated his tone reassuringly. 'Above her, your grandfather, the last prince.'

She lifted her head from examining the family tree. Again the impact of that bright gaze hit him. He'd swear he felt it like a rumbling echo inside his chest.

'Why isn't my uncle inheriting? Or my cousin, Marissa?'

'You're the last of your family.'

Her brow puckered. 'She must have been so young. That's awful.'

'Yes.' The accident was a tragic waste of life. And it altered the succession.

She shook her head. 'But I'm not part of the family! My mother was disinherited when she fell in love with an Australian and refused to marry the man her father chose.'

She knew about that? Did that explain her animosity?

'Your grandfather blustered but he never disinherited her. We only discovered that recently when his will was read.' The Prince of Ardissia had been an irascible tartar but he had too much pride in his bloodline to cut off a direct descendant. 'You're definitely eligible to inherit.'

How much easier life would be if she weren't!

If there were no Ardissian princess he wouldn't be in this appalling situation.

'I tell you it's impossible!' She leaned forward, her brow pleating as she scanned the papers.

The scent of lavender wafted to him. Raul inhaled, intrigued. He was used to the perfectly balanced notes of the most expensive perfumes. Yet this simple fragrance was strangely appealing.

'It *can't* be right.' She spoke again. 'He disinherited me too. We were told so!'

Startled, he looked down to find her eyes blazing up at him. Her chin was angled in the air and for the first time there was colour in her cheeks.

She looked...pretty. In an unsophisticated way.

And she knew more than he'd expected. Fascinating.

'Despite what you were told, you're his heiress. You inherit his fortune and responsibilities.' He summoned an encouraging smile. 'I've come to take you home.'

'Home?' Luisa shot to her feet, the chair screeching across the floor. 'This is my home! I belong here.' She gestured to the cosy kitchen she'd known all her life.

She fought a sense of unreality. This had to be an appalling mistake.

From the moment he'd mentioned Ardissia and Maritz bitter recollection had cramped her belly and clouded her brain. It had taken a superhuman effort to hear him out.

'Not any more.' Across the scrubbed table he smiled.

He really was unbelievably good-looking.

Until you looked into those cool eyes. Had he thought her too unaware to notice his smile didn't reach his eyes?

'You've got a new life ahead of you. Your world will change for ever.' His smile altered, became somehow more intimate, and to her surprise Luisa felt a trickle of unfamiliar warmth spread through her body.

How had that happened?

'You'll have wealth, position, prestige—the best of every-thing. You'll live a life of luxury, as a princess.'

A princess.

The words reverberated in Luisa's skull. Nausea rose.

At sixteen she'd heard those same words. It had been like a dream come true. What girl wouldn't be excited to discover a royal bloodline and a doting grandfather promising a life of excitement and privilege?

Luisa's heart clutched as she remembered her mother, pale but bravely smiling, seated at this table, telling her she had to make up her own mind about her future. Saying that, though she'd turned her back on that life, it was Luisa's choice if she wanted to discover her birthright.

And, like the innocent she was, Luisa had gone. Lured by the fairy tale fantasy of a picture book kingdom.

Reality had been brutally different. By the time she'd re-jected what her grandfather offered and made her own way home, she'd been only too grateful he hadn't publicly presented her as his kin. That he'd kept her a cloistered guest during her 'probation' period. Only her closest family knew she'd ever been tempted by the old man's false promises of a joyful family reunion.

She'd been naïve but no more.

Now she knew too much about the ugly reality of that aristo-cratic society, where birth and connections mattered more than love and common decency. If her grandfather's actions hadn't been enough, she only had to recall the man she'd thought she'd loved. How he'd schemed to seduce her when he realised her secret identity. All because of his ambition.

Luisa's stomach heaved and she reached out blindly for the table, shaking her head to clear the nightmarish recollections.

'I don't want to be a princess.'

Silence. Slowly she turned. Prince Raul's hooded eyes were wide, impatience obliterated by shock.

'You can't be serious,' he said finally, his voice thickening with that appealing accent.

'Believe me, I was never more so.'

Revulsion filled Luisa as she remembered her grandfather. He'd invited her to join him so he could groom her into the sort of princess he wanted. To do his bidding without question. To be the sort his daughter had failed to be.

At first Luisa had been blind to the fact he merely wanted a pawn to manipulate, not a granddaughter to love.

He'd shown his true colours when news arrived of her mother's terminal illness. He'd refused Luisa's tearful, desperate pleas to return. Instead he'd issued an ultimatum—that she break off all contact with her parents or give up her new life. As for Luisa's begging that he fund further medical treatment, he'd snarled at her for wasting time on the woman who'd turned her back on his world.

That heartless betrayal, so blatant, so overwhelming, still sickened Luisa to the core.

That was who she was heir to! A cruel, ruthless tyrant. No wonder she'd vowed not to have anything to do with her bigoted, blue-blooded family.

She recalled her grandfather bellowing his displeasure at her ingratitude. At her inability to be what he wanted, play the part.

A hand on her arm tugged her from her thoughts. She looked up into a searing gaze. Black eyebrows tilted in a V and Raul's nostrils flared as if scenting fear.

This close he was arresting. Her stomach plunged in free-fall as she stared back. Tingling sensation spread from his touch.

Luisa swallowed and his eyes followed the movement.

The intensity of his regard scared her. The beat of her blood was like thunder in her ears. She felt unprotected beneath a gaze that had lost its distance and now seemed to flare with unexpected heat.

'What is it? What are you thinking?' Gone was the smooth tone. His words were staccato sharp.

Luisa drew a shaky breath, disoriented by the arcing heat that snapped and shimmered in the air between them. By the hazy sense of familiarity she felt with this handsome stranger.

'I'm thinking you should let me go.'

Immediately he stepped back, his hand dropping. 'Forgive me. For a moment you looked faint.'

She nodded. She'd felt queasy. That explained her unsteadiness. It had nothing to do with his touch.

The electricity sparking between them was imaginary.

He thrust a hand through his immaculately combed hair as if, for an instant, he too felt that disturbing sensation. But then his dark locks fell back into perfect position and he was again cool, clear-eyed and commanding.

Swiftly Luisa turned to grab a glass. She gulped down cold water, hoping to restore a semblance of normality. She felt as if she'd been wrung inside out.

Finally she willed her scrambled thoughts into order. It didn't help that she sensed Prince Raul's gaze skewer her like an insect on a pin.

Setting her jaw, she turned.

He leaned against the dresser, arms folded and one ankle casually resting on the other. He looked unattainably sexy and a little scary. His brow was furrowed as if something perplexed him, but that only emphasised the strength of his features.

'When you've had time to absorb the news, you'll see going to Maritz is the sensible thing.'

'Thank you, but I've already absorbed the news.' Did he

have any idea how patronising he sounded? Annoyance sizzled in her blood.

He didn't move but his big body was no longer relaxed. His folded arms with their bunched muscles drew her eyes. Suddenly he looked predatory rather than suavely elegant.

Her skin prickled.

'The money doesn't tempt you?' His mouth compressed. Obviously he thought money outweighed everything else.

Just like her grandfather and his cronies.

Luisa opened her mouth, then snapped it shut as her dazed brain cells finally revved into action.

Money!

In her shock that hadn't even registered. She thought of the looming debts, repairs they'd postponed, Sam's outdated milking machine and her own rattletrap car. The list was endless.

'How much money?' She wanted nothing of the high society position. But the cash...

The prince unfolded his arms and named a sum that made her head spin. She braced herself against the table.

'When do I get it?' Her voice was scratchy with shock.

Did she imagine a flash of satisfaction in those dark green eyes?

'You're princess whether you use the title or not. Nothing can alter that.' He paused. 'But there are conditions on inheriting your wealth. You must settle in Maritz and take up your royal obligations.'

Luisa's shoulders slumped. What he suggested was impossible. She'd rejected that world for her own sanity. Accepting would be a betrayal of herself and all she held dear.

'I can't.'

'Of course you can. I'll make the arrangements.'

'Don't you listen?' Luisa gripped the table so hard her bones ached. 'I'm not going!' Life in that cold, cruel society would kill her. 'This is my home. My roots are here.'

He shook his head, straightening to stand tall and imposing. The room shrank and despite her anger she felt his formidable magnetism tug at her.

'You have roots in Maritz too. What have you got here but hard work and poverty? In my country you'll have a privileged life, mixing in the most elite circles.'

How he sounded like her snobbish grandfather.

'I prefer the circles I mix in.' Fire skirled in her belly at his condescension. 'The people I love are here.'

He scowled. 'A man?' He took a step closer and, involuntarily, Luisa retreated a pace before the fierce light in his eyes.

'No, my friends. And my father's brother and his wife.' Sam and Mary, almost a generation older than Luisa's parents, had been like doting grandparents through her sunny childhood and the darkest days. She wouldn't leave them, ageing and in debt, for a glamorous, empty life far away.

The sharp-eyed man before her didn't look impressed.

Had her grandfather once looked like Prince Raul? Proud, determined, good-looking and boy, didn't he know it!

Standing there, radiating impatience, Raul embodied everything she'd learned to despise.

Determination surged anew.

'Thank you for coming to tell me in person.' She drew herself up, level with his proud chin, and folded his papers with quick, precise movements. 'But you'll have to find someone else to inherit.' She breathed deep. 'I'll see you out.'

Raul's mouth tightened as the chopper lifted.

Thrilled! Luisa Hardwicke had been anything but. Just as well he'd told her only about her inheritance, not the more challenging aspects of her new role. She'd been so skittish it was wiser to break that news later.

He'd never met a more stubborn woman. She'd all but thrown him out!

Indignation danced in his veins and tightened his fists.

Something motivated her that he didn't know about. He needed to discover what it was. More, he had to discover the trigger that would make her change her mind.

For an instant back there he'd been tempted simply to

kidnap her. The blood of generations of warriors and robber barons as well as monarchs flowed in his veins. It would have been easy to scoop her up in his arms and sequester her till she saw reason. *So satisfying.*

An image of Luisa Hardwicke filled his mind. She stared defiantly up with flashing cerulean eyes.

Raul recalled her shirt lifting when she reached for a glass, revealing her lusciously curved bottom in snug jeans. The feminine shape outlined by her shirt when she moved. A shape at odds with his original impression.

Fire streaked through Raul's belly.

Perhaps there would be compensations after all.

Luisa Hardwicke had a wholesome prettiness that appealed far more than it ought. He'd made it his business these last eight years to surround himself only with glamorous, sophisticated women who understood his needs.

He grimaced, facing a truth he rarely acknowledged. That if he'd once had a weakness it had been for the sort of forthright honesty and fresh openness she projected.

The sort he'd once believed in.

Sordid reality had cured him of any such frailty. Yet being with her was like hearing an echo of his past, remembering fragments of dreams he'd once held. Dreams now shattered beyond repair by deceit and betrayal.

And, despite his indignation, he responded to her pride, her pluck.

It was an inconvenience that complicated his plans. Yet perversely he admired the challenge she represented. What a change from the compliant, eager women he knew! In other circumstances he'd applaud her stance.

Besides, he saw now, a spineless nonentity would never have been suitable for what was to come. Or so surprisingly appealing.

Raul tugged his mind back to business. He needed a lever to ensure she saw sense. Failure wasn't an option when his nation depended on him.

'Lukas, you said the farming co-op is in debt?'

'Yes sir, heavily so. I'm amazed it's still running.'

Raul looked back at the tiny speck that was her home. A sliver of regret pierced him. He'd wanted to avoid coercion but she left him no choice.

'Buy the debts. Immediately. I want it settled today.'

The roar of a helicopter brought Luisa's head up.

It couldn't be. After rejecting her inheritance yesterday there was no reason for her path and Prince Raul's to cross again. Yet she was drawn inexorably to the window. It couldn't be but it was. Prince Raul—here!

To Luisa's annoyance, her heart pattered faster as she watched his long, powerful frame vault from the chopper.

Twenty-four hours had given her time to assure herself he wasn't nearly as imposing as she remembered.

She'd been wrong.

Luisa had searched him on the web yesterday, learning his reputation for hard work and wealth. The reports also referred to discreet liaisons with gorgeous women.

Yet no photos did justice to his impact in the flesh. Her breath caught as he loped up the steps. Good thing she was immune.

'Luisa.' He stood before her, wide shoulders filling the open doorway, his voice smooth like dark chocolate with a hint of spice as he lingered on her name.

A tremor rippled through her as she responded to the exotic sound of her name on his tongue. It maddened her that she should react so. She pulled herself together, fiercely quelling a riot of unfamiliar emotions.

'Your Highness.' She gripped the door hard. 'Why are you here? We finished our business yesterday.' Surely he had VIPs to see, deals to forge, women to seduce.

He bent over her hand in another courtly almost-kiss that knotted her stomach. She had to remind herself not to be impressed by surface charm. *Been there, done that.*

Yet her gaze riveted on his austerely handsome face as he straightened. The flash of green fire in his eyes sent tendrils of heat curling through her. His fingers squeezed and her pulse accelerated.

'Call me Raul.'

It went against the grain but to refuse would be churlish.

'Raul.' It was crazy but she could almost taste his name in her mouth, like a rich, full-bodied wine.

'Aren't you going to invite me in?' One dark eyebrow rose lazily as if her obstinacy amused him. She bit down on a rude response. He must have good reason to return. The sooner she heard it the sooner he'd go.

'Please, come in.' She led the way to the lounge room, ignoring the jitter of nerves in her stomach.

Instead of making himself comfortable, he took up a position in front of the window. A commanding position, she noticed uneasily as premonition skittered across her nape.

She didn't like the glint in his eye or his wide-legged stance, as if claiming her territory for his own. She stood facing him, refusing to be dominated.

'You haven't changed your mind?'

She lifted her chin a fraction. 'Not if the cash comes with strings attached.'

Desperate as she was for money, she couldn't agree.

She'd spent yesterday afternoon consulting her solicitor. There *must* be a way to access some of the money she was in line to inherit without giving up her life here. She didn't trust Raul, a man with his own agenda, to be straight with her on that.

It was too soon to know, but the possibility she could negotiate enough funds to give the co-op the boost it needed had given her a better night's sleep than she'd had in ages. It buoyed her now, strengthening her confidence.

'Can I persuade you to reconsider?' His mouth turned up in the barest hint of a smile, yet even that should have come with a health warning.

Her breath sawed in her throat and her pulse quickened.

Luisa thought of the enquiries being made on her behalf.

She'd be a fool to give in to his preposterous suggestion. 'Absolutely not.' The very thought of accepting made her ill.

'That's unfortunate.' He paused so long her nerves stretched taut. 'Very unfortunate.' He looked grim.

Finally he reached into his jacket pocket. 'In that case, these are for you.'

Bewildered, Luisa accepted the papers. 'You want me to sign away my inheritance?' She'd sign nothing without legal advice.

He shook his head. 'Take your time. They're self-explanatory.'

Confused, she skimmed the papers. Unlike yesterday's, these weren't rich parchment. They looked more like the loan documents that were the bane of her life.

Luisa forced herself to concentrate. Hard to do with his stare on her. When finally she began to understand, the world spun around her.

'You've bought the co-op's debts.' Disbelieving, she shuffled the papers, eyes goggling. 'All of them!'

And in one day. Each paper had yesterday's date.

Was it even possible?

Bewildered, she looked up. The gravity of his expression convinced her more than the typed words.

Luisa sank abruptly onto the arm of a chair, her knees too wobbly to take her weight, her breath choppy.

What strings had he pulled to manage that in a single day? Luisa couldn't conceive of such power. Yet, staring up at the man before her, she realised he wielded authority as easily as she managed a milking machine.

The realisation dried her mouth.

'Why?' Her voice was a hoarse rasp.

He paced closer, looming between her and the light from the window. 'On the day you sign the documents accepting your inheritance, I'll make a gift of them. You can rip them into confetti.'

Relief poured through her veins so suddenly she shook.

He was so obstinate! He still didn't accept her rejection. No

doubt he thought it embarrassing that the heir to a royal title
was neck-deep in debt.

It was a generous gesture. One she'd compensate him for
if she found a way to access the funds.

'But I'm not going. I'm staying here.'

'You won't.'

Had anyone ever denied him what he wanted?

Impatient energy radiated off him. And that chin—she'd
never seen a more determined face.

Luisa stood. She needed to assert herself and end this nonsense. It was time he accepted she knew her mind. 'I've got
no plans to leave.'

He held her gaze as the seconds stretched out. His expression didn't change but a frisson of anxiety skipped up her back,
like a spider dancing on her vertebrae.

'Knowing how committed you are to the well-being of your
family and friends, I'm sure you'll change your mind.' His
voice held steel beneath the deep velvet inflection. 'Unless
you want them to lose everything.'

He spoke so matter-of-factly it took a moment to register
the threat.

Luisa's face froze and a gasp caught inside as her throat
closed convulsively.

Blackmail?

She opened her mouth but no sound emerged. Paper cascaded to the floor from her trembling hands.

'You...can't be serious!'

Slowly he shook his head. 'Never more so, Luisa.'

'Don't call me that!' The way he said her name, with the
same lilting accent her mother had used, was like a travesty
of a familiar endearment.

'Princess Luisa, then.'

She took a furious step forward, her hands clenching in
frustration. 'This has to be a joke.' But no humour showed
on his stern features. 'You can't foreclose! You'd destroy the
livelihood of a dozen families.' And her father's dream. What
she had worked for most of her life.

After she'd returned home to nurse her mother, Luisa had never found time to go back and finish school. Instead she'd stayed on to help her father, who'd never fully recovered from the loss of his wife.

'The decision is yours. You can save them, if they mean as much as you claim.'

He meant it! The grim determination in his granite-set jaw was nothing to the resolution in his glittering eyes.

'But...*why?*' Luisa shook her head, trying to find sense in a world turned topsy-turvy. 'You can find another heir, someone who'd be thrilled to live the life you're offering.' Someone happy to give up her soul for the riches he promised. 'I'm not princess material!'

The gleam in his eyes suggested he agreed.

'There *is* no one else, Luisa. You are the princess.'

'You can't dictate my future!' Luisa planted her hands on her hips, letting defiance mask her sudden fear. 'Why are you getting so personally involved?'

When her grandfather had made contact it had been through emissaries. He hadn't come to her. Yet Raul as crown prince was far more important than her grandfather.

He took her hand before she could snatch it away. Heat engulfed her, radiating from his touch and searing her skin even as his intentions chilled her marrow.

'I have a stake in your future,' he murmured.

Automatically she jerked up her chin. 'Really?' The word emerged defiantly.

'A very personal stake.' His grip firmed, all except for his thumb, which stroked gently across her palm, sending little judders of awareness through her. 'Not only are you the Ardissian heiress, you're destined to be Queen of Maritz.' He paused, eyes locking with hers.

'That's why I'm here. To take you back as my bride.'

CHAPTER THREE

LUISA watched his firm lips shape the word 'bride'. Her head reeled.

There was no laughter in his eyes. No wildness hinting at insanity. Just a steady certainty that locked the protest in her mouth.

Her lungs cramped from lack of oxygen as her breath escaped in a whoosh. She lurched forward, dragging in air. He grasped her hand tight and reached for her shoulder as if to support her.

Violently she wrenched away, breaking his grip and retreating to stand, panting, beside the window.

'Don't touch me!'

His eyes narrowed to slits of green fire and she sensed that behind his calm exterior lurked a man of volatile passions.

'Explain. Now!' she said when she'd caught her breath.

'Perhaps you'd better sit.'

So he could tower over her? No, thank you! 'I prefer to stand.' Even if her legs felt like unset jelly.

'As you wish.' Why did it sound like he granted her a special favour in her own house?

He had royal condescension down to an art form.

'You were going to explain why you need to marry.' For the life of her, Luisa couldn't say 'marry me'.

His look told her he didn't miss the omission.

'To ascend the throne I must be married.' At her stare he

continued. 'It's an old law, aimed to ensure an unbroken royal lineage.'

A tremor scudded through her at the idea of 'ensuring the royal lineage'. *With him.*

It didn't matter how handsome he was. She'd learnt looks could hide a black heart. It was the inner man that counted. From what she'd seen, Raul was as proud, opinionated and selfish as her detested grandfather.

The way he looked when she challenged him—jaw tight and eyes flashing malachite sparks, was warning enough.

Luisa's heartbeat pounded so hard she had trouble hearing his next words.

'It's tradition that the crown prince take a bride from one of Maritz's principalities. When we were in our teens a contract was drawn up for my marriage to your cousin, Marissa, Princess of Ardissia. But Marissa died soon after.'

'I'm sorry,' Luisa said gruffly. She searched his features for regret but couldn't read anything. Didn't he feel *something* for his fiancée who'd died?

She pursed her lips. Obviously the heartless arranged marriage was still alive and thriving in Maritz!

'After that I was in no hurry to tie myself in marriage. But when my father died recently it was time to find another bride.'

'So you could inherit.' Luisa shivered, remembering that world where marriages were dynastic contracts, devoid of love. She crossed her arms protectively. How could he be so sanguine about it?

'My plans were curtailed when your grandfather's will was read and we discovered you would inherit. Before then, given what he'd said about disowning your mother, your branch of the family didn't feature in our considerations.'

He made them sound like tiresome complications in his grand design! Indignation rose anew.

'What has the will got to do with your marriage?'

'The contract is binding, Luisa.' He loomed far too close. Her lungs constricted, making her breathing choppy.

'But how?' Luisa paced away, urgently needing space. 'If Marissa is—'

'Everyone, including the genealogists and lawyers, believed your grandfather's line would die with him. The news he had a granddaughter who hadn't been disinherited was a bombshell.' He didn't look as if the news had pleased him. 'You should be thankful we were able to find you before the media got the story. You'd have had press camped here around the clock.'

'You're overdramatising.' Luisa's hands curled tight as she forced down growing panic. 'I've got nothing to do with your wedding.'

One dark eyebrow winged upwards. 'The antiquated style of the contract means I'm bound to marry the Princess of Ardissia.' He paused, his mouth a slash of pure displeasure. *'Whoever she is.'*

'You're out of your mind!' Luisa retreated a frantic step, her stomach a churning mess. This truly *was* a nightmare. 'I never signed any contract!'

'It doesn't matter. The document is legal.' His lips twisted. 'The best minds in the country can't find a way out of it.'

She shook her head, her hair falling across her face as she backed up against the window. 'No way! No matter what your contract says, you can't take me back there as—'

'My bride?' The words dropped into echoing silence. Luisa heard them repeat over and over in her numbed brain, like a never-ending ripple spreading in a still, icy pool.

'Believe me; I'll do what's necessary to claim my throne.' His chin lifted regally, making clear what he hadn't put in words: that he didn't wish to marry someone so far beneath him. Someone so unappealing.

Why was he so desperate? Did power mean so much?

Luisa choked on rising anger. Twenty-four years old and she'd received two marriage offers—both from ambitious men who saw her as nothing but a means to acquire power! Why couldn't she meet a caring, honest man who'd love her for herself? She felt soiled and cheap.

'You expect me to give up my life and marry you, a total

stranger, so you can become king?' What century had he dropped out of? 'You're talking antiquated nonsense.'

His look grazed like shards of ice on bare skin. 'It may be antiquated but I must marry.'

She jutted her chin. 'Marry someone else!'

Something dangerous and dark flashed in his eyes. But when he spoke his words were measured. She sensed he hung onto his control by a thread.

'If I could I would. If you hadn't existed or if you'd already married, the contract would be void and I could choose another bride.'

As if choosing a wife took a minimum of time and effort!

Though in his case it might. With his looks, sexual magnetism and wealth there'd be lots of women eager to overlook the fact they tied themselves to a power hungry egotist!

His deep voice sent a tremor rippling through her overwrought body. 'There's no more time to find a way out. I need to be married within the constitutional time limit or I can't inherit.'

'Why should I care?' Luisa rubbed her hands up chilled arms, trying to restore warmth. 'I don't even know you.'

And what she did know she didn't like.

He shrugged and unwillingly Luisa saw how the fluid movement drew attention to those powerful shoulders. The sort of shoulders that belonged on a surf lifesaver or an outback farmer, not a privileged aristocrat.

'I'm the best person for the kingship. Some would say the only suitable one. I've trained a lifetime for it.'

'Others could learn.'

He shook his head. 'Not now. Not in time. There was unrest in the last years of my father's reign. That's growing. A strong king is what the country needs.'

The sizzle in his eyes stopped her breath.

'That leaves only one option.'

She was his only option!

'I don't care!' Cool glass pressed against her back as he

took a pace towards her and she stepped back. 'Let them crown someone else. I'm not a sacrificial lamb for the slaughter.'

His lips curled in a knowing smile that should have repelled her. Yet her heart hammered as she watched his eyes light with a gleam that warmed her from tip to toe.

'You think marriage to me would be a hardship?' His voice dropped to a low pitch that feathered like a sultry breeze across her suddenly flushed skin. 'That I don't know how to please a woman?'

Luisa swallowed hard, using her hands to anchor herself to the windowsill behind her rather than be drawn towards the glittering green gaze that seemed now to promise unspoken delights.

He was far more dangerous than she'd realised.

'Be assured, Luisa, that you will find pleasure in our union. You have my word on it.'

A beat of power, of heat, pulsed between them and she knew how an animal felt, mesmerised by a predator.

'The answer is still no,' she whispered hoarsely, shocked at the need to force down a betraying weakness that made her respond to his sensual promise. Why did her dormant hormones suddenly jangle into life around *him*?

For a long moment they stood, adversaries in a silent battle of wills.

'Then, sadly, you leave me no choice.' The fire in his eyes was doused as if it had never been. A flicker of what might have been regret shadowed his gaze then disappeared. 'Just remember that decision, and the outcome, are entirely yours.'

Already he turned away. Only her hand on his elbow stopped him.

'What do you mean?' Fear was a sour tang in her mouth.

He didn't turn. 'I have business to finalise before I leave. Some farms to dispose of.'

Panic surged. Luisa's fingers tightened like a claw on the fine wool of his suit. She stepped round to look up into his stern face.

'You can't foreclose! They haven't done anything to you.'

His stare pinioned her. He shook off her hand.

'In a choice between your relatives and my country there is no contest.' He inclined his head. 'Goodbye, Luisa.'

'I'm sure Mademoiselle will be happy with this new style. A little shorter, a little more chic. Yes?'

Luisa dragged herself from her troubled reverie and met the eyes of the young Frenchwoman in the mirror. Clearly the stylist was excited at being summoned to the Prince's exclusive Parisian residence. Unlike the nail technician who'd barely resisted snorting her displeasure when Luisa had refused false nails, knowing she'd never manage them. Or the haughty couturier who'd taken her measurements with barely concealed contempt for Luisa's clothes.

The hair stylist hadn't been daunted at the prospect of working on someone as ordinary as Luisa.

Perhaps she liked a challenge.

'I'm sure it will be lovely.' Another time Luisa would have been thrilled, having her hair done by someone with such flair and enthusiasm. But not today, just hours after Raul's private jet had touched down in Paris.

It had all happened too fast. Even her goodbyes to Sam and a tearful Mary, crying over the happy news that Luisa was taking up her long lost inheritance.

How she wished she were with them now. Back in the world she knew, where she belonged.

Luisa gritted her teeth, remembering how Raul had taken the initiative from her even in her farewells.

When she'd gone to break the news it was to find he'd been there first. Her family and friends were already agog with the story of Luisa finally taking her 'rightful place' as a princess. And with news their debts were to be cancelled.

Yet Luisa had at least asserted herself in demanding Raul install a capable farm manager in her place to get the co-op on its feet. She refused to leave her friends short-handed.

In the face of their pleasure, Luisa had felt almost selfish, longing to stay, when so much good came out of her departure. Yet she'd left part of herself behind.

Her family and friends would have been distraught, knowing why she left. They wouldn't have touched the Prince's money if they knew the truth. But she couldn't do that to them. She couldn't ruin them for her pride.

Or her deep-seated fear of what awaited her in Maritz.

She shivered when she thought of entering Raul's world. Being with a man who should repel her, yet who—

'These layers will complement the jaw line, see? And make this lovely hair easier to manage.'

Luisa nodded vaguely.

'And, you will forgive me saying, cut even on both sides suits you better, yes?'

Luisa looked up, catching a sparkle in the other woman's eye. Heat seeped under her skin as she remembered her previous lopsided cut. She tilted her chin.

'My friend wants to become a hairdresser. She practised on me.'

'Her instincts were good, but the execution...' The other woman made one last judicious snip, then stepped away. 'Voila! What do you think?'

For the first time Luisa really focused. She kept staring as the stylist used a mirror to reveal her new look from all sides.

It wasn't a new look. It was a new woman!

Her overgrown hair was now a gleaming silky fall that danced and slid around her neck as she turned, yet always fell sleekly back into place. It was shorter, barely reaching her shoulders, but shaped now to the contours of her face. Dull dark blonde had been transformed into a burnished yet natural light gold.

'What did you do?'

Luisa didn't recognise the woman in the mirror. A woman whose eyes looked larger, her face almost sculpted and quite... arresting. She turned her head, watching the slanting sunlight catch the seemingly artless fall of hair.

The Frenchwoman shrugged. 'A couple of highlights to accentuate your natural golden tones and a good cut. You approve?'

Luisa nodded, unable to find words to describe what she felt. She remembered those last months nursing her mother, poring with her over fashion and beauty magazines borrowed from the local library. Her mother, with her unerring eye for style, would point out the cut that would be perfect for Luisa. And Luisa would play along, pretending that when she'd finally made her choice she'd visit a salon and have her hair styled just so. As if she had time or money to spare for anything other than her mother's care and the constant demands of the farm.

'It's just long enough to put up for formal occasions.'

Luisa's stomach bottomed at the thought of the formal occasions she'd face when they reached Maritz.

This couldn't be real. It couldn't be happening. *How could she have agreed?*

Suddenly she needed to escape. Needed to draw fresh air into her lungs, far from the confines of this gilt-edged mansion with its period furniture and discreet servants.

It hit her that, from the moment Raul had delivered his ultimatum, she'd not been alone. His security men had been on duty that final night she'd slept at home. Probably making sure she didn't do a midnight flit! After that there'd been stewards, butlers, chauffeurs.

And Raul himself, invading her personal space even when he stood as far from her as possible.

The stylist had barely slid the protective cape off Luisa's shoulders when she was on her feet, full of thanks for the marvellous cut and turning towards the door.

Her thoughts froze as the Frenchwoman looked at something over Luisa's shoulder then sank into a curtsey.

'Ah, Luisa, Mademoiselle. You've finished?' The deep voice curled across her senses like smoke on the air. She reminded herself it was distaste that made her shiver.

'Yes. We've finished.' Stiffening her spine, she turned.

Clear afternoon light spilled across the parquet floor and highlighted Raul where he stood just inside the doorway. Once again his splendour hit her full force. Not just the elegance of hand-stitched shoes and a beautifully crafted suit that clung to his broad shoulders. The impact of his strong personality was stamped on his austere features.

Even knowing his ruthlessness, it was hard not to gawk in appreciation. Luisa saw the stylist surreptitiously primping.

Annoyance sizzled. It wasn't just her. He had this effect on other women.

'I like your new look.' Raul's sudden smile was like warm honey. The flare of appreciation in his eyes even looked genuine. She told herself she didn't care.

'Thank you.' Her tone was stiff.

Yet Luisa's pulse raced. She put it down to dislike. How dared he come here with his gracious smile and his fluent French, charming her companion as if he were a kind benefactor!

Finally, after a long exchange of compliments, the stylist headed to the door. Luisa followed.

She should have known it wouldn't be so easy. A firm hand grasped her elbow as she walked past Raul.

'Where are you going?'

'Out.' She looked pointedly at his restraining hand.

'That's impossible. You have another appointment.'

The simmering fury she'd battled for days spiked.

'Really? How strange. I don't recall making any appointment.' She raised her head, meeting his regard head-on. Letting her anger show.

Ever since she'd consented to go with him it had been the same. Exquisite politeness from him and deference from his staff. Yet every decision had been made for her.

At first she'd been in a state of shock, too stunned to do more than be swept along by the force of Raul's will. But her indignation had grown with each hour. Especially when she'd been told, not asked about appointments with the beautician, the pedicurist, the manicurist, the hair stylist, the couturier…

As if she were an animated doll, not a woman with a brain of her own.

His hand dropped.

'You're upset.'

'You noticed!' She drew a slow breath, fighting for control. She was rigid with outrage and self-disgust.

Luisa had spent enough time battling bullies. From her despotic grandfather to big banks eager for immediate returns. To this man who'd taken over her life.

She should have been able to stand up to him!

She'd never felt so helpless.

That scared her more than anything. And provoked her fighting spirit. She'd had enough!

'You're tired after the long journey.' Did his voice soften? Surely not.

She hadn't slept a wink, even in the luxurious bed assigned to her on the long haul flight to Europe. Yet fatigue was the least of her worries.

'I'm tired of you managing my life. Just because I gave in to blackmail doesn't mean I've relinquished the ability to think. I'm not a doormat.'

'No one would presume—'

'*You* presume all the time!' Luisa jabbed a finger into his broad chest then backed up a step, resolving to keep her distance. She didn't like the tiny pinprick of heat tickling her skin where she'd touched him. It was there too whenever he took her arm, helping her from a plane or car.

'You haven't once *asked*!' She spread her hands. 'Your staff simply tell me what you've decided.'

His hooded eyes gave nothing away, but the sharp angle of his jaw told her she'd hit home. Good! The idea of getting under this man's skin appealed. It was about time he found out what it felt like not to get his own way.

'Royalty works on a strict timetable.'

'And dairy farms don't?' She planted her hands on her hips. 'After you've spent your life getting up before dawn for early milking, *then* talk to me about managing my time!'

'It's hardly the same thing.'

'No, it's not.' She kept her voice calm with an effort. 'My life might not have been exciting but it was about honest hard work. A real job, doing something useful. Not—' she gestured to the exquisitely decorated salon and the man who stood so haughtily before her '—not empty gloss and privilege.'

A dull flush of colour streaked across Raul's razor-sharp cheekbones. Deep grooves bracketed the firm line of his mouth and his long fingers flexed and curled. Energy radiated from him, a latent power so tangible she had to force herself to stand her ground.

'You'll find royal life isn't a sinecure.' His words were glacial shards, grazing her overheated cheeks. 'Running a country is a demanding full-time job.'

Luisa refused to be cowed. Nothing excused his treatment of her. That had to change. Now.

'Under extreme duress I agreed to go to your country and accept my inheritance. That doesn't give you carte blanche to run my life.'

'Where were you going?' His question surprised her.

She glanced at the full length windows with their view of a wide, elegant boulevard and a distant park.

'I've never been to Paris.' She'd never travelled. Except to her grandfather's home and to Sydney when her mum visited specialists. Neither had been pleasant experiences. 'I want to explore.'

'You haven't time. Your new clothes are here and you need to be fitted. It's important you look like a princess when you step off the plane in Maritz.'

'In case I don't photograph well for the press?' She almost laughed at the idea of being media-worthy, but the way his face shuttered instantly at her mention of the press distracted her.

'It's for your sake as well, Luisa. Imagine arriving in the full blare of public interest, dressed as you are.'

Was that a hint of sympathy in his expression, or did she imagine it?

'There's nothing wrong with my clothes! They're...'

Cheap and comfortable and a little shabby. It wasn't that she didn't want beautiful clothes. It was the idea of pretending to be someone she wasn't, as if the real Luisa wasn't worth knowing. Yet a tiny voice inside admitted she didn't want to face a nation's press as she was.

She didn't want to face the press at all!

'Clothes are like armour.' His voice held a note of understanding that surprised her. 'You'll feel more comfortable in clothes that make you look good.'

Did he speak from personal experience? Seeing the proud tilt of his head, Luisa guessed Raul could walk naked before a crowd and not lose one ounce of his regal attitude.

Her breath hitched on the idea of Raul naked. With those long, powerful thighs and that rangy powerful torso...

With an effort she dragged her mind back on track.

'I don't need permission to go out.' She kept her voice low and even but her chin crept up. 'I don't answer to you and I *do* intend to see some of the city.'

She wouldn't let him dictate to her any more.

'Then what if I take you out myself, tonight?' Luisa blinked in astonishment. 'I have appointments for the rest of the day but after dinner, if you like, I'll show you some of the sights of Paris.' He paused for a long moment, his mouth easing into what could almost pass for a smile. 'Would that suit?'

Blankly Luisa stared. A compromise? That must have cost him!

Instantly suspicion grew that he was up to something. Yet the idea of escaping this gorgeous, claustrophobic house was irresistible.

'Agreed.'

Six hours later Luisa stood against the railing of a river cruiser, straining forward as each new sight came into view. From the Ile de la Cité with Notre Dame's flying buttresses illuminated like spread wings against the darkness, to the Pont Neuf and the glittering Eiffel Tower. Paris slid around them, gorgeous and outrageously seductive. Yet still the tension twisted through her.

She and Raul were the only passengers.

Another reminder of what his wealth could buy.

Like her clothes. Stylish black wool trousers and a chic winter-weight cream tunic. Boots and a long coat of leather so soft she had to force herself not to keep smoothing her hands over it. A designer silk scarf in indigo and burnt orange that brought colour to her cheeks.

Except her cheeks burned anyway, remembering the designer's whispered asides to his assistant about Luisa's shape, size, posture and walk. Her posture was good, apparently, but her walk! A stride, like a man's. And she had no notion how to carry off a dress. None!

Yet, despite being an apparently insurmountable challenge, she'd been transformed.

Not that Raul had noticed. He'd escorted her to the car with barely a word. Luisa's bruised pride had been lacerated that he hadn't commented on her appearance. Clearly it was a matter of the utmost indifference to him.

And this the man who'd spoken of marriage!

She drew a slow breath. Once in Maritz she'd consult local lawyers. There must be a way out of the wedding contract. Fear scudded through her at the idea of marrying—

'You're enjoying yourself?' In the darkness she saw movement as Raul stood beside her. A trickle of heat warmed her belly and she swallowed hard. She hated the way her traitorous body responded yet she couldn't douse her excitement. Even in her teens, bowled over by what she thought was love, she hadn't felt this way.

'The city is beautiful. Thank you for the cruise.'

'So you admit there are benefits to our arrangement?'

His satisfied smile set her teeth on edge. He took credit for the beauty of the city, forgetting the blackmail that had forced her hand! It was a relief to let her frustration and indignation surge to the surface.

'They don't outweigh the negatives.'

He made an abrupt movement with one hand, a rare sign of impatience that surprised her. Usually he was so calm. 'You refuse to be pleased, no matter what you are offered.'

'I don't recall any *offer*. That implies choice.'

'You would rather be with your precious cows instead of here?' His wide gesture encompassed the magical vista. 'I give you the chance to be *queen*.'

'By *marrying* you!' She backed a step. 'I'll go with you to Maritz, but as for marriage…' Luisa shook her head.

The sharp glimmer of his stare triggered her innermost anxieties, releasing a tumble of words. 'You can't give me anything I truly desire!'

Years before a man had tried to take her, not out of passion, but calculating ambition. It had left her feeling unclean. That was when she'd decided she'd never settle for anything less than love.

'I want to marry a man who makes my heart race and my blood sing—'

Strong hands closed on her upper arms and she gaped up at the starkly sculpted face suddenly so close. A passing light played over him. Far from being coolly remote, heat ignited in Raul's eyes. His expression sent adrenalin surging.

His head lowered and his warm breath feathered her face. 'Like this, you mean?'

CHAPTER FOUR

RAUL's mouth claimed Luisa's, pressing, demanding, till on a gasp her lips parted and he took possession.

Too late he realised his mistake.

The spark of indignation and guilt that had urged him to silence her grievances flared higher. Hotter. Brighter. He tasted her and heat shimmered, molten in his blood. He delved into her sweet, lush mouth and discovered something unexpected.

Something unique.

He slanted his mouth, demanding better access. Needing more. A ripple of stunned pleasure reverberated through him. He'd suspected almost from the start that there was something unique about Luisa. But this…!

His tongue slicked across hers, laved and slid and explored and there it was again.

An excitement, an anticipation he hadn't felt since he was a green boy.

Still it persisted. The feeling this was *different*.

He tugged her satisfyingly close between his wide-planted legs. His other hand slid up into the thick silken mass of bright hair that had caught his eye as he'd walked into the salon this afternoon. He'd wanted to touch it ever since.

It felt even better than it looked, soft as seduction.

The fire dropped to his belly, kindling like a coiling Catherine wheel that jetted sparks in all directions.

Tension screwed unbearably tight as her hand fluttered at his throat, a barely there touch that weakened his knees. When she slid both arms over his shoulders to clasp his neck a great shudder rocked him.

How could a kiss ravage his senses?

Trying to staunch the feeling that he spun out of control, Raul moved his lips to the corner of her mouth but she turned her head. Instead of an almost chaste caress, he found himself transfixed as her lips opened beneath his. Her body pressed close and her tongue slipped into his mouth in a move that he'd have called tentative if it hadn't sent every blood cell in his body rushing south.

Her kiss was slow and deliberate. Unbelievably provocative as she treated him to a devastating sensual exploration that almost blew the top off his head. Shivers of delight coursed through him.

Once or twice she hesitated as if unsure how to proceed. But the feel of her tongue mating with his in slow, lush pleasure soon obliterated such crazy notions.

Raul slid a hand under her long coat, over the tight curve of her bottom. His splayed fingers dragged her close, where that flicker of heat was now a blazing furnace. He tilted his pelvis and felt her welcoming feminine softness. Lust shot through him.

He swallowed her gasp, returning her kiss with growing fervour. Every nerve was sharp and aware, as if it had been an age since he'd held a woman.

Luisa tasted like sunshine, felt warm and soft and luscious like a summer peach.

Heat spiked in his groin and a hard weight surged there. The audacious notion rose that here, now, they should let passion take its inevitable course. He'd never felt such an unravelling of control.

Dimly he registered astonishment as desire blasted him. He met her kisses hungrily, her soft little whimper of pleasure driving him on even as he tried to slow down.

Luisa, with her sweet sensuality and her delicious hesitation, piqued an appetite jaded by over-eager women.

Brightness spilled over them, a wash of cold sanity.

Raul blinked in the light from an overhead bridge. He raised his head but his hands were still on her, their lower bodies welded together, even as they passed a group of sightseers peering down at the Seine.

Even now hunger gripped him.

Hell!

What was he doing, giving free rein to passion in public? It was unheard of! Raul kept his sex life scrupulously private after the nightmare scandal eight years ago. He'd worked tirelessly since to shore up his people's belief in and respect for the monarchy.

Yet he couldn't drag his eyes from Luisa, couldn't force himself to step away.

Her lips were parted. Her dark eyelashes fanned, concealing her eyes. She looked wantonly inviting and the heat in his groin intensified. His hold tightened.

Could this be the same woman he'd once thought unfeminine? She was beautiful.

Yet more was at work here than a no-expenses-spared makeover. Even if the result surpassed his expectations.

He met lovely women all the time. But none made him feel like this.

The women in his life were easy company, a pleasure to look at. They satisfied his need for sex. He treated them well and they were eager to please. Simple. Uncomplicated.

Yet with Luisa he didn't merely respond to a pretty woman. Her fire, her determination, her strength made her unique. He *felt* as well as desired.

She stirred against him and a bolt of erotic energy speared him.

No! He imagined things. This desire was so intense because he'd allowed her to provoke anger.

He avoided dwelling on the fact that in itself was unusual. He'd learnt years before to channel all his energies into his work. Emotion had led him to the brink of disaster. The eventual fallout of that error had destroyed his family and threatened the state. Now he knew better. He controlled his world. Never again would he be a hostage to sentiment.

Luisa's eyes flickered open and a jewel-bright stare skewered him. His heart thudded out of kilter as his rationalisations crumbled.

Abruptly he released her and stepped away.

What had she done?

Heat blasted Luisa and she swayed, legs wobbling, as unfamiliar sensations cascaded through her.

She couldn't—surely she couldn't have kissed the man who'd *blackmailed* her into doing his bidding?

Surely she hadn't…*enjoyed* it?

Cool air chilled her face and crept in the open front of her jacket. Yet she burned up, her cheeks fiery. Heat seared through her stomach and down to the terrible hollow throb between her legs.

Inwardly she cringed. So much for defiance. And for self-respect. What had happened to the reserve that had kept her impervious to the masculine sex for so long? The wariness borne of disillusionment and hurt?

Raul had hauled her into his embrace, kissed her and her brain had shorted. She'd gone from indignation to helpless need, craving each demanding caress.

How could she have responded to a man she surely hated?

And to have revealed her inexperience to him! No way could her shaming enthusiasm have made up for her lack of expertise. He knew now just how naïve she was. How he must be smirking. The country bumpkin, easy to twist around his little finger. Show her a taste of what she'd never had and she'd be eating out of his hand.

Sickening echoes of the past filled her brain. Hadn't she learned? How could she be susceptible again? Self-disgust was bitter on her tongue.

Reluctantly she opened her eyes.

Instantly he moved away, his brows drawing down in a ferocious scowl as if he couldn't believe he'd touched her.

Pain speared her. No doubt she didn't measure up to his exacting royal standards. Déjà vu swamped her, recalling the scathing revelations of her long-ago suitor.

'I don't want you touching me.' Her voice was raw, husky with distress.

Raul loomed taller, his frown morphing in an instant to a look of cool composure.

'That wasn't the impression you gave a moment ago.' He tugged at his shirt, straightened his jacket, and Luisa felt about an inch tall, realising she'd pulled his clothing askew.

'I didn't invite you to maul me.' Conveniently she ignored the way she'd given herself up to his kiss. Even now she held onto the railing to stay upright. He turned her bones to water.

In the dimming light as the boat slid away from the bridge, it looked like colour rose in his cheeks. But that had to be her imagination. His expression grew haughty and his eyes glittered.

'My apologies. You can be sure I don't make a habit of *forcing my attentions* where they're not wanted.'

Raul drew himself up like a guard on parade. Then with a flourish of one elegant hand he bowed formally. 'I'll leave you to your contemplation of the view.'

He turned and strode to the wheelhouse. He looked utterly calm, as if their passion had been a figment of her imagination. As if he'd felt nothing.

Surely not! He'd been as hungry for her as she'd been for him.

Or had he? She bit her lip, all too aware she had next to no experience to draw upon and that her judgement of men was flawed. Years ago she'd been dumbfounded when her ardent suitor finally revealed his true self when thwarted. His disdainful dismissal of her attractiveness and lack of sophistication was still vivid.

The possibility that Raul too had feigned desire made her want to sink through the deck.

Why should he do it?

The answer came too readily. To reduce her to starry-eyed compliance.

Luisa sagged against the railing.

It had worked. When he kissed her all her doubts and anger fled. She was putty in his hands. His kisses had been white-hot lightning, blowing her mind and leaving her body humming with a desperate craving.

She stared at his tall form as he disappeared into the darkness. Vivid as her recall was of that near seduction years ago, Luisa couldn't remember kisses as devastating as this. Was her memory faulty? Or had years focused on work and family, shying from any tentative male interest, made her more susceptible?

The trembling in her knees grew to a quaking that shook her whole body.

Her impossible position had just become impossibly complicated.

Raul thrust aside a surge of regret as Luisa emerged from her suite. It was unfortunate he'd had to force her hand. Her vulnerability and her desperate pride struck a chord with him. And her passion—

No! Last night was over. A passing weakness.

He was in control now. Impossible that his feelings were engaged by the woman at the top of the staircase. He didn't do feelings. Not any more. One disastrous mistake had cured him.

Though in her chic honey-gold trouser suit and black silk shirt, Luisa was eye-catching. The suit skimmed ripe curves he'd held just hours ago. His fingers flexed at the memories, still vivid after a night of no rest.

She cast a flickering half glance in his direction and chewed on her glossy lower lip.

A ripple of something urgent disturbed his inner calm.

Stoically he ignored it, focusing an appraising eye on how she descended the grand staircase. She gripped the banister tight, clearly unsure of herself in high heels.

As he'd suspected. She'd need help when they arrived in Maritz in a few hours. He didn't want her falling down the steps from the plane and breaking her neck.

His gaze lingered on the long line of her throat. She had a natural elegance her farm clothes had camouflaged. His hands tingled as he recalled the feel of her soft skin, the temptation of her lips, the way her eyes flashed when she challenged him.

Her gaze snared his and his pulse slowed to a weighted thud.

Raul frowned. It was one thing to feel desire with a warm woman pressed intimately against him in the night. Quite another to experience it here, with his butler waiting to usher them on their way to the airport.

Worse, this felt more complex than lust. In a couple of short days she'd somehow got into his head.

Instantly he rejected the idea. It was simple desire he experienced.

'Luisa, I hope you slept well.'

He walked forward as she reached the bottom step. She stumbled and his hand shot out to steady her, but she jerked her arm away, hurrying past him, heels clicking on inlaid marble.

Raul drew a sharp breath. After a lifetime fending off eager women he discovered he didn't like this alternative.

He recalled how she'd clung so needily last night and assured himself her response was contrived. Women were devious. Was it any wonder he kept relationships simple?

What sort of relationship would he have with his wife?

'Yes, thank you. I slept well enough.'

Liar! Despite the make-up accentuating the smoky blue of her eyes, Raul saw signs of fatigue.

'And you?' To his surprise challenge sizzled in her gaze, as if she knew he'd spent most of the night wakeful, reliving those few moments when she'd melted into him like a born seductress.

Even now he wasn't sure about her. There'd been more than a hint of the innocent about her last night.

But then feigned innocence could be such an effective weapon. As he knew to his cost. A spike of chill air stabbed the back of his neck.

'I always sleep well in Paris.' He offered his arm again, this time holding her gaze till she complied.

He covered her hand with his, securing it possessively. The sooner she grew accustomed to him the better. 'And now, if you're ready, our plane is waiting.'

He felt the shiver race through her. Saw her eyes widen in what looked like anxiety.

There was nothing to fear. Most women would sell their soul to be in her place, offered wealth, prestige and marriage to a man the press insisted on labelling one of the world's most eligible bachelors. But already he began to see Luisa wasn't most women.

He heard himself saying, 'I'll look after you, Luisa. There's no need to be anxious.'

It was on the way to the airport that Raul discovered the cost of his unguarded actions last night. The discreet buzz of his mobile phone and a short conversation with Lukas, already waiting for them at the airport, had him excusing himself and opening his laptop.

Not that Luisa noticed. She was busy pressing her nose to the glass as they drove through Paris.

He focused on his computer, scrolling through page after page of newspaper reports. The sort of reports he habitually ignored: 'PRINCE'S SECRET LOVER.' 'RAUL'S PARISIAN INTERLUDE.' 'SIZZLING SEDUCTION ON THE SEINE.'

There wasn't much to the articles apart from speculation as to his new lover's identity. Yet acid curdled his stomach and clammy heat rose as he flicked from one photo of last night's kiss to another.

He frowned, perplexed by his reaction.

It wasn't the first time the paparazzi had snapped photos of him with a woman. He was a favourite subject. Typically the press was more interested in his mistresses than his modernisation plans or regional disarmament talks. Usually he shrugged off their reports.

But this time...

Understanding dawned on a wave of nausea.

This time the photographer had unwittingly caught him in a moment of rare vulnerability. The press couldn't know, but Raul had been careening out of control, swept away by dangerously unfamiliar forces. Prey to a compulsion he hadn't experienced in years.

Eight years in fact.

Since the feeding frenzy of press speculation about a royal love triangle. The memory sickened him.

Since he'd learned to distrust female protestations of love and displays of innocence. Since he'd rebuilt his shattered world with determination, pride and a complete absence of emotion that made a man vulnerable.

His gut cramped as he remembered facing the press, made rabid by the scent of blood—*his* blood. The effort of appearing unmoved in the face of the ultimate betrayal. Of how he'd had to claw back his self-respect after making the worst mistake of his life. How day after day he'd had to appear strong. Till finally the façade had become reality and he'd learned to live without emotional ties. Except for his love of Maritz.

He shut the laptop with a snap.

The cases weren't the same. Then he'd been naïve enough to believe in romance. He'd hurt with the intensity of youthful emotions. Now, at thirty, Raul was in control of his world. What he'd felt last night had been lust, more intense than usual perhaps, but simple enough.

Besides, public interest in Luisa could be used to advantage. It wouldn't hurt to hint that there was more to his approaching

nuptials than fulfilment of a legal contract. People liked to
believe in fairy tales and it would ease the way for her.

A lost princess, a romantic interlude in Paris, an early wedding. It was the sort of PR that would focus interest on the
monarchy and dampen the enthusiasm for political rabble-
rousing in the lead up to his coronation.

He'd planned a quiet arrival in Maritz to give Luisa time
to acclimatise. Yet in the circumstances revealing her identity
had definite benefits.

He'd arrange it with Lukas at the airport.

'You can unfasten your seat belt, ma'am.' The hostess smiled
at Luisa on her way to open the plane door.

Foreboding lurched in the pit of Luisa's stomach.

The idea of stepping out of the aircraft and into the country
that had once been her mother's, and her detested grandfather's, terrified her. Some atavistic foreknowledge warned that
this next step would be irrevocable.

Again she experienced that sense of the world telescoping
in around her, shrinking to a dark tunnel where her future lay
immutable before her.

Desperately she sought for something positive to hang onto.
The determination to get legal advice on that marriage contract
as soon as she could. To find an escape clause that would allow
Raul to inherit the throne he coveted without marrying her.

'Here.' A deep voice cut through her swirling thoughts. 'Let
me.' Warm hands, large and capable, unclipped the seat belt
and brushed it off her lap.

Sensation jittered through her stomach and across her
thighs. Luisa looked up sharply to find Raul bending over
her, his eyes warm with an expression she couldn't fathom.

Her heart rose in her throat, pounding fast. The memory of
last night's madness filled her. The feel of his tight embrace
and her need for more. Despite today's polite formality, nothing
could obliterate the recollection. Even the knowledge it had
been a lie. He'd felt nothing.

He stepped back and she sucked in an uneven breath.

'It's time to go.' He extended an arm.

Luisa nodded, her tongue glued to the roof of her mouth. What was happening to her? She had no desire to fall into Raul's arms again, yet she imagined warmth in his gaze. When all he cared about was her usefulness to him.

Silently she let him drape a cashmere coat over her shoulders, then stepped to the door. The sooner she reached their destination, the sooner she could sort out this mess.

A roar filled her ears and she stopped abruptly at the head of the stairs. She blinked into the bright light, wishing she'd brought sunglasses.

'It's all right,' Raul said. 'They're just glad to see us.'

He slid an arm slid round her, drawing her to him. Instinctively she pulled away but his hold was unbreakable.

'Relax,' he murmured. 'I'm just making sure you don't trip on those high heels. Come on.'

At his urging they descended, Luisa clinging to the railing and inordinately grateful for his support. Sheer bravado had led her to wear the highest heels in her new wardrobe, determined to look as sophisticated as possible. The move had backfired when she'd come face to face with Raul and discovered the extra height merely brought her closer to his knowing gaze.

Another roar made her blink and focus on the scene ahead.

Crowds massed behind the fence at the edge of the tarmac. Maritzian flags waved and excited voices called out. Luisa's Maritzian was rusty so all she could make out was Raul's name. *And hers.*

She stumbled to a stop on the narrow stairs and only Raul's firm grip saved her. Adrenalin pumped hard in her blood. From the near fall or perhaps from the impact of meeting his intent scrutiny head-on.

'What's happening?'

He shrugged and she felt the movement against her as he kept a tight hold of her waist.

'Well-wishers. Nothing to worry about.'

Luisa frowned, battling a rising sense of unreality. 'But how do they know my name?'

Something flickered in his eyes. 'Your identity isn't a secret. Is it?'

Dazedly she shook her head, beginning her descent again at his urging. 'But it makes no sense. How could—'

The sight of a placard in the throng cut off the words mid-flow. It showed her name and Raul's, linked in a massive love heart topped with a crown.

She swung round and read satisfaction in his face.

'What have you done?' Every muscle tightened as she fought the impulse to run back up the steps and hide in the royal jet.

His brows arched. 'I authorised my staff to confirm your identity if queried. Now, it's time we moved.'

Mutinously Luisa stared up at him, her hand tightening on the rail.

His eyes flashed, then his lips tilted in a one-sided smile that obliterated the grimness engraved around his lips, making him look younger. 'As you wish, madam.'

He bowed. But it wasn't a bow, she realised as his arms circled her.

Seconds later he hefted her up against his chest. The noise of the crowd crested in a swell of approval. But Luisa barely heard it over the thunderous beat of blood in her ears.

She should hate being manhandled. She did! Almost.

'What are you doing?' she demanded, trying not to focus on the feel of tough muscle and bone surrounding her.

His smile deepened and something flipped over inside Luisa's chest. He shrugged again and this time the movement rippled around her, drawing her closer.

It scared her how much she enjoyed being held by Raul.

'Carrying my bride down the stairs.'

CHAPTER FIVE

LUISA walked across the tarmac towards the crowd. It was daunting. So huge, so excited. For an insane moment she wished she were back in his arms. To her consternation she'd felt…safe there.

Her knees shook with every step. His arm around her waist was both a torment and a support.

She swallowed hard, nervous at what she faced. And furious.

'Don't faint on me now, Luisa.'

'No chance of that,' she managed through gritted teeth as instinctively she tried to respond to the broad smiles on so many faces. 'I'm not going to swoon in your arms. Even for the sake of your audience.'

'*Our* audience.'

A barrage of flashes set up around them. He raised one hand in acknowledgement and the crowd cheered harder.

The information she'd found on the web mentioned his dedication to his country but she hadn't realised how popular he was. Cynically she did a quick survey of the crowd and noticed women outnumbered men three to one. That explained some of the excitement.

It would be easy to fall for Raul if you didn't know the man behind the gorgeous exterior.

He swept her towards a gleaming limousine. No lengthy wait for passport and customs checks for him.

They'd almost reached the car when Luisa saw what had

provoked such interest. Someone held up a page from a newspaper, with a blown up photo of a couple embracing so pas-
sionately it felt voyeuristic to look at them.

It took a moment for the truth to slam into her. The man
staring so intently down at the woman he held possessively
was Raul. His face was harsh with stark sexual hunger. Or
intense calculation.

And the woman with her kiss-swollen lips, apparently
swooning in his arms, was her!

Luisa's skin crawled in horror. Bile rose in her throat and
she swallowed frantically. She felt...violated at the knowledge
anyone else had seen that moment. Had viewed her vulnerability. Bad enough Raul knew her appalling weakness, but
to have others witness it, splash it in newsprint...

She gasped, her breath sawing painfully in cramped
lungs.

'Come, Luisa.' Raul urged her forwards. 'Don't stop here
in front of the cameras.'

The mention of cameras moved her on till she found herself
seated, shivering, in a limo. Her brain seemed to have seized
up and her teeth were chattering.

'Luisa?' Warm hands chafed her icy ones. Dazedly she
heard a muttered imprecation, then her knees were swathed
in warmth as Raul tucked his jacket around her legs.

'I don't need it. I'm fine.' Her voice sounded overloud in the
thick silence now the privacy screen had been raised. But a
chance glance out of the window to the people milling about,
watching their vehicle, made her shrink back into the soft
leather.

'You've had a shock. I apologise. I should have warned you.'
Luisa could almost believe that was genuine regret in his deep
voice.

But her brain was branded with the memory of his expression in that photo. She wasn't stupid enough to believe he'd
been overcome by passion. He'd recovered too fast and too
completely. He'd probably been calculating how successful

his seduction had been. Assessing how compliant she'd be in future.

Fury pierced the fog of shock.

'*You* did that!' She rounded on him, too angry to feel more than a tremor of surprise at how close he sat, his thigh warm against hers. 'You set me up for that photo.' How could she have forgotten her suspicion last night when he'd suggested taking her out? She should have guessed he was up to something.

Hauteur iced his features.

'I don't do deals with the paparazzi.'

Luisa shook her head. 'Someone did! They were there, waiting for us. You can't tell me—'

'I *do* tell you, Luisa.' His voice held a note of steel that silenced her. 'I have nothing but contempt for the media outlets and the photographers who spend their time beating up such stories.' His jaw tightened and Luisa found herself sinking back into her seat.

Gullible she might be, but everything from the set of his taut shoulders to the glitter in his dark eyes convinced her he was telling the truth.

'The press are always on the watch for photo opportunities. They follow constantly, though given my security detail, usually at a distance. It's part of being royal. A fact of life.'

'I don't think much of being royal then.' Her stomach was painfully tight after the sudden welling nausea.

To her surprise, Raul's mouth lifted in a rare smile that made something inside her soften. 'I don't either. Not that part of it.'

His hand enfolded hers and for an instant she knew a bizarre urge to smile back, sharing a moment of intimacy.

Except it was a mirage. There *was* no intimacy.

'I regret the photo, Luisa. If I'd realised we were visible...' He shrugged.

To her amazement she found herself wanting to believe him. 'But even if the press had reported our—' she swallowed, her mouth dry as she remembered his kiss '—our trip on the river,

I don't see why the crowd would be excited about my arrival. Surely they don't turn out to see all your…girlfriends.'

His smile faded and his grip tightened. Clearly he didn't like explaining himself.

Tough!

Luisa dragged her hand from his, refusing to notice the loss of warmth.

'I told you. I instructed my staff to explain who you are if asked.'

'But my name wouldn't mean anything!'

Silently he surveyed her as if waiting for her to catch up. 'Your title does. Princess Luisa of Ardissia.'

Luisa froze as the implications sank in. 'I'm not princess yet. I haven't signed—'

'But you will.' His voice was a rich, creamy purr. 'That's why you came, isn't it?'

She nodded, feeling again that hated sense of being cornered. Suspicion flared.

'That's not all they said, is it?' Urgently she leaned towards him, thrusting his jacket off her legs, uncaring she was close enough to see the individual long lashes fringing his eyes, or the hint of a nick on his smoothly shaven jaw. To inhale the warm scent of his skin.

'They just happened to mention the marriage contract, didn't they?'

Raul held her gaze unblinkingly and for one crazy moment she felt an echo of last night's emotions when he'd hauled her close and introduced her to bliss.

Heat scorched her cheeks and throat.

'Didn't they?'

'It's not a secret, Luisa, though the details weren't widely known.'

She sat back, her heart pounding.

'You don't give up, do you?' It shouldn't come as a surprise. Not after he'd manoeuvred her into coming here. 'What did you hope to achieve? Pressure me into agreeing?'

It was as if he'd known she still held out hope of avoiding

marriage. Wearily she raised a hand to her forehead, smoothing the beginning of an ache there.

'I won't be forced into marriage because your precious public expects it. If I pull out the story would be all about you. How you were jilted. Not about me.'

In an instant his face whitened to the colour of scoured bone. His nostrils flared and the flesh seemed to draw back, leaving his clear cut features spare and prominent. Almost she could believe she'd scored some unseen injury.

Energy radiated from him. A sense of barely controlled power. Of danger.

This time she did retreat.

'There will be no jilting.' Fascinated, Luisa saw the tic of Raul's pulse at his jaw.

'I will not leave my people to the chaos that would come if I gave up the throne.' He paused. 'Remember why you agreed to come here.'

Blazing eyes meshed with hers and any hope she'd harboured that he wouldn't follow through on his threat vanished. This man would do whatever it took to get what he wanted. How had she let last night's fake tenderness blind her to that? Or his solicitude here in the car?

Luisa pulled her jacket close and turned to face the window. She couldn't face him with her emotions so raw.

They'd left the highway for the old part of the city. Cobblestones rumbled under the wheels as they crossed a wide square of pastel-coloured baroque buildings that housed expensive shops.

The car turned and before them appeared a steep incline, almost a cliff. Above that, seeming to grow from the living rock, towered the royal castle. Dark grey stone with round towers and forest green roofs just visible behind the massive battlement.

Guidebooks said the castle was a superb example of medieval construction, updated with spectacular eighteenth century salons and modern amenities. That it commanded extraordinary views to the Alps and down the wide river valley. That its treasure house was unrivalled in central Europe and its ballroom an architectural gem.

But what stuck in Luisa's mind was that in almost a millennium of use no one had ever escaped the castle's dungeons once locked up by order of the king.

Her suite of rooms was airy, light and sumptuous. Not at all like a dank prison cell. Yet Luisa barely took in the silk and gilt loveliness.

She stood before the wide windows, staring to distant snow-capped mountains. That was where Ardissia lay. The place that tied her to wealth and position and a life of empty gloss instead of emotional warmth and security. Tied her to Raul. A man whose ambition repelled, yet who made her tremble with glorious, dreadful excitement.

Luisa trailed her fingers appreciatively over the antique desk. It wasn't that she didn't like beautiful things, or the designer clothes wealth could buy. It was that she knew they weren't any substitute for happiness. For warmth and caring and love. She'd grown up with love and her one disastrous foray into romance had taught her she couldn't accept anything else.

On impulse she snatched up the phone. A dialling tone buzzed in her ear and her heart leapt at the idea of calling home. She looked at her watch, calculating the time difference. With the help of the phone book she found the international code and rang home.

'Oh, pet! It's so good to hear your voice.' Mary's excited chatter eased some of the tension drawn tight in Luisa's stomach. She sank back onto a silk upholstered chair in front of the desk.

'We've been wondering how you are and what you're doing. Are you well? How was the trip? Did that lovely Prince Raul look after you?'

Luisa bit her lip at the memory of how well Raul had looked after her. He'd played on her vulnerability and used his own compelling attraction to lay bare naïve longings she hadn't even realised she harboured.

'The trip was fine, Mary. I even had my own bed on the plane. And then we stopped in Paris—'

'Paris? Really?'

Soon Luisa was swept along by Mary's demands for details, peppered with her aunt's exclamations and observations. Eventually the talk turned to home.

'We've been missing you, love. It seems strange with that new bloke and his son in your house. But I can't deny they've made a good start. He's a decent manager, by the look of it. And he reckons the changes you and your dad began to modernise the co-op were spot on. Well, I could have told him that! And between you and me, it's such a relief knowing that debt's going to be settled. Sam is like a new man without that weighing on him. And Josie's all agog about moving into town to take up an apprenticeship, now we'll be able to afford to help her with rent. And little Julia Todd is looking so much better these days. I was worried about her being so wan. It turns out the poor thing is pregnant again and was worried about how they'd afford another child. But now she's positively radiant...'

Luisa leaned forward to put her elbow on the desk, letting her head sink onto her hand.

Mary's voice tugged at something deep inside. The part of her that longed for everything familiar and dear.

Yet with each new breathless revelation it became clear Luisa couldn't go back. Her past, the life she'd loved, were closed to her.

The last vestige of hope had been torn away today when she looked into fathomless emerald eyes and a stern, beautiful face. Raul would do whatever it took to get the crown he coveted.

Already the people she loved were moving on, anticipating the cancellation of the co-op's debts. Luisa had understood that, but not till this moment had the devastating reality of it all hit her fully.

Luisa had no choice.

She lifted her head and looked around the delicately lovely room. *A room for a princess.*

She shuddered at the enormity of what faced her.

But her parents' example was vivid in her mind. No matter what life threw at them, they'd battled on, making the most of life without complaint.

Luisa set her jaw. It was time she faced her future.

'Raul.'

He looked up from the papers he and Lukas were discussing—disturbing reports of more unrest.

Luisa stood in the doorway. A dart of heat shot through him as he took in her loveliness and remembered the taste of her lips beneath his.

There was something different about her. Gone was the distressed woman of mere hours ago. And the woman endearingly unsure of herself in high heels. This was Luisa as he'd first seen her—confident and in control, yet with no hint of the farmyard about her.

She looked…magnificent.

He shoved back his chair and stood. 'We'll continue later, Lukas.' His assistant hastily packed up the reports and bowed himself from the study, closing the door.

'Please take a seat.'

She crossed the room to halt before his desk. 'This won't take long.' She paused, her slightly stunned gaze taking in his state-of-the-art computer equipment and the large document storage area behind him. As if surprised to discover he actually worked.

Raul paced around the desk. 'What can I do for you, Luisa?' It was the first time she'd sought him out.

Clear blue eyes met his and he felt that now-familiar frisson of anticipation.

'I've come to tell you I'll do it. I'll marry you.'

Raul breathed deep as the knot of tension that had screwed his belly tight for so long loosened.

He'd manipulated her into coming here. He'd overseen a new look for her, introduced her to his people in such a way she'd be cornered by their expectations, and still he hadn't been sure he could go through with it. Force her into marriage.

Despite his determination and his desperation, doubts had preyed on him.

'What made you change your mind?'

She shrugged. 'Does it matter?'

Raul opened his mouth. Part of him believed it did. The part that wanted to know Luisa better, her thoughts and feelings. The part of him, he supposed, that had made him emotionally susceptible all those years ago. The part he'd thought he'd erased from his being.

He shook his head. What mattered was her agreement.

'I thought not.' Her eyes blazed with what might have been anger. Then, in a moment, the look was gone.

He took her hand in his. She didn't resist.

'I promise you, Luisa, I will do everything in my power to ensure you never regret this.' His skin grew tight over tense muscles as he thought of the enormity of her decision. Of all it meant for him and his people.

He lifted her hand to his lips.

'You will have my gratitude and my loyalty.' Her flesh was cool, her expression shuttered and yet he felt the trembling pulse at her wrist. He inhaled her delicate scent. Something far stronger than gratitude stirred in his belly.

'You owe me more.'

Startled, he raised his head. She slipped her hand free and clasped it in her other palm as if it pained her.

'What do you want?'

She'd almost convinced him she didn't care for wealth and glamour. Now suspicion rose. He should have known better. Hadn't Ana taught him anything? What was her price?

'I want…' She paused and gestured abruptly with one hand. 'I *don't* want to be treated as some brainless doll. As far as possible, I want to make my own decisions. Don't expect to dictate to me.'

Raul took in the defiant glimmer in her eyes, the determined jut of her chin and felt the tension leach away.

No unreasonable demands? No tantrums or tears?

Pride stirred, and respect for this remarkable woman.

Perhaps after all Luisa was as unique as she seemed.

His lips curved in a smile of genuine pleasure. 'I wouldn't expect anything less.'

Raul saw Luisa led past the royal councillors, across the vast reception room. The soon-to-be-Princess of Ardissia was quietly elegant in shades of caramel and cream. Her back was straight and her chin up as if unfazed by the presence of so many august people. Yet she was pale and there was a brittle quality to her composure that made his brow knot.

Guilt pinched. A few days ago she'd been leading a completely different life. Had he been right to move so fast to cement this arrangement?

Raul stiffened, refusing to follow that line of thought. This was for the best. For the good of the nation. The alternative would plunge the country into chaos.

The sooner this was done the better.

He strode across the room, silently berating himself for getting sidetracked by urgent negotiations. He'd meant to support her as she entered the room.

He'd nearly reached her at the ornate desk when she saw him and started. Disappointment flared. This wasn't the first time she'd reacted as if his touch contaminated.

It took a moment to realise that in flinging out an arm involuntarily Luisa had knocked over the baccarat crystal inkwell. Black liquid sprayed across the hand woven heirloom carpet and his suit.

The room inhaled a collective gasp. In a moment Luisa had ripped blotting paper from the embossed blotter on the desk and dropped to her knees, soaking up the stain.

Servants rushed to assist but she didn't notice. 'We need something to soak this up.'

Raul dragged a pristine handkerchief from his pocket and hunkered beside her. 'Will this help?'

'Not much.' Her words were crisp. 'But it's better than nothing.' The snowy cloth joined the dark pulpy mass on the carpet.

'Excuse me, ma'am. Ma'am?' One of the senior staff appeared with materials to clear the worst of the mess.

'Luisa.' Raul took her elbow, gripping tight enough to make her look up. 'The staff will deal with this.'

She opened her mouth as if to protest, then looked over his shoulder, eyes widening. As if she'd only just remembered every member of the High Court, the royal advisors and sundry VIPs here to witness the formalities.

Heat flooded her face and she looked away. Gently he drew her to her feet.

She felt surprisingly fragile beneath his touch. Not like the woman who'd seduced him witless with just a kiss, or the proud woman who'd agreed to marry him.

'I'm sorry.' She watched the staff deal with a stain that was probably immovable, worrying at her lower lip.

'It's all right,' he murmured, leading her away to the other side of the desk.

'But the carpet! It's old and valuable, surely?' Her hands clenched tight.

'No such thing. It's amazing how well they make reproductions these days.'

He heard his butler's breath hiss at the blithe lie. In Raul's father's day, damaging an heirloom like this would have resulted in severe punishment. But, seeing Luisa's distress, feeling her arm tremble beneath his hold, Raul didn't give a damn about anything but allaying her guilt.

'Come,' he said. 'Here's a seat for you.'

She sank into the chair and Raul swept the blotter aside, motioning for the accession document to be brought forward. Reaching in his jacket, he withdrew his own pen.

Maritz needed to move with the times. There was absolutely

no need to continue the tradition of signing and witnessing important documents with old-fashioned ink pens.

Lukas presented the document which, when signed, would confirm Luisa as Princess of Ardissia, inheritor of her grandfather's wealth. And Raul's wife-to-be.

It was spread wide on the desk and the witnesses stepped forward. Raul handed her the pen.

And waited.

For Luisa didn't sign. Instead, she read the English translation, slowly and methodically. Her finger marked a difficult clause and she lifted her head, turning to Lukas who hovered helpfully on her other side.

'Would you mind explaining this reference?' she murmured softly.

'Of course, ma'am.' After a quick look at Raul, Lukas bent over the parchment, explaining the clause. Then after a few moments, another.

The audience grew restless. Raul noticed one or two raised brows among some of the more old-fashioned advisers. He could imagine what they whispered. That the woman should gratefully accept what was offered, without question.

Luisa was aware of the buzz of comment. Her cheeks grew brighter and he saw her neck stiffen. Yet still she read each line.

It should have annoyed him, this delay to his plans. Even now, on the edge of achieving what was so necessary, ripples of anxiety spread through his belly. He couldn't be completely happy till this was settled.

Yet his impatience was tempered by admiration. Luisa was naturally cautious.

Like him. He'd never sign anything without careful consideration either.

Raul recalled the advice he'd recently received. That on investigation Luisa's farming co-op was found to be surprisingly well run. That the financial difficulties were due to the economic downturn, a massive drought and a series of unfortunate health problems, including the death of her father last year.

According to the accountants, the business was poised to become very successful, once money was freed up for new equipment. Luisa had done an excellent job.

Once more curiosity rose. She wasn't like other women. He'd been so intent on achieving his ends he'd initially thought of her as a convenient bride, not a real woman. Now he pondered exactly what sort of woman he would wed.

He looked at her bent head, how she bit her lush bottom lip in concentration. Fire arced through his gut.

She fascinated him, he admitted now. Her obstinacy, pragmatism and quiet pride. Her unassuming ways and her disquieting sensuality. *How long since a woman had intrigued him so? Since a kiss had made him lose his head?*

Finally, with a swift movement, Luisa picked up his pen and signed. Only Raul, close beside her, saw the way her hand shook. It pained him to see what this cost her.

Yet relief swamped him. It was almost done. Soon the crown would be his. His destiny was within his grasp. His country would be safe.

He picked up the pen, still warm from her fingers, and with a flourish added his signature as first witness. 'Thank you, Luisa,' he murmured.

At his words she tilted her head and their gazes meshed. Heat ricocheted through his belly and groin, the reverberations spreading even as she looked away, letting her lashes veil her eyes.

Now she was bound to him, this intriguing woman so lacking in sophistication yet with an innate grace and integrity he couldn't ignore.

Theirs would be a convenient marriage. A marriage of state for the well-being of the nation.

Yet, to his astonishment, Raul registered a purely personal satisfaction at the prospect.

CHAPTER SIX

'I COULDN'T have done a better job of botching that if I'd tried.' Luisa grimaced as she followed Lukas through a maze of corridors to her suite.

She'd do better in future.

Her skin crawled at the memory of censorious eyes on her: an upstart foreigner, not only gauche but clumsy.

'Nothing of the sort, ma'am. You carried it off with great composure.'

Luisa smiled gratefully. Lukas really was a nice man. Surprisingly nice for someone in the Prince's employ.

'Thanks, Lukas, but there's no need to pretend. I saw the way they looked, and their impatience that I wanted to read what I signed.'

'It's true some of the advisers are rather old school.' Lukas cleared his throat and gestured for her to precede him down another wide corridor. 'I'm sure His Highness wouldn't mind me saying that's been one of his challenges in running the country as a modern state—bringing them along in the process of reform.'

Luisa's eyes widened. It hadn't occurred to her Raul would have difficulties. With his take charge attitude and formidable determination she couldn't imagine it.

'You talk as if he's been in charge of the country a long time. I thought the King only died recently.'

A hint of a flush coloured Lukas' cheeks. 'That's correct, ma'am.' He paused and then, with the air of making a sudden

decision, added, 'But His Highness was in many ways responsible for running the country long before that. The previous
king…left a lot in the Prince's hands.'

Luisa's mind snagged on Lukas' words, trying to read the
subtext. There was one. Something he skated around rather
than spelling out. It was on the tip of her tongue to press for
an explanation, till she read his discomfort.

'And is it still difficult?'

Lukas shrugged. 'The Prince has made his mark and even
the more old-fashioned courtiers see the benefits. But there are
some who resent change. Some who'd rather vie for personal
power than cooperate in a national effort to modernise.'

Her steps slowed. Lukas' assessment echoed Raul's words.
She'd half dismissed that as a smokescreen, veiling the fact
he simply coveted the crown. Though lately she'd wondered.
Seeing him with others, she'd caught glimpses of a reasonable
man, even a caring one.

Was there more truth in Raul's words than she'd thought?
He claimed he acted for the country as well as himself. Was
it possible? It was tempting to hope so.

Yet nothing excused Raul's behaviour towards her.

'As for today, ma'am,' Lukas said, 'I know the Prince was
very pleased with your first official appearance.'

She just bet he was! She'd signed his precious documents.
Yet she hadn't missed the way he'd hovered, eager for her to
sign and be done with it. If she was truthful, it wasn't just the
habit of reading legal papers carefully that had made her delay.
A tiny part of her had wanted him on tenterhooks, wondering
if she'd go through with it.

As if she'd had a choice! Besides, she'd given her word.

Her heart plunged at the implications of what she'd just
done. No turning back now.

'Lukas, I've changed my mind. Can you show me the way
to the gardens? I need some fresh air.'

Forty minutes later Luisa felt less claustrophobic. Wandering
through the courtyards she'd found a gardener. They'd

discussed the grounds with enthusiasm and sign language since her Maritzian was sparse and Gregor, the gardener, spoke a particularly thick dialect.

They'd toured the terraces and rose garden, where Luisa recognised the names of gorgeous old roses her mother had mentioned. They'd visited an orchard in the moat, a walled garden with fountains and arbours and the kitchen garden where Luisa struggled to identify the rarer herbs.

For the first time in days she felt as if she'd stepped out of her nightmare and into the real world, with the scent of rich soil and growing things around her.

She breathed deep as she climbed the spiral staircase in the battlements. Gregor had said, if she understood right, that she'd see the parterre garden from here. She'd read about such gardens, with their intricate patterns laid out in plants and gravel paths, but the view from the ground didn't give the full effect.

She could have seen it from the castle. But she didn't want to meet any of the disapproving VIPs who'd witnessed her accession to the title of Princess of Ardissia.

Princess! Her stomach curdled, thinking about it. Or was that because of the tower? She didn't have a head for heights and the open window beside her gave a dizzying view to the city below.

Luisa pressed a damp palm to the wall and kept moving. Soon she emerged at a low opening looking towards the castle. Someone had been working here and she side-stepped a pile of tools. The opening was so low she felt safer on her knees, her hands on the stonework.

The garden was spectacular, though overgrown. She made out the remnants of the Maritzian dragon, the one flying on the flag from the topmost turret, laid out in the hedges below. Shrubs with gold foliage denoted its eyes and a straggling group of red-leaved plants might have been its fiery breath. Its tail was missing and a path cut through one claw, yet it was still magnificent.

Enchanted, Luisa leaned a little further out.

She'd inherited her mother's love of gardens, though she'd had little time to indulge the interest.

Movement caught her eye. She looked up to see a familiar figure striding through the garden. Raul. Instantly, absurdly, her pulse fluttered.

He saw her and shouted something as he raced forward.

Instinctively Luisa recoiled, feeling as if she'd been caught trespassing. She pushed back and again that dizzy sensation hit. Only this time it wasn't just in her head.

To her horror, the wall beneath her hands shifted. Instead of rising up, her movement pushed her further out, the stone sliding forward with a terrible grinding noise.

She scrabbled back but her centre of gravity was too far forward. With a loud groan, the old sill tumbled out of her grasp to fall, with dreadful resounding thuds, to the ground below.

Luisa lurched forward, spreadeagled over jagged rock, her arms dangling into space and her eyes focused disbelievingly on the sheer drop below. Masonry bruised her ribs but she couldn't get breath to try inching back. Fear of another fall, this time with her in it, froze her.

She couldn't see Raul now and the staccato beat of blood in her ears drowned every sound. Her throat closed so she couldn't even yell for help. Swirling nausea made her head swim.

Her breath came in jerky gasps as she tried to crawl backwards, only to slide further forward as another block tumbled with a reverberating crash.

Any minute now, that could be her.

'It's all right.' The deep, soothing voice barely penetrated her consciousness. 'I've got you.' On the words strong arms slid beneath her waist.

'No!' she gasped, terror freezing her muscles. 'Keep back. It's too dangerous.' Surely Raul's weight with hers on the unstable wall would send them both plummeting.

'Don't move. Just relax and let me do this.'

'Relax?' He must be kidding. Luisa squeezed her eyes shut as swirling dots appeared in her vision.

Her body was rigid as he hauled her back, his arms locked around her. She waited, breathless, for the ominous groan of rock on rock. Instead she heard Raul's indrawn breath as he took her weight against him, dragging her slowly but inexorably to safety.

There was heat behind her. Searing heat that branded her back as he held her to him. His breath feathered her nape and his hands gripped so hard she wondered if she'd have bruises. But they'd be nothing to the bruises on her ribs from the stones. Or to her injuries if she'd fallen.

A shudder racked her and she squeezed her eyes even tighter, trying to block the pictures her mind conjured.

'Shh. It's all right. You're safe. I promise.' Yet the tremors wouldn't subside. Her teeth began to chatter.

Desperately she sought for composure. 'I n-never did l-like heights.'

'Open your eyes.' He held her away and the shaking worsened. Her eyes snapped open in protest but he was already lowering her to sit on the floor.

Luisa slumped like a rag doll, her bones water. Even now the view down to the distant flagstones was emblazoned on her brain.

'Here, lean forward.' She did as she was told and heat enveloped her as Raul draped his jacket around her quaking shoulders. A subtle spicy scent surrounded her. The scent of Raul's aftershave. Or perhaps the scent of him. Luisa breathed deep, letting the fragrance fill her lungs.

She lifted her head. He stood before her, hands on hips, brow pleated and mouth a stark line.

Luisa had seen him without a jacket only once, briefly, in the limo. Always he was impeccably dressed. It shocked her that beneath that tailored elegance was a broad chest of considerable power.

Her eyes trailed over his heaving torso, noting the way his stance drew the fine cotton of his shirt taut, moulding to a body that wasn't that of an effete clothes horse but a strong, very masculine man. Luisa's heart skittered to a new rhythm as she remembered that solid muscle pressed against her on the boat in Paris. No wonder he'd felt so good!

'We need to get you inside where it's warm.' Yet he didn't move to help her rise. Did he see how weak she was?

Shakily she nodded, drawing his jacket close. 'Soon. I need to get my b-breath.' She had to pull herself together but she couldn't quite manage it.

'Here.' With a quick stride, Raul moved behind her. Next thing she knew, those capable hands were on her again. He pulled her up and across his lap as he sat leaning against the wall opposite the gap.

Luisa should protest. She didn't want to be this close to him. But she didn't have the energy to resist and had to be content holding herself as stiff as she could in his arms. As if she could ignore the heat of those solid, muscular thighs or his arms around her!

'I hope that wall's safe!'

'It's fine. Don't worry. It's only the other side that's a problem.' He hauled her closer so her shoulder was tucked into his chest. 'Didn't you see the warning sign?'

She recalled a neat sign at the base of the tower but she'd barely glanced at it.

'The door was unlocked.'

'It won't be in future.' His voice was grim. 'Not until it's safe.' He tugged her closer but she resisted. Any nearer and her head would be on his shoulder. The idea both attracted and horrified her.

'Why did you come up here? You get finer views from the other side of the castle.'

She shrugged jerkily. 'I wanted to see the parterre garden. Gregor showed it to me, but you don't get the effect from the ground.'

'Gregor?' A steely note in his voice made her turn and meet his eyes head-on. They had darkened to a shade of rich forest-green. This close she was surprised to find a glimmer of scintillating gold sprinkled there too.

'Yes.' She found she was leaning towards him and drew back abruptly. 'One of your gardeners. He showed me around.'

The frown returned to Raul's face and his mouth flattened. But, instead of marring his features, it made him look like a sulky angel.

A quiver began low in her stomach that had nothing to do with her recent scare.

'He didn't encourage you to come up here, did he?'

'Of course not.' It was only now she realised Gregor's gestures had been to warn her away from the unsafe structure.

'Thank you for saving me.' She should have thanked Raul immediately but her brain was too frazzled.

'I'm just glad I saw you when I did.' His hold firmed and his frown became a scowl, as if he'd like to blame someone.

Luisa looked at his concerned expression and tried to remember how callous he was. That he'd forced her hand.

'Just think. If you hadn't reached me, you mightn't have had a princess to marry. Then you'd never inherit.'

A large firm hand cupped her jaw and cheek. His gaze snared hers and her breath caught. The gold in his eyes seemed to flare brighter. Or was that because he was nearer?

He shook his head slowly. 'If there was no princess, the contract would no longer bind me.' His thumb slid under her chin and Luisa's eyelashes fluttered as a strange lethargic heat stole through her. 'I'd have been free to marry whomever I want.'

'Is there someone you *want* to marry?' The notion clawed Luisa back from the brink of surrendering to his caress.

'Don't worry, Luisa.' His face loomed closer. 'You're not coming between me and the love of my life.'

'So there's no one special?' It confirmed his cold-blooded approach to marriage. But right now, dazzled by his brilliant stare, lulled by his rhythmic caress and the encompassing heat of his body, Luisa couldn't scrape the energy to be outraged. She felt...distanced from pain. Who'd have thought she'd find solace in Raul's embrace? There was unexpected pleasure in the sense that, for this moment at least, they could be frank.

'No one who matters.' His warm breath caressed her face and she struggled to find the anger that had burned within her before. Surely she shouldn't enjoy being here, with him.

'You really are ruthless, aren't you?' Her tone was conversational, curious, rather than accusing.

It was as if, after the shock of her accident, she floated on another plane where all that mattered was that she was safe in Raul's strong arms.

He shifted and she found her head lolling against his shoulder, his body cradling hers. She almost sighed at how good that felt. She felt boneless, like a cat being stroked in the sun.

'If you mean that I plan to get what I want, then yes.' His lips curved in a smile that held something other than humour. His intense focus reminded her of the way he'd watched her in Paris. Heat filled her.

'Have you always managed to get your own way?' She should protest about how he held her but it felt so good and Luisa liked this new, unreal world where she and Raul weren't at daggers drawn. Where that fragile connection shimmered in the still air.

He shook his head. 'Far from it. I was anything but spoiled. My mother died in childbirth and my father was impatient with children.'

Her heart clenched. No wonder Raul was so self-sufficient. She stared up at his perfectly sculpted mouth, just made for reducing women to mindless adoration.

'But as an adult. With women, I bet you've always—'

'Luisa.' The hand at her jaw slid round to thread through her hair and hold the back of her head. His eyes gleamed with an inner fire. 'You're talking too much.'

She watched those lips descend in slow motion. As if he gave her a chance to pull free. Or to savour their impending kiss. Excitement raced through her.

By the time his mouth covered hers Luisa's breath had

stalled, her lips opening to meet his, her pulse an insistent, urgent beat.

Their kiss was slow, a leisurely giving and receiving of pleasure. Delight swamped her in a warm, sultry wave. This wasn't like the forceful, hungry passion they'd shared in Paris.

A voice in her head tried to point out that in Paris they'd shared nothing. Raul hadn't felt anything.

But Paris seemed so far away.

Here, now, this felt like something shared. Something offered and accepted. Not dominance or submission. Not demand or acquiescence, but something utterly, satisfyingly mutual.

Luisa slipped an arm around his waist, revelling in how his muscles tensed then relaxed to her touch, testament to the leashed power of the man caressing her so gently. The realisation heightened her pleasure.

His tongue curled against hers as he drew her deeper into his mouth and the little voice of sanity subsided, overwhelmed by the magic Raul wove with his kiss, his big body, his tenderness.

Desire unfurled within her like a bud opening to the sunlight. Tendrils spread low to the feminine hollow between her legs. Up to her breasts that tingled as he pulled her closer, as if to absorb her into his body.

Her other hand rose to splay across his neck, discovering the pulse thudding heavily at his jaw. Then up to tangle in the rough silk of his hair.

Raul growled at the back of his throat. The raw sound of pleasure thrilled across her skin and sent heat plunging through her.

The languor that had held her spellbound dissipated and she wriggled against him, wanting more. The tingle of sensation at her hardening nipples became a prickle of need. The lavish, slow swirling eddy of delight in her belly grew more urgent.

Then, abruptly, he pulled back. Just enough for her to see his face. Stunned, it took a moment to read the heat in his hooded gaze and realise he was breathing heavily.

He grasped her wrist and tugged it down, holding it securely away from him.

'Next time—' his nostrils flared as he drew a deep breath '—if you want a tour, ask me. I'll arrange to come with you or have someone guide you. Agreed?'

Silently Luisa nodded, her mind abuzz, her world rocked out of kilter. Could she blame shock for the fact that she wanted to fall back into the arms of the man she'd been so sure she detested?

Two weeks later, in conversation with a gallery curator, Raul found his gaze straying to Luisa. She stood before a display of botanical studies, talking to the junior curator who'd organised the exhibit.

Raul's gaze slid appreciatively up her slender legs. It was the first time he'd seen her in a dress and he couldn't keep his eyes off her. Especially when she smiled at her companion with all the warmth of her sunny homeland.

The impact was stunning. Heat flickered along his veins and pooled in his groin.

She was blossoming into a lovely woman. That had to explain why she'd been knotting his belly with thwarted desire since Paris.

And why he'd succumbed to temptation and kissed her in the tower. His pulse jumped and a spike of something like fear drove through his chest at the memory of her sprawled out over that fatal drop. The need to hold her and not release her had been unstoppable. The hunger for another sweet taste of her lips inexplicable.

It disturbed him, the force of this unexpected attraction.

She was utterly unlike his usual companions. She was unpolished, preferring flats to high heels and avoiding even the simplest of her inherited jewellery. She had a habit of talking to anyone, particularly the staff, rather than to VIPs. He sensed she'd be as happy chatting to the gardeners as attending a glitzy premiere occasion.

Yet his heart lifted when he was with her.

He told himself that was sentimental twaddle. Yet there was definitely *something* about his bride-to-be.

Raul shook his head. Didn't he prefer his women sophisticated, assured and sexy?

Why did Luisa infiltrate his thoughts at every turn? Why had he found it so hard to release her that day in the tower? Or to pursue his own busy agenda while she began her lessons in language, etiquette, history and culture?

Because he wanted her. And, almost as much as he wanted her, he wanted her company.

Raul turned to his companion. 'Could the Princess and I have time alone to view the rest of the exhibition?'

The curator agreed enthusiastically. Such interest boded well. Two minutes later Raul and Luisa were alone. Even the guard at the door discreetly melted into an adjoining space.

'Thank you.' She turned to him and he saw her eyes were overbright. His heart thumped an unfamiliar beat and his hand closed automatically over hers.

'Are you OK?' He'd thought to please her with this visit, not upset her. Show her she *did* have a connection with his homeland.

'I didn't expect to see my mum's work on show. It was a lovely surprise.'

Raul shrugged. 'She was a talented artist. It's a shame she didn't continue her botanical painting.'

Luisa looked away. 'She dabbled but she said it was a discipline that needed dedication. She couldn't give that. Not with the farm.'

He nodded. It was clear what a toll that place had taken on Luisa's family. Her mother should have more than early works on display. She would have if she'd not embraced a life of hardship. All for the supposed love of a man who could give her so little.

People were fools, falling for the fantasy of love.

So-called love was an illusion. A trap for the unwary. Hadn't he learnt that to his cost?

'It was kind of you to bring me.' She touched his sleeve and looked up from under her lashes in an unconsciously provocative way that made heat curl in his gut. 'Lukas told me you rarely have time for such things, especially now.'

'It was nothing. It's been a while since I visited and there were issues to discuss.' The last thing he needed was for her to get the idea he'd changed his schedule for her. Even if it was true.

Luisa had been stoically uncomplaining through her first weeks in Maritz. Yet the change must be difficult for her. Despite her heavy tuition schedule he'd often glanced up from a meeting to see her wandering in the gardens and he had the discomfiting notion she was lonely, despite her ever-widening acquaintance.

Guilt blanketed him. She was here because of him, his country, his needs. What did she personally get out of it?

She wasn't interested in riches or prestige. The only money she wanted was to save her friends.

His lips twisted. She didn't see *him* as a prize, even if she couldn't conceal the passion that flared when he kissed her. Luisa Hardwicke was a salutary lesson to his ego.

'I had no idea Mum's work was so well regarded.' She turned to examine a delicate drawing of a mountain wildflower and he followed, not wanting to lose the warmth of her hand on his arm.

'Tell me about her.'

Luisa swung round. 'Why?'

He shrugged, making light of his sudden need to understand Luisa's family, and her. 'She must have been strong to have stood up to your grandfather.'

Luisa grimaced. 'Maybe it's a family trait.'

'Sorry?'

She shook her head. 'I thought she was remarkable. And so did my dad.'

Raul threaded his fingers through hers, pleased when she didn't pull away. 'Tell me.'

For a long moment she regarded him. Then she seemed to make up her mind. 'She was like other mums. Hard working, making do, running a household and doing the books. Always busy.' Luisa paused. 'She made the best cinnamon Christmas biscuits and she gave the warmest hugs—guaranteed to make you feel better every time. She loved roses and had an eye for fashion, even if we couldn't afford to buy it.'

Luisa moved to the next picture and he followed. 'She hated ironing and she *detested* getting up early.'

'Not suited to be a farmer's wife then.' The change from palace to dairy must have been hard. Had the marriage been a disaster? He frowned. It didn't sound so.

Luisa laughed, a rich, lilting chuckle and Raul's senses stirred. 'That's what Dad used to say. He'd shake his head and pretend to be scared she'd go back to her glamorous world. Mum would smile that special smile she saved for him and say she couldn't possibly leave till she mastered the art of cooking sponge cakes as well as my aunt. Dad would say no one could ever make sponges like Mary, so Mum would just have to stay for ever. Then he'd kiss her.'

Raul felt the delicate tremor in her hand and watched a wistful smile flit across Luisa's features. He knew an unaccountable desire to experience what she had. The warmth, the love. A childhood of cinnamon biscuits and hugs. How different from his own upbringing!

'But how did it work?' He found himself curious. 'They were so different.'

She shrugged. 'They came from different worlds but they made their own together. Dad said she made him feel like a king. Mum always said he made her feel more like a princess than she'd ever felt living in a palace.' Luisa swung to face him. 'Life with my grandfather wasn't pleasant. He tried to force her into marrying someone she detested, just to cement a deal. There was no laughter, no fun. Not like in our home.'

Someone she detested. Did Raul fit that category for Luisa? He told himself the country must come first, yet he couldn't squash regret.

'They were in love; that was the secret.'

It didn't take a genius to know that was what Luisa had wanted for herself. Till he'd come along.

Never before had Raul's duty seemed so onerous. He was doomed to disappoint her. He didn't even believe in love. He'd never experienced it.

'But she loved it here.' Luisa turned to him, her smile a shade too bright. 'Mum wanted to bring us one day to see it.'

'I'm glad.' He paused, clasping her hand more firmly. 'In time I hope you come to love it too. It's a special place. There are no people like Maritzians.'

'You're not biased, are you?'

'Surely that's my prerogative.' He led her towards the rest of the exhibition, regaling her with a traditional local story. It surprised him how much he wanted to hear her laugh again.

Raul strode swiftly to his study. There was a crushing amount of work to do and, though the unrest in the provinces had abated a little, he couldn't afford to be complacent.

Yet the wedding tomorrow, a small affair since the nation was in mourning for his father, would pave the way for his coronation and go a long way to solving his problems.

Taking his bride to bed would go a long way towards easing the permanent ache in his groin.

Anticipation pulsed in his blood at the thought of his wedding night to come. His desire for Luisa grew daily.

The more time he spent with his bride-to-be the more she fascinated him. She was vibrant, engaging, determinedly independent and down-to-earth. Different from every other woman he knew.

Even now he never knew what to expect from her.

Lukas approached as he reached the study.

'Your Highness.' He fell into step beside Raul.

'Yes? Am I late for my meeting?'

'No, not that.' His secretary hesitated, his mouth turning down. 'You have a visitor. I wanted to warn—'

'Raul. Darling!' The husky female voice came from the

door ahead. For one shattered instant Raul felt his feet rivet to the floor as shock vibrated through him. His hands clenched into fists. Then, bracing himself, he slowly approached the blonde draped in the doorway.

'This is unexpected, Ana. What are you doing here?'

'Surely you didn't expect me to miss your wedding, darling?' She straightened and lifted her head, her lips a crimson pout. 'Your invitation didn't reach me. Luckily I heard about it on the grapevine.'

He stopped a metre away, distaste prickling his skin. Foolishly, he'd thought he'd seen the last of her, for the time being at least.

They weren't in public so there was no need for a courteous bow. And she could wait till hell froze over before he took up the invitation implicit in that pout.

Not when she was the woman who eight years ago had dragged him to hell.

CHAPTER SEVEN

'LUISA, you look so lovely!' Tamsin said. 'This pearly cream is wonderful with the golden tone of your skin.'

'You think so?' Luisa stood stiffly, uncomfortable in the full length gown of silk. The fitted bodice covered with cobweb-fine hand-made lace. The diadem of finely wrought gold and pearls.

The bridal dress showcased the finest traditional Maritzian products. Lace from one province. Hand woven silk from another. The exquisite filigree gold choker necklace that made her throat seem elegant and impossibly fragile was by craftsmen in yet another province. Beaded slippers from still another.

Only the bride hadn't been involved in the design of her wedding clothes.

Gingerly Luisa turned to the mirror, feeling a fraud under the weight of this charade.

Yet the image awaiting her took her breath away. Could that really be *her*? A woman who till recently had spent her days in jeans and gumboots?

'You look like a fairy princess.' Tamsin shook a fold of embossed silk so the flaring skirt draped perfectly.

'I don't feel like it.' Nausea churned in Luisa's stomach. It was only through sheer willpower that she'd nibbled at a fruit platter for lunch. She whose appetite was always healthy!

'Believe me.' Tamsin clasped her hand briefly and smiled. 'You'll take everyone's breath away. Especially Raul. He won't be able to take his eyes off you.'

Luisa saw the other woman's secret smile and wondered if she was thinking of her recent marriage to Prince Alaric, Raul's distant cousin. It was clear that the big man with the steely jaw and face almost as handsome as Raul's was deeply in love with his new English wife.

For a moment Luisa let herself imagine what it would be like to marry for love. Burnt so badly years ago, she'd buried herself on the farm, shunning any hint of male interest. She'd longed to experience true love but had she been too craven to open herself to the possibility?

The day Raul had saved her from falling and kissed her so tenderly she'd allowed herself to be swept along by his deep voice, his gentle hands and the unstoppable cravings that welled at his touch.

For one fragile interlude she'd longed to believe something warm and special could grow from their union.

Then there was his unexpected kindness, taking her to see her mother's work.

But the fantasy was too painful. It scraped too close to the bone for a woman who'd been chosen, not for love or respect. Not even for convenience. But because Raul had no other option!

'It's good of you to help me get ready.' She sent a shaky smile in Tamsin's direction. Though this wasn't a romantic match it was her wedding day. The day women looked to their mother for support.

Luisa had never missed her mum more.

'It will be all right.' Again Tamsin took her hand, chafing warmth into it. 'I know how daunting it is marrying into a new world. Marrying royalty. But Raul will look after you. He's like my Alaric. Strong and protective.' She sent a speculative glance at Luisa. 'And I suspect behind that well bred calm, very passionate.'

Heat roared through Luisa's cheeks, banishing the chill that had frozen her all day.

Tamsin giggled, blushing herself. 'Sorry. I didn't mean to

embarrass you. It's just sometimes I feel like pinching myself. It all seems so unreal!'

'I know what you mean.' Tamsin was an outsider too—a commoner and a foreigner who'd married her prince in a love match that had intrigued everyone. But Tamsin had fallen in love. Luisa would face her royal marriage and the weight of public expectation without love to cushion the shock. Their circumstances were so different.

'I'm glad you're here,' she added, grateful to this initially reserved but warm-hearted woman.

'So am I! And when you settle in, after your honeymoon, I hope we can spend more time together.'

Luisa nodded, not bothering to disabuse her. Raul was a workaholic. That was why the trip to the gallery had been such a lovely surprise. He wouldn't take time off for a honeymoon. Not with a wife he didn't really want.

A wife who was simply a solution to a problem.

A cold lump of lead settled in the pit of her belly as a soft knock sounded on the door.

'It's time, Your Highness.'

The music swelled and the massive doors swung open and Luisa stepped over the threshold into the castle chapel.

Multicoloured streams of light shone through ancient windows. A cloying wave of fragrance hit. Hothouse flowers and incense and a multitude of perfumes. Hundreds of faces turned to stare. She didn't know a single one.

A rising tide of panic clawed at her, urging her to turn tail and run, as fast and as far as she could. Her heart slammed against her ribs and her knees shook.

She faltered, her hand curling into Alaric's sleeve. He covered her hand with his and leaned close. 'Luisa?'

'This is a *small* wedding?' Dazed, she saw heraldic banners, including some of the Maritzian red dragon, streaming from the lofty ceiling. The crowd murmured and it sounded like a roar.

'Courage, little one. It'll soon be over.' He paced forward

and she had no option but to follow. 'Tamsin and I have a bet on who spots the most absurd hat. Weddings incite women to wear the most monstrous things on their heads, don't you think?'

His *sotto voce* patter continued all the way down the aisle, almost distracting her from the throng of hungry-eyed guests. Watching. Judging. Finding her wanting.

Suddenly she caught a smile. Tamsin, in muted gold, giving her an encouraging nod. Behind her was another woman, platinum blonde, dripping jewels yet sour-mouthed.

Then, abruptly, they were at the end of the aisle. Bands of steel squeezed the breath from her lungs as, with a sense of inescapable inevitability, she turned her head towards the dark figure she'd avoided since she entered.

Raul, tall and heart-stoppingly handsome in a uniform of scarlet and black that made him look like the model for Prince Charming.

Something in her chest rose and swelled. Was it possible that perhaps they could make this work? The other day they'd surely started building a fragile relationship.

Then she read his expression. Austere, proud, stern. Not a scintilla of pleasure. A complete absence of anything that might one day turn into love. His mouth was a stern line, his jaw chiselled rock.

She blinked quickly, hating herself because even now, faced with his indifference, she yearned for the tenderness he'd begun to show her.

How could she? She knew what she was to him. How could she be so weak as to want the impossible?

Luisa gulped. It was like swallowing shards of glass.

Just as well she hadn't allowed herself to pretend he reciprocated her inconvenient attraction.

Her hand tightened, talon-like as Alaric ushered her forward. But Raul took her hand in his, his other hand at her elbow as she swayed.

She had to quell this anxiety. She'd *agreed* to this. She looked away, to the mass of flowers by the altar: a riot of roses, orange blossom and lilies. Their scent was too pungent for her roiling stomach.

The priest spoke but Luisa didn't listen. She was thinking that at home lilies were traditional for funerals.

'Who *is* that woman?' Luisa watched the petite platinum blonde lean into Raul, her hand possessive on his arm. Her scarlet dress matched his jacket perfectly and her plunging neckline showed a stunning cleavage. She smiled up, her face hardly recognisable as the one that had scowled at Luisa in the chapel.

'She wasn't in the reception line,' Luisa added.

Raul stood on the other side of the reception room, his back to Luisa, but from here she'd almost swear the woman flirted with him. A spike of heat roared through her. Heat and anger. 'Is she an ex-girlfriend?'

Beside her Tamsin spluttered, choking on champagne.

'Are you OK?'

Tamsin waved her away. 'I inhaled some bubbles. I'm not used to champagne.'

Luisa knew the feeling. This evening she'd sipped some, standing beside Raul for a formal toast. The wine had tickled her senses and tingled all the way down her throat. But it was Raul's presence beside her, like a wall of living heat, that had made her giddy. His stern expression had eased for a moment and his lips had curved in a heady smile as he toasted her. The impact had knocked her for six and Luisa had felt as if she were floating.

As if this were a real wedding and she a bride smitten with her handsome husband! Instead of a woman blackmailed into cooperating. That still rankled.

Luisa stiffened. It scared her that Raul affected her so. That she might be jealous of the woman pawing at his jacket. It should be impossible, yet...

'You don't know her?'

Finally Tamsin looked up. A flush tinted her cheeks.

'Tamsin?' Her new friend's expression made Luisa tense.

'The woman with Raul? No one you need worry about.' The words came out in a rush. 'She lives in the US now.'

'But who *is* she?'

Tamsin took another quick sip of wine. 'That's Ana. Raul's stepmother.'

Stepmother?

'But she's too young!' She didn't act like a stepmother. The other woman was flirting outrageously. Luisa's only consolation came from the fact Raul stood as stiffly as he had through the wedding ceremony, though he inclined his head as if listening intently.

'I think she and Raul are about the same age.'

Through her shock Luisa heard Tamsin's intense discomfort. She saw Tamsin's gaze dart away as if seeking a diversion and uneasiness stirred.

Intuition told her there was something Tamsin wasn't saying. Luisa turned back, finally noticing how the guests kept their distance from the pair. No one had approached Raul since his stepmother had claimed his attention but they all watched speculatively. An undercurrent of whispers eddied around them.

The frisson of uneasiness grew to stark suspicion.

No! Luisa refused to draw conclusions about Raul's relationships. No matter what her eyes told her.

Yet she couldn't stifle a feeling of betrayal.

As if sensing her scrutiny, Raul turned sharply, his gaze skewering her. Fire seared her blood and she felt as if she'd been caught out spying on him.

But she had every right to be here. This was *her* wedding reception. *Her* day. Even if it wasn't her choice.

Hysterical laughter bubbled in her throat. Today should be the happiest day of her life!

If she didn't laugh at the absurdity surely she'd cry.

Holding Raul's eyes, she lifted her chin and downed the rest of her champagne.

'If you'll excuse me, Tamsin, I'd better introduce myself to my mother-in-law.' Luisa passed her glass to a waiter and picked up her skirts, grateful now for the formal dress that kept her posture perfect and made guests move aside as she stalked forward.

She was magnificent. She cut a swathe through the crowd as if it didn't exist, her eyes locked with his.

A pulse of heat thudded deep in his belly at the sight of her: jaw angled, eyes glittering, chest swelling against the demure V neckline. She skimmed across the polished floor, her train sweeping magnificently behind her. Tiny bursts of fire peeped from beneath her hem as her jewel-encrusted slippers caught the light. It was as if she set off sparks with each step.

Absently Raul brushed Ana's clawing hand away. He'd done what he had to—accepted her presence publicly. But he'd had enough.

He'd had enough of her eight years ago!

He barely registered her protest as he strode instead towards the woman he'd just married and pleasure surged.

All day tension had ridden him. Worries for the state. Fury at Ana's return. Discomfort at the idea of marrying. Guilt at forcing Luisa's hand. The need to bury his thoughts deep behind a cloak of royal calm. Now the tension morphed into something that had nothing to do with concerns and everything to do with his long-suppressed needs.

And with the challenge he read in his bride's expression, her posture, her firmed lips.

Her eyes flashed azure fire and heat danced in his veins. He drew a breath, the first free breath all day.

He'd done his duty in marrying. Now he wanted to forget about duty, about diplomacy and building bridges with intransigent politicians and soothing the bruised egos of his father's cronies. About his own doubts.

He wanted…Luisa.

A smile cracked his carefully schooled features.

'Luisa, you look enchanting.' Her pace propelled her forward and he took full advantage, stepping before her at the last moment and putting a hand to her waist, ostensibly to steady her. Through the lace and silk he felt warmth and lithe muscle and the deep exhalation of her breath.

He grasped her other hand in his and lifted it to his mouth. Her eyes blazed and he almost smiled at the provocation in her glare. Instead he turned her hand and pressed his lips to her wrist. He heard her breath catch and a satisfying tremor rippled through her. Slowly he moved his mouth, kissing her palm and touching his tongue to the erogenous zone at its centre.

Her eyes widened and he felt pleasure tug through his belly. She tried to draw her hand away but he held her.

'Aren't you going to introduce me to your mother?'

He read the doubt and hurt pride in her eyes and silently applauded her front.

'You mean my father's second wife. Not my mother.'

'My mistake.' She bit the words out precisely with her even white teeth. 'You two looked so close…'

Little cat.

This was what he'd missed. Much as he enjoyed having his plans go smoothly and the tantalising sense of closeness he'd experienced with Luisa now and then, he'd missed her vibrancy. From the first she'd sparked with energy and defiance. She'd obstructed him and argued and defied him. Even consenting to wed she'd been proud as an empress.

He enjoyed her sassiness when she stood up to him. He'd grown accustomed to fireworks. He enjoyed them more than he'd thought possible. Especially when it wasn't argument that fuelled the conflagration.

Even the hint of jealousy in her tone pleased him. Did her desire match his? A bolt of excitement shot through him. He recalled her passion, the way she melted in his arms. How she watched him when she thought he didn't see.

He leaned forward and whispered, 'I'm not going to introduce her. You wouldn't like her.'

She gaped at his honesty. He wanted to kiss those lush lips till she forgot how to speak. He wanted that sizzling energy channelled in more satisfying directions.

Urgent heat swirled in his loins as he visualised it.

'Why not?' Luisa looked stunned.

'Because she's not at all nice.' It surprised him how much pleasure there was in saying it out loud, even if in a murmur for Luisa's ears alone. How long he'd been constrained by the need to keep up appearances!

'But surely I need to meet her.'

'Hardly. She's leaving for LA tonight. Grabbing a lift with her newest boyfriend, a Hollywood producer.'

Raul didn't even feel the usual simmering anger. Ana couldn't be bothered to feign mourning for her dead husband. Their marriage had been a farce, his smitten father turning a blind eye to anything in his young wife's behaviour that might dent his royal pride.

Raul was tired of pretending his father's marriage was anything but a sham. His father was dead and his ego couldn't be battered any more. Ana didn't deserve more than the merest observance of courtesy. Her attempt just now to wheedle more cash from the royal coffers had been expected but her timing had surprised even Raul, who'd believed himself inured to her grasping ways.

'Come,' he said, turning Luisa with him towards the dais where the royal throne rested. She grabbed her wide skirts and followed. The scent of lavender that accompanied her movements was refreshing after Ana's cloying perfume. He breathed deep and helped his wife up the steps.

The flush colouring Luisa's cheeks was charming. His gaze descended her throat, gorgeous in its gold filigree and pearl choker, down to where her breasts rose and fell rapidly. His palms itched to touch.

Leaving the reception early would cause a stir. But he wasn't in the mood to worry about protocol. After years acceding to duty and convention, trying to compensate for the trauma of earlier royal scandal, Raul chose for the first time to flout tradition.

It felt good. The gossips could go hang.

He reached for his wife's hand, enjoying the way it fitted his own so neatly. Enjoying her presence beside him.

'Highnesses, ladies and gentlemen.' Raul addressed the assembly. When he'd finished the sound of clapping made him turn. There were Alaric and Tamsin, smiling broadly. The applause spread.

Raul raised a hand in acknowledgement, then turned to Luisa. 'It's time we left.'

Her eyes rounded but a moment later she conjured a smile and a wave for their audience. She really was superb.

A moment later Raul ushered her out through the double doors behind the throne, held open by footmen.

Then they were walking down the private corridor, her hand still in his. The doors closed behind them, muting the swell of applause.

Satisfaction filled him. He was alone with his bride.

It happened so quickly Luisa was dazed as he led her through the labyrinth of corridors.

Only two things were real. Raul's warm hand enfolding hers and the fact she was married. Even in the chapel it hadn't seemed real. But hearing Raul tell their guests to enjoy their wedding hospitality, seeing the curiosity, the goodwill, even the envy on some of the faces staring up at her, it had suddenly hit.

She'd bound herself to this man. No turning back.

Her spurt of indignation over his stepmother dwindled. Now she felt only shock.

Raul's hand tightened and sensation streaked through her.

No, she felt more than shock. A tiny bud of something curled tight inside. Something that kept her hand in his even when she knew she should withdraw it. Something that shortened her breath as Raul halted before an unfamiliar door then stood aside, waiting for her to precede him.

She stepped in then halted. She shouldn't be here in his private apartments.

The door closed, silence enveloping them. Her breathing was overloud as she sought for something to say.

'Come.' A hand at her elbow propelled her forward. 'You need food. You ate nothing at the reception.'

'How do you know?' For much of the reception they'd been on opposite sides of the room.

'I watched you.'

She started, stunned at the idea of Raul concentrating on her all the time he'd chatted with dignitaries. The notion sent a ribbon of heat through her.

'And you had just one glass of champagne.'

Her gaze melded with his. The kindling heat she saw made her look hastily away.

'Maybe a bite of something would be a good idea.' Then she'd go. She felt too aware of him beside her.

Aware of herself too, in a new, unsettling way. Of the swish of rich fabric around her legs as she moved. Of the tight clasp of the fitted bodice at her waist and breasts as she struggled to draw in oxygen. The fabric of her bra seemed suddenly abrasive, drawing her nipples to taut peaks.

She stepped away, only to stop again abruptly. Her eyes widened. 'This looks…intimate.' It sounded like an accusation.

'Does it matter?'

'Of course it matters!' Luisa bit her lip at her high pitched response. She sounded like a schoolgirl, not a mature woman.

A low table was drawn up before a massive sofa long enough for even Raul to recline full length. Velvet cushions made it look plush and inviting. A foil-topped bottle nestled in a silver cooler. Cold lobster lay sumptuously arrayed beside a bowl of fresh ice that cradled gleaming beads of caviar.

Luisa stepped back abruptly, only to find Raul behind her. She spun round, hands planted on his chest as if to ward him off. So why did her fingers curl into his jacket?

Hurriedly she retreated. 'Is this someone's idea of a joke? It's like a clichéd set for a seduction.'

'You don't like lobster?'

'Well, yes.' She'd only tried it here in the castle and had loved every mouthful.

'Or fruit?' He gestured and she spied a platter of her favourite fruits: peaches and cherries and glowing navel oranges. Beside them was a bowl of fresh berries. Beyond that a basket of bread rolls—not the fine dinner rolls that graced the royal table but the malty whole-grain bread, thick with seeds, that she'd discovered when she'd invited herself to the kitchens. Traditional peasant fare, she was told. The best bread she'd tasted.

Luisa leaned closer. Beyond that were fat curls of butter, a board of cheeses and a silver bowl of cashews. Her favourites.

A familiar jar at the end of the table caught her eye. Mary's spidery writing on the label: raspberry jam.

Luisa blinked hard, her pulse thudding. She reached out and stroked the thick glass jar of her aunt's home-made jam, the jam she'd been helping make since she was a child. A taste of home. Luisa could barely believe he'd taken the trouble to ask Mary for this.

Raul hadn't just clapped his hands and ordered a feast. This was just for her. Something special. His unexpected thoughtfulness blindsided her.

'How did you...?' Her throat closed on emotion.

'How did I know you prefer fruit to gateaux, cheeses to chocolate?'

Shaken, Luisa turned. He stood so close she saw again that sparkle of gold in his dark green gaze.

'Because I notice everything about you.' His voice was deliciously deep. 'You are my wife now. I want you to be happy.' The warmth in his tone made her tremble inside.

Not even to herself would she admit how those words eased her wounded soul.

'But not like *this*.' Her wide gesture encompassed the sofa, the crystal flutes, the whole seductive scene. 'We agreed to a marriage of convenience!'

Was she trying to convince herself or him? From the

moment she'd stepped into his chamber she'd had the delicious sense of walking on a knife-edge of excitement.

Raul said nothing. Yet his look heated her skin. His mouth
was a sensual line of temptation she had to resist.

Luisa's heart drummed an urgent tattoo. Part of her wanted
nothing more than to touch him. To feel his power beneath her
hand. That was why she forced her hands behind her back and
kept them there.

Did he read her desire? His brilliant green eyes were hot
with an inner blaze and Luisa realised how close she came to
being singed.

'We married for legal reasons.' Her words were slurred
because her tongue was glued to the roof of her mouth. 'So
you can inherit. Remember?'

'I remember.' His voice was low, resonating through her
body to places she didn't know existed before. 'I remember
how it felt to kiss you too. Do you recall that, Luisa? The fire
between us? The need?'

She shook her head and her veil swirled between them. It
snagged on the gold braiding that marched across his tunic,
emphasising the breadth of his chest.

'It wasn't like that. You just...'

Her throat closed as he untangled her veil. His fingers
were centimetres from her breast and she sucked her breath
in, trying not to think of him touching her there.

But breathing meant movement. Her breast brushed his
hand. She gasped as sensation pierced her and she trembled.

He didn't look up but she saw his lips curve.

'I'm not some passing amusement.' She gritted her teeth,
trying not to breathe too heavily.

'I never thought you were. I take you much too seriously
for that.' His eyes snared hers and she forgot about breathing.
His hands dropped away to hold hers, warm and firm. 'You
are my bride. You'll be the mother of my children. I don't take
you lightly at all.'

His mouth curved up in the sort of smile mothers had

warned their daughters about for centuries. Luisa felt its impact like a judder of power right down to the soles of her feet.

Her heart raced—in indignation she assured herself. Yet indignation had nothing to do with the hunger coiling inside or the febrile heat flooding her body.

'I never agreed to share your bed.'

She tried to summon anger but discovered instead a jittery thrill of dangerous excitement.

'You don't want children?' His brows rose.

'Of course I want—' She stopped and tried to harness her skittering thoughts. 'One day.' Once she'd dreamed of a family. But with Raul? She'd thought this a paper marriage. Or had she deliberately deceived herself? Heat poured across her skin and eddied deep in her womb.

The trouble was he tempted her with the very thing she'd tried unsuccessfully to deny wanting: him. From the first she'd been unable to prevent herself responding to him at the most basic level.

He took desire for granted but for her it was momentous. Life-changing. She'd learnt distrust too young.

His smile would reduce a lesser woman to a puddle of longing. Luisa it merely turned to jelly. Her knees gave way with a suddenness that astounded her.

Why didn't it surprise her when he swept her up against his chest in one fluid, easy move?

'I never said…'

He crossed the room as if she weighed nothing, entering another chamber and kicking shut the door. This room held a wide bed that seemed to stretch for hectares. The sight of it dried her mouth.

He lowered her and Luisa shut her eyes, wishing she didn't delight in the friction of each slow, tormenting centimetre as she slid against him.

'I thought you had spirit, Luisa. Why are you afraid?' His tone sharpened. 'Did someone hurt you?'

Her eyes snapped open at his husky anger.

'No. I wasn't hurt.' Not physically at least.

Yet he was right. She was afraid: of these new overwhelming feelings. Afraid she'd lose herself if she gave in to this longing. That it was a betrayal of her moral code—giving herself to a man she didn't love.

Yet standing here, bereft now of his touch, feeling the heat of his breath on her face and his body so close, desire twisted deep. Hunger for an intimacy she'd never had. Would never have with love, not now she'd given herself in a cold, practical bargain.

He'd robbed her of that chance.

The realisation was an icy hand on her heart.

She'd never experience true love. Would never have what her parents had shared. That was what she'd always hoped for, especially after the disaster of her first romance.

The knowledge doused her fears and made her angry as never before. Scorching fury rose, stronger than regret or doubt.

Raul had taken so much from her.

'Is it so wrong to find pleasure together?' He voiced the thoughts that already ran, pure temptation, through her head. 'You disappoint me, Luisa. I thought you woman enough to admit what you feel.'

Luisa stared up into his hot gaze and wanted nothing more than to wipe away his smug self-satisfaction. For him desire was easy. No longing for love. No doubts or fears.

A tumble of images cascaded in her head. Turning on her heel and storming out. Or walking serenely, with a cool pitying expression on her face as she left him behind. None of them did justice to the roiling tide of emotion he'd unleashed.

Instead Luisa stepped in, slamming hard against his body. She took his face in her palms and kissed him full on the mouth. She leaned in to him till, with a flurry of billowing silk, they collapsed onto the bed.

CHAPTER EIGHT

It was like holding a flame, or a bolt of lightning.

Luisa was all urgent energy. Her touch, her body, igniting explosions in his blood.

Sensation speared through him. White light flickered behind his eyelids as she pushed her tongue into his mouth in an angry, urgent mating. There was little finesse but her hunger incited the most possessive urges.

She grabbed his scalp as if to imprison him with her scorching passion.

Raul welcomed it, meeting her questing tongue in a desperate kiss that was more like a battle for supremacy than a caress.

He felt alive as never before, caught by a throbbing force that drove every thought from his head but one.

The need for Luisa. Now.

He growled in his throat as he lashed one arm around her waist and the other lower, clamping his hand on her bunched skirts to pull her tight against his groin as he sank back on the wide bed. He was on fire.

Splayed over him, she wriggled as if she too couldn't get close enough. He pushed his hips up and felt her legs slide satisfyingly wide to surround him.

Yes!

It was as if she'd smashed the lock on his self-control. All those primitive urges that he, as a civilised man, had learned to suppress, roared to the surface, stripped bare by this woman who kissed as if she hated him.

He knew passion, used it as a release from the difficulties of life under the spotlight. But never had it been this blistering current of untrammelled power.

Again he rocked up into her encompassing heat and she pushed down to meet him with a jerky movement that spoke of need rather than grace.

Raul scrabbled at the mass of her skirts, pulling it higher and higher around her back till finally he touched silky bare skin. His pulse throbbed in his throat and his groin simultaneously as he clamped both hands to the taut warm silk over her backside. He could almost swear flames crackled around them.

The sound of her cry, a wordless mew of encouragement against his mouth, notched the tension impossibly higher.

Holding her tight, he drew her pelvis to his in a circling movement and sparks ignited in his blood.

A moment later he had her on her back, a tumble of silk and lace and femininity. Hands around her slim waist, he tugged her higher up the bed with a strength born of urgency.

She was flushed, her eyes a narrow glitter of heaven, her lips open and inviting as she gulped in air. Her breasts strained against the tight bodice and he allowed himself a moment's diversion. He covered one breast with his hand, feeling her arch into his touch, her nipple a pebbled tease to his palm. He rotated his hand, squeezing gently and she groaned, her eyes slitting shut and her body moving restlessly.

With his other hand Raul was already busy scooping metres of silk up and away to uncover her calves, her thighs. But a man could do two things at once. He ducked his head and kissed her open-mouthed on the breast, drawing lace and silk and her hard little nipple against his tongue.

Her hands clamped his head close and her breath was a hiss of delight. Beneath him she twisted and bucked as if seeking the weight of his body on hers.

He'd never had a woman so wild for him. No games, no subtlety, just a devastating need that matched his own.

Such pure passion was liberating.

Raul let his hand skim up Luisa's thighs to her panties, pressing hard and discovering damp proof of her need. It was all the encouragement he required.

Seconds later he'd loosened his trousers and freed himself enough to slide his length against her hot apex in a move so arousing he had to pause and gather his scattered wits.

Luisa wouldn't wait. She circled her hips in hungry little movements that tore at the last vestige of his control.

Propped on one arm, Raul ripped away the delicate fabric of her panties and settled himself on her.

'Is this what you want?' His voice was thick, rough with desire and the promise of unsurpassed pleasure.

Azure fire blazed from her eyes. He read passion and something fierce and unfamiliar. But her body eased beneath him. She was enticingly soft, reassuringly strong and vibrating with erotic energy.

She panted for him yet he wanted to hear the words. Why, he had no idea.

He fitted one hand to her upthrust breast and felt her jolt beneath him.

'Tell me, Luisa.' He pushed against her, torturing himself as much as her with the luscious friction of body on body. 'What do you want?'

Her eyes widened and he felt himself sink into their brilliance. She rose, tugging his head down and her mouth took his, greedily, tongue swirling and plunging.

Raul struggled against the force of her ardour and his own pleasure. But it was too much. Too close.

With a muffled groan he gave in and reciprocated, tasting her, almost taming her mouth with his then retreating so the kiss became a mutual give and take of sensual combat.

Using his thighs, he nudged her legs wider and settled himself at her entrance. He slid one hand over blonde downy hair to find the nub of her pleasure. One stroke and she shivered. A second stroke and she shuddered.

'Raul!' His name was a tiny, breathless gasp that shattered his fragile control.

A moment later, his mouth claiming hers, he drove inside. Pressure screamed through him as tight, hot, silken walls enclosed him. Tighter than was surely possible. Raul felt her tremble around him, her raised thighs quaking against his hips.

Stunned, he made to draw back but Luisa fastened her hands in his hair and kissed him with a desperation that made his head swim. Or was that from the relief of finally being sheathed in her body?

She wrapped her legs around him and he sank deeper, lodging fully in exquisite pleasure. He braced himself as the trembling spread from her body to his, making his nape prickle and every muscle quake with tension.

It was no good. Stillness was impossible. Clamping his hands on her hips, he slid back, seeing stars behind closed eyelids as sensation rushed through him.

Another second and he thrust again, harder, longer, as he gave in to the force of a desire that had ridden him ever since that night in Paris.

'I'm sorry. I can't...' His words were swallowed by the roar of blood pounding in his ears.

Dimly he heard a cry rend the air. Luisa convulsed around him, tearing at his strength and his consciousness as he lost himself in delight.

Frantically his body pumped, driven by a force so strong only Luisa's gasps anchored him to reality. His movements crescendoed, wringing out every last vestige of white-hot pleasure, till, with lungs bursting and the world spinning away, Raul sank into oblivion.

Despite his weight on her, Luisa felt as if she were floating. Echoes of incredible pleasure shimmered through limbs taut with the aftershock of tension.

Finally she gathered the strength to move a fraction and let her legs, impossibly heavy, sink to the cushioned mattress. She felt the hint of an ache in untried muscles but even that felt satisfying. Her arms clasped Raul tight. She could barely breathe but the feel of him blanketing her was…comforting.

Stunned, she thought about opening her eyes, but the notion of reality intruding on the single most remarkable experience of her life stopped her.

Even now she couldn't put a name to the feelings that had burst out of nowhere when she'd confronted Raul at their wedding reception. Or when he'd dared her to make love with him. No…have sex with him.

She swallowed, trying to ignore the strange winded sensation in the region of her heart.

If that was having sex, what would making love be like?

How could something so glorious have come out of such turbulent emotions?

Luisa waited for shame to engulf her. For regret that she'd given herself to a man who, though her husband, didn't truly care for her, didn't love her.

Yes, there was regret. Sadness that she'd never know what it was like to be with a man she loved and who loved her.

Yet she couldn't hide from the fact that with Raul she'd felt…different, glorious, powerful. The words didn't do justice to the sensation of soaring, of life and excitement and pleasure bubbling through her veins when they'd come together. Even when they argued it was there, a hidden promise that egged her on to defy him.

What did it mean? Luisa's brow knotted as she tried to work through her feelings. But she was too dazed by the enormity of what had just happened. Thinking was too hard when simply lying here with Raul was so wonderful.

A knuckle gently grazed her brow. 'Don't frown. It's not the end of the world.'

Luisa's eyes snapped open and she found herself staring into Raul's face. He looked as perplexed as she felt. A lock of dark hair tumbled over his brow, making him seem younger, more approachable. Her hand itched to brush it from his fore-head but, despite what they'd just shared, the act seemed too intimate.

He moved, easing his weight onto his elbow, and she flushed, realising they were still joined intimately. She looked away but he turned her head towards him.

'You didn't tell me.'

'Tell you what?' The lovely lax feeling of contentment vanished and her muscles tensed.

'That you hadn't done this before.' His beautiful mouth twisted.

Had it been that obvious? While the passion lasted it hadn't mattered to Luisa. All that counted was her need and the fact that Raul reciprocated with equal urgency. Had he been disappointed? Her stomach dived.

'Does it matter?' She kept her gaze fixed on his mouth rather than his knowing eyes.

His lips thinned. 'Of course it mattered. I would have made sure it was better for you.'

Her gaze flew up, colliding with an intense green stare. It was on the tip of her tongue to ask how it could possibly be better, but she managed to stop herself.

At the memory of what they'd done Luisa breathed deep, internal muscles clenching. To her shock she felt an answering throb inside as Raul stirred. His mouth tipped into a smile that was rueful and devastatingly glorious and Luisa's heartbeat picked up speed.

'I could do that now,' he offered. To her amazement, Luisa felt her body hum with answering desire. So soon!

It frightened her how easily he'd made her need him. How readily she responded. Despite his occasional devastating tenderness, to him she was a convenience.

If she tried she'd convince herself what they'd just done meant as little to her as it must to him.

She just had to try harder.

'I need to get up. This dress will be a mess.'

Abruptly he withdrew, his smile fading. Luisa bit her tongue rather than cry out for him not to move. Without his weight pressing on her she felt lost.

How could she miss his touch so soon?

Shakily she drew her crumpled skirts down over her nakedness while he stood and adjusted his trousers. She had to remember he was used to dealing with desire. With sex. For him it was nothing special.

'Here, let me.' He took her arm and drew her up to a sitting position.

Avoiding his eyes, Luisa looked down at her creased and rumpled silk. Her throat clogged. 'It's ruined.'

'Nonsense. It just needs a little attention. Don't worry, the palace has expert launderers.'

Shakily Luisa stroked the fabric, noticing a tear in the fine lace, feeling dampness at her bodice where Raul had suckled. What had seemed magnificent just minutes ago now seemed anything but. 'They'll know what we've done.'

'No one expects us to be celibate.' Once more he tilted her chin up. 'You shouldn't be ashamed of what we did.' He paused and she sensed he hesitated. 'Are you?'

Something passed between them, a surge of heat, a sense memory of passion. Luisa felt fire flicker in her belly. So, it wasn't over after all. It was still there, this...craving for his touch.

That was when she faced the truth. 'No, I'm not ashamed.' She wanted her husband still, again.

She shouldn't crave intimacy with the man who'd treated her so. Yet the feelings he unleashed subverted her pride.

'Good. Because I intend for it to happen often.' His hand slipped up to caress her cheek and she caught her breath at the gleaming promise in his look. 'Turn around and I'll help you out of that dress. You'll feel better after a bath.'

Luisa twisted sideways, telling herself she wasn't disappointed at his prosaic request.

It was only natural she'd enjoy sex with her virile, handsome husband. They were young and healthy. These...urges were to be expected. Yet she couldn't shake the feeling that nothing was quite that simple.

Luisa didn't understand her feelings. One minute he outraged her. The next he intrigued. He wasn't the sort of man she told herself she wanted, yet there were times when she liked him too much.

Perhaps she'd fallen for his expert seduction? He was vastly experienced and she a complete novice. Yet there'd been precious little seduction. He'd seemed as out of control as she. Luisa recalled the dazed look in his eyes and how he'd gasped an apology because he hadn't been able to hold back. As if she'd wanted him to!

Her lips curved and her thighs squeezed as satisfaction curled within her.

'Hold still while I get this veil.' The feel of his hands fumbling in her hair sent rivulets of heat through her. Finally he drew the veil aside and tossed it onto a plush chair, a stream of heirloom lace. A reminder, if she needed one, that they came from separate worlds. She couldn't imagine treating such a work of art so cavalierly.

Then she remembered how she'd thrown herself at him, heedless of the beautiful things she wore.

He brought out a side to her she didn't know.

The touch of Raul's fingers at her nape made her breath catch as the mattress dipped behind her.

'This will take a while.' The couturier had insisted on a myriad of buttons, each with its own tiny loop.

Raul sat close, his breath feathering her bare skin. She straightened, nipples tingling. In the silence she heard her breathing grow shallow.

'I wondered...'

'Yes?' She'd never heard Raul hesitant.

'Why were you so set against coming here? It wasn't just the prospect of marriage. From the first you were negative, instantly opposed to inheriting.'

'It bothers you that I didn't swoon at your feet?' Yet from the first Raul had got under her skin as no other.

'If I ever expected that, I know better now. Besides, I prefer you as you are.' Instead of annoyance, she thought she heard admiration in his voice.

Did her senses conspire to fool her?

His fingers brushed her back and her flesh drew tight. A coiling pulse began low in her belly. He devastated her defences. Luisa drew a sharp breath, seeking control.

'Won't you tell me?' His voice was a dark velvet caress.

She shut her eyes. What would it hurt?

'When I was sixteen my mother was diagnosed with a terminal illness. I looked after her.'

'I'm sorry. That must have been hard.'

She nodded, her throat tight. 'At least I was with her. But the point is, just before that some strangers came to the farm, wanting to talk to me. They were sent by my grandfather.' Even now she had to force that word out. The man didn't deserve the title.

'Not to see your mother?'

'No.' A sour taste flooded her mouth. 'His offer was for me alone. He invited me to live with him and learn to be a real princess.' She paused, clasping unsteady hands as she recalled the grandiose promises and the demands.

'At first I was excited. I was thrilled to see him, to be in his home. It was like a fairy tale. Even though he kept me busy at the palace, training me, he said, for when I'd be ready to take my proper place with him.'

'You actually came here? I didn't know.'

She nodded. 'No one did. Obviously I wasn't up to his high standards. But I was here long enough to get his measure and that of the people he mixed with. That put me off ever returning.' She laughed hollowly. 'I was naïve. It took a while to realise I was just a puppet to manipulate. No choices. No career. No control over my own destiny.'

The skimming touch of Raul's fingers was gentle, almost a caress. She knew a ridiculous desire to sink back against him.

'When news came of my mother's illness I saw him for what

he really was. He insisted I sever all links with my parents. He hated that my mother had walked out on the life he'd planned for her—a duty wife to some crony. He never forgave her. When I begged for help to get her better care, he was furious. According to him, she'd ceased to exist the moment she'd left her home.'

Luisa shuddered as she recalled the old man's vitriol. His cruelty.

'By marrying a commoner she'd diluted her aristocratic bloodlines. It was only his extreme generosity that enabled him to overlook my tainted birth and offer to take me in.'

A stream of low-voiced Maritzian cut the air. No mistaking its furious, violent edge.

'I knew he was old-fashioned.' Raul's voice was a lethal whisper. 'But that's just vicious.'

Luisa felt tears prickle, hearing his outrage and sympathy. It wrapped round her like a warm blanket.

She'd never told her parents. Couldn't bear to repeat it, though she suspected her mum had guessed some of it.

Relief filled her at finally spilling the awful truth.

'So you went back to the farm.'

'Mum needed me. And so did Dad. When she died it almost broke him.'

'Which is when you started taking responsibility for the co-op. I'm sorry, Luisa.'

She stiffened. 'There's nothing to be sorry for. I *wanted* to be with them.'

'I meant I'm sorry your first contact with Maritz was so poisonous. No wonder you hated the idea of the place.'

Her laugh was bitter. 'You can say that again. I thought the place full of the worst sort of people.'

'Not just your grandfather?'

She hesitated, aware she'd again strayed into territory she'd never shared.

'Luisa?' He paused. 'Do you want to tell me?' It was the concern in his tone that did it. The gentleness.

'There was a guy a little older than me at my grandfather's

palace.' She sucked in a breath. 'No one knew I was the prince's granddaughter but when we met in the gardens it didn't seem to matter who I was. We talked and talked.' She cut herself off. How gullible she'd been!

'We met daily. And I...fell for him.' He'd kissed her and she'd believed herself in love. 'He wanted to elope but I refused.' She'd wanted her parents at her wedding.

'That upset him. He tried...' Foul memories surged, chilling her to the marrow and she was grateful for Raul's warmth. 'He tried to force me but I fought him. He left with a black eye, but not before he'd explained the reason he'd bothered with me was because of who I was. He'd found out and decided to use that to his advantage. He was ambitious, you see. Marrying a princess would be a coup.'

'Luisa—' Raul's deep voice was gruff '—I'm sorry.'

'It's not your fault.'

'But it's my country, my people.' No mistaking his regret and indignation.

A touch feathered between her shoulder blades as if he'd pressed his lips there. She was so tempted to ask him to love her again till the disturbing memories receded and all she knew was ecstasy.

Raul made her needy. He made her want things she shouldn't.

On wobbly legs she stood, clasping the loose dress close. She needed to take control. She'd already revealed enough. Despite the relief of sharing, she felt raw.

'I can manage now, if you point me to the bathroom.'

'Let me help.' From behind he tugged the dress.

Resisting would tear the fabric so she cooperated, only to find her bra had somehow got caught up with the gown. Hurriedly she crossed her arms over bare breasts.

'That's enough. I—'

He dragged the cloth down till it pooled at her feet.

Too late she remembered her panties lay in shreds somewhere. She clamped a hand between her legs, feeling moisture there, a reminder of the sex they'd shared. There wasn't even a robe or a towel to cover her nakedness.

He circled before her, tall in his exquisite finery while she wore nothing but stay-up stockings. She felt vulnerable, especially before his magnificent height.

'You're stunning.' The thickening timbre of his voice splintered her thoughts. 'Let me look at you.'

The avid glitter in his eyes, the way his nostrils flared as if to drag in oxygen, spoke of a man at the edge of control. She felt his hands tremble as he took hers. He swallowed jerkily and tendons stood out in his neck.

She'd never been naked before a man. Embarrassed heat flushed her skin. But with it came a buzz of excitement, a rising sense of power.

For Raul looked...enthralled.

Again he swallowed and she saw the rapid pulse in his throat. It mirrored her heartbeat.

He looked like a starving man before a feast, not sure where to begin. She felt again that stirring of power.

With a visible effort he dragged his gaze up. His eyes had a strange unfocused look. Slowly he shook his head. He released her and stepped back.

'You were a virgin. You'll be sore. I shouldn't...'

She didn't feel sore. Not much. She felt wonderful. Because he wanted her as she wanted him? Or because he cared enough to hold back? To put her needs first.

She hugged the knowledge close. It was a small thing but it felt significant.

When he gently scooped her in his arms Luisa curled into him. She delighted in the steady thump of his heart as he carried her to the bathroom.

Minutes later she sank back with a sigh in warm scented water. It was bliss on the gentle ache of muscles.

Under lowered lashes she watched Raul strip off his jacket, roll up the sleeves of his collarless shirt and reach for a large sponge. Anticipation zinged through her.

His swirling touch with the sponge was impossibly erotic.

She gripped the massive tub rather than reach up to brush back the dark lock tumbling over his forehead. He tended her so gently. As if she were precious.

Sweat sheened his face. It trickled down his throat and she wanted to slide her hand along his skin. But his taut frown and grim mouth deterred her.

Until she noticed the bulge in his trousers. No wonder he looked in pain. No wonder his big capable hands shook so badly he'd dropped the soap more than once.

The knowledge set every nerve ablaze.

'I'm getting out.' Luisa struggled to rise.

'Wait!' Heedless of the water, Raul hauled her out with an ease that reminded her of the power hidden under his clothes. She sank into him, spreading her hands over his saturated shirt and muscled chest.

'You need rest.' His jaw set hard as if with strain.

'That's not what I need.' She tilted her chin and met his gaze. 'I need you.'

There, she'd said it and the world hadn't collapsed around her! In fact it felt good.

'*Now.*' Her fingers curled tight in his sodden shirt. She raised herself on tiptoe and pressed her lips to his.

In a flurry of urgent movement he lifted her, strode out and laid her on the bed. Seconds later he'd ripped his shirt open and shrugged it off. Luisa's pulse rocketed as she took in his sculpted torso with its smattering of dark hair. His hands went to his trousers as he heeled off his shoes. A moment later he stood naked and imposing.

She forgot to breathe as she surveyed his perfect form, felt the power radiating from him. Then thought ended as he joined her. He was like a furnace, burning hot.

He touched her all over, palms smooth, fingers teasing. He skimmed and stroked and even tickled till she squirmed and tried to reciprocate. But he held her, his thigh clamped her still, his hands capturing her wrists.

The torture began as he used his lips, tongue and teeth on her body. Minutes turned into an aeon of pleasure.

It was as if he tried to compensate for the speed of their earlier coupling. Delight piled upon delight till Luisa was strung out, quivering with need and pleasure. It was too much, too intense.

'Please, Raul,' she gasped. 'Don't tease.'

He looked up under hooded lids and her breath snagged as he tugged with his mouth at her breast. He held her gaze as his tongue circled her nipple then lapped hard, drawing hot wires of desire through her taut body. She groaned and instantly his hand slid down, stroking at her most sensitive point.

That was all it took.

She cried out as waves of ecstasy crested and crashed within her. Still he held her gaze, even as the world swirled around her and she bucked helplessly beneath his touch. It was wonderful; it left her speechless.

But it wasn't *Raul*.

Luisa clutched at his shoulders and finally, as she sagged spent against the mattress, he settled between her thighs. The feel of his hot flesh there sent a spark of energy through her lax bones and a searing sense of familiarity. Of rightness.

This time he slid home easily. She rejoiced in each magnificent centimetre, excitement stirring anew as he propped his weight above her. His solid chest brushed her sensitive nipples. Friction built to combustible levels with each measured thrust.

But it was his eyes that transfixed her. The connection between them was different this time. She read arousal and restraint in his gaze. And more. Something unguarded and raw. Something honest.

Raul moved faster and Luisa tilted her hips to meet him. Pleasure coiled tighter, lashing them together. It reached breaking point and still their eyes locked.

The climax came. Earth-shattering, mind-blowing ecstasy that went on and on. Through it all their gazes held in silent communication.

It felt like they shared as equals.

CHAPTER NINE

REALITY hit when Luisa woke.

Last night she'd almost believed they shared more than their bodies. But waking alone in Raul's bed reminded her where his priorities lay. Their marriage was about his desire for power. Sex was a bonus they shared.

Her chest tightened as she forced herself to think of it as sex. *It had felt like making love.*

Yet he'd left it to a maid to wake his bride, discreetly pretending not to notice the rumpled bed or that Luisa was naked beneath the fine linen.

Fire scorched Luisa's skin as the girl swept up the rumpled wedding gown, folding the metres of fine hand-worked veil with the reverence it deserved.

Memories seared, of Raul flinging the veil away. Of her standing with the dress at her feet as he held her arms wide and feasted on the sight of her. Of their blazing passion, utterly heedless of her exquisite finery.

Thrumming arousal beat low in her body, just remembering. Appalled, Luisa realised the need Raul had awoken was far from sated. How much she'd changed in one night!

She nodded vaguely as the maid, eyes carefully averted, pointed out the door in the panelling connecting to Luisa's room, for when she wanted to dress.

Luisa hadn't known the apartments were connected. She hadn't even recognised the corridor when Raul had brought her here! She'd been so caught up in her response to him.

Alone at last, Luisa stared at the empty pillow beside her.

She had no right to feel disappointed. She'd known what she was doing. She'd initiated it! But through a night of intimacy, curled close in his arms, she'd forgotten.

What they'd shared had been purely physical. Her skin prickled as she recalled how eager she'd been. It had been almost a relief to let anger push her into reckless desire.

She'd given herself, *knowing* where she fitted in his world. Raul viewed her in terms of her usefulness to him. Despite his tenderness, in that he was like her grandfather.

Pain cramped her belly. Her dream of one day finding love like her parents was dead. This—the ecstasy and the loneliness—would be her lot.

Maybe that was why she'd imagined the fragile connection between them: because it was easier than facing reality.

But she couldn't hide from the world for ever.

Ignoring the breakfast tray, Luisa wrapped a sheet around herself and hurried to the connecting door, determined not to yield to weak regrets. She'd made her bed and now...

She grabbed the door frame and braced herself as sudden realisation smote her. Her knees shook so hard she feared she'd slide to the floor.

They hadn't used contraception! How could she only just have realised?

It scared her—how much Raul scrambled her thoughts. How she changed when she was with him. He raised passions she'd never known. Her every emotion, from anger to joy, seemed so much more intense because of him.

Giving herself to him surely made her more vulnerable to his potent influence. But it was too late to turn back.

All she could do was try to be sensible, remembering they shared a pragmatic, convenient relationship. She couldn't afford to fall into the trap of foolish dreams.

She'd begin with contraception. She wasn't ready to bring a baby into such a situation.

* * *

'Your Highnesses, welcome.' The mayor bowed low, his bald head gleaming in the sun.

But Raul's attention wasn't on the resplendent figure before the town hall. It was riveted on Luisa. In her pale suit and with her golden hair swept up she looked coolly elegant. Yet a darting glance at her full lips and the slenderness of her throat brought waves of memory crashing in on him.

Of Luisa beneath him last night, writhing with a desperate pleasure tinged by innocent wonder that had held him in thrall despite his urgent need for completion. Of her unrestrained passion that blasted through his sophistication and years of experience and reduced him to slavering, uncontrolled need.

As if *he* was the virgin and she the seducer!

Even the feel of her arm as he guided her over the uneven cobblestones made hunger spring to gnawing life. He had to call on all his experience to mask his feelings.

That was what worried him. The fact that she made him *feel*. Not merely mind-blowing lust. Nor simply relief and gratitude that the crown was assured.

A cocktail of emotions had stirred last night as she'd spoken of her grandfather and her would-be seducer. A fierce protectiveness utterly unlike that he felt for his country. Fury at her hurts. Sadness. Tenderness he'd never known.

And joy so profound it had shocked him to the core and driven him from bed this morning, seeking work as a distraction.

Instinctively he tried to deny the intensity of his emotions. He didn't do feelings. That was how he'd survived and rebuilt his life in the face of humiliating public speculation and private pain.

What did Luisa do to him?

Even as a youth, when he'd been smitten by what he'd foolishly deemed love, he'd functioned better than this.

The crowd cheered and it was all Raul could do to remember to wave in acknowledgement. For the first time he had difficulty remembering his duty.

The realisation terrified him.

Duty had been his life. He'd devoted himself to his country with a dedication other men gave to wives and families. It gave him purpose. Had kept him going in that bleak time when his world crashed around him.

'Prince Raul, Princess Luisa, welcome.' The mayor's eyes gleamed admiringly as he bowed to Luisa.

Raul tensed at his blatant stare. He knew an unreasoning desire to pull Luisa behind him out of sight. Or take her to the castle and lock her in his bedroom.

Now *there* was a thought!

The crisp wind brought colour to her cheeks. Last night's passion had softened her lips to a lush, inviting bow that played havoc with his self-control and sent blood surging to his groin. Any minute now and the snapping cameras would catch him in rampant arousal.

'Your Highness?'

A look at the mayor's puzzled face told Raul they were waiting for him.

Dredging up his control, Raul spoke, finding calm in the give and take of official welcome. Yet the undercurrent of awareness heightening every sense disturbed him. A night of passion should slake desire, not increase it.

The mayor turned to Luisa, holding out a huge ornamental key that signified her free entry to every locked building in the capital.

'Welcome to our city, Your Highness. I hope you will be as happy here with us as we are to have you among us.' He spoke in Maritzian then English and the crowd cheered.

She looked sexy as hell. No trace now of the androgynous mud-spattered farmer. Raul imagined unbuttoning her jacket as he'd undone her wedding gown last night and—

'Thank you so much. It's a pleasure to be here.' To Raul's amazement Luisa spoke in slow but clear Maritzian as she turned towards the people lining the square. 'It's kind of you all to come and welcome me to your lovely city. I'll look forward to discovering it for myself.'

The crowd roared.

It didn't matter that Luisa had turned from the microphone so the sound blurred, or that her accent wasn't perfect. The fact that she made the effort to speak Maritzian, when everyone knew from the press release that she wasn't fluent, endeared her to them.

The mayor beamed. Streamers waved and a ripple of applause rose.

Pride surged as Raul watched her smile at the throng. Only he, beside her, saw the stiff set of her jaw and how her hands shook as she clasped the heavy key.

Only he, the man who'd forced her into leaving everything she knew and adopting a role she'd rejected time and again, guessed what it cost her to put on this façade.

Razor-sharp pain speared through him. He'd done what he must for his nation and Luisa had been the one to suffer.

A memory flashed of her pain last night as she'd spoken of her grandfather's manipulation. Raul's hands balled to fists. His own demands must have been like an echo of that dreadful time. The knowledge stirred an uncomfortable, unfamiliar sensation. *Guilt.*

He'd plucked her from her world, one where she was loved and appreciated, and dropped her into an alien place. Into a role even those born to it found challenging.

Last night they'd shared physical pleasure. But he'd persuaded and challenged her into it. Would she have come to him of her own volition?

'Here, let me.' He took the key, disturbed at the shame he felt. He wasn't used to questioning his actions. He'd spent so long sure in the knowledge he acted for the public good.

'It's almost over,' he murmured. 'Just back to the car and that's it.'

Finally Luisa met his eyes and shock sucker-punched him. Gone was the wonderment and warmth that, despite his attempts to rationalise, had turned last night into something remarkable. Something he refused to analyse.

For the first time since she'd agreed to marry, Luisa's gaze was coolly remote.

Inexplicable loss filled him. He'd thought they'd begun to share something more than an acceptance of duty. Instinctively Raul reached for her but she moved away.

At the last moment he remembered to thank the mayor. By the time he'd finished Luisa was ahead of him, her spine erect and poise perfect. That hadn't been learned in the last week. Her mother's teaching?

He followed, his gaze drawn to the slim skirt that shifted over her curves with every step. That was why he didn't see the bustle on the edge of the crowd. The next thing he knew, one of the security staff lunged across the open space while another hurried forward. Instantly alert, Raul raced across the cobbles, adrenalin pumping, ready to protect her.

He skidded to a halt beside her as she bent. That was when he saw the ragamuffin dog, all hair and lolling tongue, gambolling at her feet.

Raul's heart crashed against his ribs. When he'd seen the security men swing into action he'd feared the worst. If anything had happened to her...

'Luisa, he's filthy.' The words were brusque, sharper than he'd intended as relief flared. His wife gave him a wide-eyed stare.

His wife! The world shifted beneath his feet and Raul couldn't tell if it was from shock or reaction to the reproach in her eyes.

'He's just a harmless puppy.' She cradled the mongrel, looking down and murmuring in a soft tone that made the beast wriggle in ecstasy.

If Luisa smiled at him that way, whispering and rubbing his belly, Raul would lap it up too. His groin tightened. Damn it! This was ridiculous. She only had to smile and he got as hard as a randy teenager. He didn't understand it.

A commotion caught his eye. A small boy was trying to get past Raul's staff. Raul nodded to them to let him pass.

The kid cast a fearful glance over his shoulder then hurried forward. Raul saw a scowling red-faced man in the crowd where the boy had been.

For an instant memory side-swiped Raul. Of his own father wearing that same expression on one of the few occasions he'd deigned to spend time with his young son. Raul couldn't remember what he'd done to earn his father's wrath. Scuffed his shoes perhaps or earned a less than perfect mark in his studies. It hadn't taken much to disappoint the old man.

Bitterness welled on his tongue and his eyes narrowed.

The boy stopped before them, his head sinking low.

'Is this your dog?' Raul had to wait for a silent nod and felt Luisa's hand on his arm.

What? Did she think he'd rip into the kid?

'Yes, sir. He means no harm, sir. The cord broke and—'

'Completely understandable,' Raul said. 'With all that noise it's not surprising he got overexcited.'

The boy raised his head and stared, as if unable to believe his ears.

'He must have sensed the Princess likes dogs.' Raul found himself talking just to reassure. He'd had no idea Luisa liked dogs till he saw her cuddle this one. She smiled at the boy and crouched down to his level.

Good with children and dogs. Raul watched the boy's nervousness disappear under the warmth of Luisa's approval and realised she was a natural with both. She'd make a great mother—warm and affectionate. He watched her hand the pup over and pat the kid reassuringly.

Raul could imagine her with an unruly brood, unfazed by soccer in the gloomy royal portrait gallery on a wet winter's day or kids who wanted to run outdoors instead of perfecting their Latin before they were allowed dinner.

Something scooped a hollow deep in Raul's belly at the thought of Luisa with children. *They'd be his children.*

For the first time the idea of fatherhood appealed, even though he had no experience of real family life.

He tried to imagine Luisa carrying his child and found the notion strangely satisfying. Though not as pleasurable as having her to himself, naked and needy.

'It's time to go.' He took her arm and helped her rise. Then he steered his wife and the boy towards the beet-faced man at the front of the crowd.

He wanted his wife to himself, had wanted her since he'd forced himself to leave her this morning. But first he had business to attend to.

Luisa raised a hand to wave at the crowd pressed close to the road. Safer to look at them than the man beside her who continually bewildered her.

Self-conscious, she crossed her legs over the ladder creeping up her stockings where the pup had scratched. Then she wiped at the muddy stains on her designer suit.

'Don't fidget with your clothes. No one else can see the dirt.'

Startled, she turned. She'd thought Raul focused on the crowd on the other side of the road. Even now he didn't turn. She had a perfect view of his austere profile as he waved. Luisa found her gaze lingering on his full lower lip as she remembered the way he'd kissed her last night.

Heat spiralled inside and she swallowed hard. It didn't do any good. She couldn't quench the need he'd ignited.

Obviously Raul wasn't similarly bothered. He was utterly composed. No doubt displeased by her behaviour in picking up a grubby little dog that was anything but pedigree. Her eyes shut as she imagined the press pictures. Raul looking regal and she with a ladder in her stockings.

Well, tough! She hadn't asked to be princess. He'd stampeded her into it. Now he could put up with the fact that she didn't fit the mould.

She'd read his stern demeanour through the ceremony today. As if waiting for her to embarrass herself. Not even her carefully rehearsed lines, learned with Lukas' help, had softened Raul's severe countenance.

Had she really sought his approval? The notion of such neediness disturbed her.

Only once in the whole proceedings had his face softened. With the boy.

'Why did we go over to that man in the crowd?' She hadn't even been aware of the question forming in her head.

Raul turned and a sizzle shot through her as their gazes collided.

Luisa slumped back against her seat, heart pounding as fire roared through her veins. How did he do that? Was it the same for all the women he bedded?

The idea was pure torture.

'I wanted to make sure there was no trouble.'

'Trouble?' Luisa scrabbled for coherent thought.

'He was complaining loudly about his son being uncontrollable. And about what a nuisance the dog was.'

'You're kidding!' Luisa straightened. 'Peter was a darling, but so serious, not uncontrollable. If anything he seemed too old for his years.' She hadn't understood everything he'd said but his gravity had struck her.

Raul shrugged but the movement seemed cramped. 'Living with a judgemental parent will do that.'

It was on the tip of Luisa's tongue to question Raul's assessment, till she read a bleakness in his eyes that made her back off.

'What did you say to his father?' Raul had looked every inch the monarch, full of gracious condescension.

Again that shrug. A little easier this time. 'I congratulated him on his fine son.'

'Good on you!'

Startled green eyes met hers and for a moment Luisa lost the thread of the conversation.

'And I invited both boy and dog to visit the castle, to renew the acquaintance.'

Luisa tried but couldn't read Raul's expression. Yet instinct told her why he'd done it. 'You wanted to make sure he didn't get rid of the pup?'

For an instant longer Raul held her gaze before turning back to the window and raising his hand in acknowledgement of the people thronging the road.

'A boy should be allowed a dog for companionship. Don't you think?'

His tone indicated the matter was of no importance. Yet she remembered Peter's trembling fear and the nervous way he'd eyed his father. Raul had gone out of his way to speak to them when he hadn't made time to glad-hand anyone else in the crowd, preferring to wave from a distance.

Luisa sensed the matter was anything but unimportant to Raul. The scenario had struck a chord with him.

Frowning, she realised she knew almost nothing about the man she'd married.

CHAPTER TEN

RAUL'S mother had died in childbirth, his father had been impatient with children and Raul didn't have siblings. That was all Luisa knew, apart from the fact that he distanced himself behind a formidable reserve.

What did that say about him?

'Did you have a dog when you were a boy?'

Raul shot her a surprised look as they drove through the castle gates.

'No,' he said finally, his expression unreadable. 'Dogs and antique heirlooms aren't a good mix.'

Luisa surveyed the enormous courtyard and thought of the labyrinth of terraces, walled gardens and moats around the castle. 'There's room enough outside.'

If *she* had a child she'd let him or her have a pet or three and find a way to protect the antiques.

Shock grabbed her throat as she realised she was imagining a sturdy little boy running across the courtyard with black hair and eyes as green as emeralds. Eyes like—

'Are you ready, Luisa?' She looked up to find Raul already standing beside the limousine, offering his hand. No way to avoid touching him without being pointedly rude. Yet, even braced for it, the shock that sparked from his touch and ran up her arm stunned her.

Raul gave no sign of anything untoward, which left her wondering again if it were she alone overreacting to last night's intimacy. Sternly she told herself it was natural she'd respond to the touch of her first ever lover. But when he tucked her arm through his and led her through the cavernous entrance, it was all she could do to repress the shivers of excitement running through her body. Being this close set desire humming through her.

'Who did you play with?' She sought distraction.

One dark brow winged up towards Raul's hairline, giving him a faintly dangerous air.

'I had little time for play. Princes may be born but they need to be moulded for the role too.'

Luisa stared, horrified. But his cool tone signalled an end to the subject and he picked up his pace, leading her swiftly towards the lift.

'But when you were little you must have played.'

He shrugged, the movement brushing his arm against her. She breathed in the subtle scent of warm male skin.

'I don't recall. I had tutors and lessons from the age of four. Playtime wasn't scheduled, though later sports were included in the curriculum.'

'That sounds...regimented.' She smothered her outrage and distress. Surely they could have allowed him some time to be a child! It reinforced her resolve not to risk having a baby. No child of hers would be treated so.

Raul punched the button for the lift. 'My days were busy.'

Busy, not happy. The ancient castle was perfect for hide and seek and the fantasy games young children revelled in. Had he ever played them? Her heart went out to the little boy he'd been, so lonely, she suspected now.

Did that loneliness explain his aloof attitude? His formidable self-possession?

'Did you see much of your father?' She recalled him saying his father had been impatient with children. How had that impacted? She had no idea how royal households worked but she guessed no man became as ferociously self-sufficient as Raul without reason.

Her husband shot a warning look that shivered her skin. Luisa looked straight back.

The lift rose smoothly, so smoothly she knew it hadn't caused the dropping sensation in her stomach that came with the word *husband*.

'My father was busy. He had a country to run.'

Luisa bit down hard rather than blurt out her sympathy. The doors slid open but Luisa didn't move.

'Do you mean he didn't have time for you?'

She could almost see the shutters come down over Raul's face, blanking out all expression. The suddenness of it chilled her. Yet, far from blanking her out, it made her want to wrap her arms around him. The image of Peter, the little boy in the market square, so quaintly formal, tugged at her heart. Had Raul been like that as a child?

Her own glorious childhood, filled with laughter and love, happy days on the river or riding the tractor with her dad, running riot with a couple of dogs and even a pet lizard were halcyon by comparison.

'Why do you want to know?'

'Why don't you want to tell me? I'm your wife.' She didn't even stumble over the word. 'It's right I know you better.' Yet it was like pulling teeth, trying to get him to open up even a little.

Raul stood still, his face taut and unreadable. Then she caught a flicker in his eyes that made her thighs quiver and her stomach tighten.

'Just what I had in mind.' His voice lowered to a deep resonance that caressed her skin. 'Getting to know each other better.' Raul tugged her into the carpeted hallway and she realised they stood in front of his suite.

The glint in his eyes was unmistakable. Desire, raw and hungry. Something feral and dangerous sent delicious excitement skimming through her.

Her eyes widened. No mistaking what he meant.

Sex.

It was in his knowing look. In the deep shuddering breath that expanded his wide chest, as if he had trouble filling oxygen starved lungs.

Luisa waited for outrage to take hold. For pride to give her the strength to shove him away. Indignation didn't come. It was excitement that knotted her stomach. Desire that clogged her throat.

He'd introduced her to pleasure and she was too inexperienced to hide the fact that she craved more.

Raul must have read her feelings for his lips curved in a smile that made her pulse jitter. Wordlessly he shoved open the door, pulled her in and against him as he leaned back, closing the door with his body.

Fire exploded in her blood. Last night she'd loved the heavy burden of him above her. Now she wanted to arch into him and revel in the hard solidity of his big frame. It was weak of her but she couldn't get enough of him.

She shoved aside the memory of this morning's desolation, and the suspicion that his desire now masked a determination to stop her prying into his past.

At this moment it was Raul's passion she wanted. Perhaps because of the emptiness she'd glimpsed in his eyes when he'd spoken so casually about a childhood that to her sounded frighteningly cold. Did she doom herself to a similar loneliness, marrying him?

Yet it wasn't fear that drove her. Or simple lust.

Her heart twisted as she realised she wanted to give herself to her husband in the hope of healing some of the deep hurt she'd seen flicker for a moment in his eyes.

'Luisa? Do you want this?'

'Yes.' She didn't try to hide from his searching gaze.

When he lowered his head to graze the side of her neck with his teeth the air sucked straight out of her lungs. Thought disintegrated as she sank into pleasure.

She opened her eyes and groaned as he bit into the sensitive flesh at the base of her throat. Her hands clenched at his shoulders as his hands skimmed her jacket, undoing it and her shirt and spreading the open sides wide.

'You were magnificent this morning.' His voice was a low, throaty purr as he stripped off her jacket then kissed the upper slope of her breasts as he shoved her blouse off. Her skirt followed moments later and she shivered in sensual delight as he ran his big hands over her hips.

'I just did what was expected.' Yet she felt a tiny burst of pleasure at his words. Having accepted her new role, she was determined to do it well.

She sighed as he fastened his mouth on her lacy bra, sucking hard till the nipple stood erect and darts of liquid fire shot to her core.

Convulsively she shuddered, cradling him close, overwhelmed by the sudden need to embrace him and comfort him. This big man who needed no one.

He lifted his head and met her eyes. His own were shadowed, as if he veiled his thoughts. The knowledge pained her. He worked so hard to maintain his distance. Had he never learned to share anything? Was she crazy to think they could make this work?

Then his mouth descended and he swung her up in his embrace. Heat surrounded her. Hard-packed muscle. The steady beat of his heart.

By the time he lowered her to the bed and stripped both their clothes with a deftness that spoke of practice and urgency, Luisa's thoughts had almost scrambled.

'Contraception!' she blurted out as she sank beneath him. 'I don't want to get pregnant.'

His brows rose. 'We're married, Luisa. Having a child is a natural outcome.'

She shook her head. Despite the wonderful weighted feeling of his lower body on hers, this was too important.

'No. I'm not ready.' She gulped down air and tried to order her thoughts. 'It's been too fast.'

For what seemed an eternity Raul stared, as if seeing her for the first time. Finally he nodded and rolled away, reaching for the bedside table.

When he turned back he didn't immediately cover her body with his.

For a man who'd married her out of necessity he had a

way of making her feel the absolute focus of his world. As if nothing existed but her. His total concentration, the intensity of his gaze, the knowing, deliberately seductive touch of his hands on her body, were exhilarating.

Raul's gaze softened with each circling stroke and she felt something shift deep inside. She arched into his touch and her pulse pounded in her ears. When he leaned close his breath was an erotic caress of her sensitive ear lobe that sent sparks of heat showering through her.

'Come for me, Luisa.' His fingers delved and a ripple of sensation caught her. 'Give yourself up to it.'

Gasping, she focused on him, feeling the dip and wheel of excitement while the intense connection sparked between them. His set face, his mouth, no longer smiling but stretched taut in concentration. The furrow on his brow, his eyes...

Out of nowhere the orgasm hit, jerking her body and stealing her breath. Heat flared under her skin as he dipped his head to take her mouth in a long, languorous kiss that somehow intensified the echoing spasms.

Spent at last, she sank back into the bed.

Now he'd come to her. Dreamily she smiled, her inner muscles pulsing in readiness. Despite her exhaustion, it was Raul she wanted. The hollow ache inside was proof of that.

He moved, but not as she'd expected. Shocked, she saw him settling himself low, nuzzling her inner thighs.

'No! I want—'

His kiss silenced her. She shouldn't want more after the ecstasy that still echoed through her, but the caress of Raul's tongue, his lips, sent need jolting through her.

That was only the beginning.

Dazed, Luisa gave herself up to new caresses, new sensations that built one on the other till all she knew was Raul and the pleasure he wrought in her malleable, ever eager body. The taste of him was on her tongue, his scent in her nostrils as she grew attuned to his touch and the deep approving rumble of his voice.

Blindly she turned to him as finally he took her for himself, his rampant hardness a contrast to her lush satiation. She breathed deep, taking his shuddering, powerful body into hers as she seemed to absorb his essence into her pores.

Raul cried out and pleasure drenched her at the sound of her name in that raw needy voice. Instinctively she clutched him protectively close.

Raul lay completely spent, only enough strength in his body to pull Luisa close, her body sprawled over him.

He told himself the post-coital glow was always this intense, but he knew he lied. From the moment he'd bedded his wife he'd known the sex was different.

Why? His brain wouldn't leave the question alone.

Because she didn't meekly comply with his wishes? Because, despite agreeing to marry, she was still her own woman, not like the compliant lovers who gave whatever he wanted because of what he could provide in return?

With Luisa he had the thrilling, faintly disturbing sense that he held a precious gift in his arms.

She was far more than a warm body to sate his lust.

This was unknown territory. Or, if he were honest with himself, a little too like the feelings he'd discovered in his youth, when he'd believed in love. The thought should terrify him. He was well past believing in such things.

His lips quirked ruefully. That was why he'd seduced his wife as soon as they'd got back from the civic ceremony. Not just because he wanted her, but to stop himself puzzling over what she made him feel.

And to stop her questions. His hand clenched in the silk of her hair and she shifted delectably, soft flesh against his. Was it possible he'd used sex to avoid talking about his past? Even something as simple as his childhood?

Was he really such a coward?

His life was an open book. It had been pored over and dissected by the media for years. Yet the discomfort he'd felt answering Luisa's questions surprised him.

As did the unfamiliar need to open up to her. To share a little of himself.

He frowned. It was absurd. He didn't need a confessor or a confidante. There was no need for conversation. Yet deep down he knew he lied.

Perhaps because of the sense that he owed her for agreeing to marry?

Whatever the reason, when she shifted as if to move away, he slipped a restraining arm around the curve of her waist and cleared his throat.

'My father was interested in me only as heir to the throne.' His voice sounded husky. Raul told himself it was the aftermath of that stunning climax.

'That's awful.' Her words were murmured against his chest. She didn't look up. Somehow that made it easier.

He shrugged. 'Staff raised me. That's the way it's always been in the royal household. He dropped by just enough to remind me I had to excel to be ready to wear the crown one day.'

'And you wonder why I'm not ready for children!'

Shock smote him. He'd spoken blithely about the possibility of pregnancy, but the reality hadn't sunk in. Luisa, pregnant with his child...

'No child of ours would be raised like that.' Certainty firmed on the words.

'Really?'

Raul nodded. He'd spent years adhering to tradition as he fought to stabilise the monarchy and the nation, working behind the scenes as his father's focus narrowed to pleasing his capricious young wife. It had been Raul who'd tried to redress the damage after the fiasco with Ana.

But some traditions needed change.

'You have my word.'

He might not be a success as a father. Certainly his father's model of paternal love had been distant and unemotional. He thought of Peter, the boy with his dog. At least Raul knew what *not* to do. And Luisa would make up for his shortcomings. She'd be a natural.

He smiled, satisfied at the prospect.

'Tell me…' She hesitated.

'Yes?'

'Yesterday at the reception. Why did everyone watch you and your stepmother as if they expected a scene?'

Raul drew a heavy breath, satisfaction dissipating in an instant. But Luisa had a right to know. As she'd pointed out, she was his wife. Better to learn the facts from him than from some gossip sheet.

'Because they know I don't like her.' He stroked Luisa's hair then down her back, distracting himself just a little by the way she arched into his caress.

'Why not?' Luisa's question was a breath of sound. 'Why don't you like her?'

Raul clenched his jaw, forcing himself to answer.

'She pretended to marry him for love. He was proud and arrogant and he'd never been in love before, but he didn't deserve what he got.' Even though at first Raul had wished them both to the devil. He'd found no satisfaction seeing his father, weighed down by regret, dwindle into a shadow of the man he'd been.

'He was duped by a gold-digger half his age who wanted wealth and royal prestige. She spent most of her time with other men. His last years were hell.'

Even in his anger Raul felt a weight slide off his chest. He'd kept his views to himself so long, knowing an unguarded word would inflame the gossip and speculation he'd tried so hard to quash. The truth of his father's marriage had been guessed by many but never proven.

He'd worked tirelessly to protect his family's reputation, covering for his father as he grew erratic and less able to control his kingdom. Overcoming a desire to expose Ana for the witch she was. His country needed faith in the monarchy that kept it stable.

'There's more, isn't there? More you're not telling?'

Raul felt movement and looked down to see Luisa's bright eyes surveying him. She looked troubled.

Briefly he hesitated. But there was no point refusing to tell her. She could find out easily enough. He looked up at the wood-panelled ceiling, away from her searching gaze.

'I met Ana in my early twenties. She was my age but unlike any of the girls I knew. She wasn't aristocratic. She didn't simper or talk in platitudes. She didn't talk politics and she didn't care about court gossip.'

His lips twisted at the memory.

'She was a breath of fresh air. Vibrant, outspoken, fun. She wasn't afraid to get her hair messed riding in a convertible, or enjoy a picnic out in the open instead of dinner at a chic restaurant.' Or so it had seemed.

'I was smitten.' Raul halted, drawing a searing breath. It was the first time he'd admitted it. Strange how the memory seemed less shattering. Maybe because he saw his youthful folly clearly since he no longer believed in love.

'Oh, Raul!' No mistaking Luisa's distress. Or the tension in her body. The story wasn't a pretty one. Suddenly he wanted it over as quickly as possible.

'It turned out I was wrong about her. She seemed fresh and innocent, uncomplicated and appealing. But she wasn't what she appeared.' His mouth twisted.

'I wasn't the only one taken in. I introduced her to my father and he fell for her with all the force of an old fool for a very beautiful, very clever young woman.'

Raul remembered those days vividly. Ana had played him, holding him at arm's length once she got his father in her sights. After all, what price a prince when a king was available, with a kingdom's wealth at his disposal?

'My father married her four months later.'

Raul had thought his world had ended. He'd retreated into duty, throwing himself into anything that would dull the pain of betrayal. It had become habit to direct all his passion, all his energies into his royal obligations.

It had worked. Over the years he'd dispensed with the need for emotional ties.

'Raul, I'm so sorry. That must have been soul-destroying.'

Luisa didn't know the half of it. But it had made him stronger. He was self-sufficient and glad of it.

So why did he feel stripped naked in a way that had nothing to do with his lack of clothes?

'Do you still…care for her?'

Blindly Raul turned towards Luisa's voice, finally focusing on her troubled gaze.

'Care?' He almost spat the word. 'For the woman who deceived me and incited my own father to betray me?' A laugh tore, savage and rough, from his throat. 'For the woman who made me a laughing stock? She damned near destroyed the monarchy with her scandalous behaviour. She did destroy my father's pride and honour with her affairs.'

Raul shook his head. 'I learned a valuable lesson from her. Never to trust. Never to be gullible again. Love is a trap for the unwary.'

It struck him that what had drawn him to Ana all those years ago was what attracted him to Luisa. Her innocence in a world of political machinations. Her directness and honesty. Her beauty. Except in Luisa it was real. In Ana it had been false, designed to snare.

Ana had come to this apartment one morning just months after her wedding. She'd worn sheer black lace and even sheerer audacity and she'd expected Raul to satisfy her as his father hadn't been able to.

Rancid distaste filled his mouth. It had taken him a long time to banish the taint of that memory, even though he'd spurned her, avoiding her whenever he could.

In the long run Ana had done him a favour. Never again would he fall for the fantasy of love.

Luisa reeled from the shocking truth. The harsh light in his eyes as he'd spoken of his stepmother made her shiver.

Or was that because of the revelation that he'd once loved Ana?

Did he love her still? Despite his vehement denial, it was clear she still evoked strong emotion in him.

Nausea rose, threatening to choke Luisa. Raul had taken her with the compulsion of a man staking his claim.

Or a man intent on obliterating the past.

Had he really wanted *her*? Or had his pent-up passion been for the woman who'd rejected him yet still had a place in his life? Was Luisa a stand-in?

She bit her lip.

He'd said he didn't believe in love. Had he already fallen so hard for Ana he couldn't escape his feelings?

And if not, why did the idea of Raul, deprived of love as a child and now rejecting it as an adult, fill Luisa with sadness?

CHAPTER ELEVEN

LUISA peeked through slitted eyes as Raul dressed. She'd fallen into an exhausted sleep despite the swirl of disturbing thoughts his revelations had produced.

Hours ago they'd scaled the heights of bliss and she'd felt absurdly as if she'd found the other half of her soul in his arms, especially when he'd then begun to open up a little about his life.

But his later revelations about Ana had poisoned that heady pleasure and made her doubt.

What did Raul feel? Would she ever know?

She swallowed a knot of distress. The best she could do for herself, and the man she feared she was coming to care too much for, was be sensible—take a day at a time and try to build a workable marriage.

Easier said than done when just looking at him made her heart clench.

Hair slicked back from the shower, strong hands knotting his tie, Raul looked more potently sexy than any man had a right to.

Was this how his other lovers felt when he left them? She breathed through the hurt.

There could never be love between them.

Raul had closed himself off from that possibility. His bitterness over his father's wife skewed his emotions so much he'd admitted he'd never trust a woman, or love, again.

Who could blame him, after the devastating betrayal he'd

suffered? Pain seared her as she recalled the stoical way he'd revealed the bare bones of the awful story. But her imagination filled in some of the blanks.

What had it been like seeing the woman he'd loved living with another man—his own father? Adopting an air of unconcern in public and riding out the storm of speculation that surely must have howled around them all? She cringed thinking of the salacious gossip that must have circulated.

And facing his father—staying loyal and supporting him both publicly and, from what she'd heard, privately too, taking the brunt of responsibility for the kingdom.

She could barely imagine how bereft Raul must have felt at his father's lack of loyalty or caring.

Luisa had been scarred by her grandfather's actions, but at least she'd had the unquestioned support and love of her parents. Raul hadn't had that!

No wonder he closed himself off behind duty and a work schedule that would tax any workaholic. No wonder he found no difficulty marrying without emotion.

Was it possible he could ever learn to trust? To love?

'You're awake.' Dark eyes snared hers and something melted inside.

'You have to go?' Where had that come from? She sounded so needy.

'I'd hoped to stay here.' Heat flickered in his eyes as he took in the shape of her under the sheet. His nostrils flared and suddenly Luisa felt that now-familiar spark of desire flicker into life. Stupid to feel pleased that he obviously didn't relish leaving. It only meant her husband was virile, with an appetite for sex.

A very healthy appetite.

'There was a phone call.' He turned away to pick up his jacket. 'Urgent business.'

It was on the tip of Luisa's tongue to ask what business was so important it interrupted a honeymoon, when she remembered they weren't sharing one. Even the day after the wedding they'd been out and about on public show.

They didn't have that sort of marriage. Theirs was a convenient union. Remember?

She turned away, battling deep sadness.

'I'm sorry, Luisa.' He startled her, speaking from beside the bed. 'This is one matter I can't ignore.' She stared up into his brooding face. 'It's to do with the unrest I mentioned. I'm needed.'

She nodded. He had a country to run. That would always be his priority. Only now did she begin to understand how important that was to him. Through personal crises, his royal responsibilities at least had remained constant. No wonder he was so focused on them. Had they provided solace when he'd most needed it?

'You have a heavy schedule,' she said to fill the silence.

'You get used to it. I've been preparing for the work since I was four.'

The reminder sent a shiver down her spine. Raul had said any child of his would be brought up differently and she'd fight tooth and nail to ensure no child of hers was 'moulded' in that heartless way. She had to make a stand—for herself and for her family if she ever had one.

Luisa sat up against the headboard, drawing the sheet over her breasts and trying to ignore the flash of interest in Raul's eyes.

'I'll get up too. I have plans for this afternoon.'

'Plans? There are no appointments scheduled.'

'I want to meet with Gregor and the other gardeners. You have no objection to the parterre garden and some of the other spaces being renewed, do you?' It was a spur of the moment decision but she refused to spend the afternoon here, pining over the state of her marriage.

'No, of course not. It's overdue. But I can detail one of my staff to oversee it. It will need consultation, not just with the ground staff but with the castle historian, as well as kitchen and event staff. It's not just a matter of gardening.'

'That will be a good way to get to know them.' Luisa needed something to sink her teeth into, something to focus on other than Raul. She didn't want to think about the emotions he inspired for fear of what she'd discover.

'You don't *need* to work, Luisa.'

Her brows rose. 'You expect me to loll in the lap of luxury while you work the day after your wedding?'

'I regret that. I'd much prefer to stay.' The glint in his eyes made her pulse hammer erratically but she ignored it.

'I need something to *do*. A purpose. I'd go crazy without that. I'm used to working.'

Raul lifted a hand to his already perfectly knotted tie and for a split second she'd have said he looked uncomfortable.

'Your lessons don't keep you busy?'

'That's not enough.' She'd never been good at formal lessons. Her language skills were improving but if she had to learn about one more Maritzian monarch or the correct way to greet a grand duke, she'd scream.

Besides, the intensive lessons evoked memories of her long ago stay in Ardissia. The rigid discipline and the judgemental faces were missing, but she couldn't shake the notion she'd never live up to expectations.

Raul surveyed her, his face unreadable. 'Soon you'll be busy with official duties. As my consort there'll be plenty of events where you're required.'

'Being seen at openings and fetes?' She shook her head and sat straighter. 'That's not me.' Despite the makeover, she'd never be the glamorous clothes horse people liked to stare at in magazines. Wearing those stunning couture clothes, she felt like a fraud. Not like herself.

It didn't help, remembering Raul had bought her just as he'd bought them.

'I'll make a start this afternoon.' She met his unblinking gaze, almost challenging him to protest.

When he merely nodded Luisa took a slow breath.

If she was making a new start there was something else she had to face.

'I'm planning to visit Ardissia too.' It was time to lay her grandfather's ghost. Maybe going there, confronting the place that had meant so much to him, and held such dreadful memories for her, would help her bury her hatred.

He frowned. 'My schedule's too full right now.'

Luisa drew herself up. 'Do I need to wait for you? Aren't I Princess of Ardissia?' Much as she disliked the title, it was the one thing she'd got out of this devil's bargain: her inheritance. In her absence the province had become the responsibility of the monarch, but she was here now. 'It's time I shouldered my responsibilities.'

Raul paced towards the bed, his brows arrowing down. 'It's logical we go together. People will expect that.'

'But you're tied up every day. You just said you're not free.' A little breathing space, time to regroup after the massive changes in her life, beckoned. She'd been on a roller coaster of emotion these last weeks.

'There are matters of protocol and plans to be made. Royalty doesn't just stop by.'

Why was he against her going? No mistaking the tension in his big frame. The tantalising idea surfaced that he'd miss her. She dismissed it instantly.

'It's not dangerous, is it?'

He shook his head. 'Ardissia is safe.'

'Good. I'm sure I'll be welcome. I'll give notice I'm coming. A couple of days. Would that be enough?'

She stared into his set face, suddenly relishing the challenge of standing up to the man who'd taken over her life in more ways than she'd ever bargained for.

She needed to stake a claim as her own person lest he subsume her totally. Even now she longed for him to haul her close and forget the so important appointment that called him away. How was that for needy?

'Surely it's the right thing to do?' She worked to keep a cajoling note from her voice. 'It's only polite to visit now I've accepted my inheritance.'

Raul's lowering brows told her he didn't see it that way. The sight of tension in his jaw sent dangerous excitement zigzagging through her. As if she felt pleasure knowing she got under his skin, even in such a way as this.

Surely she wasn't that desperate for his attention?

'The timing's not ideal, but you're right. A visit makes sense. Leave it with me.'

Why did Luisa feel as if she'd lost the argument when he nodded, turned and strode out of the room, his mind obviously occupied with matters of business?

She hadn't expected him to kiss her, had she?

'This way, Your Highness.' The chamberlain ushered Luisa into her grandfather's study. She'd left it to last on her tour of the Ardissian royal palace.

She pictured the old man here, seated at the massive desk awash with opulent gilt scrollwork. Even in his towering rages he hadn't deigned to rise. Always he'd remembered his position as prince and hers as unsatisfactory, low-born grandchild.

Her teeth clenched as she recalled his poisonous words. Not merely his diatribe on her incompetence and ingratitude but his slashing vitriol at her parents.

'Thank you.' She nodded to the chamberlain, smiling despite his haughty rigidity. 'That's all.'

As he withdrew she considered the portraits lining the walls. Ancestors with remote expressions stared down their noses at her. She lifted her head, surveying the portrait of the man who'd cut off his daughter and his granddaughter when they wouldn't kowtow to his domineering ways.

'The last laugh's on you, Grandad. The farmer's daughter is Princess, soon to be Queen.'

Yet there was no pleasure in the shallow triumph. She hadn't come to gloat, but to see if she could put the past behind her and move on.

She wrapped her arms around herself, suppressing a shiver. Despite her determination to accept her lot, to dress the part and learn protocol and all the other things they foisted on her, Luisa couldn't imagine the future.

What would it hold?

Endless, empty years of public receptions and meaningless small talk? Breathtaking moments of delight when Raul treated her to mind-blowing sex? Heat curled inside at the memory of his loving.

Would she hang onto those moments, desperate for the little Raul could give her when she wanted so much more?

Would her life be sterile of friends and family?

If she had children, how could she protect them from the world that had produced a monster like her grandfather? And Raul had turned into a man of such emotional reserve she wondered if she'd ever build a relationship with him.

She paced to the window, seeking the warmth of the sun streaming in on the luxurious carpet.

Only the best for the Ardissian prince! She'd seen the run-down sections of the city and the bare amenities provided for the palace servants when she'd insisted on seeing *all* the premises. Her grandfather had spent money on his own comfort rather than his people.

Movement caught her eye. A group of young people made their way across the courtyard. On impulse Luisa opened the window. Laughter, bubbling and fresh, washed around her before they entered a door on the far side of the yard.

Wherever they were going, it appealed more than this place. She closed the window and headed for the door.

Raul drummed his fingers on the car seat as the limo purred towards the Ardissian palace. He lifted a hand to the people lining the street.

He was eager for a break after this intense week. He'd planned to come days ago, but political developments had made it impossible. Now he could please himself.

It pleased him to see his wife.

Five days she'd been away. It seemed far longer. His bed felt empty. His days regimented and predictable, despite the political crisis they'd averted.

Life seemed…less without Luisa.

His lips flattened as he thought of the day she'd announced

she'd come here. He'd only just dragged himself from the temptation of her. He'd reeled from an ecstasy unlike any he'd known. And from the unique sense of peace that came from sharing the story of his past.

Was it simply that he'd needed to unburden himself after years keeping it to himself? He couldn't shake the suspicion that the sensations of release and relief had more to do with the fact it was Luisa he shared with.

Only the most urgent crisis had forced him away, still stunned by the unprecedented sense of peace and pleasure he'd found with her.

And she'd sat there, her sweet mouth a taut line, demanding occupation. *Demanding more.*

Clearly he hadn't been enough to satisfy her!

Male pride smarted from the fact she'd been unaffected by what had passed between them, while it had knocked him completely off balance. It had been on the tip of his tongue to beg her not to leave.

Because he *needed* her! Not just sexually.

He couldn't remember feeling this way about a woman. Even Ana, at the height of her appeal, hadn't invaded his thoughts like this.

Raul smoothed his hand over the seat. At night he found himself reaching for Luisa. He felt bereft when she wasn't there.

Worse was his gut-deep sense of culpability. As the limo pulled up before her ancestral palace, her words came back to haunt him. How desperate she'd been for work to occupy her. Yet another reminder that, despite his attempts to help her adjust, this wasn't the life she'd chosen.

It was the life he'd demanded so he could inherit.

Yes, Maritz needed a strong monarch to see it through difficult times and, with the support of a democratic government, steer it clear of civil war.

But wasn't it also true he'd *needed* to be king? The monarchy had been his salvation as well as his burden as he'd worked to drag himself and his country out of the pit his father's hasty marriage had plunged them into.

And for that he'd bullied Luisa into his world.

He'd wanted to believe she'd find a fulfilling life by his side. These last weeks he'd seen glimpses of a woman who could make the role of consort her own and make a huge difference to his people, even if her way was not the traditional one.

Could she be happy here?

If he'd thought she'd be eager, waiting at the grand staircase to greet him, he was mistaken. Instead it was Lukas, whom he'd sent to support Luisa.

'Your Highness, welcome. And congratulations on the results of your recent negotiations.'

Raul smiled, allowing himself to enjoy anew a sense of relief. 'Thank you, Lukas. Hopefully it will mean peace at last.' He looked around but still no sign of Luisa.

'Her Highness planned to be here. She's delayed but shouldn't be long.' As he spoke he turned, walking with Raul inside the palace.

It was as grand and gloomy as Raul remembered.

He shuddered at the thought of Luisa here, a trusting, innocent teenager, at the mercy of the venomous old man who'd treated her and her mother so appallingly.

'Sorry?'

'I said the chamberlain has requested an audience.'

Raul stopped. 'Surely his business is with my wife. This is her property.'

One look at Lukas' face told Raul there was trouble ahead. He sighed. Days without sleep took their toll. All he wanted was his wife and a bed, in that order.

'Raul!' Luisa slammed to a stop in the doorway to her suite. She'd planned to be back earlier. Groomed and presentable, ready to greet him with calm courtesy.

One look at him, framed by the arched window, and her breath sawed out of control. Her heart kicked into a frantic rhythm. So much for calm. Just being in the same room with him shattered her composure.

She'd been so busy these last days. It was ridiculous she should miss him, but she had. More than she'd expected.

If things were different, if *they* were different, she'd run over and plant a kiss on his tense mouth until it softened in that sulky, sexy way it did when they were intimate. He'd put his arms around her and...

This was no fantasy. One look at his cool expression scotched that notion.

'Luisa.' He inclined his head but he didn't approach. Something inside her sank. 'How are you?'

'Fine, thanks.' She pushed back the hair that fell over her cheek and surreptitiously straightened her collar. She'd yanked her jacket on in a hurry. 'How was your trip?'

'Excellent.' He paused and she felt tension vibrate between them. 'Though as soon as I arrived your chamberlain came to me.'

Luisa frowned. Now she understood his disapproval. No doubt the official had poured out a litany of complaints. The man had been negative since she'd arrived.

'I see.' She breathed deep. She supposed she'd broken all sorts of rules. Now she had to face the music. But she refused to be intimidated. These were her decisions to make and she'd stick by them.

She closed the door and walked into the room. She gestured to an armchair. Raul ignored it.

'He voiced a number of concerns.'

'I'm sure he did. What did he start with? The proposal to open the state reception rooms for public functions?'

Raul shook his head, his saturnine eyebrows tilting down. 'No. It was your plan to turn the Prince's private apartments into a museum.'

Luisa's chin jerked up. 'I'm never going to use them so they might as well be put to some use.' She swept out a hand that encompassed her bright modern room with its view to the Alps. 'This is more suitable for when I visit.' She shuddered.

'All that overdecorated pomposity downstairs is too much for me.' Besides, the thought of bunking in her grandsire's bed curdled her blood.

'For us.' Raul paced closer.

'Sorry?'

'We'll visit together in future.'

What? He didn't trust her now to come here without him? She drew herself up to her full height.

'What else did he object to?' Might as well get it over, though it stuck in her craw to defend her plans.

Raul spread his arms in a gesture that drew her eyes to the expanse of his chest. She remembered his strength as he'd pulled her into his arms and taken her to heaven.

Despite her anger, heat snaked through her belly.

'He had a list. He was concerned about the plans for a children's playgroup in the eastern annexe.'

Luisa's mouth tightened. 'The premises are perfect and easily accessible from the main square. You might not know but in this part of the city there's virtually no provision for community groups. It's not like central Maritz where that's well catered for.'

It seemed her grandfather had stymied local plans to support the community, especially young people. His mindset had been rooted in the past.

'And the cooking school?'

She put her hands on her hips. 'I found students visiting the old kitchens. Their premises had been damaged when the old wiring caused a fire. The palace chef offered temporary use of the kitchens here.' Her lips firmed. 'It's a perfect match. The facilities are here, and the expertise for that matter. It's not as if there are lots of state banquets since I'm not here permanently.'

'And the same for the mechanics?'

She stared. 'How do you know about that?' She'd just come from a meeting of vocational teachers in what had been the stables but now housed an automotive workshop.

Raul stepped towards her and she read a flicker of something in his eyes that made the heat in her belly spread low and deep.

He raised a hand to her cheek. Luisa shuddered as delicious sensation stirred. She didn't want this distraction, this sweet reminder of the magic he wrought!

'It was a guess.' He held up his hand so she saw a dark stain. 'Motor oil?'

Her tongue thickened at his nearness. He was so close his body heat invaded her space.

'We were checking the facilities and I got a little...involved.'

Raul's eyes narrowed. 'I see. Like you got *involved* when you were presented with that cow?'

Luisa clenched her hands rather than spread them in a pleading gesture. The press had had a field day with that and she'd avoided reading the paper for days since. One paper in particular delighted in portraying her as wilful and disrespectful, though most seemed positive.

The animal had been beautiful, with garlands of flowers round its neck and horns and a huge alpine bell.

'It was part of the official welcome to Ardissia. Lukas explained it was a sign of great respect from the rural population. I couldn't refuse it!'

'But did you have to milk it?' His mouth tightened till the strain showed at his jaw.

She shrugged, feeling hemmed in by his disapproval. 'OK, so it wasn't proper protocol. I know real princesses wouldn't dream of it. But we got talking about dairy cattle and suddenly they offered me a milking stool and a bucket and...' She threw up her hands. 'So sue me! You insisted I do this. Don't complain now that I'm unorthodox. I'm trying. And—' she jabbed a finger into his pristine shirt '—while I'm happy to hear suggestions about these ideas for the palace, it's ultimately *my* decision. No one else's!'

'Exactly what I told your chamberlain.'

'Sorry?' Luisa was so dazed she barely noticed Raul had closed his hand around her prodding finger.

'I told him to keep his thoughts to himself until he had a chance to share them with you.'

Luisa stared. 'You don't mind?'

His nostrils flared. 'I mind very much being accosted by a jumped-up official who bad-mouths his employer behind her back. And I'm furious.'

Her shoulders sank. Here it came.

'Furious I didn't have the right to fire the troublemaker on the spot. He's your employee but he's more concerned about his own prestige than his job!'

'Raul?' Only now did she notice his other arm had slipped round to drag her close. She inhaled his intoxicating scent. It was like reliving those intense dreams that had haunted her ever since she'd come here.

'It's your decision, Luisa. But you need to consider finding someone better. Someone who can work with you on your plans rather than thwart them.'

She locked her knees against the trembling that started somewhere near her heart and spread to her limbs.

'You don't *mind* what I've been doing?' She'd been so sure of his disapproval her brain struggled with any other explanation for his tight-lipped expression.

'Why should I mind?' He rubbed her back in a circling motion that eased muscles drawn to breaking point. 'It's good to see you getting involved and listening to your people. I'm proud of what you've tackled in such a short space of time. But you're sensible enough to take advice and not rush into anything without due consideration.'

She blinked, staring up into dark green eyes that glimmered with warmth. The shock of it nearly undid her.

After the chamberlain's starchy disapproval and the knowledge her grandfather would roll in his grave at her plans for his precious palace, she hadn't been surprised to read criticism in Raul's expression.

Except now she couldn't find it.

A wave of warmth crashed over her that had nothing to do

with Raul's nearness. It stemmed from an inner glow, knowing he'd stood up for her with the chamberlain.

That he was ready to support her.

That he seemed to care.

She put out another trembling hand to his chest, spreading her fingers to capture the steady beat of his heart. His arm tightened around her and he leaned close.

'But what I most want to know, wife, is what the mayor said when you presented him with a bucket of warm milk.'

Again she caught that flicker in his eyes, the tightening of his lips. This time she realised what it was.

Raul trying not to laugh.

'He was very impressed and told me I had hidden talents.' Her mouth twitched. 'Then he showed me an old local technique he reckons gives you a better grip.'

Raul's face creased into a smile, then a grin. He tipped his head back and released a deep infectious laugh that made her lips curve and her heart dance.

Deep within Luisa something relaxed, unfurled and spread.

Happiness.

CHAPTER TWELVE

THAT happiness stayed. It was like a glowing ember, warming her from the inside and thawing the chill that had gripped her so long.

With each week Luisa found herself more content. She grew fond of her new home and its people. The nation of Maritz and even its tiny principality of Ardissia that she'd recalled as a nightmare place from her youth were growing more like home. She could be happy here.

Then there was Raul. He could be gentle and tender but there was always an undercurrent of explosive passion between them that left her breathless. Luisa shivered as erotic memories surfaced. Their physical intimacy was out of this world, and she always felt she got close then to the real man behind the façade.

The man she wanted to know better.

Raul was a loner. No wonder, with such a regimented childhood, brought up by staff rather than doting parents. Then there was his father's betrayal with the woman Raul had fallen for.

He'd spent so long cutting himself off from emotional connections; the moments when he let down his guard with her were special, poignantly precious.

More and more, Raul shared his wry wit, surprising her into giggles of shock or delight. The last thing she'd expected from the man who'd married her to claim the crown.

But as she watched him work tirelessly for his country,

every day and into the night, and saw his people respond to him, she knew he was the right man for the job.

Luisa's anger over his ruthless actions was now strangely muted. She knew Raul wasn't the unfeeling villain she'd once painted him. In some ways he was as much a victim of circumstance as she. A wounded man who hid his vulnerability behind a façade.

She felt melancholy. For, despite the way he stood up for her, supporting her sometimes unorthodox approach to her royal duties, she could never forget that for him she was an unwanted wife.

The wife he had to have.

A sweet ache pierced her and she pressed a hand to her chest. She hitched a breath and stared blindly at the newspaper on the desk before her.

It hurt because, even knowing Raul made the best of their convenient marriage, Luisa had done the unthinkable.

She'd fallen in love.

Despite the pain, happiness bubbled. Ripples of delight shivered through her till she trembled.

Love was such a big emotion. It overcame the fears plaguing her.

Surely there was a way she could make this marriage work? Make him care for her the way she cared for him?

'Sitting alone, Luisa?' Raul's voice made her jump and turn. Her heart kicked as she took in his tall frame, his sculpted features and the flare of heat in his eyes.

She yearned to throw herself into his embrace. Declare her feelings and demand he love her too.

If only it were that simple.

She sat where she was, limbs stiffening as she strove not to give herself away. He'd be horrified if he guessed her feelings. She had to be calm while inside she was a nervous jumble of joy and fear and tentative hope.

'My language lesson's over and I was trying to read the paper.' She twisted her fingers together and looked down, choosing an article at random. 'There's a picture of you but the words are too difficult.'

He stood behind her. She knew from the way her flesh prickled. Her body possessed radar tuned solely to Raul. Whenever he approached, even when he watched her from the other side of a crowded reception, Luisa felt it.

'It's a court report. Why not try something simpler?' His words were a puff of warmth at her ear as he leaned in.

Luisa shut her eyes, willing him to forget the paper and slide his arms around her.

'Luisa?'

She snapped her eyes open. 'What's the article about?' She didn't care but she had to say something.

'Just the trial of people illegally stockpiling banned weapons. Why don't we—'

'But why were you a witness?' She'd finally made sense of the caption.

'It's not that exciting.'

She frowned, finally concentrating on the piece. 'It says something about an armed raid. And a plot. A coup.' That word was familiar. She pointed at the next paragraph. 'What's that word?'

A sigh riffled her hair. He hesitated so long she wondered if he'd answer. 'Assassination.'

Luisa swung round, shock widening her eyes.

'Who did they want to assassinate?' Ice froze her feet, her legs, creeping upwards as she read resignation in Raul's expression.

Surely it couldn't have been...

'The cabinet. As many government officials as they could.' He straightened and stepped away and she felt bereft. She pushed back her chair and stood on shaky legs.

'And the Prince?' The words were a brittle rasp from her constricting throat. 'They wanted to kill you?'

To her horror he didn't deny it, merely lifted his shoulders. 'Don't worry, Luisa, it was over weeks ago, when you went to Ardissia.'

The glacial frost encroached to her heart and she wrapped her arms around herself. 'You didn't tell me.'

He strode to her and rubbed his hands over her rigid arms. 'You have nothing to fear, honestly. It's all over.'

'You think I'm worried for myself?'

Raul's eyes widened and for an instant she saw a flicker of shock. Then he drew her close. Beneath her ear she heard the strong beat of his heart. Her hands slid under his jacket, palming the muscled heat of his torso.

He was so alive. So vibrant. If anything happened to him...

Terror was a jagged blade, slicing through her.

This was the downside of love. She cared so much for Raul the thought of losing him was impossible to bear.

He moved to step back but she burrowed closer. His arms tightened till she felt cocooned and safe.

'Listen, Luisa. It really is over. These were just a handful of the lunatic fringe. The police had monitored them for some time so there was no danger. In fact their schemes have done everyone a favour.'

'How?' She arched back to meet his eyes.

'I told you there'd been unrest. It got worse in the final stages of my father's reign.' Raul paused before finally continuing.

'There were limits to what I could achieve as prince. In the last years as his marriage deteriorated, he became...erratic. He let his cronies grab too much power and didn't think strategically about the nation's well-being. Power blocs have been vying for position.'

'Lukas said you'd worked to keep the peace.'

'Did he? It looked at one stage as if the various parties might tear the country apart. The news that unstable elements saw that as an opportunity for a bloodbath made them all rethink and realise how important our peace and democracy are. It's brought them back to the negotiating table.' He smoothed his hand over her hair in a gentle caress.

'When the coronation takes place and parliament resumes, we'll be working together.'

'But what about—'

A finger against her lips stopped her words. 'It's nothing to concern you.' He turned to the newspaper. 'Let me find you something easier to read.'

Luisa's mind whirled. Raul had been in danger for his life. She'd assumed his talk of protecting the country was exaggerated to cover his desire to inherit.

Her stomach hollowed, realising how serious the situation had been. That she might have lost him.

That he hadn't considered sharing even a little of the truth with her. Even now he didn't want her to know.

And she'd thought they'd been building a rapport!

Raul might support her attempts to become a princess. He might take her to paradise with his body. But as for sharing anything more significant... How could she pretend it was possible when he kept so much from her?

Pain twisted to raw anguish in Luisa's heart. Even if he didn't carry a torch for Ana, his distrust was so ingrained Luisa saw now her chances of truly connecting with him were doomed.

He was a man she could love. The man she *did* love— strong, caring, capable and tender. But she knew no way to breach the final brittle shell of reserve he wore like armour. The shell that kept them apart even when she'd imagined they shared more and more.

She'd fooled herself, believing that after their time together he'd begun to feel something for her too.

He wouldn't want to hear her declaration of love.

He didn't want to share himself.

How would he react if she told him she suspected he'd shared enough of himself to create a child with her?

CHAPTER THIRTEEN

'THIS way, Your Highness.'

Raul followed the urban planner across waste ground, listening to him extol the virtues of the site that would become a community garden. Another of Luisa's projects.

It had merely taken mention of unused public land in a disadvantaged area for Luisa to find a use for it. Castle staff lent expertise to help the community build a place to meet, play and grow food. But it was Luisa, with Lukas' help, who'd checked zoning restrictions, negotiated with the council and met with residents.

His wife had extraordinary organisational skills, honed keeping a struggling business afloat. He'd seen with pleasure how she put those skills to use in Ardissia and here in the capital.

Raul admired her practicality, her drive to make things better.

Who'd have thought a girl off the farm would be such a success? She was a breath of fresh air, cutting through hidebound protocol with a smile, yet sensitive enough to see when tradition was necessary.

People loved her, drawn by her charm and warmth, and the royal fairy tale romance was a source of real pleasure after difficult political times.

Raul urged the planner towards the group at the centre of the site. Luisa was there, wearing her trademark casual chic clothes. He stifled a smile, seeing a couple of girls in almost matching gear.

Luisa's couture gowns were seen now only at formal functions. Instead she'd set her own trend, the first Maritzian royal to wear casual clothes to meet the people. But on Luisa casual looked so good. Today she wore slim-fitting jeans, low-heeled boots of supple scarlet and a matching jacket over a white top.

Only this time she hadn't shoved up her sleeves so she could take a hands-on role. Her boots were pristine, not even a fleck of dirt. Her face wasn't flushed with exertion and she didn't have a hair out of place as when she'd cuddled some toddler in a crowd.

He liked it when she looked a little flushed and rumpled. It reminded him of Luisa naked in his bed.

Now she looked elegant with her stylish clothes and pale, fine-boned features.

Raul's eyes narrowed. Too pale, surely?

Usually Luisa was a golden girl with her colouring and her tan. It complemented her infectious smile as she chatted with anybody and everybody.

Now, though surrounded by people as usual, she stood a little aloof, hanging back from the discussion. She looked peaky and the smile she wore wasn't the grin he'd become accustomed to.

No one else seemed to sense anything wrong.

But he'd come to know his wife.

He tensed, premonition skating down his nape as he recalled recent changes he'd preferred not to dwell on. Times when Luisa's warm impulsiveness had grown strained, appearing only in the heights of passion.

Then she was all his, just as he wanted her.

He repressed a scowl. Did he imagine she'd grown cooler? The suspicion had hit several times that she no longer wanted to share herself. As if she tried to hide the woman he'd come to think of as the real Luisa. Open, honest and exuberant.

Or as if that Luisa had ceased to exist.

An icy hand gripped his innards as he fought a rising tide of tension. A sense of déjà vu.

He squashed the thought. Luisa was *not* Ana. Only Raul's youth and the blindness of so-called love had ever convinced him Ana was the sort of woman he could trust.

Yet still he couldn't shift a sense of foreboding.

'Is everything OK?'

Luisa swung round, away from people waving goodbye. Raul had moved across the limo's wide seat to settle beside her. He'd raised the privacy screen.

Excitement zinged through her veins and drew the skin of her breasts and stomach tight. Her body betrayed her. She couldn't resist Raul, even knowing their relationship was tragically one-sided. Lately too, the more she tried to pull back and develop some protective distance, the more determined he seemed to invade her space.

Yet there was no gleam in his eyes now, just the shadow of a frown.

'Of course. Everything's fine.' With a supreme effort Luisa pasted a smile on her lips as she lied.

She teetered on a knife-edge of despair. She'd given her heart to a man who couldn't reciprocate her feelings. And now it seemed possible there'd be a child.

Her emotions were like a seesaw. One moment she was thrilled at the idea of carrying Raul's baby, at the new life she hoped she cradled in her womb. The next chill fear gripped her at the idea of bringing a child into this tiny family so unlike anything she'd dreamed of. Love was anathema to Raul yet it was her hidden secret. What sort of world was that in which to raise a child?

That was when she hoped against hope the pregnancy was a false alarm and guilt ate her, for wishing away such a precious gift.

She couldn't blame Raul. With his past it was no wonder he'd cut himself off from the deepest of emotions. She didn't even know if he believed in love!

As for his unswerving dedication to his country, putting it ahead of personal relationships, she could understand that too.

When she'd translated the papers about that trial she'd been stunned to learn the key role Raul had played in the investigation, as well as the political ramifications of the plot. Maritz needed Raul even more than Raul needed the satisfaction of fulfilling the role he was born to.

'Luisa?'

'Yes?' She looked over his shoulder and waved. 'What did you think of the garden site? It's got potential, don't you think? And the locals are very enthusiastic.' Great. Now she was babbling.

'The site is excellent.' He paused and she sensed he chose his words carefully. 'You seem...not as exuberant as usual.'

Luisa darted a glance at him then away, her stomach churning. 'I didn't think exuberance in a princess was a good thing.' She clenched nervous hands and searched for a neutral topic. 'The project's going well, don't you think?' Or had she already said that? Her brain was scrambled.

'Very well. You should be pleased.'

'I am. The volunteers have worked so hard.'

'You've worked hard too.' His brows puckered. 'You haven't been overdoing it, have you?'

Luisa's breath snagged. Had he guessed? She'd been forced from bed earlier and earlier by what she suspected was morning sickness. She didn't want Raul to see her white, nauseous and bedraggled. Especially when she didn't know how he'd react to the news.

It was one thing for him to say he'd break with tradition in bringing up a child. Another to welcome their baby with the whole-hearted love it deserved.

In that moment she decided. The idea of a trip home to see Mary and Sam had lurked in the back of her mind for days. Now the need for their warmth and unquestioning support was too much to resist. She'd visit them and discreetly schedule a doctor's appointment, something that was impossible here.

Imagine even visiting a pharmacy in Maritz to buy a pregnancy
test kit! The news would be in the press before nightfall.

Luisa needed time and space to come to grips with the
changes in her life. She'd go as soon as the coronation was
over.

'Of course I haven't overdone it. I'm fit as ever.'

He placed his hands over hers. Instantly she froze. She
hadn't realised she'd been wringing them. His warmth flowed
into her and for a moment her racing brain calmed. Perhaps
after all she could—

'You didn't cross the site to say hello to the people on the
far side of the block.'

Luisa drew a steadying breath. 'We'd run out of time. I
know you have a meeting and I'd already been there a while
before you arrived.'

'Still—' his gaze pierced hers '—normally you make time
for everyone.'

'You wanted to see them?' She'd been so eager to get away,
to find quiet in which to think.

'No, you're right.' He shook his head. 'I'd run out of time.
It just seemed...unlike you.'

Luisa flexed her fingers and instantly he released his grip
and moved away.

Pain gripped her chest.

See? It wasn't that he wanted to hold her. Except of course
when they had sex. He was just making sure she was well
enough to carry out her duties.

Raul's meeting had been endless. Time and again he'd caught
himself staring at his watch, calculating how long before he
could get away.

He should be pleased. All was set for the coronation next
week and negotiations with formerly difficult local leaders
had proved fruitful.

Yet he couldn't concentrate. Luisa had seemed strained
earlier this afternoon. This morning he'd woken to find she'd

slipped from his bed again. What had begun as an occasional irritation was now a worrying habit.

He felt unsettled when she wasn't there. He liked waking with her. Not only for the physical satisfaction of early morning sex. But because she made him feel good. Relaxed. Content.

Strange, when in the past he'd preferred to sleep alone. But so many things about his marriage were unusual.

Like the way he watched Luisa. She was vibrant and attractive, though not as gorgeous as some women he'd known. Yet he found himself watching her all the time, smiling when she smiled, enjoying her interactions with others and her combination of spunk and intelligence during their own discussions.

Though there hadn't been many of those lately. His fingers tightened on the neck of the chilled champagne bottle. Tonight would be different.

He put his head in the outer office before leaving for the private apartments.

'Clear my calendar for the fortnight after the coronation, can you?' He was determined to spend time alone with Luisa. Now things were stable he'd take time off and give her a honeymoon they'd both enjoy.

He couldn't think of anything he enjoyed more than being with his wife.

'Yes, sir.' The junior secretary took a note.

'Don't book anything else in my wife's diary either. I'll talk to her about clearing her dates as well.'

He smiled. A couple of weeks at his secluded lakeside retreat. It would be beautiful at this time of year. Luisa would love it and they could be alone.

'I'm sorry, sir.' The girl frowned. 'The princess is booked on a flight the day after the coronation.'

'A flight? It must be a mistake.'

'No, sir. I organised it myself just hours ago.'

Raul felt a curious hollow sensation deep in his chest. He strode to the computer.

'Show me.'

Silently she found the booking then turned the screen towards him. A flight to Sydney, no stopovers. No return.

The void in Raul's chest expanded and the breath seared from his lungs.

'Was there a call from Australia?' It might be sickness in the family. Luisa was close to her aunt and uncle.

But she hadn't mentioned it to him.

'Not that I know of, Your Highness.'

She bit her lip and Raul realised he was looming over her, glowering. He took a step back and forced a smile.

'That's fine. I'll talk to her about it myself.' He turned on his heel. A sixth sense chilled his flesh.

A one-way ticket to Sydney. Alone.

He forced down the instant thought that she'd had enough. That Luisa couldn't stand it here, had never forgiven him for bringing her to Maritz and planned to leave for good. *Leave him.*

His skin prickled and he lengthened his stride.

There would be an explanation. Yet his belly was a hard twist of tension as he headed for the royal apartments.

Raul tapped on the door of her suite and waited.

Strange. According to the secretary, Luisa had come here an hour ago to rest.

He knocked again and turned the handle. Perhaps she'd fallen asleep on the bed. Despite his concern, Raul's mouth kicked up at the idea of Luisa, tousled and soft from sleep.

He stepped in and slammed to a stop.

Time splintered.

He stood frozen, bile rising as his numb mind absorbed details. Déjà vu smote him and he reeled.

Yet this was worse. Far worse. This was Luisa...

Luisa and Lukas.

This clearly was no business meeting but something far more intimate.

Luisa wore a tight tank top and flirty skirt, her hands curled round Lukas' shoulders. Lukas, the man he would have trusted with his life! *The man he'd trusted with Luisa.*

Lukas held her close in his embrace, arms wrapped possessively round her slim form. Their blond heads were just a kiss apart.

Raul recalled his wife's recent coolness, the way she left his bed and tried to distance herself. Had Raul been a coward, ignoring signs he didn't want to see? Could Luisa have betrayed him as Ana had?

It felt as if someone had reached in and ripped his heart out.

Lukas had removed his jacket and tie. His collar was undone. Had Luisa done that? Had she used her nimble fingers to begin undressing him?

Roaring pain blasted Raul. It battered like a mountain avalanche till he could barely stand upright. It clamped his chest in a vice so tight he couldn't draw breath.

An explosion of shattering glass at his feet roused him from sick shock. The couple before him whipped their heads round and noticed him.

Fiery colour washed Luisa's face and her hands dropped. Lukas straightened and released her, adjusting his collar.

Raul's brain filled with an image he couldn't thrust away. Of Ana and his father, emerging from a state bedroom after his old man had taken Raul's visitor on a personal tour. Ana had coloured and looked away. His father had stood straighter, fiddling with his cuffs.

The beginning of their betrayal.

Raul breathed deep. With an effort he cleared his whirling thoughts.

This was Luisa and Lukas. Not Ana and his father.

His heart thundered and adrenalin pumped in his blood, but sanity prevailed. He forced his stiff legs to move. Ignoring the churning in his belly, he prowled into the room.

Raul watched Luisa's bright flush fade and her skin pale to bone-white.

'Luisa.' His voice sounded unfamiliar.

'Your Highness.' Lukas hurried into speech. 'I know this must look—'

Raul slashed one silencing hand through the air. It was Luisa he needed to talk with.

'But Your Highness…Raul…'

Raul swung round, focusing on his secretary. Through all the years they'd worked together Lukas had been a stickler for formality, refusing Raul's suggestion more than once that in private Lukas call him by name.

Fear churned in Raul's belly that Lukas should choose this moment to bridge that gap. To put them on equal footing.

Why? Because he and Luisa…?

No! Raul refused to let himself think it.

Yet, like a spectre, the possibility hovered in the recesses of his brain, waiting to swamp him in a moment of weakness.

'Leave us, Lukas.'

His voice was harsh with shock and a fear greater than anything he'd known.

Still Lukas didn't move, but looked to Luisa who stood, fingers threading nervously before her.

'Go, Lukas,' she whispered. 'It will be all right.'

Finally, with lagging steps he left. Raul heard the door click quietly behind him. Yet still Luisa didn't meet his eyes.

Anxiety stretched each nerve to breaking point. He clenched his hands, forcing himself to wait till she was ready to talk.

'It's not what you think.'

'You don't know what I'm thinking.' At this moment rational thought was almost beyond him. He was a mass of churning emotions. Only the voice that told him over and over that Luisa was *different*, was *his*, kept him sane.

She lifted her head and met his gaze and the familiar sizzle in his veins eased a fraction of the desperate tension in his body.

This was his Luisa. He refused to believe the worst.

'Aren't you going to ask about Lukas?'

'I know you'll tell me.' He just prayed he was man enough to hear the truth.

She paced away, her steps short, her eyes averted as if she couldn't bear to look at him. Fear knotted his brain.

'He was helping me.'

'Go on.'

'He was teaching me to dance.'

'Sorry?' Raul stared, flummoxed by the unexpected response.

'Teaching me to waltz, ready for the coronation ball.' Luisa flashed him a challenging look. 'At home our local dance was a disco in the school hall and I never learnt anything formal.' She looked at a point over his shoulder. 'It didn't matter at our wedding because the country was in mourning and there was no dancing at the reception, but this time...' She shrugged stiffly. 'I didn't want to disgrace you on your big day.'

Raul frowned. There was something so intimate about the idea of teaching Luisa to waltz. Holding her in his arms and showing her how to move her body with his.

'You could have asked me.' Surely that was the sort of thing husbands did? He'd have revelled in it.

What did it say about their marriage that she'd turned to his *secretary* to help her?

Colour washed her throat and her mouth pursed. 'And make it obvious there was another simple thing I couldn't do? You have no idea how hard it's been to try to get everything right—the protocol and customs and language—and still I make so many mistakes. Besides—' she drew a shaky breath '—it's so basic. How embarrassing not even to know how to waltz.'

She blinked quickly and his heart compressed.

'I don't care if you can't dance.' His voice was rough as he stepped closer.

'But I do. I wanted...' She chewed her lip.

'You thought anyone would care about your dancing ability? That I'd care? That's absurd!' Not after they'd shared so much. More than he'd shared with any other woman.

'Absurd?' She shook her head and spun away to pace the room again.

Raul wanted to tug her into his arms but the way she wrapped her arms round her torso and her strained expression told him this wasn't the time.

'What's really absurd is marrying someone you don't know. Giving yourself to someone who'll never care for you. Can never care for you because he never got over the woman who hurt him years ago.'

Shock held Raul mute as her words lashed him. He couldn't credit what he heard. Luisa believed he hadn't got over Ana?

'That's not true!'

He reached for her, took her arm, but she shrugged out of his grasp.

Anguish lacerated him at her rejection.

'Do you know how it feels knowing I wasn't your first choice of wife, not even your second? That you married me because of who my grandfather was?'

She drew a huge shuddering sigh and Raul felt the full weight of regret bear down on him for all he'd done to this vibrant, special woman.

All through their relationship his needs had come first. She'd given him what he wanted, more than he'd ever dreamed possible, and all the time she'd suffered.

He'd known it, had felt pangs of guilt but never before had he truly faced the full magnitude of Luisa's distress and loss. He'd conned himself into believing she'd begun to feel some of the pleasure he did in their union, shared some of his hopes for the future.

Reality hit him like a sledgehammer to the heart.

Raul shoved trembling hands into his pockets rather than reach for her. Clearly she didn't want his touch. The knowledge burned like acid.

'Is that why you've booked a flight to Sydney next week?'

Luisa's mouth gaped then shut with a snap. 'You know about that?'

'I just found out.' He waited. When she remained silent he prompted, hoping against hope there was another reason for her trip. 'Is there a family emergency?'

She shook her head and he felt hope flicker and fade.

'I wanted to go home.' Her voice cracked and it was all Raul could do not to scoop her close.

'This is your home.' His voice was rough, emotion scouring each word.

She shook her head so fervently fine gold hair whirled around her face and he'd have sworn her eyes shimmered with tears. His stomach clenched as from a crippling blow.

'I need time. Time away from here.'

Time away from him.

Something withered in Raul's breast. Something he couldn't put a name to. He'd hoped eventually she'd be happy with him, forget how he'd forced her to come here. Had he deluded himself, believing she'd come to care for him? That they'd begun to share something special?

But he couldn't give up.

'You belong here now, Luisa.'

He cut himself off before he could say she belonged to *him*.

'Do I?' She spun away, her arms wrapped over her chest. She drew a shuddering breath. 'I think it would be wise if I went away for a while. You see—'

'Running away, Luisa?' He couldn't be hearing this. Only yesterday she'd snuggled, naked in his embrace, and he'd felt... he'd hoped...

She shook her head. 'You'll be crowned. You'll have what you want.' Her voice sounded muffled.

And what if it was *her* he wanted? It struck him with the force of absolute truth that he wanted nothing more than to spend his life with Luisa.

Why had he not seen it so clearly before?

The crown, even his country, meant nothing without Luisa.

Had he lost her for good?

Unbidden, an image rose of her and Lukas. Would they meet in Australia?

He refused to consider the possibility.

'You can't leave the day after the coronation. At least put off the trip for a while.' He needed time to make her see reason. Time to convince her to stay.

She stiffened. 'I thought I should be there for the ceremony. But maybe it would be better if—'

She stopped as his mobile phone beeped insistently. With an impatient click of his tongue Raul reached into his pocket and switched it off.

'That's your private line. It's probably important.'

He stalked towards her, in no mood to be distracted. '*This* is important, Luisa.'

The sound of Luisa's landline ringing cut across his words. Before he could prevent her, she'd lifted the receiver, as if eager for the interruption.

'It's for you.' She held out the receiver to him. 'The government's legal counsel says he has to speak with you.'

Raul hesitated. They needed to discuss this now. But the matter he'd had the lawyers working on would surely help his cause with Luisa. He was desperate enough to clutch at anything that would help.

He reached for the phone.

Luisa watched Raul, so intent on the lawyer's news.

See? She'd been right about his priorities. As his wife she came somewhere near the bottom.

He'd challenged her about her trip to Australia and she'd waited, half dreading, half hoping he'd decree she couldn't go, say she had to remain, not for reasons of state but because he couldn't bear to be parted from her.

She'd imagined being swept into his arms, hauled against his hard torso and imprisoned there. Because he loved her as she loved him and he refused to release her.

Reality was so different.

'There's something I need to attend to.'

Wearily she nodded. There'd always be something more important than the state of their marriage. Dejectedly she wondered if perhaps it would be better if she left and didn't return.

'Luisa, did you hear me?'

'Sorry?' She looked up to find him already reaching for the door.

'I said we need to talk, *properly*. I'll be back as soon as I can.'

Luisa nodded, donning the mask of composure that now felt brittle enough to crack. Or was that her heart? Her last hope for a real marriage had just shattered.

CHAPTER FOURTEEN

'THANK YOU, everyone.' Raul nodded to the High Court judges, the Attorney General and the other witnesses who'd been urgently summoned two hours ago on his orders to witness this history-altering event.

In other circumstances he'd be excited at the prospect of initiating such significant change. But it was all he could do to wait patiently while they filed slowly from the chamber, leaving him alone.

So alone.

His mind snagged on the image of Luisa just hours ago in her room, pale and strained as she spoke of the need to get away. The hurt she'd felt at her place in his life.

How deeply he'd injured her, forcing her into his world.

Was he doing the right thing now, trying to tie her to him more strongly than ever? He looked at the parchment on the desk, checked, signed, countersigned and witnessed. The document he'd long planned as a surprise for Luisa, a testament of his regard for her.

The document that now represented his last-ditch, desperate effort to convince her to stay.

Did he have the right to try to hold her when life with him had made her so patently unhappy?

Until today he'd thought her content. More than content: happy.

Was he doomed never to find that emotional closeness Luisa

had spoken of so longingly? Was he simply not the right man to make her happy?

Pain seared through his clenched jaw at the notion of letting her go.

Terror engulfed him at the thought of life without her.

But who could blame her? He'd never experienced real love and surely that lack had left him emotionally flawed. Was he incapable of providing what she needed in a husband?

If she wanted to be here it would be different. Together they could face anything. If she cared for him...

His bark of raw laughter was loud in the silence. How could Luisa care for him after what he'd done to her? He'd deluded himself, believing things had changed between them these past weeks. The way she'd shied from his touch this evening said it all.

He turned to the window and looked at the glitter of city lights below. Normally he enjoyed the view of the capital he loved, the valley that had been home to his family for centuries. That sense of place, of belonging, always brought comfort.

Not now. Now all he felt was the terrible aloneness.

Life without Luisa.

He couldn't conceive it. His brain shut down every time he thought about it and a terrible hollow ache filled him. His very hands shook at the idea of her on a plane to Australia without him.

He should do the honourable thing and let her go. Release her from this life she'd never desired.

Yet he wanted to throw back his head and howl his despair at the idea of losing her. His pulse raced and his skin prickled with sweat at the thought of never seeing her again. Never holding her.

Never telling her how he felt.

Excruciating pain ripped at him, giant talons that tore at his soul.

It was no good, try as he might to be self-sacrificing, this was more than he could bear. It was asking too much.

He grabbed the parchment and rolled it quickly, heedless of the still drying wax seals. Turning on his heel he strode to the door.

Luisa woke slowly, clinging to a surprisingly wonderful dream.

After hours pacing the floor she'd retreated to bed. And still she'd tortured herself reliving the blank look on Raul's face as he'd left her, already intent on other business. The fact that he hadn't countermanded her trip to Sydney. That he didn't care.

Now she felt...safe, cocooned in a warm haven that protected her from everything. She didn't want to move.

But she had no choice. Even in her half aware state she registered the sick feeling, the rising nausea. She breathed deep, trying to force it back but it was no good.

With a desperate lurch she struggled upright, only to find her movements impeded by the large man wrapped around her back. His legs spooned hers, his palm on her stomach.

'Raul!' It was a raw croak. What was he doing here? When had he—?

Her stomach heaved and she thrust his confining arm away, swinging her legs off the bed.

'Luisa!' His voice was sharp. 'What's wrong?'

She had no time for explanations. She stumbled across the room, one hand to her stomach, the other clamped to her mouth as she tasted bile.

Miraculously the bathroom door swung open and she dived in just in time to brace herself as her last meal resurfaced. Her legs wobbled so much her knees folded and she almost crumpled to the floor.

But an arm lashed round her, keeping her upright with all Raul's formidable strength. Behind her she felt his body, hot and solid, anchoring her.

Then she bent, retching as the paroxysm of nausea overcame her. Her skin prickled horribly and searing bitterness filled her as her stomach spasmed again and again till there was nothing more to bring up.

She slumped, trembling and spent, eyes closed as she tried to summon strength to move.

Her head spun, or did she imagine movement? Next thing she knew she was seated on the side of the bath and she sighed her gratitude as every muscle melted. Raul supported her and she couldn't summon the energy to order him out. Not when he was all that kept her upright.

Then, like a blessing, a damp cloth brushed her forehead, her cheeks and throat, her dry lips. She turned her face into it gratefully.

'Drink this.' A glass nudged her mouth. Gratefully she sipped cool water. The damp cloth wiped her forehead again and she almost moaned in relief. She was weak as a kitten.

How could she face Raul now? Why was he here?

Tears stung as exhaustion and self-pity flooded her.

'You're ill. I'll call a doctor.' She opened her eyes to meet a worried dark green gaze. Raul looked grim.

She wanted to sit, basking in her husband's concern, pretending it meant more than it surely did.

'No. I'm not ill. It's perfectly normal. A doctor won't help with this.'

Belatedly she realised what she'd said as Raul's brows arched. Shock froze his features as he read the implications of her nausea.

She'd meant to tell him soon. But not like this.

'Please,' she said quickly. 'I need privacy to freshen up.' She refused to have this conversation on the edge of the bath, with her hair matted across her clammy brow.

Luisa turned away, not wanting to see suspicion darken his gaze. Pain welled and she bit her lip. After seeing her with Lukas it would be no surprise if Raul questioned the baby's paternity. He hadn't said he believed her explanation of why she'd been in Lukas' embrace.

Raul left the room without a word.

She should have been grateful but felt only despair that he'd been eager to go. So much for her fantasy of them bonding over their child!

Luisa took her time in the bathroom, but when she opened the door Raul was there. To her astonishment he swooped, scooping her into his arms.

'I can walk.' But her protest was half-hearted. His embrace was magic, even knowing it didn't mean anything. Raul was a man for whom duty was paramount. Tending to a pregnant female would come naturally.

He deposited her on the bed, where plumped up pillows sat against the headboard. He drew the coverlet over her and reached for something on the bedside table.

'Here. Try this.' It was a plate of salted crackers. He must have ordered them while she was in the bathroom.

'I'm not an invalid.' Luisa pushed them aside and fought not to succumb to the sweet delight of being cared for. Absurdly, the thoughtful gesture made her eyes swim, despite her anger and distress.

It didn't help that Raul looked wonderful. Faded denim stretched across his taut, powerful thighs. He wore a black pullover, sleeves bunched up to reveal strong, sinewy forearms. He was even more gorgeous than in one of his suave suits. Would she ever see him like this again? Her throat closed as she realised the answer was probably no.

The bed sank as he sat, facing her. Luisa's heart squeezed.

'You're pregnant.' It was a statement.

'I think so. But if I am it's your child.' She met his impenetrable gaze defiantly. 'It's got nothing to do with Lukas.'

He reached out and smoothed a lock of hair off her brow. Luisa's breath caught at the seeming tenderness of the gesture. She told herself she was a fool.

'I didn't think it had.'

'Oh.' She sank back, stunned.

'Have you seen a doctor?'

'No. It's still early.' She knew exactly when their baby had been conceived: that first tempestuous night of marriage, when she'd learned about ecstasy and heartache.

But Raul's calm acceptance surprised her. 'So you never thought—?'

He shook his head. 'I can't lie and say it didn't occur to me.' His eyes slid from hers. 'But when would you have time for an affair? It's *my* bed you share? *My* sofa. *My* desk.'

'You've made your point!' He didn't have to remind her how needy she was for him. How he only had to tilt one dark eyebrow in delicious invitation for her pulse to thrum with anticipation.

She stared hard into his face, trying to decipher his thoughts. Bewildered, she shook her head. 'I thought you'd believe—'

'That my wife was having an affair with my secretary?' Raul grimaced and placed has hand over hers. She felt heat, power and solidity, and she couldn't bring herself to dislodge his hand.

'I admit it was an unpleasant shock.' He tightened his hold and drew a deep breath that expanded his chest mightily. 'But I've come to know you, Luisa. You'd never go behind my back with another man. You're honest, genuine and caring. You wouldn't behave like that.' The words fell like nourishing rain in her parched soul.

He believed in her?

Her hands trembled with the shock of it.

'I know Lukas too,' he continued. 'We've worked together for years. How could I believe the worst, knowing you both?'

'I—' Words failed her. Such trust, when Raul had been so badly hurt before, and in the face of such evidence, stunned her. She'd expected a myriad of questions at the very least. Her heart swelled.

'I thought after Ana—'

'Forget Ana. I was a fool ever believing myself in love with her. But I got over her years ago. This is about you and me, Luisa. No one else.'

Raul's intense stare pinioned her, even as relief flared deep inside at the knowledge the other woman was no rival for Raul's affection. She'd worried about that so long! A burgeoning sense of lightness filled her.

'Luisa.' Her name was a sudden hoarse rasp that startled her. 'I want you to stay. Here, with me. Don't go to Sydney.'

The trembling in her hands intensified as tenuous joy rose. He believed in her! He wanted her!

It took a moment to realise why.

Disillusionment was bitter on her tongue. She tried to pull away but his grasp tightened.

'Because of the baby! You want your heir.' That was why he'd changed his mind about her going. This was about bloodlines. How could she have thought otherwise? She knew to her cost how important royal blood was in this place. Her heart spasmed in distress.

'Of course I want to be with the baby and you.'

She shook her head, a lead weight settling on her chest. The pain was worse now, more intense after that single moment of hope. She almost cried out.

Despite her efforts to make a place for herself here, Luisa knew she was too impulsive, too casual, too ready to bend the rules to make a good monarch's wife.

It wasn't Luisa he wanted, just her unborn child.

'Please let go of me. This won't work.' She didn't know how she summoned the strength to speak calmly, when inside it felt as if she were crumbling.

For what seemed an age he held her, his gaze sharp on her face. Then finally, when she'd almost given up on him responding, he released her and turned away, his shoulders hunching.

Instantly Luisa missed his warmth, his strength. She looked at her hands, where he'd gripped her so tightly, and it hit her she wasn't trembling any more.

Stunned, she looked to Raul, the distracted way he shoved a hand through his hair. She stared, not believing what she saw.

It was *him*. He was shaking all over.

'Raul?' Luisa's voice sounded hollow, as if it came from far away. She didn't understand what was going on. Her big, strong husband shook like a leaf.

'Raul! What is it?'

He didn't answer and she reached out a tentative hand to his shoulder. She felt the tremors running through his large frame.

'Raul!' Fear welled. Was he ill?

'I can't. I...' His head sank between his shoulders.

Frantically Luisa tugged at his upper arm, turning him towards her. She rose onto her knees and shuffled closer.

'What is it? Please, tell me.'

Finally he swung his head towards her. He was haggard as she'd never seen him, his flesh drawn too tight across the bones. Only his eyes looked alive in that spare face. They glittered, overbright.

'I can't lose you, Luisa.' His voice was a whisper of anguish that tore at her. 'God help me, I can't let you go. When you said you had to get away I knew I couldn't force you to stay any longer. But...'

'Raul?' She gulped. 'I don't understand. What are you saying?'

Luisa stared, dumbfounded, at the man she'd heard give speeches in four languages, charming, persuasive Raul, struggling to get his words out. Her grip eased on his arm and her hand slid up in a soothing caress.

'I need to look after you, Luisa. You and our baby.' Her heart somersaulted at the sound of those words: *our baby*.

'We'll come to some arrangement.' Much as the idea of part-time parents pained her, she knew their baby needed them both.

'I don't want *an arrangement*.' He lifted his head, the glitter in his eyes different, almost dangerous. 'I want my wife and child. Here.' He reached out to grab a rolled up paper from the foot of the bed. 'This will prove how much I want you here.'

With fumbling hands he thrust it at her, almost ripping the thick parchment as he hastened to unroll it.

'It's all in Maritzian.' Despairingly she skimmed the document, too distracted to concentrate properly. All she took in was the column of seals and signatures at the bottom, beginning with the flourish of Raul's formal signature and the royal dragon seal.

'What is it, Raul?' She'd never seen him like this, so agitated she wanted to cradle him close.

'It authorises a change in the royal succession from the moment I'm crowned. On that day you'll become Queen.'

She frowned. 'That's no change.'

He shook his head. 'Queen, not royal consort. You'll be my equal, my partner in ruling the kingdom.' His gleaming gaze met hers and the force of it warmed her very soul. 'How else can I prove what you mean to me? How much I need and trust you?'

Her eyes widened. 'But you can't do that! I'm not...not...I don't have the experience. I wouldn't know what to do. I—'

He grabbed her hands and held them tight. 'You'll learn. I'll teach you.' He kissed her palm and shivers of delight ran through her.

'But Maritz isn't ready for this. I'm not good at—'

'Maritz will adapt. You're capable and honest and caring. You'll make a perfect queen. For my country. For me. For our child.' His gaze dipped to her belly and heat sizzled through her.

'But I break all the rules.'

'Sometimes they need to be broken. There's more to life than protocol, you know.' He smiled, a slow, devastating smile that heated her from the soles of her feet to the top of her head.

'You're a princess to make anyone proud. Already our people respect and care for you, because they see how you care about them. You've helped them when it counted. You've helped *me*. You've changed my life and taught me hope.'

Luisa's brain whirled. It was too much to comprehend.

'Can you forgive me, Luisa? Enough to stay and give me another chance?'

She watched him swallow hard and searched her heart for a response. She loved him but was that enough to face the future? To build a life together even in the light of this momentous gesture of faith?

If he hauled her into his arms and swept her away on a tide of passion it would be easy to say yes. She yearned for that. But life wasn't so simple.

'It's not about forgiving the past. It's about the future.' She drew a difficult breath, wondering if he'd understand. 'I want a real marriage. A happy family. I want my child to enjoy being a child, with parents who really care. I want—'

'Love,' he finished for her on a husky whisper that pierced her. 'And trust and respect.' He nodded. 'You deserve it, Luisa. That's what I want to give you. If you'll let me try.'

Her breath caught in her throat at the look in his eyes.

'I love you, Luisa. I want you by my side.'

Dazed, Luisa stared into his tense face. A pulse jerked at the base of his neck and another beat at his temple. He looked like a man on the edge.

'It can't be,' she whispered, stunned into immobility.

'It's true.'

Silently she shook her head, afraid to believe.

'I didn't realise it myself.' His mouth twisted in a lopsided grimace that made her want to cuddle him close. 'I'd spent so long explaining away my feelings because the alternative was too terrifying. All my adult life I've worked to shut off my emotions. Then you came along. You made me *feel* so much, so intensely.'

Raul threaded his fingers through hers and tingling heat spread through her bloodstream. 'I've been torn, regretting the way I forced you here, forced you to marry me.' His eyes flashed. 'Yet knowing that in my heart I couldn't be truly sorry because it brought you to me and I couldn't let you go. How selfish is that?'

He thrust his other hand through his glossy hair in a

distracted gesture that made her want to wrap her arms around him. 'I'd told myself for so long that love was a fool's game. And here I was falling for a woman who had every reason to hate me.'

'I don't hate you.' The admission slipped out. She was numb, dazed.

'Really?' Hope blazed in his eyes. 'Then it's far more than I deserve.' His hand moved up to stroke her cheek and thread into her hair. Hope whispered through her.

'I've been torturing myself, telling myself I should find the strength to let you walk away and be happy.' His hold tightened.

He brought their joined hands up so he could kiss her wrist. 'But I can't do it. I have to fight for you.'

'Tell me again,' she whispered, her voice uneven. 'Tell me you love me.'

Raul lifted both hands, tenderly bracketing her face.

'I love you, Luisa. Never doubt it. I want to be by your side always. To share with you, be the one you turn to. Teach you to waltz and whatever else you want if you'll share your warmth and your laughter with me.'

Something shifted deep inside her. A tightness eased and Luisa drew breath, it seemed for the first time in an age.

'Oh, Raul!' She choked with emotion. 'I've loved you so long. I never thought…' She blinked furiously as tears welled.

'Truly?' His voice was husky with awe.

She nodded and gentle fingers wiped the wetness from her cheeks. 'Truly. Desperately.'

'My darling!' His forest-dark eyes meshed with hers. 'I didn't mean to make you cry, sweetheart. I only want to make you happy. Always.'

'You do.' She blinked and smiled. 'I've been happy here with you.'

She saw doubt and fear etched across his features. Uncertainty in the man who'd strode into her life and grabbed her destiny in his strong hands. Who ruled a kingdom with an ease anyone would envy.

'I'll make mistakes,' he admitted. 'This is all new to me. I've never felt like this.' He swallowed hard and she read a flicker of anxiety in his eyes. 'I'm not a good risk, I know. I don't have your gift of closeness and warmth. I have no experience of real family life. No role model of how to be a good father—'

Luisa's fingers on his lips stopped his words. Her heart contracted, seeing the man she loved unsure of himself.

Seeing his self-doubt, Luisa knew the truth. She had to cast off her own fear. She had to trust, in him and in herself and put the past behind her.

'I'm willing to try if you are,' she whispered in a voice croaky with emotion. It welled inside, making her whole being tremble.

Dark eyes met hers and the love she read there made her poor bruised heart squeeze tight.

'Luisa!' He gathered her close, kissing her neck, her cheeks. He held her as if she was the most precious thing in the world.

It was glorious, but it wasn't enough. Not when her heart soared with wonderment.

She cupped his hard jaw and pressed her lips full on his mouth. Instantly he responded, his mouth hungry, as if it had been a lifetime since they'd kissed. As if they'd never kissed.

Not really.

Not like this.

Raul's kiss healed. It was demanding, possessive, yet poignantly sweet. A giving and receiving, not just of physical delight but of love. True love.

Eventually they pulled apart, enough to gulp in much needed air. But Raul's arms were locked close around her and Luisa's hands were clamped tight at his shoulders.

Happiness surged so strongly she felt incandescent with it.

'I can't believe this is real.'

His shining eyes met hers and her heart somersaulted when she read the tenderness there. 'Let me show you how real, my sweet.' He gathered her close and kissed her till the world fell away.

EPILOGUE

THE ballroom was packed. Out in the courtyard more people gathered beneath fluttering royal banners, garlands and gilded lanterns.

Cheers reverberated off the antique mirrors and frescoed ceiling as the crowd applauded their new rulers: King Raul and Queen Luisa. The first joint monarchs in Maritzian history.

Goosebumps rose on Luisa's bare arms as she heard their names shouted once, twice, three times, first by the herald and then by the swelling voices of the throng.

On her head sat a delicate diadem of pure gold and dazzling brilliant cut diamonds. In her hand rested the mediaeval bejewelled orb and in Raul's, seated beside her, the engraved golden sceptre.

She breathed deep, hardly daring to believe this moment was real. But then a warm hand enfolded hers and squeezed. She turned and fell into the warm green depths of Raul's loving gaze.

It was real. The ceremony, the crowd, but most important of all, Raul's love.

He raised her hand and pressed a fervent kiss there. Instantly excitement shot through her. And anticipation.

He smiled, a devilish light in his eyes and she knew her expression gave her away. He read her feelings for him on her face. She didn't care. She revelled in their love.

And this was only the beginning…

Raul laughed and through the haze of well-being she heard the crowd applaud again.

She turned and looked down from her throne. There was Lukas standing with Luisa's new secretary, Sasha. From this angle it looked like they held hands. Then there were Tamsin and Alaric, their smiles conspiratorial. Mary and Sam were in the front row, in places of honour, beaming at Luisa as if it were the most natural thing that she should marry a king and rule a country.

She shook her head in wonderment.

'Are you ready, sweetheart?'

Raul rose and drew her to her feet. Officials appeared to take the precious orb and sceptre.

'Ready as I'll ever be.' He led her down from the dais to the polished floor where space was made for them.

'You'll be fine,' he murmured and pulled her into his arms. 'If there's a problem, blame it on your teacher.'

She gazed into his eyes, ablaze with love, felt him swing her into a waltz and smiled. The music soared and she whirled in the arms of the man she adored. She was home.

WEIGHT OF THE CROWN

BY
CHRISTINA HOLLIS

Christina Hollis was born in Somerset, and now lives in the idyllic Wye valley. She was born reading, and her childhood dream was to become a writer. This was realised when she became a successful journalist and lecturer in organic horticulture. Then she gave it all up to become a full-time mother of two and run half an acre of productive country garden.

Writing Mills & Boon® romances is another ambition realised. It fills most of her time, in between complicated rural school runs. The rest of her life is divided among garden and kitchen, either growing fruit and vegetables or cooking with them. Her daughter's cat always closely supervises everything she does around the home, from typing to picking strawberries!

You can learn more about Christina and her writing at www.christinahollis.com.

To Martyn, who makes all things possible.

PROLOGUE

LYSANDER was flying. Far below, the glitter of city lights was a diamond necklace drawn back into the velvet case of night. His lips parted in a wicked smile. He had made it to the top, and he was coming back to a hero's welcome. Nothing could stop him now, no matter how exhausted he was. His uniform was open at the neck, the sleeves turned back anyhow and he needed a shave. He dug the fingers of one hand through his tousled hair, trying to stop exhaustion shadowing his eyes. To him, tonight, sleep felt like a waste of time. He had too many things to do, and they all involved a certain person he hadn't seen for six days, four hours, eighteen minutes and counting...

Alyssa...

Her name moved around inside his mind like polished stones as he cruised over the sleeping English countryside. Several times his hand went towards his breast pocket as though to pull something out. Each time, he hesitated. His memory was enough. That snapshot couldn't affect him any more.

The intercom buzzed.

'You are cleared to land, Your Royal Highness!' a respectful voice informed him.

'That's OK.'

Lysander smiled. For the first time in his life, he felt comfortable with the title. Now he was flying through the night to reclaim what was his. This was what he was born to do. He had it all, and it felt good.

But the feeling didn't last.

His knuckles whitened as he gripped the controls of his private jet, anticipating trouble. It was a mistake to assume anything when it came to Alyssa. He didn't have everything he desired. Not yet.

That thought made him uneasy. Dragging at his cuff, he checked the watch on his smooth golden wrist. Timing this next move was crucial. He dug his teeth into his lower lip. The cause of all his sleepless nights would be in Ra'id's bedroom right now. Her changeless evening routine would be almost over. Everything would be peaceful, calm and predictable—until he dropped in.

Within seconds her neatly starched, ordered calm would be transformed into noisy chaos.

Lysander laughed. Adrenaline powered through his body, preparing him. The sort of happy homecoming he had dreamed about since he was a child was nearly within his grasp—but it wasn't guaranteed, not by any stretch of the imagination. He still had work to do. Alyssa Dene wasn't his—not yet. Lysander was a winner in his own country, but he had a different struggle in mind now. He was shaping up to confront Alyssa with what he had just done.

Lysander's mouth twitched as he considered the problem. This was going to be his hardest battle. He had already seen two tragedies in his thirty-two years, but there was not going to be a third. He was sure of that. So far things were going completely according to plan—*his* plan. But for how much longer?

His hand strayed towards his pocket again. With a sharp shake of his head, he slapped his fingers back to the controls. He was returning in triumph, secure in his position as leader of his country. He didn't want to spoil that. So the photograph stayed in his pocket, lodged like a cherry stone. He knew exactly how Miss Alyssa Dene would look right now, moving around the warm, welcoming rooms she had made her own. That was how he wanted to remember her right up to the end, whatever that might be.

His brow contracted. For the first time in his life, there was a slight chance things might not go entirely his way, but Lysander was determined. Thoughts of what he had done in the past, and how she had reacted to it, had tortured him for long enough. He was coming back to offer her the chance of a lifetime, whether she wanted it or not.

He felt his dark, strong features work with emotion, and resented it. That happened each time he remembered the angry words he had thrown at her on the night he left to secure the throne of Rosara.

I've *got nothing to prove!* You're *the one whose future is on the line...*

Lysander clenched his teeth until they ached. Snatching the damned photograph from his breast pocket, he slapped it down in front of him. As it came to rest on the instrument panel flesh and blood threatened to overwhelm him. All his best intentions crumbled to dust. When he looked at that picture, time stood still.

Suddenly it was summer in his heart again; his body and soul busy with thoughts of the woman whose presence could arouse him with desert-scorching fire. But then he had been forced to make a choice between his country, and her. She had turned her back on him, and the reason why would never go away. In the eyes of other people, Lysander was the world's most successful man. That was true—up until now. He had won the hearts of his people, but the only battle he truly cared about hadn't started yet. He exhaled heavily, trying to focus on the stellar image lying on the bulkhead before him. It was no good. He couldn't quite look her in the eyes.

Alyssa... He savoured her name as well as the sight of her tempting, toned body. The silky feel of her soft blonde hair between his fingers was such a distant dream, but this photograph brought it all back. That swimsuit was supposed to be discreet, but its sleek green gloss showed off her full breasts as provocatively as it sculpted her neat waist and warmly rounded hips.

Lysander drew in a slow, ragged breath. His hands could recognise her shape in the dark of a desert night, but the expression she wore in this picture chilled him to the bone.

She looks as poised and controlling as she did when she turned her back on me for the last time, he thought with a flicker of the falcon in his eyes. There had been little time to think over the past few days, but every second he could spare had overflowed with thoughts of her. Now he had come to a decision, and he was going to stick with it.

Lysander tried to concentrate on the instrument panel before him, not the image of a woman he had last heard telling him to go to hell. Working on automatic, he flicked switches and checked displays, but it was impossible to shut her out of his mind. He closed his hands slowly into fists around the controls. He had been away for too long, fighting through public battles and private negotiations. Now there was only one thing left to sort out. A provocative, priceless woman had trespassed into his private life, and tonight would see the showdown.

He ran a hand through his raven hair once more, and tried to pull his battle-weary uniform into some kind of order. Then he turned his ruthless stare back to the instrument panel. His mouth moved, and he almost smiled again. At last. With one twitch of his hand he set his plane on the path down to find the woman who could change his life for ever.

CHAPTER ONE

A month earlier.

THIS is supposed to be fun, Alyssa reminded herself. It should have been ideal. Everything she loved was all here in one place—solitude, a beautiful setting and time to think. The only downside was the weather. Raindrops were still rustling through the tree canopy after that last shower, but the sky was clearing. This was England in summer, after all. Changeable weather was all part of the *fun*.

She grimaced. That was the second time she had used the 'f' word inside thirty seconds, but it didn't make her feel any better. If only she could stop remembering... She shuddered.

Rebuilding some sort of existence for herself wasn't easy. This holiday was supposed to give her space and time to plan her future. Out here in the forest she had the room and the opportunity to think, but all she could do was brood on what had happened, instead of how she might move on.

She hugged her knees, trying to enjoy the feeling of being snug inside the entrance to her tent. It was hopeless. This sabbatical wasn't working. Listening to the gentle play of water welling up from the spring beside her, she shut her eyes and tried to clear her mind. This spot was a real find. It was miles off the beaten track, in a hidden valley that hadn't seen the hand of humans for years. There was wildlife, and flowers, and perfect peace—until her phone rang.

'Hi, it's only me.'

Alyssa tried her best to raise a smile. Karen, the agency manager, was a good friend, and that wasn't always a good thing. Today, it was part of the trouble.

'Look, please don't take this the wrong way, Karen, but I'd be glad if you could give me a bit of a break. I really don't need you to keep pushing work in my direction. I'm supposed to be getting away from the whole childcare scene for a bit.'

Looking back, there might have been the briefest of pauses, but Alyssa wasn't aware of it at the time.

'Who said this was a job offer?' her boss began breezily. 'I'm just ringing up to check that you're OK. Good grief, you thought I was calling to offer you the job that came in this morning? Believe me, you'll be glad you're *not* available when I tell you about it. They wanted the best, and they'll need it, but it's a poisoned chalice.'

Alyssa stiffened. 'It sounds like trouble.' Her mouth dried and she couldn't say any more.

'No, no. It's not as though the child is in actual *danger...*'

But the hint was there. Alyssa felt her blood run cold.

'So anyway, how do you feel, Alyssa? Any better?

What are you up to at the moment?' Karen said without pausing for breath.

'That doesn't matter. I'm more interested in that new job you mentioned. There's something wrong. I can hear it in your voice.'

'Rubbish! The new Regent of Rosara wants the best for his nephew. That's all.'

Alyssa gasped.

'That's *all*?'

Awful headlines had been splashed across every newspaper for days. To read about a child orphaned in a car crash while visiting his family's holiday home in England was bad enough. When A-list celebrity Lysander Kahani was named as his guardian, the story had stuck in Alyssa's mind. Glamorous Prince Lysander's link with the case had instantly snatched all the limelight from the little boy.

'The prince's people asked for you by name, Alyssa. You were recommended to them because they want the best, of course.'

'They'll need it, with that Casanova turning the poor child's home into an open house for idiots,' Alyssa muttered, her head full of all the lurid 'Playboy Gets Top Job' stories she had seen.

'But I'm going to tell them you aren't available,' Karen went on airily. 'Which is probably just as well for all concerned.'

Alyssa definitely didn't like the way the agency boss said that. 'Meaning?'

'Come off it, Lis, would you really want to work in a set-up like that? Everyone knows you're the best person in the world when it comes to taking care of children, but, let's face it, would you have been able to fit in with Prince Lysander's way of life? He's got such a terrible reputation, I knew you wouldn't want the job in a million years.'

Alyssa could feel herself being played, and she didn't like it, but she also couldn't deny it was working. Maybe this break was doing her some good after all. The only thing she had decided over the past few days was that her life had to change. Could this be where it started?

That child needed a calming influence in his life. Even in the midst of her own misery, Alyssa had never been able to ignore a child in need. Also, she had to admit to a faint flicker of curiosity—the first sign of life she'd felt for ages. What would the palace be like? How could she go about helping the little boy? *And after all*, she thought, *if I say I'm not available, they might go ahead and hire the first hopeless, brainless, wannabe celebrity they come across. Someone only interested in trailing the poor little boy around in Lysander's wake...*

That settled it for Alyssa.

'Have you actually put the royal family off yet, Karen?'

It was difficult to sound offhand when her heart was racing. Keeping quiet had wrecked her life before. And now, telling herself the only thing that mattered was what the child might be going through, she knew she had to have that job. She'd make sure little Ra'id Kahani was safe and properly looked after first, then worry about her own feelings afterwards.

'Not yet, no. I'm trying to find someone else for

them first. Telling them there *is* no one as good as you is the next thing on my "to do" list.'

'Then don't do it.' Alyssa plunged in before she had time to think about all the drawbacks. 'You don't need to ring them. I'll take the job, Karen,' she said with the blood pounding in her ears.

There was a considered silence at the other end of the line. Then her boss laughed. 'But what about the irresistible Prince Lysander? No woman is safe from his charm, apparently!'

'After what's happened to me over the past few months, I'm totally immune to men. Don't say you've forgotten one of the things that drove me to take this break from work in the first place.'

Karen hesitated. 'Of course...'

'Yes. Him.'

Jerry. Alyssa still couldn't bring herself to say the name out loud. Thinking about what that rat had done still made her feel ill. This Rosara job would be the perfect way to bury all her horrible memories. It would give her the new start she was craving so badly.

'So you think you can cope with a dark-eyed, dashing playboy?' The smile was obvious in Karen's voice.

'The only thing I'm interested in is his poor little nephew,' Alyssa said, and meant it. 'When can I start?'

'I'll tell them you're on your way.' Her boss laughed again.

Alyssa's nerve held right up until she reached the security checkpoint at the entrance to Combe House. She had worked for plenty of rich people in the past and was no stranger to being met by guards inside a home and at its doors, but never at gates so far from the house. It was a new experience for her. *But one I shall have to get used to,* she thought, driving towards the Kahanis' mansion along a curving drive that seemed to go on for ever. Starting with a new family always made her nervous, and these surroundings didn't do anything to make her feel better about the Kahani family. Untamed English woodland pressed in on all sides, while undergrowth spilled out over the gritty approach road. *They're probably nocturnal,* she thought grimly. *And too busy partying all night to care what the place looks like to daytime visitors.*

As she drove on, a huge rambling mansion rose out of the undergrowth ahead of her. Combe House had turrets, weathervanes and flagpoles, all lichenous with age. She could hardly take it all in. It was the most beautiful house she had ever seen, and the setting was lovely despite the weeds.

This whole place is like something out of Sleeping Beauty! she thought.

A little knot of sharp-suited security men stood chatting beside the great entrance doors to the house. When Alyssa rolled down her window to ask where she should park, she got a first taste of working for Lysander Kahani. One man took her car keys to save her the trouble of parking, while a second escorted her into the building. He showed her into a waiting room the size of a ballroom. Much of it was hidden beneath dust sheets while the delicate plaster details of cornices and dados could be restored, but the parts that had been finished were truly beautiful. Alyssa hoped it would take the Combe House staff a long time to find anyone to deal with her. She wanted a chance to look around the room on her own, first.

She didn't get it. An awful racket bowled through the house towards her. It was a lot of people jabbering among themselves, seasoned with the sound of ringing mobile phones.

The Kahani state circus was coming to town.

Alyssa checked her appearance in the nearest mirror, but she needn't have bothered. A cavalcade of smartly dressed staff burst into the room where she was waiting, but showed no sign of noticing her. They were only interested in the tall, lean man who strode ahead of them. He had the look of an avenging angel, while they clamoured for his attention like a nest of ravens. Common sense told Alyssa this figure must be Lysander Kahani, but it was hard to recognise him. This man didn't look much like the amused playboy prince pictured in all the celebrity magazines, and on the front pages of all the newspapers. He looked angry, dark hair tousled untidily over his brow, and he wore a perfectly fitted light grey business suit rather than the tuxedo of his photos. His tie was missing, and his plain white shirt was open at the neck. He certainly wasn't smiling, and there was a dangerous gleam in his eyes as he saw her watching him. Despite the crowd and noise, Alyssa had never felt so alone and vulnerable.

I thought the royal family were here on holiday, but you'd never know from Prince Lysander's expression, she thought.

While his rapier gaze was distracted by the arrival of yet another electronic message, she tried to study her new employer. Lysander Kahani was a six-and-a-half-foot scowl, his height impressive and intimidating, but she could only bring herself to look at the lower seventy inches or so. To make up for that, she studied him all the way up from his highly polished, handmade shoes to his dark shaded chin, and then down again. It was scarily enjoyable—so she did it again. On the return journey her eyes made their way right up to his. As she tried her best to look cool and unapproachable she saw the anger leave his face.

As his eyes locked onto hers, he spoke sharply to his crowd of followers. Alyssa didn't speak his language, but his words had a questioning lilt that was easy enough to understand. He must want to know who she was, and why she was there. His staff all fell silent and turned to stare at her as if she were another exhibit for their madhouse. Alyssa tried to concentrate on the blurry newspaper photos of the poor little boy, Prince Ra'id, who had lost both his parents and must have been shoved aside in favour of this mob. Folding her hands in front of her as a defence, she took a deep breath.

'I am Alyssa Dene. I'm here by special request of Prince Lysander of Rosara, because I'm to be his nephew's new nanny.'

The words came out louder and more haughtily than she intended. Before she could apologise, something changed in Lysander Kahani's expression. It softened, and in the face of his dark amusement Alyssa stopped thinking straight. She couldn't help it. The sight of his smile sent all the questions she had lined up for her new employer scattering like beads on a tray. It was obvious he knew the effect he was having on her. This was more fun to him than work. His taut frame relaxed. With a few words he sent his horde of advisors scuttling away. Tossing the sheaf of paperwork he was holding onto the nearest table, Lysander followed them to the door and closed it behind them. As he leaned back against it Alyssa came to her senses. She was now totally alone with a notorious man. If that weren't bad enough, somehow in the past few seconds he had become more attractive than he appeared in all his photographs put together.

She tried to speak, but no sound came out. Lysander Kahani showed every sign of revelling in the situation.

'That's more like it!' he said in beautifully accented English. 'Now I can hear myself think, and devote my whole attention to you. This job is playing havoc with my lifestyle, I can tell you.'

Alyssa swallowed hard as he prowled towards her. His wicked smile sent tremors straight through her body. It felt incredible, but she couldn't afford to enjoy it. A man without a fraction of Lysander's charm had wrecked her life only a few months ago, and she was still trying to recover. Every ounce of her common sense told her this was a dangerous situation and she ought to resist, but Lysander was looking at her as though she were the only woman in the world. The expression in his rich brown, dark-lashed eyes made it difficult not to give in and simply revel in the wonderful feeling of being admired.

'D-don't you think you'd better deal with all that paperwork first, Prince Lysander?' She faltered, looking at the chaos scattered over the nearest table top.

She was suddenly desperate for more time to prepare herself for this encounter.

'No, I don't,' he said, strolling over to position himself between her and the table. By leaning back against it he hid the heap of work from her, but she had already stopped looking at it. The fine lines of his suit and the long, strong fingers he curled over the edge of the table top had captured her attention. 'It's only parcels of trouble, tied up in red tape. Forget it. I'd much rather talk to you...*Alyssa.*'

The way he purred her name sent a shiver of anticipation across her sensitised skin. She was already nervous about starting work for such an infamous man, and his flirting set new butterflies dancing inside her tummy. The last thing she needed was this handsome stranger taking over her body by stealth before she was safely hidden away in Combe House's nursery wing. She had to show she meant business right away.

'It—it might be important, Your Royal Highness.'

'You'd like to think so, wouldn't you?' His well-shaped mouth twisted with the sulky retort. 'Maybe if it was about the important things in life I could raise some enthusiasm, but it's nothing but CRB checks, Health & Safety issues and risk assessments concerning a child I don't even know. But why are we talking about all that, when we could be talking about *you*?'

His annoyance over something so close to her heart was the wake-up call Alyssa needed. She stopped melting in the warmth of his gaze and fastened her new employer with a look of her own.

'Because I am your nephew's new nanny, and right now that paperwork *is* the most important thing—in *his* life.' *You self-centred drone!* she added silently to herself.

Prince Lysander Kahani stopped smiling, and she felt a brief spark of satisfaction. That was quickly extinguished as his dark eyes continued to ripple over her like a caress.

'You sound like a woman who knows what she's doing and have the added advantage of looking nothing like a headmistress. Goodbye, all my thoughts of a terrifying harridan, and hello to the beautiful vision that is Miss Alyssa Dene!'

With a ridiculously extravagant gesture, he reached out for her hand. Lifting it to his lips, he brushed her fingers with a kiss of long, slow meaning.

'Please don't do that, Your Royal Highness,' Alyssa said sternly, forcing herself to pull her hand out of his grasp, but unable to stop the corners of her mouth curling up at his teasing.

He gave her a mock pained look. 'Don't spoil my one moment of hope, Alyssa. You are my only ray of sunshine—the first woman below the rank of minister I've been alone with in over three weeks. Look at me!' He groaned, throwing up his arms in mock despair. 'I used to have a life. Now I'm a caged tiger, performing for the benefit of others.'

Alyssa was transfixed—a rabbit trapped in the headlights of his charm. Catching herself gazing at him, she shook her head as though waking from a dream. Angry with his effect on her, she gave a dramatic sigh and said:

'Cursed with a fortune and forced to live in a place

like this? Dear, dear—it must be absolute *hell* for you, Your Royal Highness!'

The moment the words popped out, Alyssa knew she should have kept her mouth shut. Lysander's eyes hardened to jet. The change in him was like the sun going behind a thundercloud.

Why the hell did I say that? He may be an arrogant so-and-so, but he's still royalty! What will happen to his poor little nephew if I get sacked before I've even met the child?

'In the past month I've lost my brother, my sister-in-law, and my freedom.' Lysander Kahani's voice was as cold as the shiver running through Alyssa's body.

There was nothing for it but to apologise. 'I know—and I'm sorry, Your Royal Highness, but my first loyalty is to little Ra'id—' she burst out.

'I can see that, by the way you didn't let me finish what I was saying,' he cut in smoothly. 'I was going on to tell you that picking up the pieces my brother left behind is a full-time job. It shouldn't leave me any time for self-pity.' He gave the tiniest nod of acknowledgement, and the hint of a wry smile.

Alyssa didn't like the way he interrupted her, but at least he understood why she had spoken out.

'At least when I take charge of your poor little nephew it will be one weight off your shoulders.'

His gaze had been working its way down her body with slow enjoyment, but her words stopped him. He dragged his attention back to her face. 'You say that as though you actually give a damn, Miss Alyssa Dene.'

'That's because I do. I'm here to make sure your

nephew is properly looked after, and gets a sensible upbringing.'

'And to bring a little light into my life while you do it,' he said with a widening smile. 'You can start by dropping the formalities. As we'll be working so closely together, call me Lysander.'

Alyssa hesitated. This was quite a normal request from an employer, but with a smooth operator like Lysander Kahani it might be an intimacy too far. It broke down a barrier between them, and that couldn't be a good idea. She already knew it was desperately important to keep this man at arm's length, so he couldn't affect her judgement. That had failed her in the past, when it came to adults. The only thing she wanted to rush into now was little Prince Ra'id's nursery. If she couldn't trust herself, how could she trust a womaniser like Lysander? Only thoughts of the poor child involved stopped her making some sort of excuse and escaping from Combe House while she still could. Good or bad, this man was her new employer. She had to develop a working relationship with him, and that would involve some give and take.

'All right, then…Lysander. You can trust me to look after poor Prince Ra'id as if he was my own child,' she told him.

He raised his dark, finely arched brows. 'There speaks a woman who's never met him!'

'I'm here to care for your poor little nephew, Lysander, not your feelings. So while I'm sorry about your family bereavement and the way you've been forced into becoming Prince Regent, you and I have to work together to make the best of it, for little Ra'id's

sake,' she said firmly, hoping she could be equally determined when it came to resisting Lysander's charm.

'Nobody's ever said anything like that to me before,
either.'

The crease between his brows deepened.

Alyssa realised a man would never have risked saying something like that to Prince Lysander Kahani.
Only a woman could get away with it. She allowed herself the hint of a smile. Lysander's interest in her body
was turning out to have advantages as well as danger.
It could deflect his anger—at least for the moment.

'Then I hope I can keep your nephew a bit more
down to earth.'

Lysander was beginning to have doubts about her.
She could see it in his face.

'I wish you luck,' he murmured. 'As Ra'id is my
brother's son, I've seen him now and again over the
years, but that's all. What I've heard about him from
his nursery maids is bad enough. It'll be a brave woman
who refuses that child anything, from the sound of it.'

When she didn't laugh, he shrugged and stuck his
hands in his pockets. 'Well...if you feel confident
enough to make a mad claim like that, the least I can
do is match it, and raise you. What can I do to help you
in your hopeless task, and earn your undying gratitude
when I've done it?'

She raised her eyebrows, then met his question with
one of her own.

'How do you get on with Ra'id?'

He responded with a quizzical smile. 'Me? I don't.
My family has used this house in England as a bolt hole
for years, so we've met up here regularly for holidays,

but that doesn't mean I've had anything to do with the child.'

I might have guessed, Alyssa thought. 'So you're quite happy to leave that poor mite completely in the hands of strangers?'

His expression hardened. 'Of course, when they come with qualifications and references like yours. What else would you expect me to do? I don't know the first thing about children.'

'Lysander!' Alyssa chided him, but it was only when she took a step backwards and away from him to underline her disapproval that he looked at all bothered.

Annoyed at her reaction, he moved towards an intercom on the desk. 'Ra'id has been well looked after by the general nursery staff here since his last nanny left. I think. At least, I assume… No, I'm sure that's been the case,' he said through gritted teeth.

Alyssa could tell that not knowing annoyed him. That was a detail she could work with.

'Well, you'll be able to judge that side of things for yourself when I've called someone to take you to the nursery,' he went on irritably.

Alyssa had other ideas. 'I'd rather you took me yourself, Lysander. After all, you did ask how you could help,' she said, and this time her smile was as winning as any of the looks he kept turning on her.

CHAPTER TWO

THEY were tempting words, but Alyssa's body language belied her inviting smile, and warned Lysander. He knew she was only trying to use his reputation against him again. Liking her cheek, however, he escorted her to the nursery with the indulgent smile of a man who always got what he wanted. Women generally fell into his arms within seconds, and Alyssa was the first woman in a long while to present him with anything like a challenge. Her beautiful body and long, shapely legs made this new experience very enjoyable. He was confident she would soon be running to him for comfort, and for a prize like that he was willing to be patient. Little Ra'id had sent plenty of distressed nursery maids his way over the past few weeks. Miss Alyssa Dene was different, there was no doubt about that, but Lysander was sure he only had to wait for this latest peach to fall into his lap.

As they walked he sent a series of covert glances in her direction and liked what he saw. She was tall for a woman, so the crown of her head was almost level with his shoulder. Her feminine curves were in perfect proportion, and her blue-eyed beauty was topped by a swirl of shining blonde hair. He knew exactly how that silken waterfall would feel when he released it from her prissy French plait, and looked forward to doing it.

They went straight to the nursery wing's dining room, drawn by an unholy racket. It was full of people, all talking at once. Lysander introduced Alyssa, then stood back. The crowd fell silent. The staff, like him, were watching to see what Alyssa would do when confronted with five-year-old Ra'id. The child was holding court at the head of his dining table and scowling like a little old man. When Lysander saw the peculiar collection of food on the table, he frowned, too. None of it looked edible—especially the sardines in chocolate sauce and the cupcakes spread with Marmite. He watched Alyssa sum up the situation. Then he leaned in to enjoy the fragrant sensation of whispering into her small, perfectly formed ear.

'Meet the poor little orphaned mite you're going to rescue from his wicked, uncaring uncle.'

He expected her to apologise for her starchy attitude towards him, but she didn't. Instead she hissed, 'He seems to have recovered from the tragedy well enough to have your staff on the run!'

'That's because he was about as close to his parents as I was to mine,' Lysander flashed back.

She gave him a strange look, then pinned on a smile before speaking out loud to the infant dictator.

'Good afternoon, Prince Ra'id. It doesn't look as though traditional Rosarian food meets with your approval, so we'll get rid of it, *and* all these people.'

'But he hasn't had any food yet!' A shocked voice burst out from the crowd. 'And it isn't traditional—we've brought him everything he asked for, but nothing's been good enough yet.'

'That's a shame,' Alyssa said evenly. 'But lunchtime should have been over a long time ago.'

'I'm hungry!' Ra'id said through clenched teeth.

The huddle of servants held its breath. Lysander carried on lazily watching Alyssa. She took no notice of her little charge. Instead, she started piling up plates with quick, neat movements. After an exchange of glances, the rest of the staff stepped forward to help her. In minutes the table was clear and the room empty apart from Lysander, Alyssa and the little boy.

'I'm hungry!' Ra'id repeated, this time with more of a whine.

'No, you aren't. If you'd been hungry, you would have eaten the first thing you were served. You're not to treat your staff like that, Prince Ra'id. They spent a lot of time satisfying your demands, so the least you could have done was try something. As your uncle Lysander has just told you, I'm in charge now. From today, you'll eat at regular times. Whatever arrives is what you'll eat, and that's an end to it. There will be *no* alternatives.' She glanced at her watch, then looked at Lysander. 'Do you eat high tea at Combe House?'

'For you, Alyssa, anything is possible.' He chuckled.

'Then could you order a simple meal of egg on toast for His Majesty, to be served in your dining room in half an hour?'

'I don't like egg. What is it?' the little boy piped up.

'It's what you're having for tea,' Alyssa said with

a determination Lysander wished he could see more often.

Ra'id wasn't so impressed. 'No! And I can do what I like, because I'm King.'

Lysander had consoled enough nursery maids to know that was the killer line. It always worked. He glanced at Alyssa with a grin that said *I'd like to see you get out of that!*

Alyssa didn't need to answer him. She knelt down beside Ra'id and folded her arms on the ruined surface of his miniature Georgian dining table so that her face was very close to his.

'Oho—not yet, you aren't! Listen to me, young man. Your uncle Lysander is going to be in charge of you, and everything else around you, for at least the next four thousand days, so what he says, goes. That's a long time, so get used to it. And he says you'll eat the lovely food the staff are kind enough to make for you. If you don't, you'll go hungry.' She looked up at Lysander with battle blazing in her eyes. 'Right?'

Wide-eyed and speechless, the little boy switched his gaze from Alyssa to Lysander, searching for support.

'That's right, isn't it, Lysander?' Alyssa repeated, more forcefully this time.

Lysander knew she wanted him to back her up, but he took his time. He was busy with his own thoughts, enjoying the arousal that pulsed through his body as he watched this determined and beautiful woman in action. The sensation was far more enjoyable than talking to her about nursery routine. Miss Alyssa Dene had the sort of nerve he had never encountered before. He already knew she wasn't going to roll over and submit to him like so many women that had filled his universe until now. He would have to break down her resistance to him inch by inch. It was an idea he found intensely exciting. It would make the moment she finally fell under his spell a real triumph, and a conquest worthy of his maverick skills. He allowed a slow, seductive smile to warm his face. Her need for him was so deeply buried she might not recognise it yet, but she would. Given time. He would make sure of it.

'Right...' He teased the word out slowly. 'So from now on, Ra'id, you'll do everything Alyssa tells you, OK?'

His answer satisfied her, although she laid down the law to Ra'id for a long time after that. While she rattled on, Lysander lost himself again in more luscious thoughts involving silk sheets, perfumed massage oil and Miss Alyssa Dene's soft curves. He only realised he should have been listening to her instead when she coughed politely to attract his attention.

'So, Lysander, Ra'id and I will see you in your dining room in half an hour.'

'Of course,' Lysander said suavely, still wondering if she knew what she was letting herself in for. He sent another leisurely glance over her body. The tempting reality of her promised to be even better than his fantasy.

'Miss Alyssa Dene is the best nanny in the business, Ra'id,' he told his nephew. 'And I'm looking forward to discovering what other talents she has, very soon.' He smiled, tilting his head towards her in a way that never failed to soften women. She stared at him, her cool blue eyes as assured as his own technique.

'It's a pity smiling doesn't seem to be one of them,' he went on, standing back to give her room to melt over his teasing. It had no effect.

'Childcare isn't a laughing matter, Lysander.'

Her wide-set eyes would have been beautiful if they hadn't been focusing a stare on him that was as hard as sapphires.

The last few weeks had stretched Lysander's patience so thin, it was practically transparent. He heard himself snap, like an elastic band that had been stretched too far.

'Then that's a shame. You'll need a sense of humour if you're going to work here.'

He regretted it instantly. Unleashing his bitterness wasn't the way to win over rebellious women. Stepping in close to her again, he softened his retort by patting her gently on the back. 'If only to put up with my short temper. So if you wouldn't mind giving me a few moments of your time outside so we can discuss it, Nanny—?'

His hand slid sensuously over her ribcage on its way to become a support under her elbow.

'My name is Alyssa!'

She jerked away from him so savagely, Ra'id gave a little cry of alarm. Instantly, she swooped down to comfort the little boy. Any angry remarks Lysander might have made at her overreaction died on his lips when he saw the way she reassured his nephew—that, and the way her shirt gaped a little as she bent forward. It gave him an illicit glimpse of her lacy bra as it cupped the creamy swell of her breasts. The view was so delicious, he forgave her everything.

It made him look forward to seeing a whole lot more of her, very soon.

Alyssa used a combination of psychology and her own novelty value to make tea a triumph. Comfort eating over the past few months had made her staid navy-blue nanny's uniform a bit snug. This worked wonders on Lysander. She had his full attention, although it did tend to gravitate towards her breasts. To get him back on track she told him his good manners and charm would soon rub off on his nephew. Ra'id turned out to have a big appetite, and he was so astonished that anyone would stand up to him, he was easy to manage. Food was the perfect bribe. All Alyssa had to do was to make sure he got a healthy diet, and by keeping Lysander on side she would have all the backup she needed.

She was still smiling hours later as she left Ra'id's bedroom that evening. She closed the door so quietly, it didn't make a sound. She could have laughed with relief at the end of such an exhausting, perfect day, but didn't want to wake her little charge. These first few hours in her new job had achieved what her holiday had failed to do—distracted her from the past and helped her to move into the future. It turned out she'd needed a new challenge, and she was relishing it. Ra'id was a real handful, but that was because no one had cared enough to teach him how to behave properly—until now. He was quick, clever, and underneath he had the makings of a dear little chap. Now she could relax for a few hours, and thank her lucky stars that she had

gone with her instincts rather than her emotions. She
had taken this position to save Ra'id from falling into
the hands of some wage slave who was only interested
in what the job prospects were. Now she was looking
after him, everything would be fine. The only fly in the
ointment was her unprecedented response to Lysander,
but what with her past and his present she'd certainly
never be silly enough to give into him—however wickedly tempting his smile might be...

As she entered the suite's sitting room she jumped
violently when she saw that the object of her thoughts
had made himself at home on one of the nursery's low
couches, his long legs stretched out beneath a table. A
tray set for two with fine china and a steaming cafetiere waited in front of him, untouched. A dozen down-
lighters around the walls gave the room a soft golden
glow.

'Thank you, Lysander.' Alyssa kept her voice cool
and professional, desperate not to show him how much
his presence unsettled her. She preferred speaking to
children rather than adults, but talking with Lysander
was all too easy. She tried to concentrate on tidying
the room, hoping her busyness would hide her nerves.
'When you told me you never normally had anything
to do with Ra'id, I thought it meant you didn't have any
interest in him. It was good of you to sit with us while
he had tea in the main dining room. The different surroundings made him a bit uncertain, and that really
helped him behave. Eating with you and other adults
instead of being waited on alone will really help his
manners. You'll be a great example for him to follow.

Is there any chance you could make afternoon tea with him a regular thing?'

'It'll be my pleasure, as long as you promise to always be there, too,' Lysander purred.

The room's low light gave his aristocratic features a shadowy mystery—but there was no mistaking the meaning in his eyes. During the meal they had all taken together Alyssa had been focused on Ra'id, but that couldn't stop her feeling the warmth of Lysander's interest. Alone with him now, she felt coils of attraction snake through her body. Tearing herself away from his gaze, she moved methodically around the room, picking up scattered toys and plumping cushions.

'You must have given your army of attendants the slip,' she said without looking at him.

'I told them to leave me, yes,' he said in a light, conversational way.

Remember, men like him gain your confidence, then abandon you when you're at your most vulnerable. That's how it works, Alyssa told herself firmly.

When the room was as neat as it was going to get, she couldn't think of anything else to do to avoid his eyes except pouring the coffee. Trying not to let her nervousness show, she approached the table from the opposite side to where he sat. As she reached for the handle of the cafetiere his hand closed in on hers and he lifted it out of her grasp.

'That's OK. I'll pour the coffee. You should sit down and relax, Alyssa. It's been a busy day for you. And for me, too. You've given me plenty to think about.'

Until that moment Alyssa had been careful to keep her eyes on the tray, but that made her look up and question him. He was watching her with the exotic look of a well fed panther.

It's bound to be some sort of line, but there's nothing to worry about as long as I keep that thought in mind, she told herself.

'What do you mean?'

'The way you improved Ra'id's behaviour right from the start, by laying down strict boundaries for him. That impressed me. I went back to my staff and put some ground rules of my own in place, to make my life more structured. My nicely pampered, trouble-free life, as you were quick to point out,' he drawled, smiling at her in a way calculated to melt the stoniest heart.

Alyssa tried to resist, but the crafty way he recalled their first meeting started every muscle in her face working as she tried to avoid returning his smile.

'I'd hate to be followed around by all those people the whole time.'

'I do. But that's the way my brother worked, and having all those staff hounding me from day one hadn't given me enough time to devise a better system. I think better when I'm on my own. Clearing my mind by sending them all away for a while gave me the chance to work out a sensible routine for myself. And all it took was the sight of you, taking control.' He lifted one of the little black and gold cups of coffee towards her. 'Cream and sugar?'

'Cream, please. That's all.' She felt suddenly shy, rather than scared of him.

'I prefer cappuccino myself.'

'Oh, so do I!' They both looked surprised at her quick reply, and then smiled.

'You and I will have to indulge ourselves one day,' Lysander said. 'My late brother thought frothy coffee was undignified, and out of keeping with high office.' His smile had been getting wider by the second and Alyssa couldn't resist its power any longer. She could feel her own face relaxing, too.

'Thoughts like that don't stop you?'

'Nothing stops me.' His voice was warm.

Alyssa didn't doubt it. She leaned back in her seat, trying to make the point that she didn't intend starting anything.

'This is very good coffee. Your brother may have had a point. I've heard he was very respectable. When you can drink coffee that tastes like this, why risk pushing any boundaries?' she said, making it clear she didn't only mean coffee.

Lysander wasn't about to be put off so easily. 'Akil didn't start laying down the law until he was unlucky in love and then *bang*! He reverted to the family type where many things were concerned. For one thing, when it came to women he decided they should be seen and not heard—and preferably not seen either.' He gave her another smile. 'I get the feeling you'd be happy to keep this nursery wing as your own private space. I suspect he would have approved of you.'

'All I'm interested in is giving his son a good start in life.' Glowing with quiet pride, Alyssa took another sip of her coffee. 'It's the early days yet, but I think I'm going to like it here. I already love working with Ra'id so much, I'll be quite happy to fit in with whatever you want, Lysander.'

The moment the words left her lips Alyssa went hot

all over. It was exactly the wrong thing to say to a dangerously tempting man like this.

'That's what I like to hear.' He laughed.

'Just remember, I'm not here for your benefit!'

Lysander was so taken aback by her sharp retort, Alyssa had time to organise her thoughts before carrying on.

'My interest is in children, and making sure they're properly looked after. From what I understand, Ra'id has suffered all his life from a high turnover among his carers, so I intend sticking with this job for as long as I'm needed. That's *needed*, and not *wanted*, Lysander,' she said with chilling emphasis, letting him know that she assumed infidelity ran through his veins. 'I'm not going to let anything affect the way I care for Ra'id. That's why I want to get one thing clear from the start. There have to be ground rules for us as well as him.'

He slipped her a sidelong glance. Alyssa's heartbeat accelerated, but she tried to ignore her pounding pulse.

'I mean it.'

'That's a shame, but I suppose I should have guessed.' He sighed, then took a long drink of coffee. 'I've seen for myself how seriously you take your work. Does this mean you think sex isn't a laughing matter, either?'

Alyssa swallowed, knowing she had to dodge his question. Every time she looked at Lysander she noticed some new detail about him. The slight natural curl in his dark hair, or the muscles that were hardly concealed by the fine fabric of his crisp white shirt.

'It really doesn't matter what I think about anything, except my job,' she said, with a determination to ignore his smile. 'I'm employed to care for Ra'id. You've got your work cut out caring for his country, Lysander. We both want the same thing.' She felt embarrassed about exactly how true that was, and knew she was colouring up again. It was a good job the background lighting was so soft. It hid her embarrassment as well as her feelings. 'And that's the best thing for Ra'id. It means you and I have to work together as a team, and I mean *work*.' She emphasised the last word carefully.

'And I have no doubt at all that we will,' he drawled, making Alyssa wonder what he thought of as work. 'That's why I'm going to study your methods as closely as I can. The job of Regent of Rosara couldn't be more different from the life I've lived until now. With Ra'id years away from becoming King, and despite my brother's best attempts at marrying me off, I'm still his only living relative. That means our country's succession is in a precarious state. I have to make sure nothing happens to Ra'id, while running Rosara at the same time, and I intend to succeed at both jobs.'

Alyssa saw he was deadly serious, and knew she had underestimated him. 'That's a real challenge.'

'I know, but I specialise in those.'

She had been thinking so hard about how a playboy was going to juggle two jobs like that, she didn't realise he had been leaning steadily closer and closer to her. When he laid a hand on her arm, she jumped.

'That's why I need your help, Alyssa.'

She pulled her arm away smartly. 'If there's anything I can do to help Ra'id, I will. But that's all, Lysander.'

'Of course. You've made your point, so I'll make

mine. I prefer partnerships of pleasure.' Despite her obvious anger, he didn't sound at all apologetic.

'I suppose by that you mean little and often,' Alyssa snapped.

The smile returned to his beautiful mouth. 'I've never had any complaints.'

'Until you met me, and I'm out of bounds,' she told him meaningfully. 'As long as you remember that, Lysander, you can keep your record with women—which I'm sure must be one hundred per cent perfect.'

'Oh, don't worry. One little setback in a lifetime wouldn't bother me. A single rejection among thousands of triumphs would only amount to a fraction of a percentage point,' he said with a careless smile.

'Ah, but if you don't try, you'll make *sure* you never fail—'

Alyssa had never known a man with such easy, natural charm. Those flashing eyes and that devilish smile made him almost impossible to resist, but then she remembered something. His one and only weakness would always be her greatest strength.

'And if you ever force me to give you a black eye, Lysander, it would make other girls think twice about tangling with you, until your bruises have faded.'

He stopped smiling. His eyes narrowed. He pursed his lips, thinking.

'I'm a fast healer, but...point taken.'

Alyssa wasn't going to take any chances. 'I'm serious, Lysander.'

He took another long, slow sip of coffee but his eyes didn't once leave her face. 'I'm sure you are.'

'I'm here to work, so I don't have time for

distractions. I couldn't live with myself if I didn't do my very best for your little prince. I once let a child down...' She paused, not wanting to complete the story. 'From that moment on, my job became the most important thing in my life. Do you understand?'

Lysander leaned back, resting one arm along the back of the couch. His eyes were dark and inscrutable. 'Ah...yes, I remember somebody bringing that to my attention when they were checking your references. It was truly a tragedy that that little boy died because nobody took any notice when you told them how sick he was. That was unforgivable.'

Alyssa's heart began to beat very quickly, and not only because of the way he was studying her. Talking to Jerry about the tragedy of little Georgie had been hard enough. Discussing it with a stranger would be impossible.

'Yes, it was. Which is why I'd rather you changed the subject,' she said abruptly, her breathing shallow.

Lysander's expression altered. The intensity of his gaze made her blush.

I was never this forceful until—she thought, and felt the sharp pain of sadness in her throat. *Oh, no. Why must that come back to haunt me, right now?* The events of a few months ago had snowballed until they threatened to suck all the life out of her. This job was her chance of a fresh start. She couldn't afford to weaken.

Lysander was so self-confident. Alyssa wished she had his sort of nerve, but she was at least determined not to let him see her eyes fill with tears. She looked away quickly, but for the first time since she had lost

Georgie she found that her tears were easily blinked away. Painfully, she wondered if this was the start of her recovery.

'Of course. It's no wonder you mistrust people after that.' Lysander's voice was as slow and calculated as his smile. 'Is there anything I can do to persuade you we aren't all bad?'

He had picked up on her suspicions about him, so there was no point in denying them. It wasn't good for her new employer to feel he was under surveillance, but that wasn't Alyssa's only worry. If a gorgeous man like this could see how troubled she was, her life really had gone too far in the wrong direction. She had to do something, fast, but what? Maybe she *could* do with talking about what had happened rather than bottling everything up...but this handsome, piratical prince looked more trouble than he was worth. Wanting to talk was one thing. Trusting him was something else. Finishing her coffee, she put her cup and saucer back on the tray and stood up.

'Well, thank you for the drink, but unless you have some aspect of Ra'id's care you'd like to discuss I think you'd better go, Lysander. I've got a lot to do.' She took a last look around the sitting room, then started off towards the door she assumed must lead to her own suite. 'The chap who parked my car earlier said he'd bring my luggage up but I got so involved with Ra'id, I haven't even had a chance to find where I'm sleeping.'

'The nanny's rooms are through there.' He pointed to the door. 'But that way is kept locked all the time, to stop Ra'id disturbing her during the night. You'll have to go out into the corridor and use the main door, at the top of the stairs.'

Alyssa flashed a dangerous look at him. 'And how would you know that, if you've never had anything to do with Ra'id before?'

Lysander smiled at her knowingly. 'Let's call it a lucky guess, shall we?'

'Well, the minute I find the key I'm going to unlock that door, and leave it open. That's how it's going to stay. I can assure you I'll never have any reason to stop Ra'id coming into my rooms to see me.'

'Really?' He gave her a mocking look of disbelief.

'Really.'

Her reply led him to give a casual shrug. 'Then it must be time for me to take you to your lonely suite.'

Alyssa raised her eyebrows.

'To the door and no further,' he assured her, offering his arm.

She hesitated. All day she had fought against falling under his spell. She had managed it so far. Surely she could reward herself with this one, brief point of contact? The fear that Lysander would misunderstand and assume it was the start of something warred with the excitement of being escorted by such a gorgeous, polite man. She already knew he was too much temptation, but had to find out if he was enough of a gentleman.

'Thanks, but I want you to know I'm giving you the benefit of some very big doubts, Lysander,' she told him, slipping her hand into the crook of his arm.

It was just as well she answered before the sensation of his warm, vital body rose through the thin fabric of his jacket. The feel of it shook Alyssa to the core.

She wanted to go on standing there in the middle of the room, enjoying the casual intimacy with this dark stranger. Lysander had other ideas. At the very moment she was most vulnerable, he ignored his advantage and started off towards the door.

'Would it help to put your mind at rest about me if we talked about work?' he asked her.

'That depends,' Alyssa said warily. 'Whose work did you want to discuss? Yours or mine?'

'Yours, of course. Now I've discovered little Ra'id isn't the creature from hell that everyone warned me about, I think I will want to take a more active role in his upbringing.'

Alyssa considered his words carefully. Ra'id was so full of himself, he wouldn't be helped by a fickle uncle who would be distracted by every woman who lured him away. On the other hand, whatever his motives, she didn't want to put Lysander off getting closer to Ra'id. In her bitter experience, it was better to have an adult getting in her way than taking no interest, and ignoring her professional advice.

'You've already told me that Ra'id didn't have a very close relationship with his parents. What he needs is some stability and routine in his life, not to mention some love and affection from a parent figure. If you could offer him that, it would be great. I'd love to have your help,' she continued cautiously, 'although I wouldn't want you to overcommit yourself. Why don't you try to make tea time with Ra'id a daily appointment to begin with, and see how you manage with that? Making some time available regularly in your schedule is much better than overwhelming him with attention to begin with, and then leaving him high and dry when something comes up to divert your attention.'

'I agree. I can't abide people who promise everything and then don't deliver.'

Alyssa looked at him quickly. 'That sounded heartfelt!'

'I've got good reason,' he told her, but didn't say anything else until they reached a door at the point where the nursery wing joined the main house.

'Here it is—the main entrance to your suite. To the door and no further, as promised.'

'Thank you—and I didn't promise anything at all, so that means you won't be disappointed when I say goodbye and let you go,' Alyssa said firmly, taking her hand from his arm. Going inside her suite, she turned around quickly to block the doorway in case he tried to follow her.

'I was thinking about someone else who didn't keep their word—to me.' His voice was slow and thoughtful. 'I find this hard to say but the fact is I need you, Alyssa.'

Alarmed, she took another step backwards into her rooms and tried to close the door on him. Lysander was too quick for her, and grabbed the edge of the door. 'I didn't mean to upset you, Alyssa. For once, I wasn't flirting. I meant that I need you *professionally*, because I don't know the first thing about children.'

He sounded so genuinely pained, she laughed. 'You were one yourself once, don't forget!'

'I know and I remember all too well what I had to go through. I admit, I'd rather leave all the caring to experts like you, and just be there for the fun stuff,' he said with real feeling.

Alyssa was moved. Without realising what she was doing, she reached out and patted him on the arm.

'That's better than nothing, and right now might be exactly what Ra'id needs his uncle for. It'll be great.'

'With you in charge, I'm sure it will be perfect.' His voice was a low murmur, full of possibilities. Alyssa tensed, but his hand slid from the door straight into his pocket.

For two heartbeats she thought about simply closing the door on him, but she couldn't do it. Lysander didn't move a muscle. His stillness was as arousing as the look in his darkly mysterious eyes. She knew exactly what was going to happen, but could not stop herself waiting for it.

Slowly, silently, Lysander reached out to her. She was unresisting, so he drew her into his arms for a kiss that made her forget everything—until she remembered that she was in the grip of a serial womaniser. With a heart-rending effort she forced herself out of his grasp.

'Lysander! You promised you were going to take me to my door and no further!'

He pointed towards the floor. Without knowing what she was doing, Alyssa had stepped over the threshold. She was now out in the hall again.

Lysander was already coolly backing away from her. 'I was as good as my word. That is exactly what I did. No more—but no less, either.'

With that, he blew her a kiss, turned and sauntered off.

Alyssa was rooted to the spot. She watched him go,

her fingertips resting on her lips as she tried to recapture the pressure of his mouth against hers. When he reached the top of the stairs, he stopped and glanced back. His smile told her everything she didn't want to know. It took her right back to those few delicious seconds she had spent in his arms. She responded with a sudden rush of sensual warmth. Her body would have done anything to experience his strength surrounding her again.

But her heart was too afraid…

CHAPTER THREE

EARLY next morning, Lysander appeared in the nursery doorway. His unexpected arrival threw Alyssa into a panic, but she was careful not to show it. She was briefing her members of staff when she saw him, and didn't want to betray her feelings in front of them. Luckily, this wasn't a social call. He stayed brisk and business-like as he informed them he was arranging for the royal household to fly back to Rosara in a few days' time.

'Once we get there, instead of Ra'id taking tea in my suite I thought we could take him out for a picnic every afternoon, Alyssa,' he told her.

She nodded, glad he was keeping things light and impersonal. 'If the weather's good, it'll be a great idea.'

'Don't worry about the weather, it's the company that matters,' he said teasingly, then walked off, with nothing more than a wink for the other girls.

Alyssa went back to her work in a haze of regret. She might have had more sense than to be seduced by Lysander last night, but it was a near thing. His touch had ignited a slow burning fire inside her that couldn't be extinguished. She knew she should have kept right out of his grasp. All she could do now was try and feel glad that at least she'd found the strength from somewhere to push him away. If she had given in to the temptation, let him go all the way and seduce her, how much worse would she be feeling this morning? She would be tortured by regret as well as feelings of loss. As it was, she felt as though a sticking plaster had been wrenched off her heart—the heart that her ex-fiancée had broken and Lysander now endangered once again, just as she was trying to heal. She was so afraid the edges of her mental wounds were coming apart again, too. If that happened, there would be nothing to hold back the flood of her bad memories. And then all those mistakes would return to haunt her.

Over the next few days, Alyssa barely saw Lysander. He was too busy arranging their transfer to Rosara to spend more than a few minutes with Ra'id each day, over tea. At those times Alyssa kept out of the way, using the excuse that she wanted them to get to know each other without any distractions. That didn't stop her keeping a discreet eye on Lysander from the next room. She told herself she was only being professional, but that wasn't true. The way he smiled each time she opened the door to him made her blush so furiously she could barely meet his gaze.

The rest of the time, all she got was a glimpse of him in passing now and again as she and Ra'id settled into their new routine, or she heard the sound of his clear, calm voice ringing through the house. Those tantalising hints of what might have been made him all the more desirable. All Alyssa could do was go on telling herself she had been right to push him away, and try to keep her mind off him. It was almost impossible, but packing all Ra'id's things ready for the journey to Rosara gave her hardly any time to brood. She already adored the little boy. Getting him to tell her all about his home far away strengthened their bond and cheered him up, too. While he painted pictures of his ponies and spun stories about life in Rosara's Rose Palace, Alyssa told herself life couldn't possibly get any better.

If only she could stop thinking about Lysander. And if only international travel didn't involve flying...

On the night before they were due to leave for Rosara, Alyssa sat up late. She pretended she was collecting things to keep Ra'id occupied during the flight, but the idea of sitting in a tin can hurtling through the air thousands of feet above the ground had a lot to do with her sleeplessness. Only in the early hours of the morning did she finally give in and go to bed. She had barely closed her eyes when the alarm buzzed in her ears.

Ra'id was so excited about going back home he was a real handful, but Alyssa was determined he should behave. They ate a quiet breakfast together in the nursery wing, though she barely had an appetite. Then she marched him downstairs to the entrance hall. Lysander was already there, supervising the transfer and as smartly dressed as ever.

The moment he spotted her, he strolled over to meet them at the bottom of the stairs. Ra'id was delighted, but Lysander was more interested in Alyssa.

'What's the matter?'

'Nothing, Lysander.'

'I hope you are being a good boy?' he warned his nephew.

The little boy blinked up at them both innocently.

'He's fine,' Alyssa said quickly. 'We're getting used to each other, gradually.'

'But there's definitely *something* different about you.' Lysander's hand went out to her, but he brought it sharply back to his side before it went anywhere. 'If you're still worried about what happened on your first night here—' he murmured.

If they had been alone, Alyssa knew he would have reached out to her, which could so easily have turned into something more. The urgent need to feel his touch again filled her until she couldn't speak. All she could do was shake her head.

That wasn't enough for Lysander. 'So what *is* your problem?'

'What problem?'

He gave up. 'OK. I'm taking the lead car for the drive to the airport while you and Ra'id follow in the one behind, so I'll speak to you again once we're on the plane.' Lysander rapped out the words like a warning.

Alyssa felt herself going green. Luckily, Lysander didn't notice. He was distracted by a furious wail from Ra'id.

'No! I want to go with you, Uncle Ly!'

Alyssa frowned. 'You can at least ask properly, Ra'id. Now, we've been working on this. What should you have said?'

The little boy gazed at her for a few seconds, and then remembered.

'Please, Alyssa, may I go in Uncle Ly's car?'

She smiled gravely. 'Well done, Ra'id, although it all depends on your uncle. Your Royal Highness?'

She looked up at Lysander, expecting only an answer to her question. She got a whole lot more. He was gazing down at her so intensely that, for a moment, every one of her fears vanished.

'I think that would be a very good idea, Alyssa.'

She stood up again and bowed slightly. 'Then I'll arrange to have Prince Ra'id's things moved into your car.'

'There's no need for that. I'll ride with you in your car, instead.'

Alyssa felt her face relax in a smile of relief.

'That's better,' he murmured to her as they all moved towards the front door. Alyssa thought she felt a slight touch on her arm, but when she looked down there was no trace of his hand. It didn't matter. Knowing Lysander would be sitting in the same car with them was a welcome distraction. It would give her something other than the flight to think about on their drive to the airport.

As they got to the great front door of Combe House Ra'id broke away and frolicked out into the sunlight.

'I want to sit next to the driver!'

'I thought you might!' Lysander laughed, with a quick sideways smile at Alyssa.

Unable to stop herself, she blushed. As they stepped out of the house the dazzle of bright sunlight reflecting off three highly polished limousines made her blink. It was the perfect excuse to look away from Lysander and hide her nerves. As their chauffeur settled Ra'id into the front passenger seat Lysander reached out and opened the rear door for himself. Alyssa couldn't look at him directly, but made the most of the glimpse she got of his lean, golden-tanned hand. Suddenly, he stood aside.

'After you, Alyssa. Since you're trying to teach Ra'id to be a gentleman, I will of course lead by example! For tips on gentlemanly etiquette, you need look no further than me.'

There was a twinkle in his eyes that was downright wicked and it helped defuse the tension she was feeling, Alyssa smiled back at him in spite of herself and slid demurely into the car.

'Now *that's* more like it.' He slid into the seat beside her and slammed the door. Pressing a button, he raised a partition that closed the passenger compartment off from where Ra'id was busy distracting their chauffeur.

The second they had complete privacy, Lysander lost his smile. Turning in his seat, he levelled a penetrating stare at her.

'Joking apart, what *is* the matter, Alyssa? Are you ill? You're as white as a sheet, and you look terrible.'

She managed to rally, but it was an effort. 'Well, thank you very much! I thought you said you were a gentleman?'

Twisting her hands nervously in her lap, she steeled herself to tell him the worst. It had been preying on her mind, and now it felt like the most awful, enormous problem in the whole world.

'You're right. I am worried about something.'

'Well?' He narrowed his eyes. 'Don't tell me you're having second thoughts? Watching you with Ra'id, it's obvious you're made for each other.'

She felt a wonderful rush of pleasure that made up for all her nervousness about travelling with him.

'Thank you! Looking after him doesn't feel like work to me. I love it so much, and everyone here is so friendly. I can't believe I nearly missed the chance to work for you, Lysander. It's turning out to be a dream job for me,' she said, but he wasn't taken in.

'So what has stolen the roses from your cheeks?' He raised one finger and started to trail it down the side of her face. Alyssa started. Her eyes flicked to where Ra'id and the chauffeur were deep in conversation, just the other side of the soundproof screen. Lysander raised an eyebrow, but dropped his hand. 'Not me, that's for sure. I can see by that blush.'

'I keep telling you, Lysander, it's nothing you need to worry about,' she said in a dangerous voice.

He raised a sardonic eyebrow. 'Well, have it your own way—but remember, if there's ever anything I can do to help, just ask.'

'Thank you. That's very kind,' she said as he offered her a drink from the car's chiller. Pouring some freshly squeezed passion-fruit juice into a glass filled with ice, he handed it to her with a shrug.

'One of the perks of "working for a prince", that's all,' he said with a devastating smile.

When he looked at her like that, Alyssa saw why hordes of beautiful women flocked around him despite his easy-come-easy-go reputation. She also realised her body wasn't as determined as her mind. It melted under the warmth of his gaze, despite what he said next.

'And as Ra'id's nanny, that means you'll be travelling with him and me in the private quarters of the plane, apart from the rest of the staff. You should be quite comfortable as there is a lounge area aside from my office. While there are some matters I must attend to I want to reassure you that I intend to look after my nephew properly.'

'Of course. That means we'll all be able to get some work done,' she said, trying to sound firm.

Lysander's smile became more of a rueful grimace as he nodded towards Ra'id's small, excitable figure in the front seat. 'I wouldn't be so sure about that!'

As usual, Lysander and his team were fast tracked onto the plane so he could start work straight away. He was glad of the excuse to bury himself in paperwork, because he needed time to think. Alyssa was starting to affect him far more than he'd expected. She was stealthily stripping away all his certainties about women. He loved women in all their forms and, so far, wanting a woman and sleeping with her had been one and the same thing to him. He had never met one who didn't want to gratify her desire for his body within minutes of meeting him. Alyssa was no exception, but for some reason she was determined to fight it. Despite her reticence, nothing could hide the signs. He loved watching the pupils of her breathtakingly blue eyes grow large and dark when she looked at him. When the tip of her tongue danced sensuously over her lips it betrayed her thoughts until he wanted to kiss her senseless.

He moved irritably in his seat. Trying to settle himself was impossible, especially as she passed by just then with Ra'id and gave him the briefest of smiles. It wasn't enough. He was hungry for Alyssa's laughter. No other woman looked at him like that, or stood up to him the way she did. It was the effect she had on him that concerned Lysander. Women who wanted money or status were easily dealt with, but Alyssa wasn't like that. She was an unknown quantity. Simply bedding her would pose no problem for him at all. He knew she would come to him, sooner or later. He saw it every day in her eyes, felt it in her touch and, for a few spellbinding seconds, he had tasted it on her lips. Yet each time he tried to get closer, she backed off. It seemed as though life leant too heavily on her mind to let the real Alyssa inside the starchy nanny out to play. That thought ran through his chest like a rapier blade. Lysander knew all about secrets, and the way they could lead to disaster.

He pulled a hand down over his face, blocking out the memories. He didn't want to think about the past in any more detail than that.

And that was why he found Alyssa so disturbing.

Alyssa was not happy. Ra'id's excitement made her feel ten times worse about being so nervous. She made herself join in with him, while fighting to hide her fear. She wished she could be like the rest of the staff, laughing and joking while they stood on the tarmac as they waited to board the plane. When Lysander had jokingly told her, *Cheer up, it might never happen!* she'd snapped at him without meaning to. That made her feel even worse.

Ra'id couldn't wait to be shown to his seat in Lysander's private quarters. Alyssa followed him, glad to be well away from the rest of their party. While a stewardess strapped Ra'id into his seat for the flight, Alyssa sat and shivered. She hardly noticed when

Lysander asked for a blanket, but she was soon very glad he had. Taking the seat beside her, he threw the blanket over her lap and arranged it round her. As the engines rumbled into life he slipped his hand under its folds and caught hold of her hand.

'I was right. You looked cold, and your hand is freezing. Are you sure you're all right, Alyssa?'

He sounded so concerned she shook her head, but couldn't open her eyes. Only the smallest shiver of apprehension betrayed her.

'Oh, is *that* it?'

She heard a mixture of relief and triumph in his voice. Then he gave her hand a quick squeeze and announced loudly, 'Ra'id, Alyssa has a headache, so you must be very quiet.'

Leaning close to her, he whispered very softly in her ear, 'Why didn't you tell me you're afraid of flying?'

'It seemed silly to bother you with something I have to deal with myself.'

'That's a typical Alyssa answer!' He laughed quietly. 'Good. It means you're still there underneath the nerves.'

'Thank you for understanding, Lysander,' she muttered under her breath.

'Don't mention it. Thank *you* for being so brave.'

The royal jet began to thunder down the runway. Lysander held her hand tight until they were airborne.

'There. That's all there is to it,' he reassured her, withdrawing his hand from beneath the blanket. 'Although you still look pretty frail. Why don't you go and have a lie down? I have a bedroom for long haul flights.' He indicated a door behind them. Alyssa was on her guard instantly, and saw him realise why.

'You don't need to worry about me. I'll be far too busy out here, what with paperwork, and Ra'id...you know,' he said casually.

'As kind as your offer is I really shouldn't, Lysander. It's my job to be here to keep an eye on Ra'id, and if you're busy with work—'

'Nonsense,' he interrupted her. 'I will need you to be on top form once we land and return to the palace. Ra'id is bound to be bursting with excitement then and will need some calming down. I'll get another staff member to play some games with him until I am free to entertain him myself. I'm giving you an order to rest.'

Alyssa nodded. After her restless night, the chance to catch up on her sleep and ignore her fears for a while—even if it was in the surroundings of Lysander's own room—was too tempting to miss.

He showed her into a compact cabin. It was perfectly equipped and totally unthreatening, she was glad to find. The carpet was so thick, it felt quite natural to kick off her shoes and dig her toes into its softness as she looked around. The bed was large and uncluttered with the duvet and pillows covered in a plain tan slip. The masculine theme continued through to the room's brown upholstery and the air seemed tinged with the faint suggestion of his signature aftershave.

'Stay in here for as long as you like, Alyssa.'

His guiding hand gave her a light pat.

'Thank you.'

There was nothing forced about her smile now. As she went towards the bed Lysander reached out and

pulled back the duvet for her. She hesitated, eyeing him
with suspicion. Taking the hint, he dropped the coverlet
and took a step back from the bed. With that reassur-
ance, she got in. Before she could stop him Lysander
covered her over. It was like being enveloped in a cloud.
She closed her eyes. There was a slight pressure from
his hands as he settled the cover around her. It eased,
returned again for a fraction of a second, and then was
gone.

'Try and get some rest.'

His words came from somewhere safely over by the
door. Alyssa smiled without opening her eyes. After
her long, sleepless night, she really couldn't stay awake
any longer.

Lysander didn't leave the room straight away. He
paused, then on impulse returned to her bedside the
moment she was asleep. After a second's hesitation,
he kissed her lightly on her cheek.

'Sweet dreams,' he murmured, and then quickly left
the room.

Why in the world did I do that? he wondered, making his escape. He closed the door behind him, but that
was the last sensible thing he did. He didn't stride away,
putting a good distance between him and temptation.
Instead, he stood with one hand on the door handle,
thinking.

There was only one problem with Miss Alyssa
Dene—and that was the fact that there *was* no problem. She had the body of an angel, and a mind to match.

That was the highest praise Lysander could give.
He'd known a lot of women, but they were all too easily

distracted by his money and influence. None of them had shown a fraction of Alyssa's nerve and determination. There was no doubting her courage. She didn't think twice about standing up to him, and the way she hid her fear of flying from Ra'id was so brave. When he'd held her in his arms the other night, it had aroused an urgency within his body that was completely foreign to him. And as for kissing her...well, that was something else...

Lysander forced himself to push thoughts like that to the back of his mind. He liked to retain control of his body and emotions at all times. He only had to think about his brother's disastrous love affair to see what happened when a man let his heart rule his head. But Lysander had started leaving his common sense behind whenever he thought of Alyssa. She stirred primitive feelings in him, and they couldn't be ignored. Seeing her looking so vulnerable in his bed, he had been overcome in a shocking way by the urge to possess her fragile beauty.

He was still for so long, Ra'id stopped chewing the end of his crayon and looked up from his colouring book.

'Is Alyssa all right, Uncle Ly?'

'Oh, yes.' He nodded, although his face was grave. 'She's perfect.'

And that's dangerous, he thought.

CHAPTER FOUR

ALYSSA stretched out luxuriantly, still hazy from the dream she'd just had. Opening her eyes, she lurched back to reality. This was Lysander's bed, and she was still in his cabin on-board his private plane. Only the touch of his lips had been a dream. The wonderful, guilty feeling of being held in his arms slipped away as she woke fully, leaving her alone again. It wasn't his pulse she could feel purring through the length of her body, but the soft vibration of aircraft engines.

That was enough to get her moving. She wished she could enjoy Lysander's own private space, but the sensation of being in a plane played on her nerves. She needed distraction, and was about to get up when sounds of soft movement came from outside the bedroom. She froze. Without knowing why, she shut her eyes again and rolled onto her side with her back to the door. There was something about being found awake in this room that felt all wrong, and her only defence was to play possum. Whoever was coming to investigate was bound to let her sleep on. That would be less embarrassing all round.

She heard the cabin door brush over the thick carpet as it was pushed open. She expected her visitor,

whoever it was, to retreat after a quick peek. Forcing
herself to breathe slowly despite her pounding heartbeat, she waited to hear it close again. It didn't happen. Instead, muffled footsteps crossed the room to
her bedside. Despite straining her ears she hardly
heard a sound, but there was a definite presence very
near to her. She felt it grow closer as someone leaned
over her—and she inhaled the clean fresh scent of
Lysander's aftershave. It gave her such a lift she let
her eyelashes part a fraction. When she saw the pale
shape of his hand drifting towards her cheek she drew
in a long lingering breath, waiting for his touch.

It never came. His hand hovered beside her face, then
moved down to linger over her shoulder. He was almost touching her—but his fingertips never quite connected with her body. The suspense stroked an exquisite
glow over her skin. Then she saw his fingers clench.
Abruptly, he pulled his hand out of her restricted field
of view. Her heart sinking, she waited for him to van-
ish and quietly close the door on her fantasy.

When he slammed it with enough force to demolish
the place, Alyssa didn't have to pretend to jump—she
did it naturally. She sat up sharply in the bed, then remembered she should be half asleep. Rubbing her eyes,
she pretended to be confused. Lysander was standing
in the doorway, looking carefully at everything else in
the cabin, but not her. Alyssa was glad she wasn't the
focus of his attention. It meant she didn't have to meet
his eyes.

'Come on, Goldilocks, it's time to get out of my bed.
Alyssa!' he called across the room.

Oh, why couldn't you have thought of Sleeping

Beauty instead? she thought, but deep down she knew. It was the same reason why he hadn't shaken her awake. That would have bridged the invisible dividing line between them—the one she had been so keen to draw. His bedroom was the place where it was stretched so thinly, Alyssa was glad Lysander was the one making sure things didn't get too personal. The reason for her being here in his bed was awkward enough. She already felt at a disadvantage, and wouldn't have known what to say.

'You'll have to get your seat belt on for the landing,' he announced as she checked her watch.

She sighed, but it had nothing to do with sleepiness. It was such a let-down to get up and leave all that comfort behind. Lysander's on-board office was geared up for work, not fantasy. She had experienced a lovely dream, but that was all. He had made waking her up nothing more than a chore, to be ticked off his 'to do' list. Given his casual attitude to women and her damaged feelings, Alyssa knew it was probably just as well. Trying to hide her mixed feelings about that, she busied herself getting Ra'id ready for touchdown. To distract herself, she risked a look out of the nearest window as she fastened his seat belt. If anything could take her mind off Lysander, it was the reminder that she was on a plane.

As the clouds thinned the lion-colored landscape of Rosara became visible below. Alyssa's stomach lurched, and not only through fear. She hadn't anticipated the way she would feel when seeing Lysander's country. His beautiful land appealed to her heart straight away, in the same way something about him reached out to her. It was a mystery, just waiting for her to explore…

The moment they landed Ra'id bounced out of his seat. Alyssa was glad of the excuse to chase after him. She couldn't wait to get off the plane, but Lysander caught her arm as she passed him. She looked back, and her reaction made him let go instantly. He raised his hand in a wordless apology.

'I thought you might like to let me go on ahead, Alyssa. That's all. I'm more used to the reception committee,' he began, but his cabin crew were already swinging the aircraft's door open.

She caught Ra'id's hand before he reached the top of the steps, and she was almost thrown backwards by a wave of noise. Looking out of the plane, she registered the huge crowd of people gathered around Rosara's small airport building. They were lined up around the roof, the balconies and spilling onto the airstrip. Panic almost swamped her. She gripped Ra'id's hand, but the little boy was in his element.

'Wave, Alyssa!' He laughed, but all she wanted to do was dive back into the plane. She half turned, but Lysander was right behind her. There was nowhere to run, but suddenly that didn't matter. She couldn't move. The change in Lysander was so amazing, she wasn't going anywhere. Acknowledging the cheers of his people, he seemed taller and more impressive than ever. Everything that had intrigued her about him was magnified under Rosara's golden sunlight.

Rising to the occasion, he lifted one hand to salute the crowds. They went wild with delight. Lysander must be as popular with his people as he was with supermodels and celebrities! Swept up in the romance of it all, Alyssa couldn't help being impressed. She had wondered if Lysander saved his best behaviour for abroad, making his home ground the place where he was Player King. Instead, he looked every inch the suave, sophisticated statesman. With one hand on Ra'id's shoulder, he encouraged the little boy to wave to their audience. Alyssa decided she might have misjudged Lysander. His country was bringing out the professional best in him. Maybe she would be able to relax her guard a little bit while she was here, after all...

The heat of Rosara flowed over her, filled with exotic sounds and scents. It was exciting, but terrifying at the same time. The breath caught in her throat, and she had to fight the urge to lean back against Lysander's reassuring bulk.

He had no qualms about lowering his head until she could feel the whisper of his words, warm against her neck.

'Are you OK?'

She nodded. 'Just a bit overwhelmed, that's all! Are you always greeted like this when you arrive in Rosara?'

'Pretty much. With so few flights in and out of our country, a royal arrival is always a real event. Practically the entire local population turns out to welcome us home.'

That explains everything, she thought with a rueful smile. *He's playing to the gallery. It's an easy way to impress the maximum number, with the minimum effort.*

Letting Lysander deal with the cheering crowds, she basked in the warmth of his reflected glory. It was lovely to pause, and take in her new surroundings. The atmosphere was rich, and Rosara was well named— The Land of Roses. She could smell flowers with every breath, and it was wonderful. She drank in optimism with the dry air as she walked down the aircraft steps holding Ra'id's hand. With Lysander so close beside her, her dream job was getting better and better.

'There. You've done it. Solid ground beneath your feet at last.' He chuckled quietly.

Alyssa laughed at the sensation of his breath whispering over her hair again. She was glad he had to lean so close to make himself heard over the racket.

'Yes, but you helped me more than you will know, Lysander. Thank you. And it was well worth the journey. I'm so pleased to be here at last. Isn't it terrific? All these people really love you!'

'I know. They always have, but that isn't enough any more, is it?' he murmured with an insight that made her look at him with new eyes. 'From now on, I must earn their respect, too. That's why I must get to work straight away. I should be hustling us straight to the palace.' His grimace told its own story. It was one thing to be the centre of attention, but not so enjoyable when you were in charge of all those individual lives.

Alyssa knew all about pressure. She had been under enough of it herself in the past. But this was on a massive scale.

She thought back to her first sight of Lysander, surrounded by clamouring staff all wanting a piece of him. He had looked as tense as she'd felt then, but arriving home in Rosara had transformed him. He moved today with the ease of someone who didn't have a care in the world. It was only when he mentioned going to the palace that the telltale creases reappeared around his eyes.

'The crowd are enjoying this so much, it's a shame to disappoint them by rushing away. Why don't you send someone on ahead to sort out the most urgent stuff, while you stay here and enjoy your reception for a bit longer?' Alyssa said with a smile. She guessed he might use her words as a good excuse to linger. 'Anyone can see how you've been missed. You and Ra'id really ought to let the crowd get a good look at you both before you disappear behind the black glass of one of your official cars, Lysander!'

The warmth of his presence was quite a distraction in itself, but when his hand dropped lightly onto her shoulder in response to her words, she jumped.

'There's no need for that.'

Lifting his hand again, he pointed across the tarmac. A huge black open-topped limousine was gliding towards them. Surely she wasn't expected to travel in that with him, under the interested gaze of his adoring public?

A chauffeur in full formal uniform and cap opened the car doors for them, saluting as Ra'id bounced into the front seat. Despite his regal status, Lysander stood aside with a smile for Alyssa to get into the rear seat first. She almost died of embarrassment as the crowd greeted this little touch with an extra loud roar of pleasure. From the sound of it, watching Lysander load young women into the back of official cars was a national pastime.

As they drove slowly past the airport terminal a man burst from the ranks of the crowd. The car slowed, giving him time to throw something into the car. It fell into Alyssa's lap. She jumped, then saw it was only one of the famous red roses of Rosara. It was the first of dozens. The car soon filled with flowers, all thrown by the delighted, cheering crowd.

Secure in his popularity, Lysander gave her a lazy smile.

'Wow, I've never experienced anything like this! Your people seem truly happy to have you as Regent.'

Her words had far more effect on him than the jostling press of people around the limousine. He dodged her gaze, leaning forward to reach between the front seats and tousle Ra'id's hair. 'I know. So all I have to do is to build on that. For Ra'id's sake.'

Alyssa wondered if he only tacked on those last few words for her benefit. It was easy to see it was Lysander the people wanted. It was his name they were calling, not the name of his nephew. That made her feel suddenly very uneasy, but she couldn't ask him about it in front of all these crowds. She had to wait until their car turned onto the new main road leading directly from the airport to the palace.

'I need to speak to you, Lysander.' She flicked her eyes meaningfully towards where Ra'id was chatting happily to the chauffeur.

Lysander flipped a switch, and the car's roof slid silently into position. Then he raised the partition separating them from Ra'id and the driver.

'Are you sure it's safe to bring Ra'id to a place like this?'

He gave her a steady look. 'It's his home. You don't need to worry about a thing.'

'Yes, I do. I lost a child because I didn't like making too much fuss, even though I knew in my bones it was the right thing to do. I'm never going to stand by and watch another one suffer. This time I'm going to speak out, whatever the cost to me.'

His looked at her steadily. 'Go on.'

'The people of Rosara are fond of Ra'id because he's small and cute, but most of that love and affection wasn't directed at him. It was meant for you.'

Lysander leaned back in his seat. As their car crossed the trackless wastes of desert he gazed out of the window, running one finger back and forth across his lips. 'Oh. Is that all you're worried about?'

'*All?*' Alyssa's voice was a squeak of disbelief.

'Let's just say that who the country want as their king isn't uppermost in my mind at the moment. My people want something to celebrate, Alyssa. My—our—country was marooned in the Stone Age until only a few decades ago. They don't want that any more. My late father replaced the horrible regime that killed my mother, and started improvements.'

'Your mother was killed?'

His expression shut like a trap. 'Yes. The recent rulers of Rosara don't have a good track record when it comes to wives. My parents were put together by politicians, while my late brother married for love. Both matches led to disaster and death, so I'm saving myself from that. That's why, when it comes to women, I keep moving. Everything I've seen and experienced tells me it's safer that way.'

'I thought men played around for the sake of it.'

Alyssa hid her pain so well, Lysander laughed. 'Yes, there's an element of that. Or at least there was, until my brother died and I was forced to—'

He stopped in mid flow, looked at her and became serious again.

'When I became Ra'id's guardian, and caretaker for my country. That's a job that's every bit as serious as childcare, wouldn't you say?'

'I hope you're not making fun of me.'

This time he recognised that something had touched a raw nerve in her. The half-smile he had been using to try and lighten her mood vanished again. 'Now it's my duty to concentrate on my country, and carry on the good work started by my father and brother. Once I'm up to speed on ruling, I'll teach Ra'id how it's done. Until then, I'm happy to live off my—I mean *our*—people's love until I can earn their respect. If the Rosari are happy, then the Kahani family is happy too. It doesn't matter which one of us gets the credit.'

'I want to believe you,' Alyssa said slowly. 'But when you mention Rosara, sometimes you forget Ra'id. Your instinct is to call this country your own, instead of saying "*our* country" and "*our* people".'

The look Lysander gave her was inscrutable, but he didn't silence her so she carried on.

'You said that your country is in flux. I hope there's no tussle for power going on behind the scenes. It would be terrible for Ra'id if Rosara turned into a war zone.'

Lysander's hawklike glare checked the car's intercom. Their conversation was guaranteed to stay secret, so he relaxed—but only a little. Almost as though he enjoyed keeping her guessing, he started to smile and let his expression mature in the heat of her glare. She refused to back down.

'That won't happen. I do love my country, but I didn't ask for this responsibility—frankly, I'm far more comfortable lazing about on yachts. I'll just be thankful when it's over and I can get my freedom back. Until then, it's my job to keep control of things.'

'Including me?' She narrowed her eyes.

He allowed his soft laughter to caress her. For an instant she was back in his private cabin, waiting expectantly beneath his hands.

'I only work wonders, not miracles.'

She lowered her lids in disdain, but his next words were a teasing throb of promise.

'Don't tempt me to try, Alyssa, or you'll miss your first sight of *our* palace.'

He spoke in a low, slow combination of notes that played over her body like fingertips. She turned her head away. It was one thing for her body to be preoccupied with Lysander, but she wanted to keep her mind her own. She needed distraction. Glancing out of the window, she got it.

'What's the matter?' Lysander tensed again at her gasp.

'I knew somewhere called the Rose Palace had to be beautiful…but I hadn't realised how big it would be!' she breathed.

'Do you like it?'

She didn't need to answer. Her amazed silence was enough.

The Kahani palace had been the home of Lysander's

family for centuries. It stood on the site of the best oasis in that vast, ochre landscape. The afternoon sun was already drawing gossamer shades of apricot and salmon across the sky and sand. Against this exotic colour scheme, Lysander's home stood out like a fairy tale castle spun from sugar. An enormous range of buildings glowed as white as a wedding cake against the tawny desert. Nothing Alyssa had read or seen could have prepared her for this.

It was impossible to believe that such a lovely place could exist in this sea of sand, with its brutal reefs of rock.

As they drew up at the grand south front of the palace Alyssa thought it was the most beautiful thing she had ever seen. Lysander's huge home was built around a vast central courtyard. It had been enlarged and extended over the centuries around the site of the original desert spring, which had been captured in a series of formal pools. Around them, fig and apricot trees cast lots of deep shade. This oasis of calm was overlooked on one side by offices and on the other by a residential wing. Cool, paved corridors and shady courtyard gardens running away from this living heart were the perfect place to spend hot summer days. There were all sorts of places to hide or wander undisturbed. Each large, graceful room inside the palace was more stunning than the next. Delicate traceries of pierced stonework and gold leaf were everywhere. Smiling, bowing servants in flowing traditional dress gave the whole place a fairy-tale feel. It was a completely new world for Alyssa, and she loved it.

Lysander went straight to his office, leaving Alyssa

to be shown around her new home by one of the resident housekeeping team. She was given the pick of several apartments in the nursery wing and chose one overlooking a small, quiet courtyard. Her living room had a little balcony draped with wisteria where she could sit down and relax, when she had a moment to herself. In practice, that might never happen. There were plenty of staff, but in England she had already found she could never rest while Ra'id was up and about. She didn't like to let him out of her sight during the day, and always popped in to check on him during the night, too. Each time she had run her hand over his cool, dry forehead she thought of little Georgie. That had been a rare tragedy, and with Lysander giving her total control over Ra'id's health and welfare she knew the same thing would never happen again, but the worry was always there. She knew everyone else would think she was being irrational, but it didn't feel like that to her. *I'd rather care too much than not enough*, she kept telling herself. *Except when it comes to Lysander...*

Ra'id was so exhausted after all the excitement of their journey home, he wanted to go to bed straight after his supper. Alyssa couldn't believe her luck. Once the nursery was straight, she had a long indulgent bath, got ready for bed, then allowed herself the luxury of a really early night. She was almost as tired as Ra'id, and dropped off to sleep straight away.

Alyssa had been told the nursery wing was fitted with the best alarm system money could buy, but nothing could override her years of training. Her ears were tuned to hear the slightest night-time noise. When music wafted in through her open windows, she was awake instantly. The faint, distant sound of wheels on tarmac told her exactly what was going on. Lysander was having a party. A big affair, judging by the number of vehicles arriving.

She tried to get back to sleep rather than worry about what might be going on, or how much noise there would be. From the sound of it, the party was a long way away. It must be on the other side of the palace complex. Although there was no way a nanny could have expected an invitation to one of Lysander's parties, a part of her couldn't help wishing she were there—while knowing it would be a bad idea. She had seen enough photographs of Lysander partying to know what would be going on. Half-naked starlets would be draping themselves all over the place, hoping for something more permanent than a simple photo opportunity. The more she thought about some other woman making a fool of herself over a philanderer like Lysander Kahani, the harder it was to get to sleep. In the end, she pulled the sheet over her head and stuck her fingers in her ears to block out the distant rise and fall of sound.

A loud knocking at the door to her suite was harder to ignore. Scrambling out of bed and padding over to open it, she found a footman outside. He was carrying a silver salver, and on it was a single sheet of handmade paper. It had been folded in half to hide the message. When she opened it out, she found a simple message written in a bold, flowing hand.

'Dear Alyssa, please bring Ra'id straight down to

the state banqueting hall. I'd like to introduce him to the company.'

It was signed simply 'L', with a little 'x' beside the initial letter.

Alyssa felt the unwanted stirrings of arousal within her body. A personal invitation from Lysander to visit his party, and with a kiss after his initial...

She pursed her lips. It was a dream that, professionally, she had to treat as a nightmare. He was asking her to treat his nephew like some performing animal on display!

She checked her watch, which only made things worse. It was ten past ten—hours after Ra'id's bedtime. Infuriated, she told the footman there was no reply and sent him back to the party. When he had gone, she realised a simple message would never stop a man like Lysander. He would carry on sending for her until she did as he commanded.

Fingering the mobile nursery alarm hanging from its loop at her waist, she wondered what to do. Ra'id was fine—she had checked on him the moment the party woke her, only a few minutes before. The security system was switched on, and there was no one else around. She hesitated between taking a chance, and doing nothing in case Lysander took 'no' for an answer. Assuming that wasn't very likely, she decided to take direct action. She would head towards the noise of the party, and give the first member of staff she saw another message for their prince. This time she would send a proper explanation. Slipping his letter into the pocket of her dressing gown, she marched off through the shadowy palace. *I'm not going to wake Ra'id so he*

*can be paraded in front of Lysander's feckless friends
as some sort of novelty act!* she thought angrily.

Her plan to pass on a better message didn't work.
She didn't meet anyone who could relay it. All the corridors were deserted. It was only when she reached a
landing above the great state banqueting hall that she
saw someone. A footman in uniform stood beside a pair
of wide open double doors. She hesitated, but when he
noticed her and smiled she knew there was no escape.
Creeping downstairs, she hoped no one would wander
out from the party until she had passed on her message.
Despite her dressing gown and slippers, the footman
listened gravely as Alyssa tried to explain that Ra'id
was asleep and wasn't to be disturbed. As she spoke
she caught sight of the glittering party going on beyond
the open doors and knew she had made a mistake. It
wasn't the celebrity drinking contest she had expected.
Expensively dressed, respectable couples were being
treated to silver service at a formal banquet. The music
came from an orchestra that was playing in an adjoining quadrangle while the diners chatted and laughed.
Candlelight and the fragrance of good food made her
want to linger, but she couldn't risk anyone inside the
room spotting her. Ducking out of sight as soon as she
had left her message with the doorman, she made a run
for it. Her slippers slowed her down so she had barely
reached the first landing when she heard someone thundering up the stairs behind her. They were taking the
steps three at a time. Only one person would follow her
with such silent intent.

'Lysander!'

He caught her arm before she could escape. 'Why are you running away?'

Flustered, she waved at her towelling robe. 'Isn't it obvious?'

'You should have told Gui to leave the door and come in to fetch me. Then you could have given me the message yourself.'

'I didn't want to disturb you...' She faltered.

Lysander looked so smart, it took her breath away. He was dressed in a formal black suit and a purple sash, which was studded with medals. His finery made the contrast between them all the more painful.

'You mean you didn't want to tear me away from the party where I was having so much fun?' he said wryly, making sure Alyssa saw something behind his eyes. 'But perhaps not quite as much fun as you *thought* I might be having when you stormed down here in your wrap to check up on me?' He grinned.

'I wouldn't dream of doing a thing like that!' she snapped, but his widening smile told her there was no point in denying it.

'Well...maybe you're right,' she said grudgingly. 'I thought you wanted me to parade Ra'id in front of some noisy bunch of famous halfwits.'

'You may have a point.' He cocked his head towards the state banqueting hall. The company might be more sophisticated than she had thought, but the chat and laughter were still pretty loud. 'But my real reason for making that request was to show everyone how well Ra'id is being cared for.'

His pride was obvious. Gazing at him, Alyssa forgot everything except the bond she knew was already beginning to grow between Lysander and his little nephew.

'Why don't you go back and fetch him, Alyssa? I'll take good care of him for you, and it'll only be for a few minutes.' He smiled.

It was supposed to be an irresistible request, but it had the opposite effect on Alyssa. It shook her out of her delicious trance, and back into real life.

'I don't think so. Not at ten o'clock at night. He's only five years old, Lysander. He needs his sleep,' she said defiantly, expecting him to argue.

That was the last thing on his mind. He stood back, shocked.

'I had no idea it was that late! The staff only told me about this reception an hour before it happened, when I asked to have dinner served in my suite. My late brother was so disorganised, bless him, that this household practically runs itself. They have been used to telling their king what to do at the last minute. It meant he never had to worry about making any arrangements for himself. It was safer that way. So when I wanted to offer you dinner this evening to welcome you to Rosara…' his voice took on a softer tone '…it threw everything into confusion, and I lost track of time. Of course you're right—I'll go back and tell everyone they'll have to see what a wonderful job you're doing with Ra'id another day. Maybe he could host his own little party. The staff would love to arrange that.'

'Don't make him grow up too fast,' Alyssa warned.

Lysander nodded. 'That's a good point. I had to when I was young, to make sure the staff didn't push Akil, my brother, too hard. It wasn't fun.' His lips became a thin, serious line. 'You're right—I'll tell the assembly they'll have to meet our little star another time, and leave it at that.'

Alyssa smiled. 'They'll understand. I'm sure many of your guests have children of their own. But you'd better get back to your dinner party. You are the host, after all.'

'Yes…and a lonely business it is too, despite all the racket.' He laughed, without sounding happy. 'It's almost as barren as my old celebrity circuit.'

'But much more useful.' Alyssa glanced back along the way she had come, towards the nursery wing. 'I have to hurry back. Even with this, I still worry about Ra'id.' She tapped the monitor attached to the belt of her robe.

'That's why I never need to worry about him when he's out of my sight, because I have you,' Lysander said with a warmth that was completely different from his usual flirting. 'Thank you, Alyssa.'

Dipping his head, he kissed her, in a brief echo of her wonderful dream. It was only the smallest gesture, but it was enough to send heat powering through Alyssa's veins. Instinctively she reached out her hands, sliding them up his arms. It was all the encouragement he needed. His light touch became an all consuming embrace as he crushed her tightly against his body.

CHAPTER FIVE

BEING kissed by Lysander was so much better than any dream. Alyssa relaxed into him as desire welled up within her, blotting out everything but the need to be held and appreciated. It felt so right, she knew it couldn't be wrong—not while it was happening. There would be plenty of time to worry later…

As she softened beneath his hands Lysander's kiss became fiercely possessive. His hand slid to her bottom, kneading it until the fabric of her robe reefed up and he made contact with her warm, yielding skin.

It was a defining moment. As he released her mouth to kiss the gentle curve of her neck she gasped and braced her hands against his shoulders.

'Lysander, no…'

He stopped. Leaning back, he looked at her. His eyes glittered with the need to make her his own and his breathing was ragged. It was the first time any man had looked at her with such naked desire, and Alyssa was spellbound. She knew she should break free and run to save her sanity, but she needed to enjoy her moment, and bask in the sun of his appreciation. For long, spectacular seconds she revelled in the warmth of his arms holding her close and would have done anything to make time stand still. Then he closed his eyes, and with a moan of animal intensity peeled his body away from hers.

Her heart sank as he stepped back. Lysander showed every sign of being equally disappointed. He tried to leave, but couldn't.

'You're right, of course, but...' As he leant forward to place another lingering kiss at the base of her throat his hands flowed over her again for an instant. Alyssa felt her breath catch in anticipation, but it wasn't to be. After another mind-blowing kiss he released her with a long, heartfelt sigh of regret.

'I must go. There are people waiting for me downstairs. This isn't the kind of good example they want.' He breathed, his warmth rippling over the softness of her skin and down into the shadowy depths of her cleavage.

'Yes...' Her body shuddered with a wave of disappointment. Knowing that Lysander wanted her, *really* wanted her, transformed Alyssa. The delicious feeling of power that filled her was like nothing she had known before. She wanted to enjoy all these unfamiliar sensations for as long as she could. A man craved her body and she wanted him in return, with every fibre of her being. Some ancient wisdom told her that, with one word, Lysander could be hers. She could bewitch him into a place where he would forget about his guests, his duties and his responsibilities—but this was Lysander Kahani, notorious playboy. He was a man who must look at every woman like this. A seed of disappointment germinated and grew inside her, feeding on the remains of her common sense. Yes, this was Lysander, lover of all the most glamorous and desirable celebrity women. Being seduced by him would put her in stellar company, and it would mean the world to her. But…

Seducing her would ultimately mean nothing to him. She would be nothing more than another conquest, a number not a name.

Slowly, regretfully, she detached herself from his embrace. If a dull, respectable man like her ex-fiancé could talk of love yet still leave her high and dry, what chance would she have with a rogue like Lysander? His casual approach to women was a warning she couldn't afford to ignore—but his touch was like a drug, making her hungry for more.

Catching at her hands, he drew them up to his mouth. Pressing his lips hard against her knuckles, he kissed them and she felt dizzy with longing.

'Lysander!' she whispered but he had already let her go. His easy stride quickly took him out of her reach. She was rooted to the spot, and could only watch him head off downstairs to rejoin his reception.

When he reached the open doors of the state banqueting room, he turned. Alyssa held her breath, waiting to see if he would look up to see if she was still watching. He did. There was obvious enjoyment in his knowing gaze as he glanced back at her, over his shoulder. Then he blew her a kiss and was gone.

She was left staring after him, her body alive with arousal and her mind full of regrets. Why had she let things go so far? *Because it felt unbelievably good,* a treacherous inner voice told her from its hiding place, deep within her body.

She tried to see sense. Letting Lysander get to her like that left her wide open to more pain. She knew she should have stayed strong, given him the message, then turned her back on him and walked away. Instead she had let herself taste the luxury of being desired by Lysander. Now she knew one kiss from him would never be enough. He inspired a heat within her body that needed to be fed constantly. Reliving the sensation of Lysander's broad back beneath her wandering hands, she wanted to make it reality again. Her mind was so full of him, she had forgotten she was standing in full view of the footman standing at the banqucting hall door. When she accidentally caught the man's eye, fear jolted her back to life. What had she done? Kissing her boss in full view of a witness was bad enough, but when that boss was also a man with no conscience and a country to run, it could mean nothing but trouble. Hot with embarrassment, she turned tail and dashed back to the safety of the nursery wing.

Diving inside her suite, she slammed the door and leaned back heavily against it. Her heart was beating hard and fast, but as it slowed she remembered something. The foootman hadn't looked at all shocked by Lysander's antics. She might as well not have bothered to run. Common sense should have told her that the palace staff must see that same scene, or one very like it, acted out all the time. With Lysander, it would be a new girl every night.

The thought that an escapade that meant so much to her was nothing unusual for Lysander should have made Alyssa feel better.

Instead, it made her feel a whole lot worse. She had

made a fool of herself over Lysander, and she wasn't
the only girl to have done that.

*But I'm going to be the only one who learns from
her mistake,* she vowed grimly.

Lysander strode through the huge banqueting hall towards his seat of honour at the top table. The place
was packed, and for the first time since he had been
forced into the role of Regent of Rosara his smile was
genuine. When it came to women, he had always bedded the ones he wanted, whenever he wanted them. He
might hate the loss of his free time as his carefree life
was replaced by timetables and obligations, but there
were advantages. Just when he'd thought he would go
insane with frustration, Alyssa had arrived. Right now
he didn't miss being out trawling nightclubs or film pre-
mieres. He could avoid the noisy press of nightclubs,
and the tail of paparazzi that followed his comet of celebrity. His next conquest was close enough to enjoy at
his leisure, because she was working right here in the
palace. He felt his body kick with anticipation. Perhaps
there was something to be said for his new lifestyle
after all. In his experience, women only stayed in his
life for as long as it took him to get them into bed. For
him, the thrill was all in the chase. He needed Alyssa
to go on working for him afterwards, so he would have
to be careful and very discreet—but that only added to
her allure. Breaking down the barriers she had erected
around herself would take time, but he would have her
sooner or later. There was no doubt about that in his
mind. Until then, he would enjoy pushing the boundaries a little more each time they met. It would delay

that glorious moment when at last he seduced her, and make it all the sweeter.

His smile widened. He was glad now that he had resisted every instinct to ravish Miss Alyssa Dene at the top of the grand staircase. When he finally satisfied his body and his curiosity about the delights of that delicious, tantalising woman it would be a treat worth waiting for—and he would make sure that everything about the moment was absolutely perfect. Sacrificing his old life of idleness for this new one of routine and duty didn't feel quite such a wrench when he thought about Alyssa. She was not only a delicious prospect, she liked the way he wanted to carry on the improvements to the country started by his father and brother. The idea of making her smile—and not only in the bedroom—appealed to him. It might even turn out to be more rewarding than his old shallow lifestyle on the champagne circuit. Any fool could make a girl go weak at the knees by spending money on her. It took something more to captivate a woman like Alyssa.

Lysander's feeling of satisfaction grew as he saw the way people looked at him tonight. Instead of knowing grins, most of his guests were smiling at him appreciatively. One or two looked as though they would rather be anywhere other than sitting at a formal dinner with a load of stuffed shirts. Lysander knew exactly how they felt. He saved his particularly gracious smiles for them. When they responded with warmth, it gave him a real boost. It was almost as good as the pleasurable feeling he got when he thought about Alyssa.

He had had to walk away from her tonight in favour of this banquet, but his mind wasn't going to let her go so easily. He needed satisfaction, and he couldn't get it from this formal dinner. The only way he could keep smiling at his guests was to think about her. That was ironic. Any of Lysander's entanglements that had threatened to last longer than simple physical pleasure, he had ended. Ruthlessly. It was safer that way. However, while he was still waiting for the right moment to take Alyssa, she was carving herself a place in his thoughts no other woman had managed to secure. Other conquests faded from his mind once he had satisfied his curiosity about them. With Alyssa he got the feeling that the more he found out about her, the less he knew. For instance, that all-covering robe she was wearing. The belt had been cinched in so tightly around her neat little waist it had screamed 'keep away', but he knew that wouldn't have stopped him for long. He let his mind wander in the direction his hands would take at a better time and place…

Their stolen kisses just now had almost taken his breath away. How Alyssa did it he'd never know, but her eager responses to his touch had unleashed his desire in a way that almost had him making his excuses and sidling upstairs to finish what he had started with her, a few minutes earlier. The idea of resisting that temptation was something else that made him smile. In the past he'd have had no hesitation in ditching the formal banquet.

It was exactly the sort of stunt this assembly would expect him to pull. These people were diplomats and politicians who were terrified he would make mistakes. They were all watching and waiting for his first false move. That was why he had been so keen to show off what a good job was being made with Ra'id. He had chosen the best woman for the task, and bringing up the heir to Rosara would be a joint effort. The great and good of his country needed to know its royal family was worthy of their support. *I'm definitely not going to disappoint them on that score,* Lysander thought with determination.

Alyssa barely slept that night. Thoughts of Lysander filled her mind and tormented her body. Her feelings tumbled together in chaos. She had accepted this job convinced that no man was to be trusted, least of all Lysander. That conviction was supposed to make sure she could shrug off his charms. She of all people should have been able to resist! After all the trauma in her life over the past months, she had felt immune to every human emotion. Now she knew that 'numb' was a better word to describe the way she had felt—until she met Lysander. Getting dumped by Jerry only a few weeks before their wedding had wrung out her emotions and she had vowed no man would ever be allowed to disappoint her again. And yet here she was, setting herself up for more heartbreak. Lysander had set her body free to feel again, and he was addictive. She should have walked away every single time he moved in close. Trusting her instincts and keeping him at arm's length might have kept her safe. Instead, she had let him get inside her guard. From that moment, she was as good as lost. She wanted Lysander with a fierce hunger she had never experienced before. It was infuriating and scary and she wanted to turn back time to stop herself being drawn into his web of arousal.

But this torment was so sweet, she wouldn't want to avoid it, even if she could. The only way to protect her heart was to leave this job, and that was something she could never do. The thought that Ra'id would be allowed to run wild again if she weren't there to protect him sent shivers down her spine. Whatever the personal cost to her, it would be easier to shield him from his uncle's lifestyle than to expect Lysander to change...

She sighed. A one-woman Lysander was the ideal, but it was never going to happen. She knew that, but it couldn't stop her dreaming.

Next morning, Alyssa found it hard to concentrate on anything. What she needed was something to take her mind off Lysander. Every thought she had turned to him, and how she could get to see him again. It was the worst thing she could do, but in some mad way she hoped it might frighten some sense into her confusion of feelings. If Lysander guessed how she felt, he would enjoy it so much he might try to seduce her again. If he laughed off the whole incident, she would be crushed. Either way, the idea of being a hostage to his reactions made her feel restless and insecure.

Assuming Lysander would be sleeping late after the banquet, she thought it would be safe to go for a walk. The day was already hot so she got Ra'id to take her on another guided tour of the whole palace while it was still early. It was quite a distraction. Walking through room after room of cool marble floors, silken cushions and gilding was heavenly. The whole palace was magical, but Alyssa couldn't help feeling it lacked something. There was beauty, but no life around. The place was trying too hard to be restrained and tasteful. Ra'id picked up on the lack of atmosphere, too. He was strangely quiet and well behaved.

'That's where all the offices are,' he told her as they ended their tour back on the ground floor. He was pointing along a colonnade that ran down the far side of the main quadrangle. Alyssa wondered if that was where Lysander would spend his days, when he was working. She remembered what he had said about being a caged tiger. This was a sumptuous palace, but for a man like him an office must feel like a prison cell. She looked along the airy corridor for any signs of life, but it was all peaceful.

'Aren't you going to show me inside all those rooms?' she asked Ra'id.

He gasped as though she had suggested putting his head into a lion's mouth. 'Oh, no, I'm not allowed down *there*! But I'll show you how I get the people inside to come out and play with me, if you like,' the little boy went on innocently.

Grabbing her hand, he pulled her out into the court-yard. It was a shock. The heat hit her with as much force as her embarrassment. It was only hours since Lysander had kissed her, and trespassing so close to the place where he lived his other life made her feel strangely shy.

Ra'id led her towards a pool of shade beneath a spreading fig tree. That was when she heard Lysander's voice. He was speaking in a stern, clipped way she had never heard him use before. She stopped, but Ra'id couldn't have cared less about her feelings. All he wanted to do was check out the tree for ripe figs.

As they drew level with an open office door Alyssa saw why Lysander's voice sounded so unusual. Lounging back in an executive chair, he had his feet on his desk and was talking into a small dictating machine. With a smile he raised one hand at them in greeting.

Feeling really self-concious, Alyssa stepped back. Ra'id gave a cheerful wave to his uncle and then turned his attention back to searching for figs. Skulking in the shade, Alyssa tried to become invisible. Lysander had other ideas. He stood up and strolled out of his office to lean on the low wall of the colonnade.

'Alyssa? Don't hide away in the shadows.'

Through the long, sleepless hours of night she had wondered if her memory was playing tricks. Her fantasy Lysander was so handsome and irresistible, she was half afraid the real thing might be a let-down. He wasn't. He looked every bit as good as she remembered. When he looked at her she felt her knees go weak, but that was only the start. His smile seduced her straight into saying too much.

'I have to hide. It's this horrible navy-blue uniform.' She flicked at the stiff skirt. 'I'm not accustomed to wearing a uniform but your staff seemed to think it is the done thing. I look like a relic from the fifties, and feel like I'm wearing a tent. And I'm sorry about last night,' she finished in a rush.

He leaned forward, over the low wall between them. 'I'm not...' he said as he gave her a whimsical grin '...but as for your clothes—if you don't like them, then that's easily fixed. It would be my pleasure to get something done about them.' He smiled at her in a way that explained exactly what his ideas would involve. If that wasn't temptation enough, he was looking spectacular today, despite his late night. Beautifully dressed in a lightweight linen suit, he had slung its jacket over the back of his chair. His usual gold cufflinks were missing and he had turned back the cuffs of his white shirt. They made a dazzling contrast to his bronzed skin.

'So, Alyssa—how are you getting on in your new home, apart from that?'

'Really well, thank you.' She smiled, trying not to enjoy the sensation of his gaze.

'Has Ra'id been showing you around?'

'Yes. I've seen some wonderful things.' *But your smile is the most natural yet,* she decided.

Gazing at him now brought back every stolen moment of the previous night. She could almost feel his kisses again, and so vividly the breath caught in her throat. She blushed.

'Remember what I said before we left England, Alyssa? We can take Ra'id out for a picnic this afternoon, instead of taking tea in the palace.'

She bit her lip. 'I don't know. It sounds perfect, but…' Although she was torn between work and desire, there was never any doubt about what she would say. That didn't make her inner struggle any easier. She tried to put her thoughts into words without embarrassing herself further.

'My first loyalty will always be towards Ra'id. I can't let anything distract me from his care.'

Lysander was watching her carefully.

'Of course. I understand, and I wouldn't expect you to say anything else. It's your work, exactly as showing Ra'id how to behave in public is mine,' he said in a voice so rich with meaning Alyssa had to look away. She couldn't meet his eyes. They filled her mind until she knew she had to escape. Glancing past him, she saw huge piles of paperwork and document boxes neatly stacked on his desk.

'Y-you're busy. We mustn't disturb you any longer.' She drew back, transferring her attention to the little boy. 'Come on, Ra'id—I want to see your ponies.'

'Do you ride, Alyssa?' Lysander asked suddenly. The question was so unexpected, she reacted by instinct.

'Oh, yes, but not for a long time.'

He pounced on the wistful note in her voice. 'You miss it.'

She smiled, remembering her schooldays. 'Actually yes, I do—but I didn't realise how much, until you said that!'

'Then you're in for a treat! When's your next day off?'

'Tomorrow.' She brightened, hoping he was going to tell her members of staff could ride horses from the royal stables whenever they liked.

'Then I'll make a gap in my schedule, and take you sightseeing.'

Her heart soared like a helium balloon until common sense punctured it. 'No. No, I couldn't possibly...'

'We could take Ra'id with us, as chaperone. I want to learn more about Ra'id, so it will be a chance for me to get some experience in looking after him.' Lysander's smile was innocent, but his eyes held wicked temptation.

Alyssa poked some stray strands of hair back behind their grips as she tried to give herself time to think. It would be perfect—a day out with Lysander, no strings attached. All she would have to do was keep Ra'id's best interests at heart, and that was easy enough!

'We'll order a picnic, and you'll have plenty of time to drink in the atmosphere and surroundings.' Lysander's expression was as still as a woodland pool, and equally full of promise. Time with him could lead to only one thing. Gazing deep into his eyes, Alyssa knew he was thinking exactly the same and knew that a whole day in such close proximity would be too dangerous.

'It would be wonderful, but it can't happen, Your Royal Highness. We can go out this afternoon for a short picnic at tea time as we arranged, instead. Maybe you and Ra'id could go on your own instead? You've already told me your country is everything to you. I can't expect such a busy man to find the time to take me out and about,' she said, hoping to emphasise the gulf between them again. She wanted to sound determined, but the words didn't come out like that. Instead, they were full of wistful longing.

'Stranger things have happened.'

His formal smile glittered so irresistibly, Alyssa knew she had to make a stand.

'But not many,' she told him firmly.

Lysander leaned over the low wall, watching them go. Thinking about Alyssa had got him through that tedious banquet the night before. Now it threatened to disrupt the rest of this working day. When she'd mentioned horses, his mind had instantly filled with the idea of racing across the desert sand with her. That was a first. Until now, distraction of any sort always annoyed him when he was dealing with paperwork. For once, the combination of a real flesh-and-blood woman and one of his favourite fantasies was irresistible. He was stirred by the memory of her body wrapped in that soft, ridiculous dressing gown while the expression in her eyes had conveyed that she wanted him so power-fully. It was too much. Lysander started planning for the day when he would eventually sample all the de-lights she had to offer.

One day, he would spirit her off alone to see The Queen's Retreat.

It was a breathtaking place, and the perfect setting for seduction. Bed was Lysander's cure for every rela-tionship and it had never been known to fail. Unlikely though it seemed to him just now, Alyssa's body would lose its novelty value once he had slept with her. Her mind showed signs of surprising him for as long as he lived, so he didn't have the patience to wait until she bored him. In contrast, sex with her would satisfy his body and stop it hankering after her, once and for all.

He went back to work, and smiled all the way through three drafts of a balance-of-payments statement.

Alyssa wasn't looking forward to their picnic tea that afternoon. She assumed a caravan of staff would turn it into a state visit to the desert, rather than a simple meal in the fresh air. When Lysander arrived alone to collect her and Ra'id from the nursery wing, it amazed her. Flustered, she wasn't quite sure how to react so she kept quiet and let Lysander do the talking.

'It will be just me and my nephew today,' he told her

and the other nursery staff. 'Alyssa is coming along to
see fair play, that's all.'

He sounded affable, and his audience looked convinced. That didn't stop Alyssa feeling uncomfortable.
She could barely look at him as they walked out to
the palace's garage complex. While the kitchen staff
loaded picnic things into a brand-new four-by-four, she
couldn't stand the suspense any longer. Making sure
she and Lysander were out of earshot of everybody else,
she tried to broach the subject.

'Lysander, about last night…'

He smiled, and once again Alyssa's body betrayed
her. She felt her heart accelerate, and her mouth was
suddenly so dry she could hardly speak.

'I should never have let you kiss me—and so you
mustn't think you can…' Unable to say anything more,
she flicked a glance towards Ra'id, who was bouncing
up and down in one of the rear seats of the vehicle.

'Of course I'm not going to try and carry on where
I left off. Not today…' He filled in for her, but left his
meaning hanging in the air. 'You're at work, looking
after my nephew, so I shall be on my best behaviour.'
He laid one hand gravely over his heart and dipped his
head in mockery of a formal bow. She watched him
carefully as he opened the front passenger door for her.
It was high off the ground, but when he reached out
to help her up there was nothing remotely suggestive
about his touch. Alyssa's relief was tinged with disappointment. She wanted him to go further, but told herself this was the only way—especially when he tried to
own her with his eyes, as he was doing right now. Her
heart had already been broken by a supposedly decent

man. This man was a rogue. She'd do well to remember that!

He slid into the driving seat and they started off, out into the desert. At first Alyssa was tense and watchful but Lysander didn't seem to notice. He was far too busy talking to Ra'id.

'I like picnics! I like picnics!' the little boy chanted, bouncing up and down in his seat. He was enjoying himself so much, even Alyssa began to think this trip was a good idea. The sky was blue, they had enough food to feed an army and Lysander really was making an effort to get to know Ra'id.

'I expect you have picnics all the time, living in a lovely place like this,' Alyssa said as they travelled along an ancient dirt road. She was enjoying the sight of hot, starkly beautiful desert sliding past so fast outside, while she was cool and comfortable inside the car.

'No. As far as I know the only time Ra'id went out was to travel between Combe House in England and the Rose Palace.'

'Is that why you suggested this outing?'

He shook his head. 'Having a picnic is something I've wanted to do since I was about the same size as Ra'id.' Lysander smiled, but not at her. With his lips pressed tightly together, he carried on gazing through the windscreen.

'You're not telling me this is the first time you've done this?' Alyssa could hardly believe what she was hearing.

'I've never had the excuse to do it here before. The one dim memory I have of my mother is of her, me, and my brother, Akil. We were in a park in England.

We must have gone out for the day but I can't recall her face, or what she was wearing, what we ate or anything important like that. All I remember is her voice, saying: "I wish we'd done this before. We'll have to do it again some time." But we never did.'

'That's so sad,' Alyssa said softly.

He shot her a strange look. 'The fact that the only real memory I have of my mother is of a time when she was happy?' he queried. 'What's wrong with that?'

CHAPTER SIX

ALYSSA couldn't argue with him. The quiet way he answered her question intrigued her. Was he giving her a glimpse of the man behind his public image? It was so at odds with the passionate seducer who had held her in his arms the night before. When he looked at her now, there was hardly any flirtation in Lysander's smile. She took that as a good sign, and tried to relax.

Sitting in a prestige car with a handsome prince at the wheel, she felt as though a little bit of royalty might be rubbing off on her. She even had to suppress a childish urge to wave regally out of the window. For once in her life she didn't have to worry about a thing. All she had to do was sit back and enjoy being chauffeured around. It was lovely and so, she had to admit, was Lysander. He was behaving perfectly today, as the ideal role model for Ra'id. Away from his office he was off duty, and so was the usual little crease between his brows. Now and again he even hummed along to the gentle sound of Marcello coming from the on-board CD player. With a sigh, Alyssa lay back in her seat and closed her eyes. The sun was warm against her lids and the filtered air was cool. For the first time in ages, life was offering her more than loneliness. The feeling of

Lysander at one with his car and only inches away from her was incredible.

'I suppose you went on picnics with your parents all the time, Alyssa?'

'Mmm? No...they spent most of the year working abroad, so I was sent off to boarding school. I went home for the holidays, which was about as much exposure to me as they could take.'

'Don't sell yourself short,' he said sharply.

She opened her eyes and looked at him. 'What's the matter? I expected you to laugh when I said that.'

'There's nothing funny about a child who sees themselves as a burden.'

'You're getting too fond of Ra'id for him to think that. I can see it every time you two are together,' Alyssa assured him.

'I wasn't talking about him.'

She smiled. 'Oh, don't worry about me. I've long since stopped bothering about how things are between me and my parents.'

Another look at his face told Alyssa he hadn't been thinking about her situation, either. He was staring grimly out of the windscreen at the road ahead.

'Tell me more about your upbringing,' she probed gently. 'Is the Kahani family large, beyond this branch? I meant to do some online research in my spare time to get background, but I haven't got around to it yet.'

'Don't bother,' he said brusquely, missing a gear change. That made him spit out a word in Rosari that Alyssa was glad she couldn't understand.

'No, and there's no royal family beyond me and Ra'id,' he told her. 'That's the whole problem. My father was a second son, like me. His older brother was King, and a cruel, bitter man. His rule kept Rosara in the Dark Ages. My brother Akil and I were lucky. Our part of the family was never expected to inherit the crown, so we were allowed a lot of freedom. Unfortunately, the death of our mother changed all that.'

Alyssa clucked with sympathy. 'My mother and I have never been close, so I can't imagine how awful it must have been for you to lose yours. It must have been a terrible shock.'

Lysander didn't reply straight away. Alyssa assumed it was because he was driving down a tricky, rock-strewn slope. When he spoke, she found out how wrong she was.

'Yes—and no. She was found guilty of adultery, and, as my unforgiving uncle was on the throne at the time, she was beheaded.'

Surprise catapulted Alyssa forward in her seat. 'Oh, my God!' She clapped her hand over her mouth and glanced over her shoulder at Ra'id. The little boy had calmed down enough to look at a comic, and hadn't noticed. Relieved, she turned to stare at Lysander in horror. 'When was this?'

'A long time ago. Thirty years or more—not long after the picnic I told you about, maybe? The riots that followed killed my uncle and put his brother—my father—on the throne. Father was determined things would change, and so am I. That's why I'm going to continue making improvements here.'

He was staring ahead so grimly now that Alyssa felt she had to say something. 'You're right. The sooner you can secure your country's place in the twenty-first century, the better,' she said. It worked.

'That's why I want to make sure Ra'id has a proper childhood. Akil and I never had much experience of life until we were sent to England to finish our education. Our father was quite forward thinking, but even so we had private tutors to begin with.'

'You must have been lonely.'

Lysander shook his head. 'I always had Akil to think about. He was never very worldly, so I always fought in his corner. That made me self-reliant.'

'Too much of that isn't always a good thing.'

'I don't think my brother would have agreed with you. Once he became King and inherited a band of advisors, they took over. I was surplus to his requirements and didn't have anything to do. Hitting the party circuit was a reaction to that. That was why Akil never liked the way I lived my life. He knew I was capable of so much more.'

Alyssa felt on firmer ground for once. 'Then it's a shame he never found you a job. Hard work suits you. You really looked the part when we saw you in your office.'

'Thank you,' he said, adding lightly. 'It sounds as though you actually meant that.'

'Why shouldn't I?'

Sliding a glance wickedly across at her, he laughed. 'Alyssa, I've been flattered by mistresses of the craft. Believe me.'

They crested a rise in the road, which gave them a spectacular view of the plains below. Lysander parked the four-by-four where it would cast the longest shadow, got out and opened the doors for Alyssa and Ra'id. With a squeal of excitement the little boy bounced out and careered off down the slope at top speed.

'Don't go too far!' Lysander called, but Alyssa laughed.

'He's only got little legs. With nothing but a few sparse bushes in every direction, he can't get lost. He'll be fine,' she reassured him, but kept a careful watch on her little charge all the same.

The atmosphere out in the desert was very different from the comfortable, air-conditioned interior of Lysander's car. It was hot and dry. Now and then a light breeze blew up, ruffling his dark curls and wrapping Alyssa's skirt around her bare legs. She was still wary of him, but her warnings seemed to be having some effect. Lysander's interest in her didn't waver, but he kept his distance. Neither spoke as they strolled along in Ra'id's wake. Alyssa's mind was too full of miserable childhoods and loveless lives, and the last thing she wanted to do was inflict her memories on Lysander. For a while they watched the little boy in companionable silence, but Alyssa's gaze was often distracted by their stunning surroundings. Sunlight had spent a million lifetimes baking the stony countryside into a million shades from caramel to cream, and the overall effect was breathtaking.

'It's such a beautiful place,' Alyssa was moved to say after a while. 'How could anyone prefer the big city to this?'

'A life spent in casinos and nightclubs isn't exactly hell on earth. I'm sure you'd be the first one to remind me of that,' Lysander said with dry humour.

'Do you miss it?'

He smiled, but didn't answer.

'I don't think the newspapers expected you to move back here, Lysander. If they knew how well that dinner went, and the hours of routine office work you put in, I'm sure they'd be amazed,' she said quietly.

'The Western press perhaps, but not the press here in Rosara. They've always understood that I left to avoid being sidelined, and I came back because of loyalty. I love this country, and I won't let anything disturb its peace. That's why I want to take such great care of Ra'id. Some of my countrymen don't believe he should be the next king.'

Alyssa was shocked. 'Lysander! When we were driving from the airport, you told me there was no danger to him here!'

Her first instinct was to call Ra'id straight back into her arms and head for the palace and safety. Lysander stopped her with a few simple words.

'Would it reassure you to know that I'm the one they want as their ruler? That there's a faction who think I should be King, rather than him?'

She stared at him. 'I don't know. It depends what would happen to Ra'id.'

'He's quite safe with me. You've got my word on that.' Lysander's accent thickened with honesty. 'He would stay in your care and be my heir until I had a son of my own. That's why I wanted the best nanny for him from the first. Whatever happens, I will always treat Ra'id with the respect due to my brother's son. Looking after him is my priority.'

'And mine,' Alyssa said firmly.

They had both been watching the little boy as he chased lizards over the hot desert rocks. When she said that, they turned and shared a look.

'Smiling suits you, Lysander.' Alyssa laughed. 'You should do it more often.'

His reply was quick. 'You won't believe this, but I was about to say exactly the same thing to you!'

The palace staff had packed an amazing picnic. There was a feast of things Alyssa usually kept off Ra'id's menu, such as crisps and cake, along with healthy slices of perfectly ripe melons, peaches and bunches of fat grapes. While Alyssa set it all out, Lysander produced a pair of miniature radio-controlled buggies from the back of the four-by-four. That was when Ra'id lost interest in the food—and it was the last she saw of the two men in her life until they got hungry.

It was a long time before Alyssa had a minute to herself. Once she'd put the exhausted Ra'id to bed that night and handed over to her deputy, she could officially call herself off duty for the next thirty-six hours. With a relief she didn't usually feel when faced with a holiday, she retreated to her own suite. Her apartment at the Rose Palace was lovely. It was at least twice the size of her city flat in England, and had large, airy rooms. It was a pleasure to wander around it by the light of scented candles, enjoying all the luxury. Flickering shadows danced over pale painted walls and high ceilings, while the fragrance of lilies drifted in from the courtyard garden below her open windows. Although tired, Alyssa was far too wound up for sleep. Her mind was crowded.

She roamed around hoping it would clear, but all she could think about was Lysander. The bed reminded her of his cabin on the plane, where she had imagined his kiss. Her kitchen was stocked with everything to make her feel at home, but that only brought back the way Lysander had helped her to coffee and snacks at their picnic. And every time she felt her pulse speed up, she thought of his kisses…

That moment on the palace landing felt like a life-time ago. She had seen a side of Lysander today that was at odds with his playboy image. She liked to think her common sense might be having some influence on him, but she couldn't ignore the obvious reason for the change in him. He'd had no time for flirting today. Both he and Alyssa had been too busy taking care of Ra'id and laughing along with him to think of anything beyond their shared interest in the little boy.

She tried to see that as a good thing. Today could so easily be a one-off. Lysander had been taken out of his natural habitat. That might be having the same effect on him as the change in routine did with Ra'id. It gave them both more to think about than mischief. Alyssa tried to see that as a good thing, but the memory of Lysander's eyes burning with desire for her on the night of his banquet was impossible to forget.

She wondered what the next day would bring—more respect, or more temptation? Setting her alarm, she lay down and tried to sleep. The days were long in Rosara, but she was determined to make the most of every second of freedom.

Everything was perfect, right down to the jug of fil-tered water in her bedside fridge, but she still couldn't switch off. After what felt like hours, she gave up, untangled herself from the sheet and got out of bed. One long, cool, bubbly bath later, smelling of rose petal attar from the royal perfumier, she pulled on a thin cotton blouse and light, summer-weight trousers. Pouring herself a large glass of orange juice fresh from the palace citrus groves, she strolled out onto her balcony. If she couldn't sleep, she could at least suffer insomnia in comfort. Settled on piles of silken cushions specially designed for lounging, she gazed past tendrils of wisteria draped around the balcony rail, and down into the courtyard below.

The night was warm, and heavy with the fragrance of citrus and jasmine. It was heavenly. She stretched her limbs luxuriously across the downy pillows. It felt so good, she needed only one thing to complete the picture. That was a glimpse of Lysander. She hoped their happy afternoon hadn't been a one-off, but she was wary that it might have been designed to weaken her resistance to him. Her body was definitely drawn to his, but she couldn't let that lead her astray. Instead, she fell back on fantasy. Lysander's worldwide reputation as a playboy made him too hot for her to handle in real life, but dreaming was free. She sighed. The man was a twenty-four-carat rogue, and a genuine heartbreaker. You only had to look at him to see that.

She smiled at the thought of his handsome face this afternoon. She had never seen him look so relaxed and happy, especially when he was showing Ra'id how to take pictures with his smartphone. Not even in all those press photographs, where he had a new woman hanging on his arm in every shot.

It was interesting to think he might really change now he was back in Rosara…and it was safer, too. She had heard from other staff at the palace that no woman could expect to keep Lysander interested for long, but maybe that would change, too. As long as he stopped tempting her everything would be fine, although it was impossible not to wonder what it would be like to be on Lysander Kahani's menu…

Alyssa had never met any other man like him, either in looks or character. And whatever his faults, he was always a gentleman. If he wanted, Lysander could have charmed her into his bed at any time over the past few days, if he did but know it! He made her feel so special. *But then,* she thought, *he must have honed his skill at making women feel unique on a thousand other conquests.* A man like that would be an expert at playing games with hearts. Every time she felt tempted, Alyssa relived the mental torture of her breakup with Jerry all over again.

It was supposed to keep her own heart closed to Lysander, but it didn't work. She sympathised with him, and could understand why he was so restless. He needed some form of escape within his gilded cage, she could tell—but she didn't dare try and find out what it was.

Lysander couldn't sleep. He tried paperwork. He went back to his office and shuffled documents, but it was no good. The palace had a complete movie theatre, but trying to watch films only made him feel worse. However hard he tried to distract himself, nothing worked. It couldn't take his mind off the events of that afternoon.

He cursed loudly. What had Alyssa done to him? He couldn't even be truthful with himself any more. It wasn't the picnic that had affected him so much, but *her*. When it came to women, he was a professional. This afternoon he had gone out of his way to act as though their kiss had been no big deal for him. He had tried to pretend it was a mistake he had already forgotten about. That couldn't have been further from the truth. Lysander enjoyed heightening his desire in any way he could. Resisting temptation was a new strategy. It was proving to be the most arousing *and* the most difficult thing he had ever attempted. Alyssa's smile, the scent of rosewater on her warm skin, that little habit she had of twiddling a lock of her hair when she was thinking—details kept coming back to haunt him as night fell. Tiny things about her he hadn't realised he had noticed seethed through his mind until he could hardly think straight. The woman was disrupting his thoughts and stealing his sleep. How was he supposed to work towards a better Rosara, with thoughts of her pressing in on him from all sides?

This had gone far beyond a joke. *No one can be allowed to get inside the mind of Lysander Kahani like this,* he thought with grim determination. He had to put a stop to it as soon as possible, and, being Lysander, he knew exactly how to do it. The sooner she was in his bed, the better.

The palace was winding down for the night. Alyssa got to her feet, knowing she should try to go back to bed. Still she lingered, enjoying the richly fragranced evening air for a few more moments. The sound of a bubbling fountain down in the quadrangle was wonderfully restful. An old apricot tree dripping with fruit scented the air with its sweetness. The evening was so quiet she could hear the soft sounds of the last few servants going off to bed. The rustle of a robe or the click of sandals on marble floors were the only human intrusions into a scene dominated by nature. A warm breeze caressed her skin, insects sang in the shadows and as always there was the scent of the roses that gave Rosara its name.

It was heaven—and then she heard hooves clattering across cobblestones, not very far away. She listened as the sound changed, and knew the royal horses were being led in for the night. Sleep still felt so far away. The stables were close, and she couldn't resist visiting them.

Leaving her rooms, she padded through the silent palace. As she cut through the inner courtyard below her balcony a lighted window on the ground floor caught her eye. She saw a tall and unmistakable form pass a pair of open French doors. It was Lysander. The angle meant she couldn't see his face, but that didn't matter. What she saw was arousing enough. He was pacing around in bare feet, his white shirt hanging loose and unbuttoned. Her heart lurched as she realised he must be in his own suite, on his own territory.

As she was enjoying the sight he suddenly swung out into the courtyard garden. As if sensing the heat of her gaze, he looked straight across to where she stood watching him.

There could be no escape. Alyssa thought of all the photographs she had ever seen of him. None of them did him justice tonight. While he was always snapped with the world's most glamorous women, tonight she was scrubbed clean of make-up, perfumed only with bath oil and dressed in chain-store casuals. She blushed furiously, but before she could melt back into the shadows he spoke.

'Alyssa? What a lovely surprise. I was just thinking about you. You can't sleep either?' He chuckled, his voice as warm as melted chocolate. 'I know how you feel. Our afternoon together was so good, it seems a shame to end this special day like any other.'

He smiled, in a deliciously unthreatening way.

'Wait there—I've had a great idea...'

CHAPTER SEVEN

LYSANDER vanished back into his suite, but reappeared seconds later. Fully dressed now, complete with breeches and boots, he was still buttoning his shirt as he strode across the courtyard towards her.

'I don't need to ask what brings you outside on this beautiful evening, do I, Alyssa?'

'I couldn't sleep, and when I heard the horses I had to go and take a look.'

'Enticing, isn't it?' His voice was full of its old mischief, but that was as far as it went. He stopped while he was still several feet away from her. 'Why don't we go out for a moonlight ride? If you think this palace is beautiful, wait until you see the place they call The Queen's Retreat. It's too beautiful a night to waste an opportunity like this. The gardens there are full of the most stunning plants and flowers, brought from all corners of the world.'

Alyssa stared at him. 'Don't you think it had better wait until morning?'

It was obvious he knew exactly what she meant. A man and a woman in a beautiful garden, caressed by the warm desert night…

He smiled in a way that told her he had already made

up his mind exactly what was going to happen, but he was still careful not to get too close. 'No. It can't wait.'

Alyssa's entire body began to glow. This was her wildest fantasy brought to life. Apart from dim lamps set around the quadrangle, the only lights showing were in his suite. Every other window overlooking the courtyard was dark and blank.

No one would see them leave the palace together. No one would know.

But I will, she thought with a pang, *and so will my poor battered heart.*

'That doesn't sound very sensible…' she ventured.

He shook his head, and spoke in a rich undertone. 'It's possibly the most sensible thing I've done in my life so far.'

Alyssa tried to answer, but couldn't. Desperate to know what he was talking about, she didn't have the confidence to ask. Lysander at arm's length was exciting. Any closer than that, and he was sure to be trouble.

He gave her a little bow and her senses went into overdrive.

'What if someone sees us?'

His dark eyes glittered like jet in the soft evening light. He chuckled softly. 'Little details like that never bother me. When I want to do something, I do it. There's never any point in hesitating. There comes a time when the waiting has to stop—and that's now.'

Alyssa didn't know what to think. Taking a step back, she wrapped her arms around her waist and stared down at the toes of his highly polished riding boots. To look at anything else would lead her into all sorts of trouble.

'I'm not sure…'

'I am—and if we're going at all, it needs to be soon. If we go now we'll be in time to see a full moon rise over the mountain ridge. It's a breathtaking sight,' he murmured, reaching for her hand. 'We should take our chance while we can. It's a perfect night—and we'll use my special short cut.'

Alyssa tried to refuse, but Lysander was impossible to resist. He guided her towards the open French doors of his apartment. She couldn't have complained if she wanted to. Her heart was pounding too hard. She could hardly take it all in—his breathtaking confidence, the faint drift of his aftershave and the enticing glimpses of his private life as she was whisked straight through his suite.

The hall beyond the royal wing was deserted. Lysander melted through the shadows, leading her where he must have led countless other women in the past. They made it to the stables without picking up any of his security team. From there, it was easy. Communicating by the lightest of touches, Lysander helped Alyssa saddle up a beautiful bay mare, and then found his own horse. Together, they escaped into the night.

The royal animals were bred from tough, fast desert bloodlines that Lysander's family had guarded jealously for centuries. Alyssa laughed with delight, but desert breezes stole the sound from her lips. The only sound was the drumming of hooves on hard-packed sand. They galloped across a landscape veiled in the mauve and lavender shades of dusk, to an island of rock in the sea of sand. Cresting a final dune, Alyssa saw the stark silhouette of a royal palace pasted against the clear ultramarine sky.

Lysander led her on, but as they reached the shadow of those great stone ramparts Alyssa reined in her horse. It turned and fretted as she looked up at walls as high and solid as cliffs. Lysander was a little way ahead but when she stopped he wheeled his stallion around and went back to her side.

'Come on—I don't want you to miss a moment!' he called, urging her on past the last security post and up the sloping switchback path that led to the castle gates. As they clattered beneath a final arch, roosting doves exploded with fright across an inner courtyard. Alyssa jumped, but Lysander was there to reassure her.

'There's nothing to be scared of here. It's the safest stronghold in my country. I visit when I want to get away from people,' he confided, which shocked Alyssa.

'But everyone knows you're the original party person!' she blurted out. 'Why would you of all people want to escape?'

'Everyone needs quiet sometimes, and, anyway, I don't have time for partying any more. There's so much to do for Rosara. It fills up all my time, and the change from player to manager is a difficult adjustment.' He leapt from his horse and went to help her down. 'I've always liked my own space. It's especially important to me now. I need a place where I can leave the restrictions of palace life a long way behind.'

Lysander's strong, tanned hands slid around her waist and drew her gently from the saddle. His touch lingered over her for a little longer than protocol would have liked, but here the boring rules of palace life felt far away. For once, Alyssa was in no hurry to remind him about them.

Two men came out from a gatehouse to greet them. One took care of their horses, while the other handed Lysander a flaming torch.

'What a gesture!' Alyssa said, trying not to watch the firelight dance over the impressive, gleaming muscles exposed by Lysander's open-necked shirt.

'It sets the scene perfectly,' he told her. 'There's no electricity here. The Queen's Retreat was the last word in gracious royal living in the fifteenth century, but not now. Queens today want more in the way of hundred-watt lighting, satellite TV and walk-in fridges.'

He held the torch high and looked around with real fondness. Alyssa couldn't help wondering about all his ancestors, living, loving and laughing in this beautiful haven. Inside the perimeter wall was a large courtyard. In the centre rose the castle, but Lysander led her to one side of the main building. As they went he touched his torch to others set up along the way. When they reached a wrought-iron gate set into the stonework, he opened it and let her go through first.

She walked into a beautiful garden, laid out behind the main castle. It was a wonderland of rustling trees and tangled undergrowth, rioting around a large circular building with a high domed roof.

'That's the observatory,' Lysander told her in passing. 'This is the perfect place to study the stars, and I like to relax in style.'

Everywhere was studded with the luminous pale flowers of roses and lilies, sparkling with fireflies that danced in the dark.

Alyssa drew in a deep breath, rich with all the wonderful perfumes of flowers and oil from cedar trees.

Before she could say anything, a nightingale began sobbing from deep in the heart of a rambling rose.

'Legend says that is the lament of an adulterous queen who was banished here,' Lysander said in a low voice.

'Who could be unhappy when they can listen to that?' Alyssa whispered, afraid to spoil the moment. 'Unless she regretted putting her trust in someone who betrayed her?'

'It sounds as though you know what you're talking about,' he whispered back.

'Shh.' Alyssa put her hand on his arm. It was only a touch, but it was enough to make him tense. When she felt that, Alyssa looked at him quickly. Their eyes met, and in the silence a second nightingale sent a stream of silvery notes into the evening. For long moments they waited until the song died away. Then Lysander's hand slid over hers.

'Come on, or we'll miss the real show.' He squeezed her fingers, but then moved away.

Light-headed with the effects of his touch, Alyssa followed. He led her over to the Eastern wall, where a golden glow was already spreading above the horizon. Climbing a steep flight of steps to the sentries' walkway, Alyssa gasped at the perfect view of the night sky it afforded.

'It's lovely and you can see for miles!'

Lysander put out the torch he was carrying, then leaned his folded arms on the breast high wall.

'Yes, but can you imagine spending every day and night here, for the rest of your life?' he said quietly. 'Marooned far away from the city, the bright lights and all your friends?'

'I'd love it,' she added, smiling at the confession he had made.

'I had a feeling you would. It isn't for everyone, and that's part of its charm. My brother Akil wanted to update this place and make his wife move here, but she hated it.'

'I wouldn't have bothered waiting for the renovations. I couldn't have got here fast enough,' Alyssa muttered.

He laughed. 'You're the first woman who hasn't run screaming from the thought of being stuck here at The Queen's Retreat without so much as a power shower to bless herself with.'

'I'm a nanny. We can cope with anything!' Alyssa joined in his laughter.

'Then you're the only woman I've met who could. Most of them have fainted at the thought of a hangnail.'

Alyssa put her elbows on the wall beside him and cupped her chin in her hands. 'Then you've only met some rather silly women! I'm glad I'm not like that.'

'So am I,' he said, then looked away quickly and cleared his throat. 'This place is so beautiful, I'm determined to make it happy, too.'

'It feels wonderful to me already,' Alyssa said dreamily. A light breeze whispered in from the desert, but the castle's ancient stones had been storing up the sun's fierce heat all day. Dusk drew enough warmth from the walls to keep them comfortable, but Lysander was obviously enjoying his role as host.

'Let me know when you've had enough. For myself, I could stay here all night.'

'So could I,' Alyssa sighed. As they watched the

glowing moon rise slowly over the stark line of the distant horizon she shivered with the romance of it all—the nightingales, the flowers and Lysander, all bathed in moonlight.

It was the only encouragement he needed to slide an arm smoothly around her shoulders.

'Let me keep you warm,' he murmured, his voice low with desire.

Without a word Alyssa stepped sideways, just far enough to slip from his grasp.

Lysander paused. Alyssa's refusal to be taken for granted was one of the first things that had appealed to him. Now it was starting to get tired. Women never refused him. It simply didn't happen, but, more than that, he knew Alyssa was longing for his touch. He toyed with the idea of simply walking away without risking his dignity any further, but decided that wasn't an option. If he did that, he knew his memories of Alyssa would haunt him for as long as his life lasted. While there was the smallest chance of softening her bewitching eyes with satisfaction, he knew he would never be free from her.

It was the simplest thing in the world to reach out to her again. This time she flipped his hands away with more determination, even as she quivered with longing.

'Please don't!'

He was getting frustrated with her now; he could sense that she wanted him as much as he wanted her, so what was holding her back?

'Why do you do that, Alyssa?'

'It's nothing personal.'

'Exactly!'

She had been gazing away across the plain, refusing to look at him. When he said that she whipped around. His expression stopped her doing anything as silly as laughing. He was tight-lipped with arrogance; humour was the last thing on his mind tonight.

'You are *unbelievable*, Lysander Kahani!' Her eyes flashed.

'You make it sound like a character reference.'

'Then congratulations. I'm sure you're delighted.'

'Of course I'm not! This is ridiculous,' Lysander countered. '*You* are ridiculous. How can my touch possibly make you so unhappy? Good God, woman—why the hell did our paths have to cross? Why couldn't you have settled down with a nice, respectable middle-class man in an English suburb and raised a flock of nice, respectable middle-class children before I ever set eyes on you?'

Alyssa shuddered. 'No, thanks. I've been there, and done most of it.'

'And what is that supposed to mean?'

She dug her elbows into the weather-worn stones of the wall and dropped her chin onto her hands again. 'I'm not telling you. Why should I tear myself up about it all over again, when you've just told me you wish we'd never met?'

'I never said that!'

'Why should I torment myself by raking over my past when you'll only tell me not to be so stupid and that I should pull myself together and get on with my life?'

Her words instantly made him suspicious. 'That's not the Alyssa I know speaking! Why put someone else's words into my mouth? I...' he said, straining his frustration through clenched teeth, 'I…would *never* say that to you.'

'Huh.'

She went on staring fixedly into the distance.

Lysander could only see her in profile, but he knew the defiant glitter in her eyes had nothing to do with the reflection of the moonlight. He fought the impulse to pull her together himself, and none too gently. Instead, by taking several deep, considered breaths he managed to summon up a scrap of tact.

'You're cold, Alyssa,' he growled. 'Come into the observatory. A full moon isn't ideal for stargazing, and supper will be waiting for us.'

Pivoting on his heel, he stalked off to the circular building in the heart of the garden. Sliding back a panel in its wall, he revealed a huge telescope trained on the night sky. Then he turned to call her closer and was shocked to find she had already done as he said. She stood a few feet away, watching him guardedly.

'Come in, and tell me all about it.'

He was making an effort, and wondered how far he could carry it. From her expression, Alyssa was curious about that, too. Without a word, she followed him into the observatory. It was as richly furnished as the Rose Palace, and tonight its central table had been hurriedly set with a delicious buffet and armfuls of fresh flowers. Lysander opened a bottle of champagne, poured a glass and held it out to her.

'So you've been married, Alyssa?'

She shook her head. 'No. I—I was engaged to a guy called Jerry, but that ended months ago. He was married to his job, but then so was I. It worked when things were going well, but then...'

She faltered. At that moment the nightingale's song swelled up with such power, it seemed to inspire her. She accepted the glass from him, and took a quick sip. Then her chin went up and she looked him straight in the eyes.

'I've got nothing to be guilty or ashamed about. I did nothing wrong—he was the one who had an affair.'

'Some men do that,' Lysander said, though he'd always been careful to make sure one dalliance was over before the next one began.

She looked out towards the rose thicket where the nightingale carolled on. 'I know that now, so next time I shall be ready—' She began strongly enough, but couldn't carry on. Suddenly words failed her in a cry of pain.

This wasn't part of Lysander's game plan at all. Alyssa was supposed to throw herself into his arms, not dissolve. There was only one thing to be done, so he did it. He grabbed hold of her, pressed her head against his chest and let her cry.

'But there will be a next time,' he reassured her softly. 'You know that, don't you?'

She nodded, and that was his cue to hold her tighter still.

Alyssa was lost. She cried and cried until she was too exhausted to do anything but let her last few tears trickle away. Only her ragged gasps went on, bouncing her face against the warm solidity of Lysander's chest. All he did was hold her close and stroke her hair, but that was exactly what she needed. She knew she was making a damp, salty patch on his shirt yet she went on clinging to him, trying to put off the moment when she would have to apologise for falling apart on him.

Lysander was in no hurry to let her go. He lowered his head until it rested against hers. Sliding his hands around her body, he drew her closer. Her breathing slowed as she tried to decide what was happening, and what she wanted to do about it. Lysander was holding her in a way that Jerry had never done—like a true friend. It was a lovely, safe feeling and so far outside her experience she felt happy and scared at the same time.

'I'm sorry,' she sniffled at last.

'Don't be. You're so brave and kind and resourceful it comes as a relief to find you're human after all. I was beginning to think you had supernatural powers.' He chuckled, still holding her gently against him.

With the side of her face pressed against his chest, she felt his words as much as heard them. 'That's a wonderful thing to say. Thank you, Lysander.'

'It's my pleasure.'

Alyssa could believe it, from the way his arms were wrapped around her. She could have stayed like that for ever, but knew if she gave herself up to him now she could say goodbye to her independence. That frightened her. If she lost control and surrendered to her desires now, the inevitable would happen. Lysander would be the one calling the shots. His reputation as a womaniser made her determined not to melt, however strong her urge to become liquid beneath the firm pressure of his hands. Her confidence had been so badly battered, she didn't want to open all her old wounds again. She wanted Lysander, but not simply as a sleeping partner. Her feelings for him ran so much deeper and stronger than the indistinct fantasies of white lace and babies she had known with Jerry. Her need for Lysander was a hot, passionate desire, seething through her veins like liquid gold. She wanted him body and soul, or not at all. If she couldn't have the whole man, she had to resist the only part of him on offer tonight.

Determined to make her point, she moved. It was a wrench, but she forced herself to pull away from him.

'This is a first for me. Standing in a queen's garden, in a prince's arms!' she said, making herself chuckle.

He released her, slowly and gently. When he looked down into her face now, his dark eyes were glowing. 'It's a novelty to find someone who isn't desperate for me to do anything more than this. I never usually touch a woman without an ulterior motive.'

He spoke carefully, but after what she had been through Alyssa knew better than to expect too much in the way of real support from any man. She took a deep breath and tried to compose herself.

'You were comforting me. That was reason enough.' She gave a watery chuckle.

'Yes. And tonight it's the only motive I need,' he whispered, before pulling her back into his arms and kissing her until the sky went dark.

CHAPTER EIGHT

ALYSSA couldn't fight her feelings any more. When Lysander released her, she was so breathless with desire she couldn't speak either. It didn't matter. There weren't enough words to describe the way she felt. When he claimed her mouth with his own a second time, she sank into his arms without a care in the world. She had waited so long to feel the touch of his lips against hers again. Every fantasy flew from her mind as she relaxed into the total experience of his kisses. This was so much better than dreaming. The whole sensation of his body cradling hers and the touch of his tongue against her teeth, teasing the soft warm recesses of her mouth, was beyond wonderful. She was fully aware now that every second since she'd first laid eyes on Lysander had been leading up to this moment. The anticipation grew within her body, waiting to be satisfied by his expert touch...

Lysander knew this would be unlike any other lovemaking. The time for waiting was over. No woman had ever made him suffer like Alyssa. When she walked into his life with her beautiful body and her determined resistance to him, she had become a challenge he couldn't ignore. When she revealed her tragic past salted with tears, there had been no way he could fail to be moved. And now the touch of her peppermint-cool lips against his own… It was sublime. Everything about her was so much better than his fantasies. She surpassed all the women he had seduced before. He wanted to take his time, and make these moments last for ever so that each movement in the concerto of their desire would be turned into something special. Alyssa would be no ordinary conquest. He could feel her whole body tremble at his touch. He drew her close, and sent his fingers rippling up and down her spine. She gave a little moan of pleasure. That made him smile. She had brought him so many new experiences since they first met. Now it was time to take things to a whole new level for them both. Anticipation smouldered within him, turning his voice into pure temptation.

'Once upon a time you were afraid I might be able to read your mind. Does it worry you that I could be plundering your thoughts right now?'

'Mmm…but I know you aren't.' Her reply was low with desire. 'You're too kind to do it without asking.'

'Other women will tell you differently.'

'My common sense has been warning me off from the moment you burst into my life, Lysander. Tonight, I can't resist you any more.' She sighed, moving her cheek rhythmically against his. His skin was stippled with stubble, and teased her with a thousand points of pleasure.

'Alyssa, you drive me wild…'

'Good, so it's your turn to suffer,' she murmured

deep into his ear. 'Bringing me to the world's most romantic place to tempt me like this—'

'You deserve it.'

He nuzzled her ear, his words sending warm shivers of excitement right through her body. Nibbling down her neck until he reached her blouse, he dragged it aside with his teeth.

The thin fabric was no match for him. Alyssa gasped as one side of it fell away. Now there was nothing but a filigree of lacy bra between her left breast and his gaze.

'This is so wrong,' she breathed.

'Not if it's what you truly want...' His voice was running on pure testosterone.

Her answer was one long, wordless moan of longing. Lysander took her in his arms for a kiss that set her body on fire. She melted into his caresses until they were engulfed in pure, hot passion. This was like nothing she had ever experienced before. There was no room for thought, only action—Lysander's action.

'I can send you right up among those stars and planets, making you forget everything but the pleasure of my body, and yours. Is that what you want?' he asked, the earthy vibration of his voice almost more than she could bear.

Her fingernails drew tracks through his thick dark hair, pulling his head still closer.

'Yes...yes!'

'Then I will make love to you until every celestial light goes out...' he whispered, his breath dancing over her skin.

* * *

It was exactly as Lysander promised. Beneath that moonlit sky with its scatter of a few diamond stars, he made love to her in the most perfect sense of the word. Again and again her cries of exultation rang out into the desert night.

Finally, when pleasure had drained every sound from her, Lysander lowered his head to sip one last kiss from her lips. With it came a final question.

'Now?'

She looked up at him, sated with desire and wanting only his pleasure. The flickering firelight that danced in his eyes ignited her smile.

He exploded with a cry of ecstasy that echoed around the ancient walls of the observatory like a song. Alyssa arched to accept his body as wave after wave of pure pleasure carried them both beyond thought.

'Perfect—absolutely perfect,' he whispered when it was over, resting his cheek gently against her shoulder. Alyssa couldn't speak. There were no words to tell him how she felt, how he had made her feel. Instead, she rolled her head until she could bury her face in the soft, sweet smelling luxuriance of his dark hair.

'This is how it should be. Always,' she said, waiting for him to answer.

But he said nothing.

Lysander had lost track of time, of place, of everything. His whole existence contracted into The Queen's Retreat, a place that had unexpectedly come to represent everything good about life. Alyssa intrigued him with her independence. From the moment she walked into his life, her quiet, well ordered way of doing things had become a calm centre in the whirlpool of his new existence. She knew what she wanted, and now she had surrendered to him. As they lay together, his arms protecting her from the chill of the desert night, he smiled, and then wondered why. This seduction was supposed to defuse his desire for her, but it wasn't going to plan. Hours and hours after first contact, his need for her still burned as hot as ever. He consoled himself that the feeling would pass, eventually. It always did. He had made love to more women that he could remember, but their attraction never lasted beyond bed. Alyssa would be no different. She couldn't be. Last night she had been at a low ebb, and he merely stepped in to comfort her in the best way he knew how. There was nothing more to it than that.

The lust rising within him this instant, as her supple sleeping body moulded itself to his, was nothing more than a reaction to the warm pressure of her naked skin.

Sympathy for her is the only reason I'm not back in my own suite at the palace right now, he told himself. Not even Lysander was immune to hearing about a woman being abandoned by a rat of a fiancé. It was no wonder he was still here. How could he leave her so soon after learning about her tragic past? Alyssa was hurting because a man she had trusted had betrayed her.

Lysander might have specialised in having a new lover every night, but at least he was honest with them. They all knew better than to accept commitment from him. Alyssa was no exception—she had never made any secret of the fact that she didn't trust him an inch. That should have made him feel better. *This pity event was nothing more than a comfort to make her feel better,* he assured himself. *She'll understand.*

But would she?

He turned the matter over in his mind. She was a sensible woman, who knew his past. There could never be anything more than sex between a woman like her, and a man with his reputation. That should be obvious to anyone. Alyssa was far too down-to-earth to have any illusions, wasn't she? A night with him was guaranteed to make her forget her pain, and it would get his head back together, too. That was all. They were both level-headed people, and after these few supreme hours of satisfaction the two of them would plunge straight back into their totally respectable careers, and move on. After all, they both used their work as a substitute for adult relationships, and Alyssa worked as hard as he did. Those two facts united them against the world. He knew she was bound to feel the same way as he did about this incredible evening.

Nobody expects a one-night stand to create any emotional baggage, do they? Lysander thought, convincing himself there wouldn't be any fallout. Like him, Alyssa would write off this escapade as nothing more than a pleasant little blip for them both.

Wouldn't she?

Through the hours of darkness, Lysander spent a miraculous time giving Alyssa all the physical comfort any woman could ever need. They got no more sleep that night than the nightingales. They made love continuously beneath the golden moon, breathing in the intoxicating scent of the Queen's garden. It was only when they rested that Lysander had time to work on his excuses. *I'm only doing what she wants. It doesn't matter, as long as she's calling the shots. She's known what I'm like, from the start...*

'People will be wondering where you are,' Alyssa told him sleepily early next morning. She was stroking his hair as he lay with his head resting against her neck.

Lysander was safe in the knowledge he could walk away from her at any time, but that time wasn't now. It was a shame to stop her doing something that made her so happy.

'Let them wonder. And as it's your day off, I don't have to get you back to the Rose Palace until midnight tonight. We can stay here having fun for as long as we like,' he murmured drowsily.

'I shall need some clothes!' She giggled.

'Not for anything I have planned.'

It was his own sleepy reply that shocked Lysander wide awake. He was supposed to be escaping to check his emails and chair a steering committee. Having fun with naked women wasn't supposed to feature on his agenda any more.

Drawing his body away from hers, he got up. He felt Alyssa shiver at the loss of him, and was aware of her moving to try to see what he was doing.

'There's something wrong, Lysander. What is it? Can I help?'

Her concern brought him up short. A woman who was *really* interested in him as a person, not a bank balance? That made a change. It gave him a sense of security he had never felt in the presence of a girl be-

fore. He paused, and thought about her question before answering.

'No. I'm fine.'

Knowing he could have dropped everything and
gone straight back into her arms was faintly worrying.

Groping among their scattered clothes for his mobile, he distracted himself by making a quick call.

'Breakfast will be served as soon as they can get it
here,' he told her when he had finished.

'I'm hungry for only one thing, Lysander.'

'Me too,' he murmured, pulling her into his arms.
'That's why I'm taking you outside to the arbour, for
one last experience before my staff gets here.'

It was a long time later when they wandered in to
breakfast, through the swell of sweet-smelling flowers that filled the queen's garden. The old building had
been transformed again. The table had been cleared
and laid with fresh fruit and pastries, while changes
of clothes were laid neatly over the back of a couch.

'After breakfast I'll show you the spa. It's a natural
feature fed by hot springs, and it's the only luxury in
the place.'

'You're my luxury, Lysander.' Alyssa blushed, adding quickly, 'I'm sorry about last night. The crying, I
mean.'

'Those were unique circumstances,' he said
brusquely. 'Don't worry about a thing.'

'You're right.' Her voice was small.

'Deep down you'll never forget the reason for
those tears, but the pain will pass.' Lysander looked

uncomfortable, and she saw he was making himself speak when he would rather have stayed silent.

She nodded.

He draped a robe carefully around her shoulders, then put one on himself. Sitting down on the nearest couch, he stared at their laden breakfast table.

'This is the first time I've ever envied my brother Akil. He was always much more sensitive than I am when it comes to women—at least until he took the cure.'

'What was that?' Alyssa enquired, puzzled.

'He got married.'

'Oh, dear!' Trying to laugh, she poured him a cup of coffee. Last night had been a spectacular experience, and she wanted it to last as long as possible. Despite all her fantasies, Jerry's treachery and her broken engagement had taught her that happiness was painfully short-lived. She knew that the sooner they parted today, the faster Lysander's interest in her would die.

He accepted the cup and helped himself to a couple of pebbles of unrefined sugar. They took a long time to dissolve, and for a while the only sound was the gentle caress of his silver spoon against the bone china cup. Alyssa was determined not to ask any more questions unless he wanted to talk.

'You don't share my curiosity about people, then?' he said after his first sip.

'As I said, I meant to do some online research in my spare time to get background, but now I know what happened to your mother I'm not sure I want to know anything more about your family. Unless it would help my work with Ra'id, of course,' she said without looking at him. It was enough to feel his eyes watching her every move, stripping her soul bare in the same way he had removed her inhibitions during that spectacular desert night.

'Of course,' he said, then muttered another word in Rosari that Alyssa was glad she couldn't understand.

'For one thing, it was useful to find out that Ra'id isn't the only candidate for King,' she said carefully.

He didn't reply straight away. Alyssa tensed. Watching him wonder how much to tell her was almost as bad as imagining this strong, capable man pacing about his state rooms like the caged tiger he had talked about.

'History has a way of repeating itself, but I'm not going to recreate the mistakes of the past,' he said grimly. 'Times change, but mankind stays the same. Loving too much killed my mother. She may have been in the wrong, but the people of Rosara hated the way she was treated. Father was determined things would change. He even allowed my brother to marry for love, rather than selecting a bride for him. Of course, that didn't work out any better than the traditional system of an arranged marriage,' he said with obvious disgust. 'While he was King, Akil continued to make improvements to Rosara. Now it's all been left to me. Life was so much simpler when my father or Akil did the work and I was left to enjoy myself! There's not much joy in juggling guardianship, running a country and making sure the succession doesn't rely on Ra'id alone.'

'It's such a shame he doesn't have any brothers or sisters.'

Alyssa sighed.

'His parents' marriage had already broken down before he was born. My brother thought marriage should be for ever, so, although he eventually let me convince him to separate from Ra'id's mother, he refused to consider fathering more children with another woman. He was old-fashioned enough to think that would set a bad example to his country.'

'And of course he never expected to die before Ra'id was old enough to take over. That's such a shame.' Alyssa clicked her tongue. 'Things would have been so different, if only the late king had remarried and had more children.'

'So you don't think marriage should be for ever?' Lysander placed his cup down, carefully matching its base to the small depression in his saucer so he didn't have to look at her.

'Of course I do—but things don't always work out so well in the real world.'

Lysander hunched his shoulders in weary resignation.

'How long were you engaged?' he asked quietly.

'Just over three years.'

Naked astonishment wiped the last trace of anger from his face. 'Good God! What was *wrong* with the man?'

Alyssa thought for a while before answering. She had only just started to admit the truth to herself. It was hard to know whether sharing it with Lysander would be a good idea. Her feelings were still so delicate. Admitting that she had slipped into the relationship because it was a step on the way to achieving her dreams rather than her ideal destination would be hard.

'It wasn't his fault, it was mine,' she said eventually, and was overcome by a great rush of relief. She had done it. Now the dam was breached, she could let a whole torrent of words follow.

'I was in love with the idea of love. My working life was filled with other people's babies and children, and I enjoyed it all so much I couldn't wait to start a family of my own. In my fantasy world they would adore me, and shower me with all the affection I'd never had from my parents. When I met Jerry, he fitted my identikit picture of an ideal father. He was solid, hardworking and had his future as an accountant all mapped out—complete with career database, objectives, the lot! My parents were so impressed by him, it spilled over to me—finally I had their approval. I was on top of the world, looking forward to the wedding of the century, and starting the perfect family.

'Then little Georgie died and as I fell apart, so did our relationship. We didn't have enough in common to sustain it. Jerry couldn't understand why Georgie's death hit me so hard. I couldn't explain that the grief was bad enough, but knowing that I could have done more to save him made it ten times worse...'

Her voice broke. Lysander grabbed his clean jacket, and pulled a neatly pressed handkerchief from its breast pocket. He pushed it into Alyssa's hands. She thanked him with a smile, but her eyes were dry.

'When we couldn't talk about it, Jerry lost interest in me,' she continued. 'Not long after that, he broke off our engagement. That was when I found out he'd been messing around with one of his office juniors for quite a while.' Expecting to need Lysander's handkerchief at any second, she squeezed it into a thousand creases.

The tears didn't come, because there weren't any left. *This really must be the beginning of a new chapter in my life,* she thought.

'I know exactly how you must feel.'

If anyone else had said that to her, Alyssa would have bitten their heads off for being patronising. When it came to Lysander, she knew that wasn't what he intended. His life was full of flings. That meant he could put more understanding into his words than there had been in the whole of her long engagement. It would have been funny, if it weren't so sad.

'I hated Jerry for doing that, but now I can see there were faults on both sides. I was only using him as a way to get the life I'd always wanted.'

'So you lost the chance to bag the rich husband of your dreams?' Lysander replied in a flat voice.

'That was the last thing on my mind when I looked at Jerry. I've got my own career—why would I be interested in his money? It's not as though I'd need to pay for childcare...' She tried to laugh, but couldn't do it. 'Looking back, I can see now that I agreed to marry him only because he asked me, not because of anything he could give me beyond children.'

Lysander picked up a plate from the table and offered her a ripe fig as a peace offering. It was so sweet compared to her memories. She savoured it for as long as possible. Then Lysander handed her a finger bowl and a soft, scented towel for her hands.

'And there was another problem.' She warmed to her theme. 'As an accountant, Jerry worked long hours. He had no interest in my work, and the feeling was mutual. I didn't have the first thing in common with any of the other accountants' wives and fiancées, either.'

'Yes. I can imagine,' Lysander said darkly. 'I've met a few of those at the parties we've held for firms who work for us. The best trophy wives don't seem to have an independent thought between them.' He smiled, until Alyssa had to join in.

'Or careers,' she added. 'I liked my life the way it was…but then it all went wrong.'

'The other woman.' Lysander sighed with world-weary certainty.

'Yes—and the worst of it was, I might never have found out if it hadn't been for what happened to Georgie.'

'Your loss must have been devastating,' Lysander said quietly.

Alyssa nodded, hardly expecting Lysander to be any more understanding than her ex-fiancé.

'For that little boy to die of meningitis was the worst possible tragedy. For everyone around to have ignored your warnings until it was too late must have struck you so hard.'

She looked at him, glad that tears still felt a long way off. 'You make me sound like a control freak.'

'I wouldn't go as far as that, but I *have* noticed you share a stubborn streak with my late brother. Wait— that's not necessarily a bad thing!' Lysander added as she got ready to fly off the handle. 'Akil's rigid determination was a great asset in a king, but not so good in a human being. Some things about you remind me of him. He never knew when to relax, be more flexible and let go.'

'Which is something *you* can do better than anyone else in the world,' Alyssa rejoined sharply, a little wounded by his quick assessment. 'How can a man like you ever feel comfortable in the role of regent, let alone king?'

A quick flash of consciousness in Lysander's eyes showed that her shaft had hit its mark, but a moment later he had smoothed his expression out and answered blandly:

'I intend to continue my brother's work, not his life choices.' The dark eyes took on a more thoughtful depth. 'Alyssa, I wanted to ask you something as a newcomer to the country. Have you heard any rumours about my late sister-in-law's affairs?'

Alyssa's eyes widened. 'No…what are you suggesting? That Ra'id may not be Akil's son?'

Lysander gave her a long, steady look. 'You catch on fast. But remember—you said it, not me. It's another good reason why our country is entering a troubled time—the power of the rebels continues to grow. It's not dangerous yet, but I must take as much responsibility for Rosara as the people want to give me.'

Alyssa gazed back at him, wondering if that was the reason he had kept his distance from Ra'id until he took her to the nursery in person on that first day. It must have been so difficult for Lysander to have lost his brother, and then be forced to care for a child that might be no blood relation at all, and nothing more than a cuckoo in the Kahani nest.

Then she saw something about Lysander's dark eyes that reminded her of Ra'id. They were so alike...

That was when she felt her own eyes getting bigger and rounder by the second.

Lysander noticed, and made an irritable noise in the back of his throat. 'Alyssa! If I hadn't become hardened to all the gossip years ago, I would be very offended by that look.'

'I never said a thing!' she retorted, ashamed he could read her thoughts so easily.

'You didn't need to.' He clapped his hand loudly to his chest. 'But I'm blameless in that direction, if no other. I never laid a finger on my late sister-in-law, nor ever wanted to. You have my word on that.'

He looked so genuine, Alyssa couldn't help but believe him. 'I'm sorry, Lysander. I shouldn't have judged you,' she said, then rallied: 'Although don't forget, you only took offence because you were searching my mind through my eyes.'

His reply was quicksilver. 'I do it because I can't help keeping a *very* close check on them, all the time.'

'And I thought your mind was supposed to be full of nothing but work!'

'You've been in danger of eclipsing that for me from the first moment we met.'

His voice was like a breeze through cool ferns. Alyssa was hypnotised by his dark stare, feeling as well as seeing it travel to her lips. Then, with a sigh full of regret, he looked away from her.

'My country is my work, and nothing can be allowed to distract me any more. Nothing. Although I will show you something that comes very close...'

As he took her hand such a powerful thrill of excitement ran through her body he must have felt it. Drawing her out into the garden again, he looked back at her over his shoulder. In that moment, his expression almost stopped her heart completely.

'Dawn in my country is as spectacular as the full moon,' he whispered.

Alyssa could believe it—as long as she was sharing it with him.

Helping her up to the highest lookout point on the castle walls, he sheltered her with his body against any chill breeze off the desert. The rising sun was already staining the Eastern sky with colours of pomegranate and peach. Down in the gardens, nightingales still sang. Their music was a grace note for Alyssa's perfect fantasy, and she relaxed into Lysander's embrace. No woman had ever felt so adored. As she felt his kisses on her hair and looked out over the ageless scene she allowed herself to imagine being this happy for ever.

Then without warning she was woken from her beautiful dream. A tiny sound had begun, far out in the desert. It grew faster than the daybreak, careering towards their happiness. Lysander was the first to realise what it was. While Alyssa was still wondering, he stiffened and pushed her gently away from him. The cold morning air flooded the space between them. Needing his closeness, she followed as he went to stand with his hands on the coping stones of the castle wall.

He was intent on something far out across the sands. A vehicle was hurtling at breakneck speed over the hard-packed desert. With growing horror, Alyssa saw that their paradise was about to be wrecked. Suddenly

Lysander strode away from her, back down the steps the way they had come. She ran to catch up, breathless with fear now, rather than expectation.

'What is it, Lysander?'

'For someone to be heading this way so fast, it must be a message from the palace.'

His words were terse and businesslike. Alyssa stopped. Lysander didn't notice, and certainly didn't wait for her. His mind was miles away, already centred on his work. This realisation sent her powering after him again. She knew what it was like to be driven, and wanted to share the responsibility with him.

'What can I do?' she called, but it was no good. He was completely absorbed by the arrival of a big new four-by-four in the blue and gold palace livery.

The vehicle skidded to a halt in the courtyard and the driver jumped out. Hustling the man out of her ear-shot, Lysander began an animated exchange with him. Alyssa could only stand by and watch. They spoke in Rosari, so she had no hope of understanding more than a fraction of what they were saying. From the speed at which the message was delivered, she guessed it was bad news. When the messenger jumped back into the vehicle and started gunning the engine, Lysander strode back to where she waited for an explanation.

It didn't come.

'I'm sorry about this.'

'You have to go,' she said, her voice as flat as the plain that isolated them from real life.

'Yes.'

'But you'll come back to me?'

He stared at her as though she were the one speaking

a foreign language. Then he lifted his gaze to look at the sky. She couldn't help wondering if it was for inspiration.

The rising sun was now high enough to light his face. Reaching out, he took her by the shoulders.

'I must get straight back to the palace now. I'll try to call on you later.'

His words pushed all the air out of her lungs. Logically, she knew that their time together was only fleeting, but somehow she had expected the pleasure to last a little longer than this before the pain kicked in.

'Are you expecting me to count the minutes?' she said in a bitter undertone as he turned his back on her.

It was one tiny act of defiance, a kick against the tomorrow she could not avoid. She didn't expect him to either hear, or care. When he turned and pierced her with a look, she froze. She could do nothing but watch as he prowled back across the courtyard towards her. Her thudding heart counted down the seconds until he was towering over her, his eyes brilliant with something she had never seen in them before. Ice ran through her veins as he leaned close...and then closer still. The warmth of his breath rippling over the delicate skin of her face and neck caressed an unwilling excitement over her body. A flush suffused the pale skin of her cleavage as she became aware that he was awakening her nipples to hard peaks all over again. Dimly aware of his hand moving past the corner of her eye, she tensed. Extending one lean, tanned finger, he pushed a stray skein of hair back from her brow. From there, his finger traced a leisurely path around the curve of her cheek. When he reached her chin, he lifted it so she was compelled to meet his eyes again.

'Yes.'

CHAPTER NINE

Lysander's voice was low and rough, but this time he studied her lips with cool, professional interest. Alyssa held her breath. Her heart pounded on. She wondered if he could hear it, amplified as it was by the powerful surge of desire thundering through her body. As he brought his head nearer and nearer to her, she watched until she was dizzy with desire. Then her eyes closed. She waited one…two seconds, but the kiss she was aching for never came. Instead she felt him take her hand. Her eyes flew open again. She saw his dark head bent over her fingers at the moment his lips brushed her skin in the lightest of formal gestures. Alyssa was so aroused, a little moan of longing escaped from her lips. A heat far more powerful than all the strength of the sun turned her body to a molten mass. It was frightening—almost as frightening as his smouldering gaze.

The memory of everything they had shared brought her straight back into the present. All that pleasure had been swept from his face and his manner, and now he was preparing for business as usual. He looked every inch the king. Alyssa couldn't imagine what had possessed her to tell him to concentrate on Ra'id rather than his own chances for the crown of Rosara.

'Yes…you must go, Lysander,' she told him, but the meaning in her voice was far more powerful than her words.

He let her hand slip from his grasp. As his expressive dark eyes held her captive he placed one finger on the soft cushion of her lips. Tracing their outline with a touch as light as thistledown, he watched her fight the temptation to reach out and start caressing him again. She still wanted him, and her attraction grew like a flower. She might try to hide it, but her unsteady breathing and dilated pupils told Lysander everything. His own perfectly sculpted mouth fluctuated into a smile.

'I'm sorry,' he drawled. 'Duty must come first.'

Kiss me! Alyssa's body sobbed silently.

She reached up, wanting to ruffle her fingers through his soft dark curls once more before he left. He responded by pulling her close, moulding her body against his own so she could feel how much he wanted her, how much his body would like to stay.

'Take care, my love,' she whispered.

His hands had been running over her back, shoulders and hair. When she said that, he stopped and drew back. His eyes were now filled with a watchful look that frightened her.

'I'm always careful. Very careful.'

Cupping her shoulders with his hands, he interrogated her with a long, cool look. Alyssa returned it with a smile. She knew he could read her mind, but this time his expression was closed to her.

'Lysander? What is it?' She put her hands up to his

face again, but was too slow. He had already broken contact with her and was turning towards the car.

'Nothing. I hope.'

He dived into the four-by-four and rapped on the dashboard as a signal to the driver. In a crash of gears, Lysander was swept away from her in a squeal of burning rubber.

Alyssa waved as the vehicle became a comet at the head of a dust cloud, but he never once looked back.

A bleak, black mood enveloped Lysander. He was used to playing dangerous games, but now he had been ambushed into doing something unforgivable. He had planned the perfect seduction to cure his gnawing need for Alyssa. Instead, raw emotion had overwhelmed them both and made the situation much, much worse. Alyssa's silent, hidden vulnerability touched him. Her tears had been an unexpected tidal wave, washing away all his defences. What else could he have done, but take her in his arms and make everything all right again in the only way he knew how?

He watched her image in the nearside wing mirror. It shrank until it was hidden by the swirling dust thrown up by his vehicle. He could only hope she was every inch the woman he believed her to be. She was so unlike all the others...she was bound to understand, wasn't she? Like him, she knew from hard, horrible experience that long-term relationships were impossible.

They were both free spirits. That would help. When she had burst into tears last night, it had been only a simple mistake on her part—he had put that right and solved his own problem, too. The last thing he should have done was start to feel genuinely sorry for her. That was his mistake, but it was understandable.

When he thought about it like that, his lapse didn't feel quite so bad. He dropped his hand onto his thigh and relaxed his shoulders. All he had intended was a quick tumble in a beautiful place. Offering Alyssa sympathy had been delicious, but he had never wanted to get in so deep. Sex was supposed to be fun, not serious. That was why this call back to the palace was such a godsend.

Uneasily, he realised abandoning Alyssa this morning for anything less would have been impossible. That made things tricky. An affair wouldn't be right for either of them. Lysander was certain of that, in the same way he knew he would have to get Alyssa right out of his life as soon as possible—to save his sanity.

Alyssa ran back up the steps to the lookout point on top of the castle walls. From there she could watch Lysander's car and its thread of dust fade from sight across the plain. When it had disappeared into the low jumble of buildings making up the palace, she turned and headed for the spa. There, she stripped off and slipped beneath the warm waters. Her spirits soared up to the clear blue sky, exhilarating, yet terrifying. She had wasted so much time mourning her broken engagement, it had blinded her.

It was far more than simply desire she felt for Lysander.

When Lysander got back to the palace he blazed his way through the corridors of power. *I should never have abandoned my work. I should have come straight back here last night,* he told himself, but it was hopeless to deny the attraction that had held him prisoner at The Queen's Retreat for so long. He had been bedding Ra'id's nanny when he should have been putting his country first. Now his past and future were on a collision course. A rowdy faction of hill tribes was on its way to the palace, ready to proclaim their own King of Rosara, rather than wait for his nephew to grow up.

Lysander's word was already law to them. He was confident that he could control the situation, but that didn't make it any easier. When Alyssa got to hear of this, she was bound to be scared. He already knew how good she was at hiding her feelings, but he had just spent a whole night breaking down her resistance. This situation meant he had to focus. It was time to let her go, like all the others.

But she wasn't like them. And what if Ra'id picked up on the atmosphere this was bound to create? How would *that* affect their working relationship? If they still had one…

His veins ran with ice water as he remembered how Alyssa had mentioned the L word—love. He knew what that meant. Seduction might not have slaked his thirst for her, but when a woman used words like that it had to mean the end of everything. There was no question about it. When love came in the door, common sense flew out of the window. He had too much experience of that, and it was a painful experience. It had condemned his mother to death, and broken his brother's heart. Lysander had to prove he was bigger than either of them. There was only one way to do it—make a clean break from Alyssa while he worked things out in his mind.

He would double the guard on Ra'id and go to intercept the rebels on their own ground. He was interested in results for Rosara, not in honour for himself. Alyssa would understand that. He could tell that the country was beginning to hold almost the same importance for her as it did for him...

Suddenly, he realised it wasn't going to be easy to prise his thoughts away from her. If her voluptuous image could haunt him while he was preparing for a council of war, he didn't know how it could be exorcised. He had to send her away.

The Queen's Retreat was a beautiful place to idle away her day off, but Alyssa soon got restless. After Lysander's lovemaking, everything else was second best. Life felt almost impossible without him now. Lounging in a swing seat beneath the rose arbour, she hummed to herself. A billow of single pink daisies flounced around the trellis. Picking one as she rocked gently to and fro, she began pulling off the narrow petals one by one.

'He loves me, he loves me not...'

Going through the old rhyme felt deliciously wicked. Princes weren't supposed to carry their staff away into the desert. Nannies ought to concentrate on the next generation, not fool around with men of their own age.

She went on reciting the rhyme until there were only six petals left.

'He loves me...'

A commotion far away in the palace's gatehouse

made her stop. She listened, and then suddenly a guard was running across the courtyard, calling to her. She couldn't understand what he was saying, but recognised the sound of her own name.

Whatever the news, it wasn't good. She looked down at the flower in her hand, with its half-dozen remaining petals.

'Miss Dene! You are recalled to the palace!' the man called to her in broken English. 'Prince Lysander insisted that you were sent for. Your day off is cancelled! You must take the child back to England immediately!'

'Isn't Prince Lysander coming back to fetch me himself?'

'No, he's far too busy!' The guard sounded shocked, as if Alyssa was the last thing on the Prince Regent's mind. She tensed.

'Why? What's happened?'

'The time has come. Prince Lysander is going to confront the rebels and Prince Ra'id's household is all going back to England, where they'll be safe.'

Alyssa took the news like a blow to the stomach. The queen's garden was suddenly full of people. They swarmed around her like ants, emptying the observatory of all the lovely things she had enjoyed with Lysander. She stood in the eye of the storm, her mind already a maelstrom. Opening her hand, she looked down at the daisy that had been giving her so much innocent pleasure.

A quick calculation told her everything she didn't want to know. She pinched five petals together and pulled them off. That left only one.

He loves me not...

So there it was. Not even a child's game worked in her favour any more. She couldn't manage to keep that final, fragile petal, either. It was snatched out of her fingers by a chill breeze rippling across the garden.

For a moment, all the birds fell silent.

Lysander had been so understanding about Georgie's death and Jerry's treachery, but his silver tongue had lured her into making another mistake. Alyssa shut her eyes, trying to blind herself to the truth in the same way he had done. It was impossible. She was as big a fool as ever. Bigger, as experience should have taught her not to be so stupid a second time. She had allowed herself to be seduced, knowing all the time that Lysander's lifestyle and morals were totally different from her own. Her ex-fiancé had cheated on her while she was still grieving for Georgie, and when she had needed him most. Why should she be shocked when ruthless, single-minded Lysander Kahani did exactly the same?

She stood up. The remains of the daisy, already wilting in the warmth, tumbled from her lap. She didn't notice. All she could think about was the way she had made a fool of herself over a man—again.

A car came for her, eventually, but there was no sign of Lysander. When she got back to the Rose Palace, it was in chaos. Lysander was nowhere to be seen but she couldn't block out the sound of his voice, calm but loud, echoing through the building. Staff scurried about all day relaying his instructions, and she picked up the story bit by bit. Lysander was leaving with the army for the hills. His plan was to make contact with the rebels who had sent an ultimatum about Ra'id. To keep his nephew safe, the royal household was being shipped back to England. Alyssa didn't want Ra'id upset by all the tension, so she kept him in the nursery, but the last thing she wanted to do was merge into the background.

For once, she was determined to stand up for herself. She had to talk to Lysander. Although her attention didn't waver from Ra'id, she made sure they always played close to a window where she could keep a watch on the courtyard below. Lysander didn't appear. She texted him. He didn't reply. All day she watched and waited, but it was no good. Finally, with Ra'id packed and ready, she had an excuse to go and find out what was happening.

The palace's grand foyer was stacked with travelling boxes and crates. Alyssa spotted Lysander instantly. The sight of him stopped her dead, halfway down the stairs. He was always impressive, but in combats instead of his usual designer suit and tie he was daunting as well. In contrast to his staff, he moved around with cool assurance. They rushed backwards and forwards in a panic while he tried to keep the situation calm by giving each one a few reassuring words.

Alyssa waited for him to turn his head so she could attract his attention. He didn't so much as throw a glance towards her. When anger overcame her shame at being fooled twice in her life, she started down the stairs. Each step was heavier than the last. When she finally thumped to ground level, Lysander was heading towards the door.

'I'd like a word with you, please, Your Royal Highness.'

The staff stopped, guessed what was going to happen

and then put their heads down to carry on with what they were doing.

All except Lysander. Hands on hips and without any sense of urgency, he strolled over to where she stood.

Alyssa's face barely came up to his breast pocket, but that didn't stop her standing up to him.

'I want to speak to you.'

'I know. I saw you leave the nursery wing.'

That surprised her. 'You didn't make any effort to come over while I was waiting on the stairs,' she snapped, feeling awkward that she had misjudged him. Only hours ago, she had felt there might be some kind of mystical link growing between them. *Fat chance, when I can't even notice him looking at me*, she thought.

'Is it something about Ra'id?' His eyes were guarded.

'No.'

'What, then?'

'You mean you don't know?' Alyssa burst out.

He stood before her, tall, proud and very still. 'I hope I can't guess.'

Now that she was face to face with him, Alyssa couldn't think of how to begin. Eventually, she said in a quiet voice, 'I thought you were coming back to The Queen's Retreat.'

'I was needed here.'

'Of course you were.' Alyssa had heard about threats to Ra'id's future from the driver sent to collect her. The country was unsettled, angry, looking for a strong leader. There were bound to be those who might want to take a short cut by removing any opposition. That put Ra'id quite literally into the firing line.

She fought to keep calm. Only twenty-four hours ago the three of them had been having a wonderful time, picnicking without a care in the world. Now her universe had contracted to a tiny bubble that wasn't large enough to keep both Lysander and Ra'id safe at the same time. Bubbles were so easily burst. She would have to let one of them go, and Lysander wouldn't allow her to keep him. This was the job he was born to do, after all. She understood a sense of duty and how he felt about it, but this situation was so dangerous her feelings burst out in spite of herself.

'Please don't go, Lysander. Send someone else—'

A tiny muscle twitched as he clenched his jaw. 'Are you suggesting I should hide away, just so *you* aren't worried about my safety, when the future of both my country and my nephew are at stake?' The bitterness in his voice and his assumption that she was thinking only of herself cut through Alyssa like a whip.

'Don't flatter yourself—or me,' she struck back. 'Obviously my opinions aren't of any interest to you. How stupid of me to forget that for you women are nothing but playthings! Well, I'm worth more than that, and I'm not trying to save you for myself. See sense. If you're going to keep your country in one piece, Lysander, you have to keep yourself out of harm's way.'

'My country needs me to be strong, and I have to set an example. This is how it must be.'

'You idiot, Lysander!' Emotion made her throw her hands towards him but he stepped smartly out of her reach.

'Speaking like that to me at a time like this is treason.'

They stared at each other, his look becoming a glare. 'This will be my life from now on, Alyssa. There are times when I have to leave everything—and everybody—behind. I can't do my duty to my people if I have you to worry about as well. There isn't room in my life for any distraction right now.'

Breath caught in her throat, almost choking her. 'So that's all I am to you—a distraction.'

He stared at a point somewhere over her head and far away. 'Don't take it to heart. If anything, you should be glad I'm leaving before things go any further. I've had so many other women, Alyssa. I've abandoned them all sooner or later—' He tore his eyes away from the middle distance but still refused to meet her eyes. 'I don't want to hurt you like that. You're too good...'

She took a step forward, daring him to flinch. 'You say that—but I was stupid enough to let you seduce me!' she blazed. 'You coward! You're walking away from me in the same way you've abandoned all those other girls over the years—to prove that you can. Don't deny it!' she spat furiously.

The look transforming his face told her she was right, but that he hadn't realised it himself until then. Seeing his sudden shock was unnerving. Lysander didn't notice. He was on an adrenaline high and struck back instantly.

'*I've* got nothing to prove!' he roared back. '*You're* the one whose future is on the line if you stay here. Go, now! It isn't safe for you here!'

'I'm going! But not because of anything you've said or done, Lysander Kahani,' she hissed. 'My first loyalty is to Ra'id. As far as I'm concerned, *you* can go to hell!'

'Good! That's exactly how it should be! I don't damn

well employ you to put me off my stroke!' he shouted
over the racket of helicopters dropping onto the apron
outside the palace, but it didn't make any difference to
Alyssa. She was running back upstairs, desperate to
get away from him.

Alyssa was in such turmoil she took refuge in organis-
ing. Packing and timetables were facts and figures she
could control. Lysander might have thrown her on the
scrapheap, but she had to bury that at the back of her
mind. Ra'id was upset by all the confusion and change,
and her first duty was always to him. Her own future
looked bleak. The little boy was Lysander's number
one fan, with all that meant. If he wasn't talking about
his uncle, he was waiting for that one special visitor
to the nursery. Alyssa would never be able to escape
the influence of a man who had lifted her up and then
dropped her from a great height.

  The only silver lining was that, while she had so
much to do for Ra'id, she didn't have time to get in
a state about their hastily arranged flight home to
England.

For the next few days, Alyssa spent her time trying to
forget Lysander. It was impossible. By the time they
got back to Combe House, the place was buzzing with
news. Every bulletin started her fussing over Ra'id so
she wouldn't have to hear, and bundling him away from
every TV and radio. She said it was to stop the little
boy getting upset. The truth was, she didn't know what
would be worse: to hear that Lysander was in danger, or
to find out that the emergency was all over and he was

back home, looking for a new distraction. Either way, her heart would be pierced. Finally, the time came when she couldn't run any more. One morning she woke up while it was still dark outside to hear a television blaring away somewhere close at hand. Dragging on her dressing gown, she stumbled through the door connecting her suite with the nursery sitting room.

Ra'id was bouncing up and down on the couch, alight with excitement. He didn't notice that Alyssa's scowl would have curdled milk, and that she was pale with lack of sleep and loss of appetite. He had the TV on full blast, and launched straight into his great news.

'Uncle Ly's won!' he squealed with excitement.

'I've told you before not to switch the television on yourself!' she began, but Ra'id was far too excited to take any notice.

'Uncle Ly's won!' He kept on repeating it, but Alyssa couldn't bring herself to feel anything but dread. Ra'id's delight made it hard to pick out many details, but the words 'royal wedding' came through loud and clear as he pointed towards the giant TV screen. 'Now we can go home, and he can get married!'

Alyssa was shocked into life. She whirled around, and was confronted by Lysander's life-sized image moving over the huge TV screen. It twisted a knife in her stomach. His smile was exactly as she remembered; she could almost believe he was gazing straight at her. But he wasn't. He was sharing a joke with a rebel leader seated beside him at the conference table.

'He's getting married?' Alyssa's voice rose uncontrollably.

'Of course. He's going to marry Princess Peronelle.' Ra'id's smile reached from ear to ear.

Alyssa barely heard. She was frozen with horror, watching Lysander—the man who had cradled her, and made love to her until all her pain had gone. He was smiling and nodding wisely, ranks of photographers and film cameramen catching his every chuckle.

'He's…in love with a princess?' Alyssa felt faint. Suddenly the floor felt as if it were made from rubber. She caught hold of the nearest chair for support.

'Prince and princess, king and queen. That's how it goes,' Ra'id announced happily. 'The TV says King Boduan is sending Princess Peronelle on an official visit to Rosara as soon as Uncle Ly gets back there next week. It's inked,' Ra'id announced. He had picked up that delightful phrase parrot-fashion from one of Lysander's briefing team.

Alyssa was falling through space, helpless and alone. Her mouth was so dry she could hardly speak. 'Prince Lysander's going to get married?'

'I keep telling you. It's Princess Peronelle. *Everyone* knows that!' The little boy laughed.

'Since when? I didn't,' Alyssa said faintly, wondering how she could have been so deaf, blind and stupid.

'That's probably because it happened a long time ago,' Ra'id decided. 'I wasn't supposed to be listening. They thought I was playing. My father said Princess Peronelle had a good pedigree, whatever that is, but Uncle Ly said what good had that done our family in the past and that she was a…' he rolled his eyes with the effort of remembering '…a perfect clothes horse.'

A long time ago. So Lysander must *have known*

about his engagement before he carried me off to The
Queen's Retreat and...

Alyssa couldn't bear to think back over what had
happened. She had seen all those magazine photographs of Lysander escorting beautiful women around
the world. She knew the type only too well, but a hid-
eous need to know more about one in particular overwhelmed her.

'What's she like?'

The television coverage switched to other news, so
Rai'd lost interest in it. Instead of bouncing up and
down on the spot he was now catapulting from cushion to cushion along the length of the couch. Alyssa
had to repeat her question before he took any notice.

'The princess? She's not as nice as you.'

That made Alyssa feel worse, not better. The
only prize for coming second in the competition for
Lysander's love was a broken heart, and she already
had one of those.

'Have you met her?'

'Sort of. She came to the palace once. She walked
past me. She's all rustly, and smells like shops. She
didn't stop or talk to me or anything, but her ladies-
in-waiting did. They gave me sweets. Lots of sweets.
And chocolate. And marzipan. Lots of that, too. Then
we went into dinner and I was sick on the table and the
princess screamed and ran away.'

Alyssa might be dying inside, but that little picture
made her smile like a jealous jaguar.

'Oh, dear. Was it just on the table?'

Ra'id nodded.

'That was a shame,' Alyssa said with real feeling, but not the sort Princess Peronelle would have liked.

Lysander had some damned nerve, seducing me when he had a royal bride already lined up for himself, she thought, covering her face with her hands. *Now I know why he was so keen to send me back here without talking to me—I'd served my purpose.*

Despite everything, she felt strangely calm. Since Georgie died, she had always known that getting too fond of anyone was a mistake. So why had she let Lysander break her heart twice over? He had the words 'love rat' written all over him, he was fully aware of his own worth, and he was beautiful with it. She only had herself to blame for ignoring all the warning signs, but that couldn't stop her hating him.

'What's the matter? Have you got a pain?' Ra'id stopped bouncing and looked almost as stricken as Alyssa felt.

'Yes,' she said.

But she didn't tell him that pain was called Lysander Kahani.

CHAPTER TEN

THERE was no escape. From that moment on, Combe House was filled with talk about the forthcoming royal wedding. The newspapers seemed to know more than the staff did, so each morning a copy of every title was brought in. Everyone but Alyssa pored over them to discover the latest rumours. The ceremony was going to be held in the vast chapel at the Rose Palace in Rosara. All the talk was of which royal families and TV celebrities would be invited, what they would eat and which designer would be dressing the bride. Ra'id was so excited at the thought of his uncle Ly getting married, he talked about it non-stop. Egged on by the footmen, he decided he would be the official ring-bearer. His happy chatter wrecked every second of every day for Alyssa—until someone showed him the official photographs of his parents' wedding. Ra'id took one look at the lace encrusted, Rosari court dress their little page-boys had been forced to wear, and went strangely quiet.

Once he discovered how he would be dressed for the big occasion, Alyssa had no more trouble with Ra'id. He had spent hours trampling over her feelings and nagging to be involved. Now he couldn't wait to retreat with her to the spa wing. He didn't mention either Lysander, or the wedding, again.

Alyssa had to cope with his disappointment while keeping her own agony locked deep in her heart. Letting Ra'id fool around in the ball pit, she tried to drown her own sorrows in the warm, rose-perfumed waters of the Combe House pool. Whatever was happening back in Rosara, Lysander didn't want her any more. That simple fact drained all the life and hope out of her. She had never known a pain like it. What she was forced to endure now showed up her old heartbreak for what it was—a fuss over nothing but vanity. When Jerry had admitted his affair, she had felt viciously cheated of her big day and the happy ever after she assumed was her right—but that was all. She could see it now. Losing Jerry hadn't been the cause of all her anguish. Any feelings she might have had for him had shrivelled and died on the day he had told her to pull herself together after Georgie died. She deserved better, but looking back now she could see why Jerry had strayed. They had both been playing parts: hard-working professionals planning a safe, predictable future like all their so-called friends. It had been Alyssa's shattered dreams and damaged pride that had hurt the most. Jerry had almost been an optional extra in her plans for the perfect wedding.

The way she felt about Lysander had nothing to do with promises and party favours. She had known from the start he would have no interest in either, but for a little while he had been kind, and funny, and a spectacular lover. She had ignored all the pointers in his past and her own experience, and now she was paying the price. What more could she expect?

Despite everything, she found herself worrying as well as hurting. Whatever else he might have done, Lysander had listened, and comforted her. His own very special brand of kindness was impossible to forget. He had led a charmed life so far, but there was still a chance his luck would run out before he got back from his mission to the mountains. Alyssa couldn't bear to think of him being injured or killed. She knew she shouldn't care, but she did.

If he could seduce her while knowing about the plans for his arranged marriage, he must think she wasn't good enough for anything more than a bit part in his life. It hurt—but, thinking about it, she realised her parents and Jerry must have thought about her in much the same way.

It was a turning point. She had got over those disappointments. It felt as though she would *never* get over this, but there was one thing she could do to start on the road to recovery. If Lysander came back expecting to take up where he'd left off, he'd be out of luck. Alyssa's recent experiences had made her damned sure of one thing—she was too good to be nothing more than a mistress to him, and if she got the chance she wouldn't be afraid to say so.

The sound of an approaching microlight cut through her pain like a buzz saw. Rousing herself, she waded to the side of the pool. Ra'id always liked to be called out to see anything like that. As she climbed the steps a two-man machine swept low and slow over the trees surrounding Combe House. It swung around like an irritating horsefly, getting lower with every circuit. Alyssa was already angry and upset. She thought things couldn't possibly get worse—until she heard one of the riders call out to her. She looked up, and saw a long lens.

She ran to the ball pit to keep Ra'id inside the spa, but the damage was done. There could be only one reason why the press were buzzing Combe House. They had run out of rumours about the royal wedding and now needed to dig deeper for their daily fix. Everyone's life would be made a misery in the search for pictures and stories.

Especially mine, she thought with a chill of dread. Once the paparazzi arrived at a scene, everyone was fair game. The media feeding frenzy surrounding the Kahani wedding would need to be stoked every day. If there were no fresh details about the bride or groom, the circle would widen. Sooner or later, a slow news day would throw up Alyssa's name, and her part in Georgie's tragedy. It would be filed as a 'human interest' story, without any humanity at all. Her past pain would be raked over again, trapping her in a hell of her own making.

Lysander had proved he was the only one who could free her from that—and he was getting ready to marry someone else.

The succulent image of Alyssa in her sleek green swimming costume was a gift to the press. It went around the world in moments. Lysander, still deep in political arrangements, eyes tired from endless diplomatic discussions and smothered in yards of royal red tape, saw it and felt something break inside him.

Akil had nagged him for years about changing his wild ways. Lysander had never listened, and now he was glad he hadn't. It had taken only one night with Alyssa to upset his carefully crafted public image, and make him consider something beyond his body's prime reactions. Akil hadn't managed that in a lifetime of moaning. Lysander had been perfectly happy enjoying himself, with no thought for anybody else. There hadn't been room in his busy social life for conventional things like a wife and family. Considerations like that were for other people, not him.

Then Alyssa had walked into his life, and sent his perfectly regulated life haywire. In the long, restless hours since he'd abandoned her, he'd come to a decision. A lot had to change—and his own attitude was top of the list. Alyssa thought he cared more about his image than anything else. That might have been true before they met, but things had moved on for both of them since then.

At first Lysander had found the idea of ruling anything, much less a whole country, a bleak and lonely prospect. Watching Alyssa dealing with Ra'id had changed his thinking. He saw there must be give and take, but within limits. His head was beginning to tell him that being a royal needed two people who liked to be involved with others while staying aloof from them, and didn't mind hard work or long hours. His heart filled with the warm glow of certainty as he thought of the only person he needed and wanted to fill that special place by his side.

One sleepless night later, he had everything straight in his mind. When all the official communiqués were drafted and sent, and all the phone calls fielded, he called a press conference. He had never cared about what the media said about him in the past, but that was before he became the undisputed ruler of Rosara, until Ra'id came of age. It wasn't simply his own feelings he had to think about now. He needed to put on a good act for everybody today, and a spectacular show for the only person who really mattered to him.

When the meeting was all over, Lysander pumped the rebel leader's hand for the last time and walked away. He had achieved nearly all his objectives. Ra'id was safe from idiot rebel attack now the people of Rosara had a strong leader. Lysander was in command, and everyone was on his side. From this moment on he could go where he liked, and do what he wanted. Everything was within his power, but somewhere along the line glamorous bars and nightclubs had lost their appeal. When he looked back on his old life, it felt so shallow and incomplete. Happy it was behind him now, he didn't want to waste time wondering why or when he had started to think differently. A vital part of his future was missing, and he was going back to England to reclaim it.

Commandeering the nearest vehicle, he set off to find Alyssa.

The past week had been one of the worst of Alyssa's life, but it was about to be eclipsed in spectacular fashion. It was late. Time and again over the past few days she had tried to put away the memory of Lysander and his moonlit kisses, but it was no good. Nothing she could do was a big enough distraction to obliterate thoughts of him. They were fixed in her mind like a full-colour, life-sized photograph of the event. Right now she was standing in the shower, but torrents of water could not wash away the contrast between her paradise then, and her living hell now. Lysander's disdain for her must be ice-cold. It was a side of him he had kept hidden with soft words and careful promises while they were together, but he'd more than made up for it since then.

She came out of the bathroom still towelling her hair dry. Keying commands into a remote-control handset, she plunged her living room into darkness and sent its heavy velvet drapes scurrying apart. She was tired, and would normally have walked straight through to her bedroom. Tonight, though, something made her hesitate. She went over and looked out of the window instead.

Combe House was so isolated, the countryside outside was completely black. All that gloom beyond the windows reflected Alyssa's feelings exactly. She stared into it until her eyes became accustomed to the dark, and she could make out shapes on the horizon. The pillowy silhouettes of oak trees to the east would soon show some hope of morning. As she watched she noticed a single point of light in the distance. She couldn't see any other stars, and wondered if it was a planet— Venus, maybe. That was supposed to be the morning star, after all. She couldn't find it in her heart to really care. She wondered again how she could have wasted so much time grieving for the broken engagement that had brought her here in the first place. That pain had been nothing, compared to the agony of losing Lysander.

The trauma of seeing him with another woman would be too much, but she would never be able to avoid it. She couldn't hand in her notice—she had to stay here and care for Ra'id. What would happen to him if she resigned? It wasn't only her conscience talking, it was her heart. She really loved the little boy, and this Princess Peronelle hadn't treated him very well the first time they'd met. That was unlikely to change when she became Queen of Rosara, or, as Alyssa already thought of her, the Wicked Stepmother.

Letting her imagination sweep her away, Alyssa sighed. She picked up the pieces of shattered childhood dreams often enough in her line of work. Prissy Princess Peronelle would be all over Prince Lysander, leaving him no time for Ra'id. A woman like that might employ any kind of help, just to keep the little boy out of the happy couple's way. Alyssa shuddered every time she thought about what it could be like. At the very least, she'd have to wait and see whether the Wicked Stepmother really lived up to her name. Worst of all, the idea of betraying Lysander's trust in her held her captive. He had admired her attitude and her work before they slept together, and he had always wanted the best nanny in the world to look after his nephew. Lysander's high opinion of her work was something that would never change. She didn't want to destroy those feelings in him by nailing her broken heart to her sleeve. At the first sign of snivelling he would lose all respect for her, and she would feel the same way about herself.

As she dredged through all her unhappy thoughts

the distant bright light played hide and seek among the trees. Soon, it didn't seem so far away. She opened the French doors to get a better look and the sound of a low-flying plane flickered through the air. It grew louder, focused on that single bright point.

Suddenly Combe House burst into life. Every security light on the estate blazed. The plane swung around to approach the estate's private landing strip. As it slid sideways through the floodlight beams the royal blue and yellow crest of Rosara on its side told everyone that this wasn't a drill. It was the real thing. The Prince Regent had arrived.

Transfixed, Alyssa stood and watched the plane disappear beyond the lime trees in front of the house. Lysander was here at last. The urge to rush out, throw herself into his arms and thank him for getting back safely almost overwhelmed her. Only self-respect held her back. She had broken down in front of him once before, and look where *that* had led…

Gripping the window sill, she felt her palms dampen. With a snort of derision she dragged the curtains closed again and snapped on the light. The dazzle made her see sense. There could be any number of reasons why a plane of the king's air fleet might drop in. Lysander didn't have to be on-board. He had no reason to come here in person any more, when he could be lording it in the Rose Palace like every previous King of Rosara. He would have too much to do, preparing his stunning home for Princess Peronelle.

She shut her eyes. Her fury couldn't sustain itself when she was running on empty. For six days she had put on a brave face. Now all she wanted to do was crawl into bed, pull the covers over her head and stay there.

She didn't get as far as her bedroom. A thunderous rapping on the door of her apartment rattled her nerves as hard as it shook the windows.

'Alyssa?'

It was him. Lysander.

She thought about running into her room and locking the door. That wouldn't work. He sounded in a mood to come straight after her and, in any case, Alyssa suddenly realised she didn't want to run away. Facing him with what he had done to her and how he had betrayed her was the only way to fix this. All the rage fermenting inside her bubbled to the surface and wouldn't let her retreat. She marched over to the door and flung it open.

There he stood. Lysander. He looked magnificent in his uniform—and slightly out of breath. She glanced over towards the closed curtains so he wouldn't see what she was thinking. It was quite some way from the landing strip to the house. He must have sprinted all the way.

'I'm here to take you home, Alyssa.'

'What for? As your second-best woman?' she seethed. 'Sorry, you've come to the wrong place. Save the fairy tales for your nephew. I'm through believing in your stories.'

Her voice dripped acid as she tried—and failed—to slam the door in his face. It bounced off his boot as he kicked at the gap.

'I've spent the past week putting Ra'id's interests

first. It's you I'm interested in now, Alyssa. I've come for *you*.'

She froze. Lysander was a master of shock tactics, and used her momentary pause to wade straight into the attack. He spoke quickly, his chest rising and falling as though he didn't have time to catch his breath.

'You told me to go to hell—well, I've been there, and now I'm back. I've proved I can do my job better than any other man alive—'

'And now the Kahani inheritance is safe.'

'Yes.'

'How does it feel? Any better than turning your back on me at The Queen's Retreat?' Alyssa stared at him, very still apart from the crimson blush firing her cheeks.

'I had to do that.'

'Why? To prove you could?'

He turned all the power of his blazing eyes on her. After a long pause only fractured by his roughened breathing, his answer bruised the silence.

'Yes. Great empires have been brought down by women who weren't fit to look you in the face, Alyssa. It's happened in Rosara, too—twice in my lifetime. The first time it was my mother, the second time Akil's wife was the cause of all the trouble. I've never wanted to risk making the same mistakes other men in my family did. I needed to show the world—and myself—that I could put my country before my heart.'

'And what about *me*? What part are you expecting me to play in the Lysander Kahani Appreciation Society?' Alyssa forced the words past a growing lump in her throat.

'My people need strong leadership. Rosara has that now, and I must start building a team to take it into the future. I have to be the managing director of a whole country—'

'Or an engineer, calculating how to get rid of dead weight?' The chill in her voice reacted with his anger to make him hiss with exasperation.

'I came here to explain things to you, Alyssa. Can't you at least let me have my say?'

'I don't need explanations. I don't even want to *look* at you!' She turned her back so he wouldn't see her tears. 'You've got everything you want. Rosara, a fiancée hanging on your every word, and now you've come back to tie up the last inconvenient loose end—*me!*'

There was a pause. She heard him walk around so he could take up a position in front of her again. When she refused to raise her head, he bent down and looked up into her face. He was running his teeth over his bottom lip, perplexed. She closed her eyes to get him out of her sight. After an agony of silence, she heard him retreat.

'No...' he said eventually. 'I can't say I understood a word of that.'

'And I always thought your English was so perfect,' she snapped.

'Yes. It's about as good as your manners.'

The sound of him pacing backwards and forwards across her room was almost enough to make Alyssa open her eyes. Before she could gather the strength to do it, he started talking again.

'You're right about the loose ends, at least. It was unforgivable, shutting you out so completely. I had to force myself to do it. Alyssa, you were everything to me that night and while I've been away I've kept you close with every heartbeat. You're right—sending you back to England with Ra'id was partly a test. I had to know if I could carry on being everything to my country while you were affecting me so much. When we were together—when we made love, I forgot everything but you.' His voice became a whisper as he searched her face for any change in her feelings. 'That…frightened me. It was, after all, the same kind of madness that led to my father breaking down in tears every time my mother's name was mentioned.' A spasm of pain passed over his face. Shocked by the violence of his reaction, Alyssa automatically threw out her hands to him, but with a shake of his head he turned away.

'You've never dealt with that?' she whispered in horror.

He shook his head a second time, but still couldn't face her. 'Or the thought of how my brother was fooled by his ex-wife.'

Alyssa felt her heart hammer a warning against her ribs. Lysander was hurting, but then so was she. *He's gone from having a new woman every night to having a fiancée—and me,* she thought viciously. *Two pretty permanent fools, and both on strings.*

'So whatever made you turn to seduction as a career, Lysander? It sounds like you've grown to hate women over the years.'

'I don't hate them. I love them. But only on my own terms. I could never afford to let them get too close.' He looked at her then, biting his lip as though realising he had said the wrong thing.

Alyssa folded her arms as though that could protect her from him. 'I came here determined never to let you within a million miles of me, ever again,' she said, staring at him as the darkest pain of his past began to ebb from his expression. It was a moment of absolute stillness—until a huge crash made them both start and look back at the door connecting Alyssa's suite to the nursery.

'Alyssa! Come and hear what's on the radio—' Ra'id burst in, fresh out of bed and heading straight for her. Seeing Lysander, he squealed with delight and changed direction. Alyssa was already half crouching, ready to scoop the little boy up in her arms. As he threw himself at Lysander instead she slowly straightened up. Her original aim had been to see them happy together, but for the first time watching someone else's family bloom, without her, didn't ease her pain.

'Uncle Ly! You're on my radio, and you're here, too!' The little boy was jiggling up and down with excitement. Lysander was having trouble keeping hold of him, but neither of them seemed to care. They were both laughing. Alyssa took a step back, leaving them to enjoy themselves. This was family time. There was no room for a nanny at moments like this, but she had never given a second's thought to this part of her job before now. Now it hurt to know that Ra'id would always have a place in Lysander's heart, while she had none.

Lysander was getting his smartphone out of a pocket and holding it up to show Ra'id. 'Now I'm back, you don't need to listen to the radio. You can see what I've been saying to people on here.'

'It's me! Look, it's a picture of me!' Ra'id bellowed, grabbing Lysander's phone hand and wrenching it round so Alyssa could see the display, too. The little boy was focused on the one thing that meant anything to him, but that was only a small part of a much bigger picture. The phone showed film of Lysander, giving his last press conference in Rosara. Projected onto a screen behind him as he spoke was a photograph he must have taken during their last picnic. Alyssa was hugging Ra'id, and they were both in fits of laughter. As the camera moved away from the backdrop and zoomed in on Lysander's face Alyssa didn't know how much more she could take. She pushed her words past the blockage in her throat.

'Perhaps Your Majesty would like to put the prince back to bed himself?'

Ra'id put his arms around Lysander's neck as the successful conqueror nodded at her and set off towards the door connecting Alyssa's suite to the nursery.

'I'm coming back to carry on where we left off, Alyssa, right after I've put Ra'id back to bed,' he said firmly, disappearing into the bedroom and closing its door behind him.

Alyssa was so angry and emotionally exhausted she couldn't think what to do. She stood staring at the door blankly. When, after a long time, it opened again, she was alert to the smallest detail. Lysander locked the connecting door behind him to make sure they wouldn't be disturbed. Alyssa made a noise of disgust.

'Typical! I wonder how often you've done that in the past.'

'I've come back for you, Alyssa. What's wrong with that?'

'Because, like a fool, I let you seduce me despite the fact I've always known what you were like.'

Lysander said nothing to begin with, but she could tell he was angry. He betrayed it in the rigid set of his jaw and the iron intensity of his stare. It was a long time before he could trust himself to answer. He stood, trying to collect himself while her nerves stretched to breaking point.

'That's why you're different, Alyssa,' he said in a ragged voice. 'You've always seen the man in me, not the image.'

'Really? And which bit of you do all those women in all those glossy magazines get to enjoy?'

'What can I say?' He hitched a weary shoulder. 'I've told you—I like women. They like me.'

Alyssa's voice was carbon steel. 'I've noticed. I wonder how Princess Peronelle will feel about that.'

He looked at her askance. 'Why should *she* care?'

'When she's your wife, she'll do more than care. Be careful she doesn't stab you through that wicked black heart of yours, Lysander Kahani.'

His careful study became a frown. Alyssa's fists were balled, waiting for him to try something. What he did was so unexpected, she didn't have either the time or the sense to react. Taking her gently by the arm, he led her to the nearest chair. Putting his other hand to her forehead, he felt her temperature. She shook it off angrily.

'Don't do that to me!'

'I'm worried about you, Alyssa.'

'Oh, don't give me that! You sweet-talked me and seduced me in a moonlit garden, while all the time you were getting ready to make vows of undying love to another woman in the chapel of the Rose Palace!'

'Alyssa, you aren't making sense...' His refusal to come clean infuriated her.

'Yes, I am! I'm sick of making a fool of myself over you, when all the time I was nothing more than a stopgap until you married Princess Peronelle. Well, good luck to you both—and you'd better tell her not to bother running to me when you start tearing *her* heart to shreds!' Alyssa bounced out of her seat, her sense of injustice growing by the second. 'I'd rather have taken my chance in Rosara and been blown to bits a thousand times than watch you wreck another woman's life!'

He gazed at her with those steady dark eyes that had always spoken straight to her heart—until now.

'What in the hell are you talking about, Alyssa?'

'Don't give me that! You had the cold-blooded nerve to seduce me, when all along you knew you were lined up to marry Princess Peronelle!'

'Who told you that?'

'Ra'id. He said his father arranged everything, before he died.'

With that, all the weariness fell away from Lysander's face and he gave her a look of naked disbelief.

'You're not telling me you believed what a five-year-old boy told you? Or that I ever, in my entire life, did anything simply because my older brother thought it was a good idea?'

'Of course I believed it!' Alyssa exclaimed. 'It's all over the news! Everyone's been saying how King Akil picked you out the perfect bride, years ago. Ra'id just filled in the details for me.'

'That little monkey...' Lysander said in a slow, faint voice. 'Oh, Alyssa...my brother was always dreaming up schemes to make Rosara great. I didn't agree to a fraction of them when he was alive, and once he was dead I conveniently forgot the ones that didn't interest me. There has been so much more going on in my life since that was discussed. Time has passed, I had to come to terms with Akil's death while making sure Ra'id was well cared for, and then I had to get used to the idea of being Regent—an arranged marriage never crossed my mind. You didn't really think I'd be party to something like that, did you?'

'Of course I did.'

'But the whole idea is ridiculous! I've never given it a minute's consideration.' He put a hand over his eyes. 'Although I'm sure the people of Rosara thought there was nothing they'd like better than a royal wedding between me and Peronelle, until I told them in that press conference about something much more exciting.'

'Is that why you let the English-speaking media get away with printing all the details of your wedding, right down to who would be designing the bride's dress?'

He raised his hands to the sky. 'I have been fighting for my family's birthright. How the *hell* was I supposed to find the time to read newspapers?'

Alyssa felt her temperature heading off the scale again. 'You didn't need to—and neither did I. The press must have been following you everywhere. Didn't they say anything?'

Wearily raising his hands, Lysander went to cup

her face. She took a step back. Fury flared in his face. His arms shot out and he caught her by the shoulders. Pulling her close, he trapped her body as well as her gaze.

'My mind has been full of other things. I've told you—I've been too distracted to care about rumours, tales and lies.'

'It was a shame *I* couldn't manage to distract you better than I did.' Alyssa's words crackled like static.

So far, Lysander had been on the defensive. Her accusation changed everything.

'For one brief moment in my country's history, you were far more distraction than I could handle. I thought the pleasure you brought me would dilute my sense of duty. It was only when I managed to put some distance between us, I could get things into perspective.' He hesitated, and looked almost embarrassed as he added quietly, 'Things like…the way I feel about you.'

'That I was a handy stand-in until your honeymoon with Peronelle?'

Alyssa's granite stare was as abrasive as her words. She couldn't risk falling for his lies a second time.

'Oh, Alyssa! When you and I… What *do* you think I am? Doesn't the fact that I came back to fetch you home prove that you mean more to me than any other woman in my life? You're the only one who really matters to me, Alyssa,' he said simply.

Alyssa wanted to believe him, but there was something that didn't quite fit. 'You said there's only one thing your people would enjoy more than a royal wedding. You never said what it was.'

'A love match, of course. So that's what I'm going to give them.'

He sounded as cool and resolute as he had on the day when he had abandoned her in Rosara. For good or bad, his mind was made up about something. Alyssa had to know his decision and who was involved, but she hesitated. Did she really want to know the name of her rival? It would be an unendurable pain, but surely it would be better to hear it from him, rather than at second hand.

'Who with?'

'You, of course.'

From the moment Lysander had walked into her suite she had matched him verbally, blow for blow. Now his words silenced her completely. He had befriended her, helped her—and then inflicted a wound so deep she knew she would never recover. Only the furious memory of the way he had bundled her out of Rosara had got her this far. Now a growing anger at her own idiocy kept her staring straight at him. She had always known he would never marry her. If he was offering her a taste of what might have been, she would have to refuse. She couldn't agree to be his mistress, kept as first reserve until next year's model dazzled him into dropping her. That was what he was offering, surely. She wasn't worth anything more—all her experiences showed that. She had to drive him away, quickly, before she succumbed.

'Check your schedule, Your Majesty. You're already pencilled in to marry Princess Peronelle at the Kahani chapel, in six weeks' time.' She spat the words straight into his face, but he didn't blink.

'Then hand me an eraser. I want you.'

'Yes, but everybody knows you need a suitable wife.'

'I don't care what "everybody knows", and I don't want a wife, suitable or otherwise. I want a partner—someone who knows my mind. An intelligent, independent, thinking woman I can work with.'

His stare was as hard and resolute as his words. They confronted each other until the tension began to have a very strange effect on Alyssa. In her imagination she saw his eyelids flicker. His jaw relaxed, and the thin compressed line of his lips softened with the movement. He spoke, and that was when Alyssa knew she must be dreaming.

'I want *you*,' he repeated, and this time there could be no doubt about it. 'That's what I told everyone at the press conference. That's why Ra'id heard me talking about a queen. You're the only one I want at my side, Alyssa.'

They stared at each other, each determined not to give in. Alyssa blinked first, and it gave Lysander the break he had been waiting for. He added something, but had to turn away to say it. His voice was so faint Alyssa could barely hear, but the movement of his beautiful mouth gave him away.

There were only two words she could fit to those faint sounds, and they were so unlikely the idea kick-started her own voice.

'*What* did you just say?' she breathed. He slowly turned around and seized her hands in his, his eyes blazing into hers with dark emotion.

'Marry me.'

Lysander's voice was uncompromising. It was an

order, not a request, but in his eyes there was a flicker of something that took her breath away. Surely not, but it looked as if he was...nervous? Alyssa felt dizzy, as though the ground had suddenly been turned upside down.

'Lysander! But...I can't...' Half a dozen reasons dug their spiteful claws into her, but they were all variations on the same theme. 'You rule Rosara. I'm a nanny.'

'Do you think I care about that?'

'You should.' Alyssa took a deep breath, hardly able to believe what was happening. 'I want to marry you more than anything else in the world. But you know what my problem is. I want children, and a family— all the things you've spent your life avoiding. I want to keep working. And how could I go on doing that, when I'm married to you? Without my job, without caring, I'm nothing.'

Lysander's grip became gentler.

'You could never be a woman defined only by the work she does, Alyssa. Don't you think I've thought about that? Care for me. For Ra'id and, in time, for our own children. You'll be the perfect, dedicated mother, and that's one of the reasons I love you.'

He coloured slightly and his reply momentarily shocked Alyssa into speechlessness. She had never imagined Lysander using a four-letter word like love. Now his country was safe, it seemed it wasn't only his lifestyle that was changing.

'I never knew you could blush, Lysander!'

He passed one hand over his face, then looked down at her as resolutely as ever. 'It isn't something I intend doing a second time. And I'm not likely to repeat what I've just said, either.'

Alyssa felt a smile start to spread across her face. He was searching her face, his expression earnest. 'I want you to work *with* me, not simply *for* me. Children are our future, Alyssa, whichever way you look at it. Ra'id needs a settled, loving home life. I want him to live with us, as our son. In your spare time—if he gives you any—Rosara needs someone who understands that the care our children get decides our country's future. You can be their champion.'

He paused, but it was Alyssa who had to take a breath. The look in his eyes had softened to melting chocolate.

'I need a woman by my side I can rely on—one who can help me achieve all I want to do. So this time I'm not so much presenting you with a job, as asking you to work with me. For life.' His eyes blazed with a certainty Alyssa couldn't face. She had to look away.

'You know I'll never be a Princess Peronelle, don't you? With me, what you see is what you get,' she said quietly.

Relief flooded his face, and he smiled for the first time. 'I know. That's why we'll be happy together. You'll carry on being the independent woman who always tells me what she thinks and only laughs at my jokes if they're funny, and that's exactly what I want—and need. So…what's your answer going to be? Could you take us on? Me and my world?'

Alyssa looked up at the ceiling, pretending to think.

'Hmm. Well, knowing you, if I don't accept we'll be here all night arguing…so I suppose I'll have to say—yes!' She laughed up at him, loving the way his eyes had lit up with joy. 'Of course, you'll have to dismantle the rumour machine and survive telling Princess Peronelle the fixture's scratched, first.'

'I don't intend telling anybody anything, for a very long time.' Catching her hand, he pulled it to his lips and kissed each of her fingertips in turn. 'Unless it's you, Alyssa.'

His eyes were full of the slow-burning passion she knew so well, but tonight it was misted with deep emotion. Slipping her arms around his waist, she laid her head against his chest.

'So you'll be disappointing all those supermodels as well as the princess, then?'

'I'd rather satisfy you.' He laughed. And then he did—perfectly.

* * * * *

MILLS & BOON®

Want to get more from Mills & Boon?

Here's what's available to you if you join the exclusive **Mills & Boon eBook Club** today:

- ✦ *Convenience – choose your books each month*
- ✦ *Exclusive – receive your books a month before anywhere else*
- ✦ *Flexibility – change your subscription at any time*
- ✦ *Variety – gain access to eBook-only series*
- ✦ *Value – subscriptions from just £1.99 a month*

So visit **www.millsandboon.co.uk/esubs** today to be a part of this exclusive eBook Club!

MILLS & BOON®

Need more New Year reading?

We've got just the thing for you!
We're giving you 10% off your next eBook or
paperback book purchase on the Mills & Boon
website. So hurry, visit the website today and type
SAVE10 in at the checkout for your exclusive

10% DISCOUNT

www.millsandboon.co.uk/save10

Ts and Cs: Offer expires 31st March 2015.
This discount cannot be used on bundles or sale items.

MILLS & BOON®

Why shop at millsandboon.co.uk?

Each year, thousands of romance readers find their
perfect read at millsandboon.co.uk. That's because
we're passionate about bringing you the very best
romantic fiction. Here are some of the advantages
of shopping at www.millsandboon.co.uk:

* **Get new books first**—you'll be able to buy your
  favourite books one month before they hit
  the shops

* **Get exclusive discounts**—you'll also be able to buy
  our specially created monthly collections, with up
  to 50% off the RRP

* **Find your favourite authors**—latest news,
  interviews and new releases for all your favourite
  authors and series on our website, plus ideas for
  what to try next

* **Join in**—once you've bought your favourite books,
  don't forget to register with us to rate, review and
  join in the discussions

Visit **www.millsandboon.co.uk**
for all this and more today!